FROZEN ORBIT

FROZEN ORBIT

PATRICK CHILES

BAEN

FROZEN ORBIT

Copyright © 2019 by Patrick Chiles

A Baen Books Original

Baen Publishing Enterprises
P.O. Box 1403
Riverdale, NY 10471
www.baen.com

ISBN: 978-1-9821-2430-4

Cover art by Bob Eggleton

First printing, January 2020

Distributed by Simon & Schuster
1230 Avenue of the Americas
New York, NY 10020

Library of Congress Cataloging-in-Publication Data:

Names: Chiles, Patrick, author.
Title: Frozen orbit / by Patrick Chiles.
Description: Riverdale, NY : Baen Books, [2020]
Identifiers: LCCN 2019046167 | ISBN 9781982124304 (trade paperback)
Subjects: GSAFD: Science fiction.
Classification: LCC PS3603.H5644 F76 2020 | DDC 813/.6--dc23
LC record available at https://lccn.loc.gov/2019046167

Printed in the United States of America

10 9 8 7 6 5 4 3 2 1

For Melissa, Nathan, and Matthew.
You are the reason I do this.

1

History's turning points are often nothing more than a chain of otherwise unrelated events, set in motion by individuals who would rather be somewhere else at that moment.

The young captain of the Russian Aerospace Defense Force could have charitably been called ambivalent about his present moment, having just left his young wife and baby in their small Moscow apartment for his turn as watch officer at the Sofrino Missile Defense Complex. After driving far beyond the outskirts of the city, he parked his rattle-trap Lada sedan in a lot carved out of the forest. Trudging around mounds of dingy slush, he made his way toward an immense slab rising above a remote clearing in the predawn gray. The building's trapezoidal facade was covered with the circular panels of phased-array radars, its roof was a thicket of antennae. There were no windows, only a single door centered at the building's base which looked cartoonishly small in comparison.

The captain mechanically returned the salutes of unsmiling sentries and made his way through the first bank of security gates, thankful to be out of the cold. Following a circuitous route of corridors deep into the building with more security at every turn, he finally arrived at a single reinforced door. He swiped his ID badge across the digital lock, steeling himself for another twelve-hour shift of monitoring satellite traffic.

He hung his wool uniform cloak on a worn coat stand behind the door and settled into the watch officer's desk, returning a nearby junior officer's greeting with an acknowledging grunt. His station overlooked a small auditorium with rows of identical dull-gray consoles, all facing a wall full of oversized monitors that tracked every known satellite and piece of space debris transiting the skies above Russia.

As he rubbed the sleep from his eyes, the aroma of black tea insinuated itself into his nostrils. He looked over to the senior watch sergeant. The man always seemed to know what he needed almost as well as his wife did, as a good NCO should. "Thank you, Sergeant."

"And how is your little one, sir?" The sergeant had already been through the travails of newborns now three times over. Popov had thought he'd been tired while standing alerts in Ukraine; he was learning that combat tours were sometimes easier than parenthood.

"He started walking last month," the captain yawned, "and climbing last night."

The sergeant laughed. "It doesn't get any easier as they get older, I'm afraid."

The junior watch officer next to him, unattached and oblivious to the old-timer's banter, handed Popov a canvas-bound notebook. "The watch log, sir."

As he skimmed through the usual mundanities, his eyes were drawn to specific instructions highlighted for his personal attention and initialed by the commanding general: He was to retrieve a particular set of orders from the safe in the commander's office prior to 0530 Moscow time.

He glanced at the digital clock above the situation displays: 0524. Six minutes. The old combination lock on that safe was already meant to be difficult and years of use had left it temperamental. If the orders were that important, why not just brief the previous watch officer? He called for the senior sergeant to follow him; the one man he could rely on to coax the thing open in a hurry.

With a few careful spins and a deft touch on the release lever, the sergeant cracked the heavy door open on the second try. A manila envelope bound with red tape sat inside an otherwise empty safe. Curious. "You have my thanks once more. That will be all."

As the sergeant excused himself, the captain tore the envelope free and closed the safe. It was labeled with the current date and addressed to the Duty Officer, A-135 Battery, 9th Aerospace Defense Division. He checked his watch: 0528, two minutes until whatever deadline had been imposed on him.

He untied the string clasp and shook the contents into his hand. While the outer packaging was clearly new, the inner packaging was clearly not: Another, much older envelope fell out. He drew the blade of his pocketknife across a seam that had been yellowed and softened by the years to find a single sheet of paper within.

The message began with an otherwise unremarkable string of numbers and abbreviated prefixes. Even without the prefixes, the captain recognized them as a table of astronomical coordinates. Right Ascension, Declination, Altitude, Bearing . . . a targeting solution.

His cell phone began ringing at 0530 sharp, startling him. Even more startling was the incoming caller: Commanding General, 9th Division.

"A-135 Battery, Captain Popov." He felt like an idiot, snapping to attention for a telephone call.

"I believe you have a fire mission, Captain."

"Yes, sir," he swallowed, contemplating the intercept orders which appeared to be older than he was. "It appears that the vectors and release sequence have been determined for some time."

"Yes, I found that hard to escape notice as well."

The younger officer studied the intercept vectors as he returned to his station in the operations center and scrolled through a catalog of known objects. "But there is nothing there, Comrade General," he whispered into the phone, meaning that *of course* nothing occupied that point in space at this particular time; rather, there was nothing in their database of potential threats that should be anywhere close to that region of space in the next twelve hours. Not with the approach angle these numbers implied. Where did they think this phantom target was coming from?

"You have your orders, Captain," the general said, "and I have mine. If you are for any reason unable to carry them out, then *my* orders would be, let us say, regrettable. Do you foresee any difficulties?"

He didn't, yet the thinly veiled threat frightened him anyway, as unspecified dire consequences from a flag officer tended to do. Why wouldn't he carry out his orders if it was just to intercept old space junk? If the general hadn't called, he'd have assumed it was a long-planned live-fire exercise.

"Captain?"

"No, sir," he insisted. "There will be no difficulties." He looked back at the specified countdown sequence and then up at the chronograph above the control center's giant wall screens. "If that will be all, sir, I must see to my duties."

"Good man." The call ended at the other end with a firm click.

The target emerged on the Siberian early-warning net within seconds of the predicted time. Popov saw it appear on his own monitor before the watch chief notified him of a new target. "Very well," he answered, and noted the new velocity vector now flashing above as it began continually updating. "Designate target Zulu-One and track to intercept, Sergeant."

"Intercept, sir?"

He was taken aback at how rapidly the tracking solutions were changing. The target had appeared at the very edge of their deep-space network's range and it was nearing a firing solution, just as the countdown sequence had instructed. No wonder he'd been ordered to spin up the anti-ballistic missile interceptors an hour ago.

"You heard me, Sergeant. That object has been designated a threat and we are to eliminate it. This is why we are here. Remember Chelyabinsk." Whatever this thing was, the memory of a meteor whose effect had been indistinguishable from an airburst nuclear bomb could be counted on to motivate them to protect their homeland.

"Of course, sir. It is moving rather fast but tracking radars are keeping up."

Popov watched the intercept solution unfold. As the sergeant had noted, it was moving improbably fast. He'd made certain to mark the time it had appeared in order to deduce its orbital elements when this was all done. With enough data points, reconstructing the object's trajectory would be simple.

"Sir?" the sergeant interrupted his thoughts. "Target Zulu-One is emitting a coded signal on S-band."

"*What*?"

"Very faint, but the time lag and doppler shift are consistent with the target's relative motion. It's a transponder beacon, sir."

Deep inside the object dubbed Target Zulu-One by the Aerospace Defense battery, an electronic brain had sprung to life for the first time in decades. Weeks earlier the vessel's solar wings had felt the Sun again after years of darkness, recharging its batteries and triggering an automated countdown sequence that had been programmed decades before.

As once-frozen thrusters rippled to life with bursts of hypergolic fire, the antennas that fed its primitive nervous system registered a sudden bath of laser and radio energy washing over them. Being nothing the vessel hadn't been programmed to expect, it returned the electronic greeting by activating its transponder in reply. It couldn't know that it had just marked itself as prey, a yelping pup lost in the deep woods.

Had the vessel's occupants still been alive, they would have registered alarm at the salvo of antisatellite weapons rising to meet them: wolves emerging from the shadows of the forest. If the little ship's brain could have seen and felt and somehow reasoned beyond the limits of its simple arrangement of magnets and silicon, it might have flinched as the first of a half-dozen fragmentation warheads bit into it. The solar wings—its fragile limbs—were first to succumb. It was not long before the rest of Soyuz TMK-1 was ripped apart by the mechanical wolfpack of the *Kosmicheskie Voyska Rossii*.

It would be many days later before the event was reported in popular media and soon forgotten as yet one more obstinate Russian display of force. American early-warning satellites registered the unexpected ASAT launch, followed by a series of bright flashes high above the Russian steppes. The official line was that they had intercepted a previously uncatalogued Near-Earth Object that threatened the Motherland. Professionals among the various national space programs publicly accepted their explanation and congratulated the Russian Aerospace Force for its dedication to planetary protection.

Amateurs knew better. As fanatic and dogged as HAM radio operators, the global network of amateur astronomers and satellite sleuths may not have seen the approaching NEO but some had noticed the odd electromagnetic noise from a point in space that should have been dead quiet. After a sudden anonymous data dump from a Russian IP address that just as suddenly went dark, the group's social media eruptions had been epic:

OMG DID U GUYS SEE THAT! IT WAS A SPACECRAFT!
WTF? I MEAN WHAT THE EFFING EFF?
LOL UR HIGH DUDE. CHK UR DATA.
CHK UR MOM. IT'S A SOYUZ TM TRANSPONDER.

Soon after, the Russian government was forced to admit it had been the culmination of a long-planned exercise to hone their NEO intercept skills.

Owen Harriman, casually interested internet lurker and full-time NASA project manager, had come to a different conclusion after his own perusal of data he'd developed on his own. What the radio sleuths hadn't seen was the object's approach angle and initial velocity. Too crazy to believe, he'd run his numbers by a trusted flight planner in The Trench, the front-row consoles in Mission Control where frighteningly clever mathematicians worked their spells of trajectory analysis.

Owen was shocked when the math wizard agreed. "You're certain? There's no way I could have messed this up?"

"Only if your initial conditions were off, which they weren't. It's solid, bro."

Owen chewed his bottom lip as he worked through the implications. "A Russian spacecraft . . . "

"Soviet," the wizard corrected. "That was an old TM-model freq."

"*Soviet* spacecraft, forty years after the fall of Communism, appears out of nowhere aimed at their LZ in Kazakhstan," Owen said.

"Don't forget the part about interplanetary return velocity from Pluto's orbit."

Owen rubbed his eyes with his palms. "You're not helping."

The trajectory wizard laughed nervously. "Ivan was not screwing around, bro," he said, tracing a finger along the reconstructed orbit. "If you don't call APL, I will."

"You never saw this," Owen warned him. "All for the good of the program, of course," he ended with a wry grin.

As the digital images were dusted off—that is, pulled from whatever compressed file they'd been stored in and processed anew—the few managers from Johns Hopkins Applied Physics Lab briefed into Owen's scheme reminisced over their own unlikely but hugely successful project.

After nine years of sailing across the solar system, faster than any other machine NASA had yet hurled out of Earth's gravity well, the robotic probe *New Horizons* had finally entered Pluto's fragile sphere of influence for a fleeting encounter back in 2015. Despite carrying the hopes and career expectations of so many, the event itself amounted to not much more than a cosmic one-night stand.

"Would've been nice to put that little guy into orbit," one mused while the images compiled.

"Only way to do that would've been to keep it slow enough that we'd all be retired or dead before it got there," an engineer retrieving the data scoffed. "You forget how hard it was to get it out there in the first place."

"Neither one of you knows how hard it really was," the lead scientist said. "I was there for the budget hearings."

Owen wished he could have just brought up a couple of good backroom techs for this. He knew how these guys could ramble. "I remember that," he said. "I still can't believe you got it past Congress." After a whirlwind of begging and pleading, a small yet determined group of scientists had prevailed upon D.C. politicians to fund their little mission before it was too late.

At almost the eleventh hour they had managed to convince the Budget Committee that Pluto's tenuous atmosphere, barely detectable from Earth, would freeze into ice crystals and collapse onto the tiny planet's surface within the next decade as it migrated farther away from the Sun.

"It got me to praying for the first time since forever," the scientist continued. "You wouldn't believe how hard it was to convince them this was going to be our last chance for a couple of centuries."

"How many times did you have to repeat the same answer?" Owen asked.

The scientist slid his glasses down to the end of his nose as he relived the moment, mimicking a dullard senator who'd tormented him during the budget hearings. "*Exactly* how long until it reappears?" he said, mimicking the senator's exaggerated drawl. "You had to see his body language. It just shrieked '*and why should we care?*' I kept telling him two hundred years, give or take a few decades. I guess he was suspicious that we somehow couldn't precisely model atmospheric phenomena for a dwarf planet forty AUs away that no one had ever laid eyes on."

Almost no one, Owen thought to himself.

"But I'm just a planetary geologist," the scientist continued. "Took just enough physics to screw my GPA good and hard. Funny how they can never find any actual English speakers to teach it."

"Should've gone to UC," the engineer teased. "We didn't have that problem. Not much."

The other scientist laughed. "But then you'd have been in, you know, Ohio." His wrinkled-up nose unambiguously telegraphed how he felt about the benighted Midwest.

The engineer rolled his eyes. "At least people can afford to live there. Baltimore rent is more than my parents are paying for a mortgage on an actual house with a yard, not just some renovated motel that slapped a 'condo' sign up front."

Owen started thinking about finding those techs again. More work, less drama. "So, you said you were a planetary geologist . . ." he prodded.

"Yes. But since I was a geologist, the senator was compelled to ask the physicist seated next to me," he said, and jerked a thumb at his partner, "who in turn had to produce a meteorologist to verify our assumptions."

"An actual, working meteorologist," the physicist interjected. "No PhD, just a grad student interning at NOAA while he worked on his masters. The kid protested that he didn't know squat about extraterrestrial climatology, which is what the senators were really asking about. We explained to the kid that they're too bloody stupid to know the difference. He finally agreed that, yes, Pluto's thin excuse for an atmosphere would indeed freeze and fall to the surface as the planet moved farther away from the Sun. And no, we couldn't know when for certain because we didn't know the complete makeup of the atmosphere."

"It won't matter once you're within a few degrees of absolute zero," the engineer joked.

"And no, it would not become warm enough to reappear for another two centuries," the geologist concluded. "Only after the kid dazzled them with sophomore-level physical science did we finally get the funding."

And so, *New Horizons* had been slapped together largely from off-the-shelf components and dispatched to the edge of the solar system. It had resembled nothing so much as an ambitious gradeschooler's vision of what a deep-space probe should look like: about the size and shape of a grand piano wrapped in gold foil and topped with a massive dish antenna.

Launched from Earth in 2006, after a quick pass by Jupiter to steal some energy from the gas giant's gravity well—which it wasn't going to miss all that much—the little probe went into hibernation until being awakened by its masters back on Earth. That this golden piano, the first to encounter the solar system's most distant planet as it zipped past at forty thousand miles per hour, would be in a position to see what it did, and that what it saw was in a position to be seen in the first place, was difficult to describe as anything other than *miraculous*.

Owen flipped through the reams of observation notes. "And these gamma transients didn't get your attention back then? I mean, to have something that hot . . . "

"Like you said: transients." The physicist pointed at the thick printouts in Owen's lap. "We were drinking from a firehose. We're *still* correlating images against observational data. What are we looking for, anyway?"

Owen was afraid to voice his suspicions, lest they laugh him out of the room. "Not sure."

"Whatever. Can I see the coordinates again?" the engineer asked. "Need to make sure I'm in the right grid here."

Owen slid the top binder over to him. "Are you sure there's imagery?"

"LORRI was slaved to RALPH during approach. If there was something worth seeing, it would've snagged it."

"English please," Owen said. "I can only keep one center's acronyms in my head at a time."

"Sounds kinky if you don't know the lingo, right?" the engineer smiled. "LORRI's the Long Range Reconnaissance Imager," the engineer said deadpan. "RALPH's the infrared spectrometer. No idea where the name came from."

"Because the UV spectrometer was named ALICE," the physicist said.

The engineer entered one final command. "Got it. We have imagery correlated to that radiation transient."

He pointed at a mass of gray and white pixels suspended in the center of a black frame. "Looks like you found a new moon, Mr. Harriman."

Owen perked up. "How's the resolution?"

"At that distance? This thing's maybe the size of a boulder. I can't believe you even had a clue where to look." If likened to a game of cosmic billiards, they'd just hit a blindfolded double-reverse bank shot.

"Irregular shape," the geologist noted, "consistent with it not being big enough for gravity to make it spheroid."

The physicist leaned in for a closer look. "If it were a shard from a larger body then I might expect that much residual heat, but it would've had to be recent to be that energetic."

"Maybe energetic for a sheared-off planetoid," Owen muttered, just loud enough to be heard. "So it would have to be something else."

The scientist's latent skepticism flared, which the engineer ignored as he kept working to refine the image. "What 'something else' explains a localized source this warm?"

"Could be volcanism. Like Io," the geologist said, "but without Jupiter-sized tidal forces? I don't see how. It's too small."

"I agree," Owen said, not meaning what they were thinking. "Remember how everyone was convinced that Mars was devoid of water? The atmosphere was too thin. Then we discovered a naturally occurring antifreeze below the surface. Just because a phenomenon doesn't agree with what we've come to expect doesn't make it impossible."

The now wide-eyed engineer raised his hand warily, as if it might get snapped off. "Umm, yeah. About that." The image had taken on a more definitive shape: symmetrical, if somewhat irregular.

The geologist leaned forward. "It's almost like a . . . dragonfly."

The physicist was unconvinced. "You're delusional. Seeing what you want to see."

"Speak for yourself," the engineer shot back, silencing them by shifting the image into the visual spectrum. The object resolved to a washed-out olive green with dull highlights of bare metal and a cluster of bulky gray protuberances ending at a battered disk.

"Is that *writing*?" Barely discernible in faded Cyrillic letters was the acronym *CCCP*: the Union of Soviet Socialist Republics.

To a chorus of groans, the engineer glibly summed up their discovery: "That's no moon. That's a space station."

2

Even in late springtime Moscow remained brutally cold. Low clouds scudding across the sky cast a monochrome pallor on the equally gray, equally dismal apartment blocks that seemed to march forever across the cityscape. The architectural style, such as it was, had been called "brutalism." Leftovers from the country's long, abusive relationship with collective economics, they were nonetheless left standing only because all those people still needed to live somewhere. The fall of communism and the fascist kleptocracy in its wake had not created much incentive to build anything else. Large populations were easier to manage if they were all clustered in one place.

If architecture revealed a culture's character, then the deeper Owen Harriman wandered into this canyon of dingy concrete the more he longed to flee from it. He wasn't sure what spooked him more: the vaguely threatening air of an unfamiliar neighborhood in a country they were barely civil with, or the realization that the same authoritarian urges could just as easily be found in his own country. Random scraps of loose garbage tossed about by the wind heightened his anxiety. All that was missing was the sound of a dog howling in the distance.

And at that, a distant canine did indeed begin howling. Owen told himself it was just the wind.

He shook off the chill as a welcome splash of sunlight opened up along the face of the next building. As luck would have it, the block number matched the one on the note tucked in his coat pocket. Owen decided to take that as a sign of encouragement. That, and the place looked a little more tended to than the warren of dull cement he'd just navigated to get here. Maybe that was a way of protecting certain people.

The man's apartment was just one floor up—he guessed a ground-floor entry was too inviting for burglars—and not that far of a walk. Owen's facility with Russian was perfunctory, just enough to manage what little reliance NASA still maintained on Roscosmos's launch systems. He hoped it would be good enough to at least start a conversation on friendly terms.

He knocked on the door, trying to make it sound as non-threatening as possible and realizing how ridiculous the effort was.

There was no answer. He tried again. After a moment, there was a faint shuffling noise as a shadow moved behind the threshold. Owen sucked in his breath with nervous anticipation and mentally ran through his rehearsed greeting as the door creaked open.

A wizened old man, stooped by time, regarded him with skepticism.

"Doctor Rhyzov?"

The little man just stared, dark eyes darting beneath brows unruly as overgrown hedgerows.

"Anatoly Rhyzov?"

Without a word he began to shuffle away and pull the door shut behind him. Owen leaned in and tried one last time, perhaps a little too loudly:

"*Arkangel.*"

The door stopped moving, then inched back open. The old man still wouldn't speak.

"Doctor?"

"I am Rhyzov," he sighed in a voice turned gravelly by the years. "What is it you want, *Americanski*?"

That was interesting. "How would you know I'm an American?"

"You are rude. Noisy, too. Heard you coming upstairs and down hall. No hoodlum makes such racket. That is why they are dangerous, whereas you are simply annoying."

Owen smiled, he hoped disarmingly enough to keep the conversation moving. "Please accept my apologies if I come across as impolite, Doctor. But if this neighborhood is as dangerous as you say, then may I come in before somebody sneaks out of a dark corner to mug me?"

Rhyzov grunted. "Only because he would then move straight past you through my open door," he said. "Very well, then. Inside."

"Thank you," Owen said as he slipped past. Round one was over, a tie if not an outright win. After months of background research and diplomatic palm-greasing, he was standing in Anatoly Rhyzov's living room. It was small and tidy, painstakingly cared for and decorated with what had to be several generations' worth of family heirlooms. In one corner was an open study which was much more cluttered: An old computer sat atop an older desk, surrounded floor to ceiling with shelves stuffed full of engineering texts and loose notebooks. Scattered among the academic detritus were the hallmarks of a life spent in the Russian space program: plaques, paintings, models, even bits of equipment that must have been pulled from old Soyuz capsules. Owen thought they appeared quite heavy to have ever been used on a spacecraft. The rocket equation didn't discriminate between competing ideologies: Weight was the enemy which stalked every mission, no matter whose flag it flew.

"So," Rhyzov grunted as he studied Owen. "You come a long way, Mister . . ."

"Harriman. Sorry," he said, and extended his hand. "Owen Harriman. I'm with NASA."

If the old man was surprised, he didn't show it but for the slight lifting of those bushy eyebrows. "What do you do for your space agency, Mr. Harriman?"

"I'm a mission manager in the operations directorate," he replied, attempting an appeal to the presumed Russian respect for authority. "I'm in charge of something called Project HOPE."

Rhyzov studied him quizzically.

"Human Outer Planet Exploration," Owen explained.

"Ah. This I have heard of. Deep-space exploration vehicle, correct?"

"Correct. We're on track to have the spacecraft *Magellan* depart for Jupiter in three years."

Rhyzov nodded. "I hope for your sake it does not become rabbit hole."

"Excuse me?"

"I may be old, but I am not foolish. Neither am I naive. You appear to be earnest young man, Mr. Harriman. Your agency has wasted a great many men like you on grandiose projects that never left drawing board." The old man leaned in closer. "Tell me, does that frighten you? The prospect of devoting your life to a goal that may disappear from your grasp?"

He was a cantankerous old fart, blunt in a classic Russian way. Owen realized he wasn't out of the rhetorical woods just yet. "That is a risk in any scientific pursuit, Dr. Rhyzov."

A grin cracked his weathered face. "That is the difference in our philosophies, Mr. Harriman. Spaceflight is engineering, not 'rocket science,'" he said, wagging a finger. "You know this. I know this. Yet your superiors pretend it is somehow about science when research is secondary. What does scientific discovery matter if you cannot get to where you're going in the first place?"

Owen was taken aback. Rhyzov was right, and there was the gulf between their cultures laid bare. It was too easy to fall into the stylistic traps laid by decades of Public Affairs attempts to sell NASA to the taxpayers.

"You are very quiet for one who has traveled so far," Rhyzov prodded. "Yet you come asking of this Arkangel business." The grit in his voice made it clear this was a subject he didn't enjoy.

"I'm not sure it was a question, to be honest. But here we are. So may we speak?"

"We are speaking now."

Good Lord but this guy liked the wordplay. It was time to cut the crap. "Doctor," Owen began, catching his breath while ceremoniously pulling a manila envelope from his overcoat. "We've found it."

The surprise in Rhyzov's eyes said it all. His hands shook as he took the proffered envelope. "This is certain?" he stammered. "How did you know where to look?" Left unsaid: How did you know it even *existed*?

"We didn't," Owen said. "Chance encounter, which we didn't even see until reprocessing some imagery a few weeks ago. We'd never have found it without the radiation signature. Even after this long, that pusher plate's pretty hot."

Rhyzov glared up at him from beneath those unruly eyebrows. "You deduced our drive system?"

Owen laughed. "Are you joking? What else could it be? And I must say, that's an awful lot of nukes to absorb without having it glow like a neon sign."

"It was long ago, as you said yourself. As was your probe to Pluto. Yet you wait until now to have brought evidence."

"We didn't know there was something worth looking for until your air force blew up that inbound Soyuz a few months ago."

Rhyzov's dark eyes shifted. "What Soyuz?"

Owen maintained his best poker face. So the old guy didn't know? "The transponder squawk we intercepted was consistent with Spacecraft TMK-1, callsign *Dnepr*, a long-duration variant that conveniently disappeared from your tracking databases after the collapse of the Soviet Union in 1991. Appeared out of nowhere, headed for your landing zone in Kazakhstan. It was coming in fast, too."

"You say it was intercepted? Why?"

"That we don't know," Owen said in a little white lie fed to him by the intel briefers. "But between us, it sure looks like they were expecting it. Those ASAT batteries were spun up pretty fast."

Dread descended on Rhyzov like a cloud. "What was its orbital period?"

"Forty-four years and five months, give or take a few days," Owen said. "Consistent with a low-energy insertion from Pluto. Wasn't TMK outfitted with a Block D service module?" It was a long shot, but if the old guy bit . . .

"*Da*," Rhyzov said. He still remembered the details. "Needed for deep-space missions. More delta-v and extended life support."

So it had been manned; one more data point he'd needed. "Our information suggests it could support three cosmonauts for thirty days," Owen said, though the idea of three people being stuffed into those tiny capsules for more than thirty hours sounded crazy.

"*Da*," he said again, wheels turning behind his eyes.

"They'd have needed at least one correction burn after breaking orbit, once they'd been headed sunward a while." Thirty days might have been too soon. But if it held enough consumables to keep three men alive for thirty days, then it could keep two for sixty. Or one for ninety.

There'd been at least one live cosmonaut on that old Soyuz, if only to make sure it had remained pointed in the right direction. It might have been his—or their—last action as a living human being. "So our question for you is simple: Why?"

Old eyes flared with long-simmering anger. "You ask me why, when I just now learn at least one of them tried to come back? It would have been suicide, when they could have just come back with my ship."

And there it was, the source of the old man's recalcitrance. He'd poured his life into a machine that had been concealed from history along with his professional reputation, all no doubt due to politics. It was old Soviet Russia, after all: *Everything* was political, a miserable lesson the United States had recently begun to learn.

Owen watched as Rhyzov leafed through the grainy photographs and read the rudimentary information they'd been able to deduce: dimensions, mass, duration . . . the most shocking feature, despite being something they all knew a nuclear pulse ship could achieve, had been the assumed velocity. The Soviets had managed to build a massive spacecraft capable of achieving a measurable fraction of light speed, enough to fly a grand tour of the solar system in under a year. And nobody had known about it.

"Impressive work," Rhyzov finally said, "though your crew complement is too generous by half. The rest of your information is largely correct."

They'd flown this beast with just three cosmonauts? "You know this business, Doctor. Once you have enough data points, reverse engineering isn't that hard. We just couldn't quite believe its origin."

"Math is math," the old man shrugged. "Is hard to argue," though his words hinted at a history of having to do exactly that. Owen saw something change in his eyes, like a barrier had been breached or a vault unlocked. "Please, Mr. Harriman of NASA, we have bantered enough," Rhyzov said as he shuffled toward the study, waving Owen along. "Come, we have much to discuss."

As his host poured tea, Owen wandered about Rhyzov's crowded little office. It spoke of a life filled with family and work. Two families, really, because if a man loved what he did, it didn't feel so much like work. Owen suspected there had been precious few opportunities like that in the former Workers' Paradise. Yellowed photographs of children, cousins, and grandparents were interspersed with those of other men and the massive rockets they had constructed together.

His arm rested along Rhyzov's desk next to an ungainly contraption of lenses and polished aluminum tubes. He guessed it was some type of sextant, perhaps built for an aircraft, more likely from a spacecraft given where it now rested. He wondered if it had in fact been flown in space.

"You like?" Rhyzov asked as he sank into a well-worn chair beside him. "It is from Zond L1."

"The one you guys flew around the Moon?" Owen admired it with newfound awe—this was actual flown Soviet lunar hardware. "So it wasn't just an empty capsule?"

"No, not empty," the little man sighed. "It was fully equipped for human occupants. If they had listened to us, it would have carried a cosmonaut and your Apollo would have been also-ran. Moon race, over. Mother Russia for the win, as you might say."

Owen laughed. "You were a graduate student on the navigation team then," he said, letting Rhyzov know they'd done their homework. "Quite an accomplishment, though nothing compared to your nuclear pulse drive."

"Ah. Now we get down to business, Mr. Harriman. You have dossiers on me as well as Project Arkangel."

Owen answered with a knowing smile. "Took a while for the spooks at Langley to tease that one out," Owen said. "Suitably imposing name, too. I'm surprised the party leaders were okay with using Christian imagery for something this grandiose."

He dismissed it with a wave. "Random codeword. Arkhangelsk is city in Siberia, near Murmansk. We often name projects for cities. But again, you would not be here if there were no questions."

"Questions are the one thing we aren't short on." Owen tapped the file. "This project had a level of secrecy I've never seen. If our government knew about it, nobody's owned up to it."

That drew a laugh. "Someone knows. Someone always knows. Perhaps right people just wouldn't pay attention, or someone who should have didn't and hid his mistake."

"You're probably not wrong," Owen sighed. "There had to be some signal intercepts. Maybe it was lost in the noise at NSA." His dive into decades-old intelligence uncovered long-forgotten suspicions that the Soviets had been building an orbiting military complex that eventually became Arkangel, believed to be abandoned in the late eighties along with any CIA interest. Owen presumed some bureaucratic dweeb hadn't figured it out fast enough and hid the evidence just to avoid professional embarrassment.

"Communications and telemetry were tightly controlled," Rhyzov explained. "Encrypted signals, burst transmissions at random intervals. Ship was too far away for us to control mission anyway."

The old heads at Star City must've loved that, Owen thought. "Still, we should have at least seen the evidence when you lit up that pulse drive."

"Chemical stage pushed it out of Earth orbit," Rhyzov explained. "Nuclear stage ignition timed to occur behind Moon's shadow. Would not have seen."

"But it burned a lot more than that one time," Owen said. "Even if our early-warning satellites weren't looking in the right direction, astronomers would have noticed."

"Recall that gamma ray bursts were thought to be confined within galactic plane until your Compton satellite demonstrated otherwise," Rhyzov pointed out. "Late 1991."

Right about the time when Arkangel went dark. "So those bursts within the plane weren't natural." Or as far away as everyone thought.

"Who can know?" Rhyzov smiled, enjoying the game. "We had advantage of launching vehicle before most of your orbiting observatories were operational. Lost in noise, as you said."

Owen wondered how many astronomers were going to have to reevaluate data from back then. "I keep coming back to one question: Why do something this monumental and then sit on it? Why didn't they come back? Was there some catastrophic failure?"

"Failure was not in spacecraft." Rhyzov creaked open a drawer to remove a thick bellows folder. Ruddy brown and worn by age, it was held shut with a simple string clasp. Dust wafted up from its creases as he dropped it onto the floor between them. "Was crew. *They* malfunctioned. And if your NASA superiors are considering a similar adventure then you must be ready for whatever it may bring. We certainly weren't."

3

This is Mission Control.

After three years of intense preparations, we are at L-minus two days and counting until the Magellan II *crew departs Earth for their expedition to Jupiter and the outer solar system.*

Astronauts Roy and Noelle Hoover, Jack Templeton, and Traci Keene have spent the last week in prelaunch quarantine at Kennedy Space Center and are now conducting their final integrated simulation with the flight control team here in Houston. Once their spacecraft Magellan *is under constant acceleration from its advanced pulsed-fusion engines, within days they will have traveled well beyond any timely communication with Earth due to the signal delays over such great distances.*

After they have crossed the orbit of Mars and traversed the asteroid belt, they will make a close flyby of Jupiter for one of the most critical events of the mission. As they enter Jupiter's influence, they will intercept the Cygnus cargo ship which is already racing toward its own encounter with the gas giant. The following day, the crew will launch a series of probes into the planet's turbulent atmosphere and across its icy moon Europa before performing a gravity-assist maneuver to increase their velocity and shift the plane of their trajectory for Phase Two: the mission to Pluto and the Kuiper Belt.

Their flyby of the gas giant promises to be a momentous time for the astronauts of the Magellan II *expedition and America's Human Outer Planet Exploration program. Today is the crew's final opportunity to test themselves before they must perform this for real at Jupiter.*

◆ ◆ ◆

The simulated *Magellan* control deck, from its overhead lighting to its touchscreen instrument panels, was awash in red. The lighting the crew had dialed in to preserve their night vision accentuated the simulated planetshine of Jupiter, filling the small cabin with a carnival glow. The high-definition screens outside their windows presented towering cloud formations in swirling pastel streams of orange and purple, their digital tops sheared away by simulated supersonic winds. When time came for the actual flyby in a few more weeks, the real view promised to be spectacular and completely ignored. That so many mission-critical events would coincide with their sideswipe of one of the solar system's most remarkable sights was one of many cruel realities of spaceflight.

Mission pilot Traci Keene almost hoped for a primary control failure during the actual supply intercept, as it would give them an opportunity to hand-fly the ship if they were forced to revert to the backup plan. "*Cygnus*'s docking target just pinged us. LIDAR is locked on. Relative velocity four meters per second."

"Rog." Roy Hoover showed no such desire to look outside. His Zen-like discipline might have come effortlessly in the sims but it was a no-less-vital trait for a mission commander. While he might have been indifferent to computer-generated visuals, his crew also knew he was that much of a stoic.

"He means, 'Yes, I acknowledge your report and concur we are on target for rendezvous,'" came a soothing voice from behind her. Noelle Hoover was accustomed to filling in her husband's unfinished thoughts; her crewmates were convinced it was the main reason they'd been assigned to the mission together. Without her, two years in deep space would be agonizing with a boss who conserved words like water in the desert.

"We appreciate the translation. They're gonna miss you at Capcom, especially the Europeans. They won't have anybody left to gossip with in their own language." If the big shots in the Astronaut Office had wanted another crewman who was the commander's polar opposite, they could scarcely have done better than Jack Templeton.

"Perhaps I'm the one who will need them back here to gossip about you."

"That'd be a mistake," Traci said. "Jack's been listening to French language lessons in his sleep."

"And how is it you know this?" Noelle quipped.

"Focus, people," Roy growled over Jack's snickering while Traci searched in vain for a good comeback. "SIMSUP's throwing us a nice softball right across home plate. Screw this up and we'll get to spend our last night on Earth practicing intercepts." It was the most consecutive syllables he had uttered all day.

"The oracle speaks."

"I'm serious, Templeton." His tone carried a warning.

"So am I, boss. I'd rather be sitting at the beach house with a cold beer. It's the girls cutting up this time," Jack protested. "And by the way, relative velocity's down to three m-p-s. We're standing by with the claw." One of Jack's duties as *Magellan*'s flight engineer was to grab the resupply vehicle with their remote manipulator arm in case the two pilots somehow lost primary control.

"Can you behave, Mrs. Hoover?"

"Yes, love," she groaned, and turned off her intercom to lean in toward Jack. "You think he's cranky now, wait until we've been living off of freeze-dried food for a year."

"He'll be even crankier if we blow this sim," Jack said, "and he's right. It's kind of a tradition for the trainers to take it easy on our last run, so we need to lock down the grab-ass. You ready?"

"I am." Jack always found her Mediterranean French accent to be soothing. It hadn't been the least bit surprising when she and Roy had announced their engagement not long after a joint tour on the Space Station—she'd probably lulled him into hypnosis.

Putting a married couple on the agency's longest-duration mission had been the obvious choice. As for Jack's and Traci's assignments, he hadn't been so sure. Maybe it was the center director's idea of social engineering. Two years' worth of training alongside each other in close quarters had offered as many opportunities to learn each other's quirks as marriage would for anyone else.

"Visual on the care package at two o'clock," Traci said. "I've got her centered in window one right."

Jack spotted the computer-generated stack of gleaming aluminum cylinders in the porthole by his flight station behind Traci. "Tallyho. I have visual on *Cygnus* in window two right."

"I have positive control with the remote," Traci said. "RCS check." She tapped a control stick and the animated supply vehicle pitched and rolled in response as pixelated reaction jets puffed along its length. If all went as planned, the stack of logistics modules and propellant tanks would dock itself with the portals nested inside *Magellan*'s open support truss. Failing that, Traci could remotely fly it in. If the whole system went belly-up, Roy would bring them in close enough for Jack to grab *Cygnus* with the manipulator arm. If that failed and they missed their resupply rendezvous, they'd be forced to turn tail-first and slow down enough for Jupiter to sling them back toward Earth while looking forward to long weeks of basic rations during the flight home.

That was a whole different level of simulation which Jack was certain the others were just as sick of as he was. After two years of near-continuous rehearsals of every critical event and conceivable failure, it was nice to have everything working as planned for once.

"Twenty meters, closing at point five," Traci said in her coolest, nothing-but-a-thing pilot voice. "Cargo ship's still responsive. Switching back to auto."

"Arm is secure," Noelle said, just as cool for different reasons. "Docking nodes are clear." *Are we sure we can't stay at Jupiter for a while?* she left unsaid.

"Ten meters," Roy said. "Hang on."

The simulator rocked gently as their virtual cargo hit its imaginary target. There was a series of dull thuds as their displays told them the craft had seated itself against *Magellan*'s spine.

"Hard dock," Jack said. "All latches are barber-poled. Stand by for propellant transfer check . . . okay, there we go. Positive pressure in the manifolds. That's all, folks."

"Roger that," Roy said. "Waiting for acknowledgment from Houston."

"Can we hit the 'time warp' button for that one?" Traci chimed in. "Because I really have to pee."

A new voice sounded over their radio net. "Not necessary. SIMSUP is closing this session. Congratulations, guys."

There were whoops from the technicians out in the sim bay as they began shutting down the platform. Jack blew out a relieved sigh and sank into his flight couch. No words were spoken as they celebrated with a round of silent fist bumps. Traci tossed off her headset and fluffed her hair. "How about that beer, partner?"

◆ ◆ ◆

Launch day breakfast had been a tradition since Al Shepard's first fifteen-minute hop above the atmosphere. It would be their last face-to-face human contact without being surrounded by technicians before leaving the planet for two years, so today was especially significant. While grand send-offs threatened to become melodramatic clichés as spaceflight became more routine, today's gathering had been kept more private than usual. Perhaps because they were about to leave for the outer edges of the solar system, the mood at the astronaut beach house was subdued.

As they shuffled into the dining room, Jack was struck by how few people were here. His launch to the International Space Station years earlier had hosted more people. Today there were only three guests: Grady Morrell, head of the astronaut office; Owen Harriman, their mission manager; and one rumpled old guy he'd never laid eyes on before. Jack stole a glance in Roy's direction; their mission commander's pursed lips signaled that he was just as surprised.

Other than their unexpected guest, everything else was normal: pitchers of juice and coffee, a plateful of fruit, platters of scrambled eggs and breakfast steaks all laid out on a buffet behind them. A single sealed envelope sat at the center of the dining table.

They each took coffee and sat without a sound, eyes locked on their hosts. Owen, to his credit, didn't waste time. "I'm sorry to spring this surprise on you but it was unavoidable," he said as he pushed the envelope across the table at Roy. "This is going to be a bit of a working breakfast."

Roy's gaze remained fixed on Grady and Owen as he turned the envelope over, cocked an eyebrow and tore open the candy-striped "Eyes Only" security tape.

Owen narrated while Roy began pulling out briefing papers. "Inside you'll find mission-critical information that we've been forced to withhold until the very last minute. We apologize for the secrecy, but once you've had a chance to digest it I think you'll understand."

"That remains to be seen," Roy grumbled.

Jack peeked over Roy's shoulder and saw that most of the contents were in Russian. He looked back across the table. "Who's our guest?"

Owen laid a hand on the old man's shoulder. "Dr. Anatoly Rhyzov, formerly of the Aviation and Space Agency of the old Soviet Union." He paused as the crew did a double take and Traci almost spit her coffee.

"Dr. Rhyzov was enjoying his retirement in Moscow until I found him and screwed it all up." The thin smile that crossed the old man's face suggested he hadn't been all that bothered by it. "The state department agreed to give him a worker's visa, and he's been our guest in Houston for the past three years." Almost the same amount of time they'd been in near-total immersion training for the *Magellan II* mission.

Noelle spoke up. "Should we assume the doctor has some particular relevant expertise?"

Jack reached over to lift a stack of the Russian-language papers from Roy. "A good astronaut never questions the pretzel logic of crew assignments," he said, staring over the files at Grady. "But at this point I suppose it's worth the risk." He waved the papers for effect. "I'm assuming this has something to do with my spot on the crew?"

"Of course it does, genius," Grady drawled. "You used to be a Russian cryptologic linguist. That put you at the head of the line."

Jack scanned the cover sheet and flipped through the first few pages at random. "Nothing coded," he said laconically, "but lots of 'Top Secret' banners in Russian. It's about a project called 'Arkangel.'"

Owen leaned forward to speak before the Russian laid a wrinkled hand across his arm. "I ran Arkangel, very long time ago. Any questions you have, I will answer."

Jack began to spread the papers out across the table and stopped with a foldout diagram of what appeared to be a space station with a Soyuz crew capsule mounted on its forward node. The rest became less familiar the closer he looked. "This looks like an old DOS-7 core module," Jack said. "Same thing you guys used to build the Mir and Almaz stations, right?" He traced a finger farther along the diagram. "Docking node's at the top of the stack, not centered in the core. Everything's linear, along a single axis . . . " His voice trailed off as he stopped at an enormous disk at the base of the complex, mounted to the spacecraft by a brawny cluster of pistons. "Is that what I think it is?"

Roy took the foldout, impatient to see for himself. "Good Lord. You actually built a nuclear pulse drive?"

The Russian beamed like a proud grandfather patiently watching the children connect the dots. "*Da.* Other than shock accumulators, most difficult part was strengthening the docking node against torque."

"Thus the linear arrangement," Jack said. "Everything's stacked along the axis of thrust to handle all that power. Same way we had to build *Magellan*."

"Correct," Rhyzov said. "But mass tradeoffs were still difficult. There was no point in building *Arkangel* if we could not also carry a lander and laboratory module."

Jack continued studying the layout. There was the lander, on the opposite end of the forward node: an old LK of the type first built for their defunct Moon program. So not all of them had ended up as museum items. He pointed at a squat cylinder covered with antennas. "And this lab module, on the opposite side of the docking node. Is that what I think it is?"

"Was Kremlin's idea." There was sorrow in Rhyzov's eyes.

Roy leaned over for a better look. "You guys couldn't build so much as a fishing boat without turning it into an intel trawler, huh?"

"Not in those days," Rhyzov agreed. "Is much the same now. Too much same."

"Got that right," Roy muttered. He turned to Owen. "How'd you get him here to begin with?"

"It wasn't easy," Owen said with a glance at Rhyzov, "especially given their Middle East mischief. In the end, it all comes down to the fact that they need our help. Mother Russia wants her sons back, plus whatever stuff they found out there."

"How far out is 'out there'?" Noelle asked, thinking she already knew the answer. If that thing was still parked at Jupiter, could their second-phase mission out to the Kuiper Belt have all been an elaborate ruse?

Owen coughed. "Pluto."

It was a testament to the crew's discipline that they didn't explode with disbelief. Instead, they each leaned back against their chairs and looked to Roy in a show of unity that carried more weight than words.

Roy drummed his fingers against the table. He took a sip of coffee, glaring at Owen over the rim. "Interesting how that's our final destination," he finally said. "I always wondered why that 'Phase Two' option was added, considering the risks and departure window constraints. What I'd like to know is why the hell are we finding this out right before launch?"

"It was a condition of funding the mission," Grady Morrell said. The chief astronaut had been silent through this whole exchange. "A big chunk of it came out of the Pentagon's little black book. I owe the Air Force the next two dozen seats." At the glacially slow rate NASA was adding to the astronaut corps, that would leave them on the hook for a very long time.

Owen pushed another envelope across the table. "These were taken by the *New Horizons* probe during its Pluto flyby in 2015. The operators trained its cameras on this region because of some unexpected radiation signatures they picked up during approach phase three. I'm not sure what anyone expected to find, but it wasn't this."

They each took a photo of the metallic green dragonfly orbiting Pluto.

"So it was still generating heat?" Noelle asked. "After how much time?"

"At that point? About twenty-five years."

Jack almost choked on his coffee. "This thing's been out there since, what . . . the eighties?"

"Almost," Owen said. "Since most of us were kids. The age of big hair and parachute pants."

Jack turned to Rhyzov. "So, when you talked about doing this back in the old days . . . "

"Was not joking," Rhyzov said. "Arkangel was first proposed to Brezhnev in seventies after they learned of your Air Force's research. Was finally approved by Andropov. Gorbachev didn't even know about it until the radioactive propellant was ready to launch."

"Let me guess," Jack said. "Launching a few thousand warheads at once needed the chairman's personal approval."

"Sending a payload of nuclear weapons into orbit was major treaty violation," Rhyzov explained. "To his credit, Gorbachev was more reluctant than his predecessors about it."

"A bomb is a bomb, even if they were built to propel a spacecraft," Owen said. "It took multiple launches; one Energia booster for each propellant magazine. If there'd been a failure, all those warheads would've come crashing down along a straight line from China to Oregon. Gorbachev put all his trust in Dr. Rhyzov's team to not accidentally start World War Three."

"It figures the USSR would be the only ones crazy enough to build one of these things," Jack said. "So what was the mission? What did they want with a pulse drive, besides a nifty way to disguise a weapons platform?"

"Final mission was grand tour of outer solar system and demonstration of maximum sustained acceleration. Original mission was less scientific," Rhyzov chuckled. "Kremlin would spend anything on intelligence gathering, especially under Andropov. Remember he was KGB."

Jack scratched his head. "What intel value does this have? It doesn't do anything that a good recon bird couldn't."

The old Russian gave them an impish smile. "Unless your leaders think it can intercept signals from the future. Alters calculation considerably."

"That's the stupidest thing I've ever . . . " Jack began. His mouth hung open for a beat until he began laughing. "Oh man. They couldn't be—have been—*that* ignorant."

It was ludicrous enough to get a rise out of Roy. "That's not just stupid," he said, "that's weapons-grade stupid."

"Never underestimate *nomenklatura*'s ability to overestimate themselves. Politburo was convinced *Arkangel* could accelerate to a high fraction of light speed out of the solar system, collect radio and television signals from future Earth, then bring them back to use that information for unimaginable advantage."

"Unimaginable is right," Jack said. "Nobody explained that relativity doesn't work like that? Someone must have pointed out that time dilation only goes in one direction."

Rhyzov's features seemed to darken. "Of course someone did. My predecessor in the advanced propulsion directorate. After they took him to Lubyanka, I never saw him again. That is how I became project leader."

Just as the Nazis had refused to accept general relativity because it wasn't "German" science, the Soviets had also twisted science to serve their own political ends: Lysenkoism had led to the starvation of millions since everything ultimately ran headlong into the ineluctable laws of nature. It was a matter of time, which would have offered scant consolation to a man rotting away in the notorious KGB dungeon.

Rhyzov continued. "We kept building. Constructing ship wasn't problem. Let cosmonaut crew or bureau director explain failures to party chairman afterward." He then stabbed at the air for emphasis. "It *wasn't* going to fail because our ship didn't work."

"All those resources," Traci wondered. "Everyone thought it was our military buildup that ground the Soviet Union into the dirt. There was more to the story."

"Ah," he said with a dismissive wave, "there is always more, but you could also say this was part of our reaction. KGB and GRU elements were in charge by then. They were desperate for any advantage."

"But that's laughable," Traci said. "To think no one was able to talk sense to Andropov . . . "

"You did not know Andropov. Whole world thought Saddam had biological weapons, too."

"Good point."

"Exactly!" Rhyzov wagged a bony finger at them. "*You* thought he did because *he* thought he did. And Saddam believed he did because anyone who could tell him truth was afraid to." He drew the same finger across his neck to finish his point.

"Feet first into an industrial shredder," Jack said. "They had a nasty way of dealing with naysayers."

"As you Americans say, 'military intelligence' is an oxymoron. Fortunately for us, we still had a ship which was only limited by the mass we could launch to it. Once it was fully equipped, we could send it anywhere. Gorbachev approved final mission because he was desperate for his own standing."

"At least you no longer had to be so afraid of failure," Traci said, ever the optimist.

The old man's countenance darkened. "One is never too far removed from fear in such a system. Differences are in severity of consequences," he explained. "In this case, consequences fell upon crew."

"They're still out there. What happened?"

"We do not know," he sighed. "Though some suspect it is because of what they found."

That's not creepy at all, Jack thought. He shrugged off the chill working its way up his back. "What did they find?"

"Once again, unknown. Spacecraft 'went dark,' as you say, in 1991. For such an ambitious project, there was much we could not learn. In the end, we know the mission commander survived an apparent crew mutiny." Rhyzov took a long pull from a cup of tea as he studied Jack. "They tell me you are fluent. *Viy izuchayu Roosski yiziyk?*"

Jack shot a glance at Owen and Grady. "Two years of total immersion at the defense language institute." It had been followed by six more years of sitting in an Air Force van listening to intercepted signals along the Russian frontier. "Long before all this astronaut stuff."

Rhyzov considered him for a moment. "Your man will do fine," he finally said to Grady, who even at this late hour still needed convincing. "The commander, Colonel Vaschenko, was diligent about sending his personal observations with encrypted mission updates. Over time his transmissions became erratic. Eventually they stopped. Those who knew him best believed he kept private journal aboard spacecraft. He almost dared us to come find them."

"Which brings us back to the original question," Jack said. "Why didn't they come back?"

The old man became lost in his thoughts. "We do not know," he said after a time. "Isolation can do frightening things to the mind. Whatever it was, it drove our most trusted cosmonauts completely mad."

The normally convivial prelaunch breakfast became subdued. The crew ate in silence, each savoring their last fresh-cooked meal for the next two years while contemplating what they'd just learned, and what lay ahead. The excitement they'd begun the day with was now tempered by the harsh reality of the knowledge that they would no longer be, and in truth never had been, *first*.

Even more galling was that they would have to maintain the public facade until whenever Public Affairs might decide to let the secret out. For at the farthest reaches of the solar system, they were going to encounter the last thing they could have imagined: another crew of explorers over forty years dead.

Roy's frustration, while not quite boiling over, bubbled out from under the tight lid of his cool temper during the van ride out to 39A. As they trudged down the walkway, sealed up in their spacesuits and waving to the crowd with beaming faces that might as well have been prosthetic makeup, it had been impossible to ignore the throng of protestors lining the sidewalks.

"'No Nukes in Space'?" Roy groused. "Don't they know space is full of even worse stuff all by itself?"

"I seriously doubt anything those goobers think they know," Traci said. "The stuff they're screeching about is already in orbit. It's not coming back here."

"If they had even half a clue about what we were going out there to find," Roy chuckled. "A spacecraft powered by nuclear bombs. I swear, don't any of these people have jobs?"

"Read the news lately? Not enough of them," Jack said, not ready to join in the hippie-bashing just yet. His mother and sister might have been out there among them if he wasn't riding out to the launchpad.

"You're such a buzzkill," Traci said with a shot from her elbow. "Still can't get your head out of the real world, can you?"

"Just enough to make me glad we're leaving it for a while."

4

Mission Day 1

The Deep Space Vehicle *Magellan* awaited their arrival at three hundred kilometers' altitude, covering thirty thousand kilometers each hour in its fall around Earth. They'd been chasing it for most of the day in their Dragon III capsule; a tighter window could have put the two ships in close proximity sooner, but the mission planners had other ideas. They wouldn't be leaving Earth orbit any earlier and there was still a great deal of work ahead to check out their spacecraft in orbit before taking it along on their journey.

Sunlight poured into *Dragon*'s cabin through big oval windows that could have been lifted from a Gulfstream jet, almost obviating the need for its warm indirect lighting. It had taken many sim sessions for them to get comfortable with the little spacecraft's minimalist touchscreen controls; the single design concession for NASA was a good old-fashioned control panel mounted along the bottom with backup gauges, an eight-ball attitude indicator, and hardwired switches.

The sunlight spun across the cabin from an unplanned roll as Traci stifled a curse. "It's not a video game," Roy reminded her. "You can't always fly it with the keyboard." She nodded her understanding and reached for one of the joysticks that had been mounted on each of their seat arms at Roy's insistence.

Jack pushed away from the window by his seat to float up between the pilots. "I still think we should name her," he said. "This is a spacecraft all its own, after all." Word was the NASA administrator had been irritated to no end by the agency naming every single module of the ISS and decided that christening their first deep-space vessel the *Magellan* was good enough. "It's bad luck to take out a ship with no name."

"Superstitious Navy crap," Roy said as he followed their target through a long-focus telescope mounted behind the flight station. "But feel free to entertain the idea," he added, signaling that he was in fact open to it despite HQ's official discouragement.

Jack had been thinking on it a while but had more fun casting about for suggestions. "Anybody have a favorite cartoon character?"

"Going lowbrow right out of the gate?" Traci said. "You can't come up with anything inspirational?"

"My two favorites were taken before I was even born," Roy said. "If I can't use Charlie Brown or Snoopy, count me out."

"Who else traveled with Ferdinand Magellan?" Noelle asked. "Did he have any shipboard pets?"

Traci snorted. "You're asking the funny pages guy for historical trivia?"

"I'm just playing to my audience," Jack said. "Looks like I underestimated you guys."

"You're the first Lit major astronaut. I'm sure you have some ideas."

"It was a minor," he protested. "How come everyone conveniently forgets the 'applied math' part? But yeah, I had a couple ideas. My first thought was Smaug."

"Not Puff the Magic Dragon?" Roy said.

Jack continued. "Then I realized that was too obvious. Too pedestrian. So, I went deep," he said, and paused for dramatic effect. "Fafner."

The other three traded confused looks.

"It's from Wagner," he began to explain.

"The composer?" Traci wondered. "He wrote about a dragon?"

"Sort of. It was from one of his operas, but that's digging too deep. Then I thought of Grendel."

Traci frowned, trying to place it. "Hansel and . . . ? No, that's not it."

"*Beowulf*," Jack explained. "Grendel was something like a dragon."

"It also sounds like something I'd blow out of my nose," Roy said while Noelle stifled a giggle. He remained still at his station as a thin smile creased his face. "Let's table this discussion for later. I've got our new home in sight."

They continued falling around Earth, steadily closing until *Magellan* lay less than a kilometer ahead. Even a few meters' difference meant they orbited at different speeds, and therefore one would have to overtake the other. The trick was to get ahead of it and raise their altitude until it matched their target's enough for it to gently drift into them.

It required a bit of backward thinking: In order to speed up, one first had to slow down. Braking for just a few seconds in the direction of flight lowered their altitude and shortened the distance of their orbit, which increased their speed as they drew closer to Earth. Once they'd pulled ahead, they could accelerate to regain altitude and increase their orbital period which slowed them back down to meet *Magellan*.

Decades' worth of video from space had a deceptive tendency to make vehicles jetting about in orbit appear as benign as toys floating in a bathtub, when in truth spacecraft massing several hundred metric tons between them were whipping along at a good four or five miles per second within arm's reach of each other. Go that fast in the atmosphere and they'd be on fire.

The low relative motion often made it just as deceptive for the people inside the spacecraft. As Traci flew them along *Magellan*'s length, Jack was struck by the contrast: *Dragon* might have been roomy for a space capsule but it was nothing compared to the ship they were about to mate with. Over twice as long as the old Space Station but with half the livable space, most of its bulk consisted of cryogenic propellant tanks and utility modules. There was no mistaking that it was meant to go somewhere. Had gone somewhere, in fact: Mars, with a flyby of Venus on the return leg. While many had laid claim to the term before, *Magellan* was NASA's first honest-to-goodness spaceship: built to be reused and reoutfitted as new technologies put new destinations within reach.

Not as graceful as the massive vehicles SpaceX was building for their own Martian expeditions, it hadn't been designed with wealthy adventure tourists in mind either. *Magellan* resembled nothing so much as a flying umbrella stand built from an elaborate Erector Set. Forward, it was protected by a domed canopy of ballistic fibers that shielded them from micrometeor strikes which would become more hazardous as they gained speed. At their final velocity of over a million kilometers per hour, a pebble could hole the ship and leave a trail of ionizing radiation in its wake.

Behind the dome were the crew's living areas, a cluster of aluminum cylinders stacked side by side around a central hub. This hub held the command section, where the daily work of piloting *Magellan* would happen.

The hab modules were dwarfed by the complex of foil-wrapped cryogenic tanks mounted three abreast and centered along the saddle truss that ran the length of the ship. Even with fusion power, constantly accelerating to Jupiter demanded that over eighty percent of the ship's mass was propellant which would still have to be replenished if they were to continue on to Pluto and the Kuiper Belt. The tanks' dazzling golden skin had made *Magellan* the brightest object in the sky for months, outshone only when the Moon was full.

This freight-train-sized mass of fuel tanks fed the reactor plant and fusion drive, nestled behind a conical radiation shield at the end of the ship. If the forward dome protected the crew from the random hazards of outer space, the drive cone's shield protected them from the predictable hazards created by their own ship. Magnetic exhaust nozzles at the end were like mechanized tulip bulbs with louvered petals set within a wreath of coolant loops and control vanes. When their nuclear fire was finally lit, the exhaust plume would make *Magellan* visible in broad daylight.

"She is one big beast," Jack whistled. His face was pressed against one of the big oval windows like a kid checking out the Christmas display at a toy store.

"You've seen her before," Traci said with the practiced calm of a pilot who couldn't afford to be distracted from her mission, which in this case was to fly them nose-down along *Magellan*'s length without running into the hundred-thousand-ton complex now filling their windows. She couldn't forget that their situation was relative: Weightlessness might feel gentle, but there was an awful lot of mass and velocity between the two spacecraft.

"Haven't seen it with the new hab and drive modules. Last time I was up here they'd just brought back the Mars expedition," Jack said. "That fusion engine's a lot bigger than the old one." The ship's original VASIMR thrusters had been removed and repurposed as the core of the Cygnus interplanetary cargo tug, which for the past year had been racing ahead for their rendezvous at Jupiter.

It all seemed great until he remembered that the Russians had beaten them by several decades with an even bigger ship that had flirted with relativistic speeds. Jack had almost managed to convince himself that none of that mattered—they were still about to be the first to visit Jupiter on the way to recovering secrets from a derelict ship that had been waiting at the edge of the solar system since before he was born. If theirs was now a salvage mission, so be it.

"Topside visual checklist's complete," Roy said after several minutes of no noise but circulation fans and the occasional thump of a thruster. "You guys see anything we may have missed?"

"Nothing to report here, love," Noelle said. "Let's move in." The scientist was ready to get going.

After a thumbs-up from Jack and Traci, Roy keyed his mic. "Houston, *Dragon*. Exterior inspection complete, no anomalies observed."

"Copy that, *Dragon*. You are go for transposition and docking."

"Acknowledge we are go for docking," Roy said, then glanced over his shoulder at his crewmates. "And Houston, be advised we've elected to change our radio callsign. All comm with *Dragon* will now go by *Puffy*."

The hiss of air that came with opening *Magellan*'s inner hatch carried with it a faint aroma of iron oxide, a leftover from the previous expedition.

"So that's what Mars smells like—a rusty car?" Jack wondered.

"Just the airlock," Roy assured him. "And the flight deck. And the equipment bays. But we'll have a brand-new hab to live in."

"Don't forget the hydroponic garden," Noelle said. "I plan to spend every free minute in there."

"Good thing we'll be on opposite shifts or you'd have to fight me for it," Traci said as she dogged down the hatch behind them. The odor was stronger in there, where the previous crew would've kept their EVA suits in between surface sorties on Mars. She wrinkled her nose. "It smells like a Mojave Desert scrapyard."

"Even fresh filters can't get rid of everything," Roy reminded them as he powered up the flight stations.

A chime sounded as the onboard computer announced its readiness, just loud enough to get their attention. A synthetic female voice, its timbre painstakingly calibrated by teams of psychiatrists and audio engineers, greeted them.

WELCOME ABOARD COMMANDER HOOVER. ALL SYSTEMS ARE NORMAL. THERE WAS A TRANSIENT VOLTAGE SURGE IN MAIN BUS A DURING REACTOR WARMUP WHICH WAS ABSORBED BY THE SECONDARY CAPACITOR BANK. A PRELIMINARY ENGINEERING ANALYSIS FROM MISSION CONTROL IS AVAILABLE AT YOUR DISCRETION.

"You know better, Daisy," Roy said, not hiding his suspicion of talking computers that were always listening. The spacecraft was up and running on its own thanks to their "fifth crewman," the Distributed Artificial Intelligence and Surveillance Environment. As the time lag for communications with home would eventually be measured in hours, DAISE would likewise take over the monitoring and rapid-fire troubleshooting of Mission Control.

For different reasons, the idea hadn't sat any better with the controllers in Houston than it had with Roy. "Talk to Templeton."

OF COURSE, the voice replied. HOW ARE YOU, FLIGHT ENGINEER TEMPLETON?

"Jack works fine. Just like the sims, okay?"

A-OK.

"No need to be cute."

I THOUGHT IT WOULD BE USEFUL TO ADOPT THE APPROPRIATE IDIOM. WOULD YOU LIKE TO SEE THE ANALYSIS OF MAIN BUS A?

"Anything in there you disagree with?"

NO. IN FACT IT HAD OVER A THIRTY PERCENT PROBABILITY OF OCCURING.

Jack looked back at Roy as he switched on the flight engineer's station. "That won't be necessary, then." He lowered his voice. "And once we get settled, let's you and I keep our comms private. No need to irritate the boss."

He was answered by a light buzz on his wrist. A message appeared on his smartwatch: UNDERSTOOD.

"Good girl."

Traci leaned over his shoulder. "It's not like she's a dog. She's not even a she."

"Not now. This is already getting weird." He looked at the bag floating over her shoulder. "More stuff? How'd you get all that approved?"

"It's light. Still below mass limits." She pulled the zipper open. "See?" Stuffed amongst the stash in her "Personal Preference Kit" were strings of multicolor LED lights and inflatable decorations.

"Christmas in July?"

"Key West," she said. "It'll be a long trip."

"It will be." Jack surveyed the cabin as he floated down to the crew deck. As promised, the hab module felt brand new. Divided into three levels, each had its own common area built around an access tunnel down the center of the module. The first held their galley and rec room, and so was mostly open living space. The middle level's common area was much smaller, hemmed in by sleeping quarters and lavatories. Since half the crew was expected to be resting at any given time, this level was kept spartan to encourage their privacy. In other words, there were no TVs or treadmills right outside their bedrooms. The lower level was the most crowded, being set up for equipment storage and onboard laboratories.

"Flight stations, people," Roy announced as he flew past, heading forward to the control deck. "Five minutes."

Jack ducked into his room and strapped his duffle to the bunk. At over twenty kilos, it could cause a lot of damage once they were under thrust if just left floating around. He closed the privacy screen, which was much too flimsy to dignify calling a "door," and pushed off for the center tunnel. It was a quick flight up through the hab and back to the control deck.

The Flight Control Room, "FCR" for short and more popularly known as "Mission Control," had not held crowds of this size since the Mars expedition or the first Moon landing. The visitor's gallery was brimming over with VIPs maneuvering for space against the glass that looked out over the busy control room.

Anatoly Rhyzov dreaded being hemmed in by the pressing crowd and so was all the more surprised when his young friend Owen swept them past the security screens and straight into "manager's row." The old man seemed confused as Owen escorted him to an empty chair at his mission manager console behind the flight director. He'd been given a front-row seat.

Rhyzov risked a furtive glance toward the VIP gallery before leaning into Owen with a gravelly whisper. "Are you sure this will not upset somebody?"

"Don't much care if it does," his host replied.

"I saw your Vice President in there."

"The VP's kind of in charge of the space program, traditionally if not officially."

"He is not bothered by my presence?"

Owen smiled. "Who do you think approved your visa?"

Rhyzov looked up at the gallery, stunned, as the Vice President of the United States gave him a conspiratorial wink.

Owen's smile grew both wider and mischievous. "You represent the whole reason we're here, Anatoly. The boss understands that. The rest of them don't know enough to be upset about it."

"You are happy about this." The old man's voice carried an air of mutual understanding.

"There's a lot to be happy about today, assuming they don't blow themselves up," Owen said, just loud enough to earn an angry look from the flight director at the next console.

"You joke, no?" Rhyzov understood *Magellan*'s fusion engines well enough to know they were in essence just a more sophisticated version of *Arkangel*'s nuclear pulse drive. Both used controlled nuclear detonations to push their payloads around the solar system—the difference was that NASA's version relied on plasma jets and magnetic nozzles instead of a fixed supply of repurposed tactical warheads.

"I joke, yes," Owen said. "You checked our math, remember?"

"Bah." Rhyzov gave a dismissive wave. "Lucky for you I can still remember." While studying their test results, Rhyzov had devised a method to keep the drive running at close to its rated specific impulse even when its plasma injectors were out of sync. The downside was the heightened risk of an uncontained nozzle failure, a "rapid unscheduled disassembly" in engineering vernacular. To the general public, this was known as a "thermonuclear explosion."

Owen nodded. "Good backup procedure, though," he said, earning another skeptical glance from Flight.

"That remains to be seen," Flight grumbled as he turned back to his console, a signal for Owen and the other big shots along Manager's Row to zip it while his controllers got to work. He leaned forward and thumbed his comm loop. "Gold Team: once around the horn for TJI go/no-go."

Jack reached out for a handhold to stop his forward momentum and spun into his flight couch at the engineer's station, a six-pack of flat screens on which he could track every system on the spacecraft, including the maintenance bots that moved along rails on its spine. If anything broke, Jack and his bots could fix most of it from here.

He pulled his shoulder harness and lap belt tight and plugged his headset in. Roy was already asking for status reports as he pushed in his earpiece. It was noticeably noisier than the simulator as the spacecraft came to life. Traci turned to give him a playful wink as if this were just another spin in the sim. Roy was silent as usual, except when giving orders or needing information. Jack's own experience in the Air Force had left him indifferent to the service's "fighter mafia" but it had been a valuable lesson in managing a personality type that NASA teemed with.

Before Roy could start peppering him with questions about the plasma injectors or lithium coils, he sent an automated status report over to Roy's master display. "Hey, boss. Got any Beemans?"

"Not now, peckerwood," Roy deadpanned, unable to hide his anticipation as the final poll of flight controllers in Houston buzzed in their headsets.

"Retro?"

"Go."

"FIDO?"

"Go, Flight."

"GNC?"

"We're go."

"EECOM?"

"Umm—stand by, Flight. Little glitch here."

◆ ◆ ◆

"Talk to me, EECOM."

The electrical and environmental controller leaned into his console, as if his body language might help reveal some clue hiding in the data. "Flight, I've lost one of their telemetry feeds. Looks like Bravo-one antenna is misaligned."

"Any chance that's an instrumentation problem?" the flight director asked. The chance of losing an antenna before even breaking orbit should have been almost nil. Working on a hunch, Flight didn't wait for an answer. "Booster, what's your status?"

"Engine two had some flux in the containment field when the nozzle magnets were spinning up, Flight. Danced with the yellow band for a couple seconds before settling down."

Flight's scowl telegraphed a concern that Owen was well aware of. *This is what we get for relying on propulsion that was barely into operational testing, on a mission that promises to be one whopper of a test.* "Understood, Booster. EECOM, you hear that gouge on number two?"

"Got it, Flight. I'll get back to you." He dropped off the loop and started talking to his backroom team. Flight gave Owen and his guest a quick side-eye and returned to polling the rest of his team. Owen looked down at his own screens, taking in the unfiltered glimpse at what DAISE was doing up there with his astronauts. He decided to enjoy the lack of a signal delay for the next few hours. Rhyzov, for his part, sat transfixed by the quiet intensity surrounding them.

"Secondary antennas are just inside engine two's radiation shadow," Jack said. "That magnetic flux must've spoofed the relays." On a hunch, he typed a command into one of his screens and brought up a trace log of the engine and electrical systems. "Yeah. Time stamp's consistent with that power spike Daisy told us about." He'd been holding a finger down on his private comm link as he spoke, making sure the AI understood him. Daisy buzzed his watch once to let him know it was on the case.

Roy chuckled at the exchange on the ground. He covered his mic with one hand and turned to face Jack. "Should I just tell 'em to fix their little problem and light this candle?"

So the big guy was capable of playing along after all. "All we have left is to open the injectors," Jack said. "Question is, are you guys sure we're pointed in the right direction?"

"We are," Traci said, sounding a little defensive. She'd been updating their departure vectors the whole time.

"I always know where I'm going," Roy said. "I'm just not always sure how I got there."

Jack tapped some commands into the keypad by his armrest and Daisy answered right away. "Just in case anyone's keeping score, the onboard diagnostics agree. It's antenna interference. Magnetic flux spoofed the transmitter. Recommend we reset STE to AUX."

"You said STE off?"

"*Aux*," Jack corrected. "Auxiliary."

"That your call, or Daisy's?"

Jack wasn't ready to admit the AI had suggested it first. "Umm . . . both. And I think she's right."

"So it has a gender now?"

Noelle had made it a point to stay out of the debate until now. "I don't know of any men named 'Daisy,'" she said, "not even in France."

"She's got a point, boss," Traci said. "It saved our butts plenty of times in the sims."

Roy was unconvinced. "It's a computer outguessing another computer. So what?"

The crackling radio interrupted their spat. "*Magellan*, we recommend you switch STE to AUX."

Roy shook his head in surrender and glared at Jack, relaying the command. *Flip the switch, already.* Jack reached for the electrical panel and did as both human and computer had suggested.

Their headsets beeped as Houston came back on the frequency. "That did it. You're go." Capcom's tone then changed; there was a new gravity in his voice: "*Magellan*, you are go for Trans-Jovian Injection at thirty-six hours plus five-one."

Roy covered his mic with one hand and turned to face Jack. "Any last words, smart guy?" As Jack shook his head no, Roy returned to his flight controls. "Houston, this is *Magellan* Expedition Two; understand we are go for TJI." He stabbed a command on the master display and synched their countdown timer.

Ignition came within a fraction of a second. Jack winced as he felt the first controlled explosion of plasma push at his back. "Ignition, and the clock has started."

◆ ◆ ◆

Far behind them, cryogenic hydrogen flashed into ionized gas which was pumped through a series of magnetic injectors before it could melt the surrounding machinery.

Every few seconds a fresh cloud of this hydrogen plasma was injected into the thrust chamber, where it was met by a magnetically driven shell of lithium which instantaneously compressed it down to almost nothing. As two atoms of anything can't occupy the same space at the same time, hydrogen fused into helium in the same explosive reaction that had been powering stars since the beginning of time.

But even this wasn't enough on its own to propel *Magellan*. Besides fusing the hydrogen plasma, the lithium foil added its mass for the simple Newtonian response necessary for a rocket engine to work. The resulting explosion was channeled through electromagnetic nozzles at just the right speed to move the spacecraft away before blowing itself up. While more elegant than just throwing nuclear bombs out its tail, the process wasn't all that different than what the Russians had done with *Arkangel*.

In adjacent orbits, camera-sats broadcast the departure of NASA's first mission to the outer solar system. One, a shoebox-sized remote piggybacked into orbit on an earlier CubeSat launch by an anonymous Eastern European videoblogger, had maneuvered in close for a look straight up *Magellan*'s main engines. Any threat this electronic interloper may have presented disappeared as it was vaporized by the miniature sun that ignited just a few hundred meters away. The live feed was spectacular for the fraction of a second it lasted.

Vibrations coursed through the spacecraft as its nuclear thrust built upon itself. The plasma injector's electric hum was replaced by a brisk shudder until the dampeners adjusted themselves. After that first kick, acceleration was smooth as Roy brought the engines up through their full range of power.

"Thirty percent," Jack reported. "Acceleration one-quarter *g*."

A dull thrumming had worked its way up through the truss and into the crew modules. As their thrust increased, the pulsing engine's frequency rose in kind. "Fifty percent now, point six *g*."

"Velocity change?"

"Passing nine thousand meters per sec," Jack said with some

surprise. He'd lost count of how many times they'd practiced this, but the rapid acceleration still caught him short. He searched for a suitably witty comment and failed. "Wow. We're really moving."

Roy acknowledged him with a nod and unlocked the throttles, taking over from the computer's programmed burn sequence. "Houston, CDR override."

They could hear the question in Capcom's reply. "Umm . . . roger that, *Magellan*."

It was one more thing for Flight to be irked with. "GNC, can you confirm Roy just went manual?"

"That's affirm. He's manual, Flight."

Flight cursed under his breath, feeling the gaze from the rows of VIPs in the observer's gallery. "Capcom, get Cowboy Roy under control."

"Not sure how I'm gonna do that, Flight." An astronaut himself, the capsule communicator was thinking he'd have wanted to do the exact same thing.

"You'd better figure it out before we—" the tirade bubbling just below the surface was interrupted by another call.

"Flight, FIDO."

"Go." He bit the word off.

"For what it's worth, Roy's flying this right down the middle. He's not wasting an ounce of propellant."

"Then what's he thinking?" Flight said, glaring at Capcom.

"*Magellan*, you've got a lot of guys getting nervous down here."

"Not like we haven't done this in the sims, Houston," Roy answered brusquely.

"No complaints from my side," Traci said. The pilot in her wished she were the one flying. "It's like we're on rails."

"You doubted me?"

Jack pulled up the nav director cues that Roy was following on his station, electronically looking over his shoulder. The digital eight ball followed Roy's miniscule control inputs as he kept them centered on a floating target vector. That was Daisy, continually updating the aim point they needed to follow to leave Earth's influence on their way to Jupiter.

He gave Noelle a quick shot from his elbow to point out what he was seeing: Roy wasn't feeling out the spacecraft, he was testing the computer's ability to react to unpredictable inputs and compensate for them.

"I know," she said. "He's been practicing that at home on his desktop sim."

"Thrust coming up through one hundred percent now," Jack said as the mounting acceleration pushed ever harder into their chests. "One *g*, velocity eleven thousand point one . . . point two . . . wow. And there's escape velocity."

Roy thumbed his mic. "Houston, *Magellan*. We have breakaway at five minutes, fifty-eight seconds."

Capcom replied right away: "*Magellan*, Houston; we agree. Show your present velocity eleven thousand, four twenty. Acceleration steady at one point one gees. Confirm your gimbals, over."

"Angles are stable at X plus four-one, Y plus two-zero, Z is at zero. Drift is null," Roy said with no small amount of satisfaction. "What's your read on our residuals?" he asked, which was the real test. They were thrusting away from Earth on a constantly moving heading that would eventually bring them to Jupiter. Any mistakes in velocity or direction would start compounding fast.

"Copy those gimbal angles. Stand by."

Roy made a show of twiddling his thumbs while he waited for their answer. Jack felt like he could already hear the time lag building and the signal getting weaker.

"And *Magellan*, we confirm zero residuals." Capcom let the remark hang for a beat, knowing Roy deserved a moment to bask in his triumph over technology. "Flight says you are go for throttle down, and recommends you switch nav mode back to auto."

"Copy. In that case I think we'll switch back to auto," Roy said, and motioned for Traci to return control to the flight computers as he let go of the manual throttles. Now that they were going fast enough to escape Earth's gravity, they could keep accelerating at lower thrust while burning less propellant. This made the task of navigating between worlds even more complicated than usual as the balance between velocity, mass, and gravity would change with each passing minute.

Jack immediately felt the change as the press of gravity subsided and the vibrations settled into their own subtle rhythm. He felt instantly lighter as their acceleration ebbed into a comfortable one-tenth *g*. Though a mere fraction of Earth's, the sensation of up and down would remain a welcome companion offering a resemblance to normal life they'd never enjoyed in spaceflight. "And that's all, folks. We're in cruise. Anybody remember to bring a magazine or something?"

Roy twisted in his couch to face his wife. Their biologist and resident medic had naturally gravitated to managing the ship's life support. "Environmental systems?"

"Water reclamation and air exchangers are still nominal. Backup fuel cells and ECLSS test bed are on standby."

He gave his wife a wink and turned to Jack. "Reactor systems?" That would be the one that threatened to keep him awake at whatever passed for night out here.

Jack hadn't really stopped looking, but still made one last scan of the outputs and mass flow. "Ready for handoff," he said. "I ran one more check of the control rods and scram system just in case. Output levels and heat gradients are steady in the green."

"All right, then." Roy keyed his microphone. "Houston, *Magellan*; we are ready to hand off control for the first rest cycle."

"We've got you, *Magellan*. Flight says get some shut-eye and to not touch anything that looks complicated."

"See?" Roy beamed with a victorious grin. "It ain't bragging if you can do it," he said as they stifled their laughs.

5

Mission Day 2
Velocity 14,810 m/s (33,129 mph)
Acceleration 0.981 m/s^2 (0.10g)

Sleep was even more elusive than Jack expected. His body ached for it after being up for almost a full day but his mind was so keyed up that rest would come only when there was no more stopping it.

The porthole by his bunk wasn't helping. Jack's room just happened to be on the side facing back toward Earth thanks to one more odd fact of spaceflight: Flying along an orbit toward a planet that was also moving along its own circle around the Sun meant they wouldn't be pointed at their destination almost until they arrived. For the next several weeks, his personal window on the universe would always be looking back toward home. After having no time to waste looking out the window, now he'd have a solid twelve hours with it right in front of him when he was supposed to be sleeping.

Even now, Earth had receded enough for most of the globe to fit in the window. By the time he woke up they'd have crossed the Moon's orbit. How weird would it be to see *both* bodies in that little window? And yet it would still take most of the next month just to get past Mars' orbit.

Later, Jack told himself. He snapped down the window shade, making for one less distraction.

He puttered around his sleep compartment—an appropriately impersonal, functional name for a space about the size of a walk-in closet—and began unpacking. This was going to be home for the next couple of years and he might as well make it feel that way now.

His experience on the ISS had taught him that the pressure to just keep everything working in the unforgiving environment of space would relentlessly eat into his personal time as their mission drew on.

He didn't have much to unpack: a few pictures with his mother and sister, all of them in the mountains up and down the Pacific. Now that he was living in a flying soup can, he couldn't help but be reminded of his family home. His mother had been a true believer in the old "tiny house" fad and had never abandoned it after others moved on, mostly due to Seattle's stratospheric real estate prices as he'd figured out later.

Growing up like that made living in a cramped space like this familiar if not comforting. There might not be open spaces and fresh air, but he'd learned a lot about getting the most out of close quarters.

The clothing likewise reminded him of outdoor technical gear: all multifunction, antimicrobial, breathable synthetics designed to be worn several times over before going in the trash. Out here, there would be no laundry service. Water was at a premium, and a washing machine would've just been one more contraption to keep spare parts for. Filling a storage module with fresh clothing was easier and carried a lower mass penalty. Jack arranged this month's clothing allowance in a set of collapsible drawers underneath his bunk.

He unzipped a padded sleeve and removed a tablet and keyboard. Two years' worth of entertainment was contained in that little slate and Jack had made it a point to avoid any new books, movies or television series ever since he'd been assigned to this mission. Not that their training had allowed much free time, but now he'd have plenty to catch up on if the ship behaved itself.

Beneath that were a couple of surprises. It had become tradition for the mission managers to let family members slip a few items in their loved one's PPKs. With a wide grin, he lifted out a hand-knit afghan and a personalized, two-year calendar made of old vacation photos.

Finally he got to a small collection of books including *Robinson Crusoe, The Count of Monte Cristo*, a pocket New Testament, and a text on Zen Buddhism. The first two he'd cherished as a kid while the others he'd barely opened, and then only when asked. A bizarre combination from his mother, who held a unique Northwest Hippie amalgam of beliefs.

Mom.

Jack bunched up the blanket at the head of his bunk and curled up on the mattress with a slow-motion hop. He set the tablet into a mount on the adjacent wall and plugged it into the ship's radiation-hardened network. The tablet flickered on and he typed in his password. He'd planned to keep his personal machine off the network for now but the information that had been sent up with them was too juicy to wait. The soft electric hums he heard coursing through the thin walls told him his crewmates were thinking the same thing.

"You guys should be getting some sleep," he said, loud enough for them to hear.

Traci's muffled voice came through the partition: "So should you. We've got first watch."

Jack lay against the back of a small closet that also served as his headboard and rapped his knuckles against the wall, something that had driven Traci nuts during their weeks in isolation sims. She answered him with an annoyed mule kick from the opposite side.

"Stow it, kiddies," Roy's voice resonated from the opposite side of the crew deck.

"Yes, Dad," he heard Traci whine. If the mission commander and his wife were going to be the parents on this road trip, Jack and Traci were already falling into the brother/sister role with incessant taunts and tormenting schemes.

Jack slipped on a pair of headphones and tuned out the background noise. First up was a file with *Arkangel*'s layout and technical specs. Another file held a separate set of dossiers on the crew. Otherwise, there were no menu selections. They were going to get this in whatever order HQ thought best.

❊ ❊ ❊

TOP SECRET-SCA // EYES ONLY //
FROM   NATL SECURITY COUNCIL
TO   MAGELLAN EXPEDITION II CREW
VIA   NASA ADMINISTRATOR
SUBJ   PROJECT ARKANGEL
1.   DEEP-SPACE EXPLORATION PROJECT
              UNDERTAKEN BY FORMER USSR SPACE AGENCY
              CIRCA 1985 BASED ON "ORION" TYPE NUCLEAR
              PULSE-DETONATION DRIVE.

2.   CONSTRUCTION AND ON-ORBIT CHECKOUTS
            COMPLETED LATE 1990. SPACECRAFT DEPARTED
            EARTH ORBIT JAN 1991 BY DISPOSABLE
            CHEMICAL UPPER STAGE TO AVOID DETECTION
            BY USAF EARLY WARNING SATELLITES. [NSC
            NOTES: WISE MOVE. PROBABLY AVOIDED WWIII.]
3.   PROPELLANT MAGAZINE CONTAINED +5,000
            REPURPOSED TACTICAL WARHEAD CORES W/
            MINIMUM 0.3 KT [MSL] YIELD. SPACECRAFT
            MAINTAINED AVERAGE 0.7 G ACCELERATION FOR
            FINAL VELOCITY 0.10 C.

※   ※   ※

Whoa. That was a lot of nukes, no doubt most of their tactical arsenal. But *ten percent* of light speed?

Here he sat in the most advanced spacecraft ever built and it had been beaten by a clapped-together heap of fifty-year-old Russian tech propelled across the solar system by a load of repurposed nuclear bombs. It was as high tech as low tech could get, a real Wile E. Coyote Super Genius solution.

"Steampunk starship," Jack muttered.

The British Interplanetary Society had tried to whip up enthusiasm for such a project back in the '70s, and why not? Assuming you didn't blow yourself up first, an Orion drive could boost a ship to an impressive fraction of light speed given enough fuel. And by "fuel" they of course meant bombs, and lots of them. But their Daedalus starship concept had been ridiculously large, and the rest of the spaceflight community had stopped taking it seriously.

While the western countries may have laughed off the idea, the Russians had quietly embraced it. Should anyone have been surprised that they'd been the only ones crazy enough to try it? They had the heavy lift rockets and expertise in long-duration spaceflight, keeping cosmonauts on the old Mir station for over a year at a stretch. Plus they were sitting on enough nukes to slag the whole planet three times over. According to the briefing notes, some in the Politburo had seen it as a clever way to get rid of a bunch of miniaturized tactical warheads they weren't supposed to have anyway. He continued reading:

❋   ❋   ❋

4.   SATURN FLYBY ADDED 26 KM/S DELTA-V FOR
       OUTBOUND COAST TO PLUTO. RETURN PLAN
       ASSUMED FLYBYS OF NEPTUNE AND MARS.
5.   SIX WEEK 0.7 G BRAKING BURN PLACED SPACECRAFT
       IN ORBIT AT PLUTO.

❋   ❋   ❋

So they'd blasted *Arkangel* clear out to the edge of the solar system and just left it there? Jack flipped through the electronic files: no hint of the kind of catastrophic failure that would've stranded them out there. And the orbit they'd followed: hyperbolic, well above solar escape velocity with a flyby of Saturn. No one had bothered to even send pictures?

The level of secrecy was stunning. How had *no one* ever heard of this before? Just getting the film back would've been the PR coup of the century. The USSR had trumpeted every dubious achievement from inside the Workers' Paradise; something this stupendous ought to have made the front pages of *Pravda* and been dutifully picked up by sympathetic western news outlets. Sitting on this had to have driven the Kremlin nuts.

The Soviet Union had collapsed in the middle of the mission. Might that explain it? If anything, the old guard Commies would have broadcast any good news they could find if it might help them hold on to power. Even better if it happened to be true, unless it somehow undermined that power . . .

He tapped the screen, opening the next folder. Vehicle specs, which he'd already seen. He wasn't ready to digest that yet, so he swiped over to the next folder: more mission data, event timelines and crew activity plans. On to the next folder.

That was when he stopped. Now it was getting interesting.

❋   ❋   ❋

Arkangel **Commander's Log**
08 January 1991

A glorious day for the Motherland! We embark on the greatest adventure yet undertaken by humanity, spreading our reach far into the solar system. It is a destiny that could only be fulfilled by the Soviet Man. When our feats become known, the world will both delight and tremble in righteous fear of this achievement for all the Soviet peoples!

❄   ❄   ❄

Good Lord. Had he actually written this garbage or was it scripted by some political officer? It was easy to forget how heavy-handed their propaganda had been. Scrolling ahead, Jack saw the early log entries were filled with more of the same eye-rolling bombast that was guaranteed to please their political masters. Millions of miles from Earth and they still behaved as if they were on a very short leash.

Insufferable as it was, it showed how even the most agile minds could be manipulated given enough time. If he were being honest, it was easy enough to spot in his own country: Political partisans and religious fanatics held beliefs all bent in different directions by their rules and expectations. That anyone so obsessed could think clearly at all was amazing. How hard must it have been to visualize and build a machine like *Arkangel* while pretending loyalty to such a system?

The answer was that of course they hadn't all been pretending. There were always just enough true believers to maintain the illusion and keep the agnostics off balance. And if the true believers held the power, then the unconvinced soon learned to play along for their own well-being.

Jack flipped over to the crew dossiers and found the author: mission commander Vladimir Ilyeivich Vaschenko, colonel of the Soviet Air Force, who'd spent most of his uniformed service as a cosmonaut in Star City outside Moscow.

Had Vlad been a true believer? Jack scrolled ahead, hoping to find some stray comment that might reveal a telling detail or let him tease out some hidden meaning.

❄   ❄   ❄

11 Jan 1991

Spacecraft checkouts are complete. We only await word from Star City to begin our journey. Our vessel is massive enough that this will require burning two Block D kick stages in sequence to first raise our orbit and then achieve escape velocity. We could easily do this with the pulse drive, but chemical rockets will not attract unnecessary attention from our adversaries. It is a pity we cannot yet demonstrate the power of this vessel for the whole world to see. That time will come.

※　※　※

Jack sighed. If there were any hidden treasures, they would have to come later. Much later, as in when—if—they boarded *Arkangel* and he could see Vaschenko's original diaries firsthand.

※　※　※

14 Jan 1991

We have finally traveled far enough from Earth that it is safe to engage the pulse drive. The trajectory planners calculated our departure window to place the Moon between us and Earth, ensuring that no one will be able to observe our drive plume when it ignites.

With the Americans and NATO so preoccupied with their imperialistic adventure in the Persian Gulf, it seems doubtful as to whether any early-warning satellites could possibly be looking anywhere in our direction. I suppose their Hubble telescope poses a potential threat, although we had a good laugh at the Americans' expense when it was discovered the primary mirror was misconfigured! GRU insists this is no cover story, either: The vaunted NASA buggered it up that badly. That is the sort of thing one should check *before* the launch, comrades!

I must admit some sympathy for them, being in such proximity to the Moon they abandoned two decades ago. We were all quite thrilled to watch it pass by close enough to fill our windows; I can only imagine what other wonders await us at the outer planets.

※　※　※

15 Jan 1991

Ignition!

With the very first detonation, we could feel the plasma jet firmly kick our backsides. The second followed in quick succession and continued that feeling seamlessly. With each detonation we could sense our velocity building as gravity returned with it. We gaped at each other as our instruments confirmed the magnitude of the force we felt.

It is too grand to put into words. After being used to spaceflight only in freefall while coasting between destinations, to be accelerating for so long is exhilarating. Even flying a MiG-31 in full afterburner doesn't compare. We thought watching Earth fall away under the thrust of chemical rockets was profound. To see it recede so quickly now? Indescribable. We are living a science fiction tale.

On another note, Alexi learned a hard lesson about securing loose equipment before igniting a massive rocket. We assured him the bruise on his forehead will eventually heal.

❊　❊　❊

Somebody forgot to stow his gear before they lit the candle? Cute. Reminded him of a story from one of the Moon missions, when Al Bean took a head shot from his camera. Maybe that's what made the guy decide to become a painter?

❊　❊　❊

19 Jan 1991

We are so very isolated out here as our ship continues to propel us along a nuclear vapor trail, now well beyond Earth's sphere of influence. Though still distinct in color and shape compared to the stars beyond, home is just another point of light in the window. A sapphire grain in a sea of diamond dust.

Our velocity increases daily by astounding increments, even with the mandatory shutdown periods. We have found these quite useful for both checking up on the ship's health and for recalibrating our navigation instruments. Despite our shock dampeners, there is no way to entirely null the vibrations from our pulse drive.

Under full thrust, Arkangel rumbles like a speeding train. Once settled into its natural resonance it can be just as soothing, but we did not fully appreciate how much this rhythm might affect our inertial guidance platform. The magnitude of accumulated error threatens to overcome the regular calibration which is part of the daily activity plan. The inertial units have been quite reliable in the past—that is, in a customary free-fall environment. It is one thing to function in Earth orbit, it is another matter entirely to use such sensitive instruments under constant acceleration.

I have added periodic sextant sightings to our automated star tracker's input to reduce our gross navigation errors. We have had to perform a complete realignment of the inertial platform, but I believe as time goes on we will find ways to compensate for errors without such drastic steps. These deviations must be contained before we begin transiting the gravity fields of the planets on our itinerary.

⚜   ⚜   ⚜

So things got shaky almost from the start? That was interesting.

In his previous career of listening in on encrypted Russian military channels, Jack had brought a mathematician's discipline to his reading. This made him loathe to jump ahead to the ending, fearing he'd miss some important context along the way. Whether from fatigue, impatience or curiosity he nonetheless flipped ahead a few pages at random.

⚜   ⚜   ⚜

22 Jan 1991

Only two weeks into our journey and we are crossing the orbit of Mars! It is ironic that the planet which for so long was assumed to be the next goal for men to explore is on the opposite side of the Sun now. Instead of its warm ruddy glow to encourage us along our way, our isolation becomes more evident as we continue ever faster. We will have to wait for it to welcome us home on our return leg.

One imagines it would still be possible to simply turn around and go back. Alas, that is not how the great discoveries were made, not how the western lands were conquered. The great Pyotr Alekseyevich did not turn back against the Ottomans or the Swedes . . .

⚜   ⚜   ⚜

Peter the Great? Now Vladimir was showing some balls. Back in the bad old days, your average Ivan had to be mighty careful about referencing Tsarist history, even when it came to the man who'd dragged Russia out of the Dark Ages. In reality, renaming St. Petersburg to "Leningrad" had been a warning for the proles to not get too uppity.

Vaschenko's poetic side was starting to peek through as well. Jack imagined him hunched over a table with an ice-cold bottle of Vodka and a half-eaten loaf of black bread by his side. Who knows, maybe he'd actually had some? The Russians had always been a little more liberal about keeping a ration of the good stuff aboard their spacecraft. A long duration mission just about guaranteed there'd been a stash of hooch aboard. Maybe they'd get lucky and find some still there.

❈   ❈   ❈

. . . nor did our brothers and sisters give up at Stalingrad. The Motherland did not press on to crush the Nazis through timidity. It is raw courage which propels us.

❈   ❈   ❈

There we go. Good boy, back to licking the master's hand. The old survival instincts always seemed to find their way up through the haze. Vlad was setting up the apparatchiks for some less-than-happy news.

❈   ❈   ❈

As we become more adept at deep-space navigation, our ability to keep the inertial guidance units in tune has likewise improved. Gregoriy, bless him, has taken particular pride in his "spacemanship." If my phrasing is clumsy, it is because I have yet to find a better term. He has become so adept at navigation that he manipulates the sextant as a violinist would a Stradivarius. He outsmarts the automated systems on a regular basis, and I have come to trust his solutions over the computers.

Yet we must treat our vessel with utmost care. The pulse drive exacts a punishing demand upon this great ship; it is the price for such marvelous speed.

❈   ❈   ❈

Yeah, this looked promising. Here we go . . .

❈   ❈   ❈

Our flight engineer is examining the ablative coatings on each propellant casing for any anomalies, however we are limited by the onboard test equipment. We can detect impurities in the coatings with spectral analysis, but an X-ray machine is needed for a more complete picture.

❈   ❈   ❈

Good luck finding one of those out here. So the string of low-yield nukes they were setting off behind them was making for a rough ride? Not surprising, given twentieth-century Soviet technology. There wouldn't have been any way to make it a smooth ride even with the best equipment: The drive used shaped nuclear charges with ablative material on both the bomb casing and the ship's pusher plate. Each bomb's detonation was directed at a tungsten plate atop its casing—they'd taken to calling them "slugs"—which was vaporized by the blast into a fast-moving jet of plasma against the pusher plate. They could maintain constant acceleration for as long as the crew could stand it until they ran out of slugs.

By Jack's reckoning, their betters in Moscow presumed that would be quite a long time. The poor bastards would've gotten pummeled.

*   *   *

We have adjusted the timing between detonations to limit our acceleration to one-quarter g until the propellant casings have been inspected. There is only time for random sampling if we are to remain within reach of the outer planets and not exceed the constraints of our life support and consumables. The pressurized access tunnel may eliminate the need for repeated spacewalks, but the inspection ports' limited visibility makes a thorough check time consuming.

Otherwise, crew activities remain as planned. With signal delay times increasing each day, we have taken notice of the increasing level of detail included in the daily activity plans from Mission Control.

*   *   *

I'll bet you did, Vlad. That was a laugh. Russian flight controllers were notorious micromanagers. As *Arkangel* sped farther and faster from the Motherland's reach, he imagined their directors in the Mission Control Center, or "TsUP" as translated from Russian, becoming a little more freaked out as response times increased with each passing day. They'd have had no time to react to events, which would've driven the flight controllers crazy.

The cosmonauts, on the other hand, no doubt savored being so far out of reach. Such were the lengths some men had to travel to finally gain their freedom.

It left him with one thought that he couldn't shake, something the old man Rhyzov had said: *They found something out there. Something that drove their most trusted crew mad.*

b

Mission Day 3
Velocity 53,658 m/s (120,030 mph)
Acceleration 0.981 m/s^2 (0.10g)

Sleep, when it finally came, had been fitful: dreams of long-lost cosmonauts and nuclear bombs and unknowable secrets. The images dissolved as soon as he forced himself awake.

Jack yawned and stretched against the weak gravity. Years of astronaut training was still not enough to overcome the inertia of deep sleep and a lifetime in Earth gravity. As he planted his feet on the deck to stand he pushed off like he would on any normal day. But "normal" on Earth was too much here by a factor of ten, and he ended up rocketing into the ceiling head first. At least the fall back down was gentler.

Rubbing the fresh knot on his head, Jack hopped lightly across the crew berthing deck and climbed a ladder up to the galley into the adjacent recreation area. It was nice enough, with an exercise bike, treadmill, and a weight machine loaded with resistance bands. He'd have to think of a way to partition the gym from their dining room and made a mental note to pay extra attention to the air exchangers on this level. It all looked hospital-clean now, but it was going to get ripe in here over the next couple of years. At least this deck had plenty of windows for natural light, not that they'd ever be able to open one to air the place out.

The indirect lighting on the crew decks adjusted their color palette depending on the relative time of day. "Mornings" and "evenings" bathed them in warm light that shifted spectrums between blue, yellow and red with occasional hints of orange and purple for effect. The electrically tinted windows completed the illusion of twilight, dimming the relentless sun while they were still close enough for it to matter. A nice touch, but it couldn't overcome the astringent smell of artificial air.

Jack turned the lights out to let the sun do its thing. For the first time in days, he had some unoccupied minutes to catch his breath. He had the luxury of being able to pay attention to things other than whatever life-or-death task wasn't right in front of him. Sunlight streamed in from one side, the ring of portholes lighting up the room. Jack closed his eyes and leaned against the padded wall, basking in the sunlight. The acoustic insulation in here wasn't as dense as down in the berthing deck, and so he was able to feel the comforting hum of the spacecraft at work.

Downstairs, the only sound all night besides Roy's snoring had been the quiet hiss of air circulators. Here in the galley, the change was dramatic. It was still quieter than ISS had been but the abrupt return of all that mechanical background noise made it seem louder. Another level up, the control deck was much the same. Turning back aft, past the crew quarters and far down an access tunnel, the logistics and equipment spaces were calamitous as the pumps and valves and solenoids supplying a dozen utility modules made for an orchestra of mechanical racket.

Jack shoved a spill-proof mug into their hot drink dispenser and pressed the "coffee" button. As the machine hissed, he stared through a nearby porthole. It took a minute to find Earth, now shockingly small. What had been basketball-sized last night was now the size of a marble. The dim gray pebble of the Moon was separated from it by a couple of hand widths. In one day they'd sped beyond cislunar space and Earth's shine had dimmed enough for the brighter stars to become visible.

Jack tapped his watch, summoning Daisy. "How far out are we?"

The computer's feminine voice generator answered from a nearby intercom panel, artificially eager to please and a tad too loud for his comfort: WHAT IS YOUR DESIRED REFERENCE FRAME?

He frantically waved his hands at the panel. "*Shh!* Inside voice, please!"

PLEASE EXPLAIN "INSIDE VOICE."

"It means be quiet. People are sleeping." Had no one thought to put a simple volume knob on the intercom?

UNDERSTOOD, it said, matching his volume and logging a new subroutine to do the same in the future. DO YOU STILL WISH TO KNOW OUR DISTANCE FROM EARTH?

"Now that's interesting," Jack said. "I never answered your first question about frame of reference."

IT SEEMED LIKE A REASONABLE GUESS, DESPITE OUR ORBIT BEING SUN-CENTERED.

"You guessed right. And whole numbers are fine." He'd have to ponder over what process led it to a "reasonable guess" later. This could be an interesting side project if they ended up going the full distance to Pluto.

AS OF TWELVE HOURS MISSION ELAPSED TIME, MAGELLAN IS EIGHT HUNDRED SIXTY-NINE THOUSAND, FOUR HUNDRED SEVENTY-FOUR KILOMETERS FROM EARTH'S BARYCENTER.

"Thanks. Back to sleep now." A status light by the speaker blinked from green to amber.

Overnight they'd sped out to over three times the distance to the Moon. In just a few weeks they'd cross Mars' orbit, though the planet itself would be a million kilometers distant during their passage. A few weeks after that, they'd have a first-person look at Jupiter while using its gravity to add more velocity. Even after all that, it would be another six months to Pluto. It had taken *New Horizons* nine years to make the same journey. Swift as they would be, the distance was still intimidating. Space was just too big.

"Save any for me?"

Traci's voice startled him. Jack looked up to find her hopping off the ladder and into the galley. "What?"

She laughed. "Coffee. Java. Breakfast of champions." She pointed to his mug, still sitting in the machine. "Is that for me, or do I hope for too much?"

"It's mine," he said, and removed it from the dispenser. "But you're welcome to it. I haven't contaminated it with sugar yet." A quivering glob of black liquid spilled out in the low gravity, which he managed to sweep the cup underneath to catch before it had a chance to splatter in slow motion onto the deck.

"Keep it," she said with amusement, and reached for her own

mug. "So what's up? We spent too much time together in the sims for you to be getting weird on me this soon."

"Am I?" Jack shook his head and slid into a seat at their small table. The gravity from their constant acceleration was just strong enough to make him clumsier than usual. "Guess I didn't sleep much," he said.

"I knew it." Learning from his mistake, she carefully lifted her mug out of the machine and sat down opposite him. "You got all wrapped up in those briefing docs, didn't you?"

"You didn't?" He pulled his tablet from the cargo pocket of his utilities and slid it across the table.

Her eyes widened as she opened up the bookmarked folder. "What the—?"

"Someone didn't do her homework," he teased. "These are the official transcripts of *Arkangel*'s commander's log, straight from Star City's archives in the original Russian."

She set down her coffee and looked through his reading assignment. "You got a different file, then. Mine are just the English translations." Even for the little Russian she understood, the added mystery was fascinating. "You're in for some long nights. Might need to break out the sedatives."

Jack rubbed his eyes. "Great. Am I that obvious?"

"Just keep pounding this bean juice," she said. "If you need a break today, I'll cover for you. But you have to do one thing for me."

"I'm almost afraid to ask."

She smacked the table, maybe a bit too hard as the low-*g* reaction pushed her up in her seat. "Tell me about it! What's in there?"

"Nothing much. The usual vast conspiracy to infiltrate the West and enslave humanity under the iron fist of communism. Otherwise it's pretty typical stuff. Predictable."

Traci leaned in, her body language suggesting she wasn't buying it. "Come on. It's got to be better than Cold War propaganda."

"Okay, not quite typical," he said. "Owen keeping it from us until now might've given Roy a case of the red ass, but it's giving me the creeps."

She stared at him over the lip of her mug, silently urging him to go on.

Jack hesitated. "Congress fought tooth and nail over funding the

Jupiter expedition, until all of a sudden they didn't," he said. "Next thing you know they're letting NASA throw the Hail Mary pass, adding a high-speed run to the Kuiper Belt without a question why. Two different presidents made sure they kept the money flowing and stood on Owen's throat to keep us on schedule. They had to know what was out here."

"No chance they just finally saw the light and realized if we were going to have a space program, that it needed a purpose?"

Jack wasn't used to her usurping his usual role as devil's advocate. "Fat chance. The agency hasn't been able to put a new vehicle into service since Apollo without someone else dragging it across the finish line. We wouldn't have had the space shuttle without Pentagon money, and now here we sit in a for-real interplanetary spaceship for the same reason. Because once again, the Russians beat us." He lifted his mug in salute.

"They only did it sooner because they didn't care about the consequences of putting nukes into orbit," Traci said. "If they'd had anything resembling an open society, people would have lost their minds."

"You're assuming the Kremlin would have cared. One of the advantages of totalitarian police states is you don't have to give a crap about public opinion."

"On the other hand, they put a lot of effort into molding ours. They convinced a lot of our own people that we were the bad guys." She gestured toward the tablet. "Anything in there about purpose?"

"What do you mean? Rhyzov told us."

"And you believe that?"

"No reason not to," Jack said. "He had no need to lie."

"I didn't mean that," she said. "Think about the context. Back then, the Kremlin was scared to death of us building an antimissile system that would've neutered their nuclear force."

"So they counteract that by taking most of their tactical warheads off the planet? I don't follow."

Traci rolled her eyes. Jack was thinking like a technician while she was talking strategy. "A pulse drive is just a really big gun that shoots nukes out of its tail. How easy do you think it would've been to repurpose something like that into a weapon?"

Jack blanched at the thought. The original purpose, to create some kind of brute-force way-back machine that could read our mail from the future, was just too absurd. Nobody, not even old commie fossils like Andropov, could have possibly believed that. So was it all in fact a cover story?

She pressed the point. "What if we're looking at this all wrong? What if it was a weapon to begin with?"

Jack leaned back and rubbed at his temples. "You're making my brain hurt." *Could some kind of orbiting nuclear battleship have been their actual goal? How close would that have brought us to an extinction-level war*? "They wouldn't have needed a ten-meter pusher plate for a nuclear cannon. Getting something that big into orbit in the first place shows commitment."

"Dual purposes, then. They would've had a lot of incentive to make it look benign, even to the point where they could demonstrate its use as a drive system. C'mon, you're the engineer."

Jack scratched at the fresh stubble around his chin. "A propulsion system that powerful is going to be indistinguishable from a weapon of mass destruction, ours included. The only difference is which direction you point it."

"Especially when it's loaded to the gills with actual WMDs for propellant," she said. "Maybe the crew understood that and took matters into their own hands."

7

Mission Day 21
Velocity 73,935 m/s (165,388 mph)
Acceleration 0.981 m/s^2 (0.10g)

Jack snapped the cover down over a fresh air filter and logged the event in his tablet, dutifully reporting the event to Houston. Already, the daily routine promised to become achingly dull. Wake up, eat, check in with Houston. Take care of whatever shipboard housecleaning or mechanical hiccups appeared overnight, then settle in at the control deck to spend the next twelve hours watching the spacecraft fly itself.

One thing he was thankful for was that limits on both mass and human workload dictated that the sort of middle-school public relations experiments that had taken up too much of their time on the ISS were almost nonexistent here. The real science would happen after they seeded Jupiter and its moons with autonomous probes. Then would come Pluto, where until recently they thought their time would be dominated by surveying the planet and its moons from *Magellan*. If they found solid terrain that wasn't just frozen nitrogen, there would be a landing attempt with *Puffy* which they'd drilled in the sims. It had been billed as a "contingency" mission, which now seemed like much more of a priority. Maybe the prospect of a real surface expedition with her husband to the farthest known planet would excite Noelle enough to forget about how little time they'd have at Jupiter.

Jack had been one of the few to have welcomed the psychiatrists they'd brought in to sort potential crewmembers for compatibility, even though it had chapped Grady Morrell's ass. Especially if it had burned Grady's ass. If it were indeed possible to predict and measure personal chemistry, the agency had moved Heaven and Earth to find out. The more stubborn old hands remained unconvinced, but he thought it beat the traditional method of individual experience sprinkled with a heaping dose of internal politics and personal prejudices. It had gotten to the point where phony enthusiasm and forced camaraderie had become normal behavior and one could only maintain that facade for so long before the cracks emerged. It too often manifested itself in astronauts who either couldn't function on long duration flights or worked themselves to exhaustion.

And that had been on the space station, where home lay just beyond the windows, where the wait for a ride down was measured in hours if necessary. Out here there was no sense dwelling on it. They'd long passed the point where they could scramble into their docked crew capsule and execute an emergency burn back to Earth. In a few more months they'd pass PNR—Point of No Return—where it would be impossible to make a rapid return to Earth without exhausting their fuel.

That didn't imply it was impossible to get the vehicles back, of course. A good mission planner could work out a low energy transfer orbit, as even the weakest gravity could be used to guide a craft around the solar system. The problem was time—even though the Dragon spacecraft's extended life support and stores could last weeks, a low-energy orbit home would take years. The mathematician in him loved the elegance of orbital mechanics, the great celestial pinball game of moving about the solar system. That it wasn't his primary discipline perhaps made him all the more enthusiastic, like a hobby he was able to indulge at work. Sometimes the people who approached complex problems as a pastime found more enjoyment in it than the ones who did it for a living.

Cryptography, for instance. Jack had spent his early adulthood in drone control vans, teasing out subtle linguistic cues from surveillance intercepts. When he wasn't doing that, he was unwinding complex encryption algorithms. It had been satisfying work, even if it had involved an awful lot of drudgery before arriving at the "eureka" moments. Sometimes they never came.

❈   ❈   ❈

Arkangel **Commander's Log**
23 Jan 1991

Alexi has completed inspections of magazines 1 and 2 and all propellant slugs are within tolerance.

It has become necessary for me to assume many of Alexi's duties in order for him to inspect the remaining magazines. Therefore, at this point I must insist on exercising commander's privilege over the daily activity plans. We have received and understood today's transmission, but will not be able to accomplish the tasks as scheduled.

If our high-speed run after Saturn is to be successful, it is imperative that we eliminate the threat of resonance vibrations. The dreaded "pogo" effect could come more suddenly than any of us might be able to detect. With half-hour signal delays, it would only be apparent in the control center after it was too late. By the time a resonance event appeared in the telemetry, we would be a cloud of debris adding its mass to the asteroid belt. I have not been communicating beyond our hourly check-in with Mission Control for this reason.

It is for similar reasons that I have insisted Alexi take a day off from his efforts. In addition to working himself to the point of exhaustion, I have become concerned that he may be hiding his personal dosimeter. He has a strong sense of duty, though too often at the risk of his personal safety.

❈   ❈   ❈

It all sounded too familiar. Hadn't they learned anything from Chernobyl?

He'd seen it enough on the ISS: dedicated professionals who'd worked and trained together for years on the ground became different people after a few weeks in orbit. The job attracted classic overachievers who over time tended toward one of two polar opposite reactions: They either became moody and withdrawn or were overbearing control freaks. And the more things didn't go their way, the worse they became. Throw in a misbehaving spacecraft and things could get interesting.

❈   ❈   ❈

26 Jan 1991

After a valiant effort, Alexi has surveyed the contents of each propellant magazine and found no anomalies. As to the source of the vibrations, at this point we must resume normal operations and continue to troubleshoot.

We are weary but determined to proceed with the next phase of our mission. Our most recent star sightings and gimbal angles should have arrived in the data packet preceding this transmission. We are prepared to increase acceleration once the flight dynamics group confirms our sight reductions and alignment figures.

My concerns for Alexi's safety were well-founded as he has exceeded his maximum daily dosage twice now. He won't be sprouting tumors any time soon, but he also understands that he is now at a much higher cancer risk later in life. Of this, he does not seem concerned. It is as if we are discussing the probability of a severe weather event or the outcome of a hockey match in twenty years' time.

❈   ❈   ❈

30 Jan 1991

Despite confirming the integrity of our propellant slugs, we continue to be beaten almost senseless by the incessant hammering of the pulse drive. It is time to confess that this takes a heavy toll on our sleep cycles. This degrades our alertness and is leading to unnecessary tensions.

I have therefore shut down the drive to conduct a visual inspection of our shock accumulators. Perhaps fatigue is affecting my own judgment, but that is a matter for others to determine when we return. We must isolate this problem now if there is to be any hope of mission success.

❈   ❈   ❈

"Beaten almost senseless?" It must have been a real teeth-rattler for Vlad to slip that line into the official logs, much less shutting down the drive. Mission control must have had fits.

Surprising? Maybe not. They were simply human and a long way from home. Wouldn't be the first time a cheesed-off cosmonaut told Star City what he really thought.

❈   ❈   ❈

2 Feb 1991

Gregoriy and Alexi's external inspection revealed premature signs of wear around the second-stage accumulator's vacuum seals, however the rest of the drive section appears to remain in tolerance. This would not only account for the severe resonance vibrations, it should also explain the previous gross navigational errors we discovered.

You will have no doubt noticed from our telemetry that we did not engage the pulse drive immediately after their EVA. In this matter I must once again exercise commander's privilege. Whether due from legitimate professional differences or simple accumulated fatigue, Gregoriy and Alexi had a spirited disagreement over the precise nature of the problem and what actions to take. Either the vacuum seals are threatening to fail, or they are misaligned and therefore not performing optimally. This is not something I would ordinarily report, but time is precious and we need to complete preparations for their next EVA. They spent six hours inspecting the thrust structure; now we must plan for which actions to take. Gregoriy is the more experienced cosmonaut, but I tend to put more trust in our flight engineer in this case. What comparable experience is there for a ship such as this?

Since Alexi will be conducting the actual repairs, I believe it is right to defer to his judgment. I was prepared to do this myself so as to not put him at risk of more radiation exposure, but both men's dosimeters showed them to be well within the daily limits. This is no doubt due to the problem being isolated to the second-stage piston assembly. If they'd had to spend more time around the first-stage assembly next to the accelerator plate, radiation exposure would have been more concerning. Lucky for Gregoriy I suppose, though it would have been nice to stick my head outside of the spacecraft.

We will continue to coast for at least the next duty cycle as I want everyone rested and clearheaded tomorrow.

❈   ❈   ❈

A "spirited disagreement"? Now that was some good old Russian understatement. Was it the first sign of a crack in their veneer, or was it the normal course of human relations?

Jack realized that's what was bugging him: They seemed perfectly normal, not a crew prone to mutiny or whatever Moscow had termed "madness." Amazing as their journey was, there was nothing that far out of the ordinary in here. If anything, this was a testament to a dedicated, even-tempered crew.

❈ ❈ ❈

4 Feb 1991

Success! The source of our problem was found to be misaligned seals in the second-stage piston assembly. Quick work for a wrench ape like Alexi!

With the updated position data we were able to confirm our initial state vectors with confidence and resume operations per the agreed schedule, which is no doubt apparent from telemetry by now.

After experimenting with a range of detonation timing, we are able to maintain a steady 0.7 *g* cruise. This seems to be a level the ship is "comfortable" with. It is my intent to remain at this acceleration factor until we fully understand the resonance effect and its impact on the inertial guidance system.

Our spacecraft no longer flies like a freight train. If anything, it is like riding in a fine railcar on the Trans-Siberian. If I seem giddy it is because this will be our first full sleep period in almost a month, and I find it difficult to remain awake.

We are tired but determined and eager to proceed with the next phase of our mission. It is perhaps fortunate that we were forced to coast through our transit of the asteroid belt, as the micrometeorite impacts have been much more numerous than anticipated.

❈ ❈ ❈

Good to know, Jack thought, *since we'll be following in your footsteps soon.*

Dozens of probes had traversed the asteroid belt with minimal course corrections: It wasn't exactly Han Solo evading a flight of TIE fighters amidst clouds of floating granite—which he had to admit would be pretty awesome. But the largest of those probes had been about the size of a school bus, and while blisteringly fast for the time, had still remained in coast mode after leaving Earth.

Besides saving propellant and also not overtaking the resupply ship now a few weeks ahead of them, the belt was one reason they'd soon stop thrusting to coast the rest of the way to Jupiter. It was also why much of their mass budget had been used to rock-proof *Magellan* to the point where they could fly it through a hailstorm at full throttle and come out the other side none the worse.

So it turns out that navigating a spacecraft the size of a submarine at relativistic speeds through the same region wasn't quite as simple . . . perhaps the belt wasn't as sparsely populated as the eggheads thought.

Daisy's chime alerted them to an incoming transmission. Traci's eyes brightened at the sound: mail from home! Jack squelched her excitement by pointing out the time; it was just the daily news feed, which always started with the NASA Public Affairs happy talk:

❈ ❈ ❈

This is Magellan Control, mission day twenty-one.

In less than one month, the deep-space vehicle Magellan *and her crew have traveled farther and faster than any known humans before. Still accelerating at one-tenth gravity, their present speed is in excess of one hundred thousand miles per hour. Now covering almost two and half million miles each day, they have passed the orbit of Mars and are now traversing the asteroid belt while speeding toward their encounter with Jupiter.*

❈ ❈ ❈

"Did you catch that little qualifying phrase PAO slipped in there?" Traci asked over her breakfast. She pushed her tablet across the table. "We're now 'faster than any *known* humans.' They're setting people up for the big reveal."

"You mean that we're not the first." Jack put down his tray and took her tablet, regarding it with suspicion. "You're seriously reading those Public Affairs releases? Did you already run out of actual books?"

"I like to keep up with the news," she protested. "I like knowing what they're telling the folks back home."

Jack theatrically cleared his throat. "Yesterday, flight engineer Jack Templeton repaired another balky CO_2 scrubber while mission pilot Traci Keene spent her entire shift binge-watching her favorite TV shows while the spacecraft flew itself," he recited in his best leaden anchorman monotone. "You're right. That'd be pretty boring."

"It was two episodes, and I was speed watching!" she said, pouting. "Sometimes this boat runs a little too well."

"And now you've just jinxed us," he said, wagging his finger at her. "We won't have new spare parts for another year. We need this thing to run like a Swiss watch until then or I'm going to get very cranky."

"You're cranky now. Personally, I don't think you have enough to do."

"You may be right," he admitted. "I'm seeing way fewer glitches pop up on the daily squawk list than I'm used to."

"What's 'usual' out here?" she asked. "You can't compare this to Station, or even DSV. That thing was built out of spare ISS components."

She had a point. The first DSV, uninspired government-speak for "Deep Space Vehicle," had been a cumbersome stack of ISS leftovers: One of the few completed Orion spacecraft was docked to a pair of unused logistics modules and mated to a Centaur kick stage. They'd sent it out to a couple of near-Earth asteroids after a flyby of Venus to pick up speed along the way.

Magellan, on the other hand, had been purpose-built almost from scratch. That fresh money had been allocated for it should've alerted them to the fact that there might be an ulterior motive behind its construction, but the dwindling astronaut corps had welcomed the new ship without question.

"New technology," Jack said, drumming his fingers on the polymer tabletop. "It always makes me nervous. We don't know what we don't know . . . you know?"

Traci smirked at the pun. "You've kept that one pretty close. I'm surprised."

"Didn't want to jinx us," he said. "If I voice my deepest fears then they're almost certain to come true."

"That is such a load of crap. You're quite possibly the *least* superstitious guy I know."

"Not superstition," he argued. "Not even delusion. It's probability."

"That because you speak something, it somehow comes into being? You know my family went to a church like that."

"That's a whole different kind of superstition," he said, watching for her reaction. "I believe we voice those things that worry us once we've mentally gathered enough evidence to be convinced it's something worth worrying about," he explained. "We say the crap's about to hit the fan when it's plainly obvious there's an incoming turd."

"So we haven't realized it's happening until it's unavoidable?"

"Precisely." Jack gestured at a monitor on the opposite bulkhead, where their ship was a glowing triangle moving along a bright green arc. Surrounding it were circles with arrows of different lengths projecting outward: Each marked a known asteroid and its vector relative to theirs. "We know with certainty where each one of those things are, and flight dynamics spent months fine-tuning our trajectory through the Belt. Our nav radar is lighting up everything within a thousand-kilometer bubble and the pressure hull is wrapped in enough micrometeor shielding to stop a fifty-caliber round. Do you think I'm the least bit worried about us getting holed by a stray rock?"

"Not that I can tell."

"Not to mention we have the two best pilots in the solar system keeping tabs on it around the clock," he said, making her blush. "I'm not worried in the least. But get me to thinking about the environment or water reclamation system and I'll be up all night."

"What does all this have to do with jinxes and probability? You're awfully superstitious for an engineer," she teased.

"It's not superstition," he said, more put out than he ought to be. "And that's my whole point—most people don't voice their fears until it's staring them in the face. That's when they create self-fulfilling prophecies."

"So I should just share every worry I have with you ahead of time? Because that kind of sounds like fun."

8

Mission Day 29
Velocity 110,350 m/s (246,846 mph)
Acceleration 0.981 m/s² (0.10g)

Arkangel **Commander's Log**
7 Feb 1991

Saturn is marvelous even from this great distance, better than the view from the finest telescopes at Pulkovo. Already the ring system is opening itself up in amazing detail. Soon our speed and proximity will combine to make the planet grow by the minute in our windows. It is tragic our portholes are so small.

This has made LK-M a popular location. With the lander docked perpendicular to our axis of travel, Saturn is centered in its enormous window. I have been forced to ration access in the interest of maintaining the duty schedule.

It is unfortunate that we will soon have to keep our attention inside the spacecraft. It is vital that our intercept vector remain within tolerance for the slingshot maneuver. We are navigating to a precision as yet unknown, flying our craft between the planet and its rings for maximum energy benefit just as Oberth discovered. The distance between them is tremendous, even more than the distance between Earth and Moon, but such high velocity greatly reduces our margin for error.

Yet I am tempted by Alexi's suggestion of an impromptu EVA. We have all yearned for a more expansive view as our faces are pressed against the portholes or we reluctantly give up a turn in LK-M.

Recognizing that he is scheduled to be off duty prior to our close approach, he has asked to exit the spacecraft for the purpose of recording our passage. He admits it is a great sacrifice but one he is willing to make for the Motherland.

It was difficult not to laugh. I would gladly have him take my position in the control block for such a feat myself!

Alexi has raised a valid consideration, however. While our current mission is of the highest secrecy, we look forward to the day when it is revealed to the world. Even a single photograph of *Arkangel* against the backdrop of Saturn would define our people for the ages. While I might envy Alexi for such a glorious undertaking, I must also find a way to make this possible. Our constant acceleration requires that he must remain within the airlock while opening the door to take some pictures. It will not be so simple as allowing him to give up part of his sleep cycle for a jaunt outside—he must don his Orlan suit and pre-breathe pure oxygen for several hours. Even a two-hour EVA requires four hours spent in the confines of a spacesuit. Afterward, he will still have to assume his normal duties in the control block instead of taking a well-deserved rest. Gregoriy and I will need to adjust our duty schedules accordingly, yet I believe it will be worth the trouble.

❈   ❈   ❈

Now that was an unexpected turn. They risked a spacewalk at *Saturn*? The radiation environment wasn't as dangerous as Jupiter's, but man . . . would he have done this, given the chance? Jack wondered. His stint on ISS had ended with a ride home on an old Soyuz, and the idea of having the most majestic planet in the solar system confined to those teensy Russian portholes was heartbreaking.

Jack fiddled with the dosimeter clipped to the chest pocket of his flight suit. He decided that getting zapped with a few extra rems and the risk of a surprise tumor later in life just might've been worth it.

Jealousy tugged at him, wishing that they could be visiting Saturn themselves. Given their direction, even a fusion drive wasn't of much help if the planet was on the wrong side of the solar system.

Ah well. Maybe the next crew. For this one they'd have to settle for the comparative backwaters of Jupiter, Pluto, and the derelict spacecraft still in orbit out there.

❁   ❁   ❁

9 Feb 1991

Saturn now fills both our windows and our imaginations.

The video we beam home cannot convey the majesty of its ring system. Alexi performed a short EVA so that he might capture better photographs. Even though he simply opened the outer hatch to stand upright in the airlock, I am jealous of my crewmate! Perhaps I should have claimed commander's privilege again.

While we remained inside with our faces pressed against the portholes like impatient children, he stood in the open airlock and experienced what must be the most spectacular sight any human has ever been privileged to behold. Fortunately for us, his 70mm camera recorded it all. The film canister was moved to a shielded container which now holds an honored place among our return cargo. I am sure the wait to develop these images will be worth it.

He promises me that the photographs down Arkangel's length against the backdrop of Saturn will be worth the risk, dwarfing anything the Americans brought home from their vaunted Apollo missions.

Of their magnificence I have no doubt, though I was quite relieved to see him return inside. For the inconvenience he has caused us, Alexi has "volunteered" to take over lavatory cleaning duties for the next month. I suspect he considers it a small price to pay. I would.

It is enough of a challenge to describe being in Earth orbit. To describe a world dozens of times as massive, yet made of nothing but whirling clouds held in check by gravity? And the rings . . . words fail me. How they vanished in the planet's shadow, yet could dominate all in sunlight? Perhaps we need to bring a poet on the next expedition.

I cannot imagine the spectacle Alexi enjoyed during his jaunt outside. He has been as rambunctious as a schoolboy on holiday, unable to sleep yet tireless in his duties at the flight control station. The spark in his eyes is impossible to ignore, and I dearly wish it had been possible to bring a photographer's darkroom out here with us. Until our return, his priceless film rolls will remain locked away in a radiation-proof container.

❁   ❁   ❁

Traci might have been speechless if she hadn't been so astonished. "One of them got outside for a selfie . . . " she marveled, "at Saturn?"

Jack nodded and passed his translation notes to her: *Yep*.

"And no one has ever seen the photos?" If they managed to board *Arkangel*, finding those film canisters would be a priority and getting them safely back to a darkroom on Earth would make the trip home feel more urgent. She stared through the porthole by her shoulder. Compared to where her imagination was taking her right now, infinity felt kind of boring.

"Space is just too big," Jack said, sensing her inner struggle. "People back home think of the view, but when I try to tell them it's mostly just black and empty their eyes glaze over."

"It feels like we're at the end of nowhere," she agreed. "Hurts my head sometimes. That's why I keep the lights down."

"Migraines?"

"Sightseeing. Otherwise all the stars are washed out. Just so you know, when we get to Jupiter I'm asking Roy to run the cabin dark. I want to take in the whole thing."

Jack pressed his face against a porthole. Still weeks away, the giant planet was close enough now to show its disk instead of just being another point of light in the black. The clarity through their onboard telescope was stunning even at this distance. Details in its cloud bands were easily visible, as were its most prominent moons. "Think Roy would let me pop open the airlock to go outside and take some pics, like that Russian?"

She laughed with a very unladylike snort. "Maybe he will if you get under his skin enough. The radiation would cook you like a microwave burrito." She turned back from the porthole with a sigh. "We'll be lucky if there's enough time to even look out the window."

❧   ❧   ❧

12 Feb 1991

Our incredible machine takes us farther and faster than even Tsiolkovsky or Korolev could have imagined, and we have coaxed it on ever faster after our slingshot around Saturn.

We managed to sustain a full 1g burn throughout periapsis, adding Saturn's considerable potential energy to our expelled mass. We eagerly await the trajectory team's final confirmation, but it appears we executed the necessary plane change to intercept Pluto and added 26 km/s delta-v at Saturn's expense.

So on second thought, perhaps not Tsiolkovsky. He would have certainly imagined this. Indeed he would have expected us to do so!

I relinquished my traditional role as mission commander to allow Gregoriy to navigate us through the gap between the rings and the cloud tops below. He is a masterful pilot and has become perhaps the best celestial navigator in the cosmonaut corps, whereas my greater concern was with the overall condition of the ship. While Gregoriy piloted, Alexi and I watched for any signs of resonance vibrations. While it may seem obvious from telemetry, I am pleased to report that Arkangel performed magnificently during this fiery test. It will require more analysis, but we believe that the strong centripetal forces of our maneuver dampened the vibrations we experienced earlier. Engineers will have to decide how Arkangel "felt" but I can describe what it was like for us.

As we approached the planet its cloud tops filled our windows with a milky yellow glow. The lightning-fast wink of a shadow told us we had passed beneath the rings. Gregoriy had us close enough to an optimal path that his pitch adjustments were minor; the only forces we felt were the nuclear fire at our backs and the tide of inertia pulling us outward as we whipped around the planet.

Half of an orbit later, we emerged unscathed on the other side only for Nature to astound us one final time. While we caught our breath and boisterously slapped each other on the back, another shadow crossed our windows. Something massive had just come between us and the Sun. Of course it was the planet we had just left behind, but now from a perspective no one had yet seen: in silhouette, with its rings illuminated on either side like handles on a teacup.

I have never seen men turned so utterly silent by the face of Nature.

❧ ❧ ❧

"I suppose a month of scrubbing the space toilets would've been a fair trade," Jack said as he fought with a stuck impeller on one of the water recyclers. "It's all scut work anyway."

Traci put down the tablet she'd been reading from to join him. "Someone has a case of the Mondays."

He backed out from under the housing to turn a sour gaze her way. "You know how much I hate that phrase. It's like the fourth or fifth time you've used it today."

"Am I wrong?"

"Yeah. It's Wednesday." He nodded at his tool kit. "Oil, please."

She shrugged and handed him a bottle of machine oil. "That bad, huh?"

Jack answered with a frustrated grunt and carefully sprayed beneath the balky part. He didn't like having unnecessary globs of lubricant floating free in his spacecraft. "We're not using it enough. Everyone's afraid to overtax the system but it needs to work. Otherwise seals get dry and moving parts seize up."

"So flush the toilets more?"

"And quit the bottled water," he said, noticing the telltale bulge in her hip pocket. "No sense relying on that stuff anyway. It's going to become a scarce commodity."

His mind settled on the image of an unknown cosmonaut scrubbing toilets after what had to have been the most spectacular spacewalk no one had ever heard about. Zero gravity lavs were notoriously complicated, so how'd they get the thing to work under constant acceleration? The inventive reputation of Russian engineers had a lot to do with their relative lack of resources. That they'd managed to build a functioning crapper for both zero and constant *g* deserved an award.

"I'm not ready to drink recycled pee just yet," she said. "I need a few more weeks."

"In a few more weeks Jupiter will be in our rearview mirror. You won't have a choice."

She smiled. "Exactly my point."

He closed up the pump housing and stretched. "I wish they wouldn't have stocked that stuff in the first place," he said, pointing at the bottle in her pocket. "All of the things they pick over in the mass budget, why add more of what we already have?"

"Yet you're about to ask me for a drink anyway."

"Consider it a design trade. That mass has to go somewhere, it might as well be me."

"You're rotten." Yet she still handed over the bottle.

Jack took a long, grateful gulp and handed it back. "Okay, that was good. But I'm still saving mine for the float after Jupiter."

Unlike *Arkangel*, their mission profile would have them stop burning a few weeks after doing a slingshot around Jupiter and coast until it was time to start burning in the opposite direction. They'd have to turn the ship and slow down toward their destination for the same amount of time as they'd sped up, despite coasting for months. Even Jupiter's massive gravity well wasn't enough to slow them down for a nice drift into orbit, and Pluto itself was barely two-thirds the size of Earth's moon. The dwarf planet could do nothing to capture something at their speed short of running straight into it.

The Russians had been faced with the same dilemma but using nuclear bombs for fuel gave them more options. They could fly the outbound leg at one *g* and suck up a harder braking burn at one of the larger outer planets like Uranus, anything with a gravity well deep enough to do the rest of the work for them. It would've shaved weeks off of their trip.

The striking clarity of vision that had driven the *Arkangel* project was almost comical in its classic Soviet brute force approach. Like strapping multiple boosters to the side of a rocket just to get more throw weight: Can't build a giant engine like the American F1's? Then just cluster a few dozen smaller ones for the same result. Of course, the added complexity hadn't worked out too well for them— every known N1 booster had exploded not long after launch. One had been spectacular enough to cause a mass freak-out in Washington's intel circles, as it had looked for all the world like a nuclear burst.

The spacecraft core had been launched by an Energia booster in the late eighties, officially an antimissile laser platform that never reached orbit. Using a couple of small nuclear bursts to get the pusher plate into orbit wouldn't have been a stretch; it was the Orion drive's original operating concept and they'd been crazy enough to try a lot of things when no one was looking.

Arkangel was a model of simplicity compared to the machinations they'd undertaken to orbit all of that mass in secret. The Russians had serious long-duration spaceflight experience, and they'd learned how to keep both machinery and the people inside functioning for months at a time.

How far they could go with it all depended on the drive system.

Chemical rockets were out of the question for a number of reasons, not least of which was their disastrous experience with the N1. Nuclear thermal was a decent alternative, but if one was going to start violating treaties then it made sense to go all-in for something spectacular. Something that would forever change the public understanding of spaceflight.

The Russians were known to be ruthlessly pragmatic but Jack couldn't argue with the basic philosophy: Go big or go home.

9

Mission Day 34
Velocity 320,485 m/s (716,904 mph)
Acceleration 0.0 m/s^2 (0g)

After a year of being sped along by its electric VASIMR engines, the cargo carrier *Cygnus* had reached Jupiter's sphere of influence and matched *Magellan*'s velocity as both ships hurtled toward the gas giant. Once *Magellan* had captured the ship with its cargo modules and propellant tanks, they would be clear to follow its course around and behind the planet with a hard burn at closest approach for a dramatic increase in velocity.

Still half a day ahead, *Cygnus* careened ahead of *Magellan* along its own hyperbolic orbit. Fast enough to be free of the Sun's influence, it was still not fast enough to prevent its path from being shaped by gravity. The Sun and Jupiter battled for dominance, the gas giant winning out thanks to its proximity.

Gravity was not the only force that made Jupiter so formidable. The planet's core of molten hydrogen was in constant motion, rotating about its axis to generate an immense electromagnetic field that channeled charged particles from the solar wind into invisible belts of radiation powerful enough to kill an unprotected human in minutes. Even when protected, the less time spent within the Jovian belts the better. And that was how they'd planned *Magellan*'s trajectory since no humans had yet traversed it.

This was a dangerous environment for machines as well, particularly the kind of fragile silicon-based electrically powered contraptions flung by humans into deep space. Already hardened against the harsh electromagnetic environment, flying anywhere near Jupiter demanded an extra measure of protection.

It was impossible to protect against everything, which became most apparent when designers needed to trim mass. Encase the vehicle in enough dense metals like lead and it'd be fine, it just would be too heavy to send anywhere. Thus a few millimeters of aluminum and Mylar foil was all that stood between *Cygnus'* electronic brain and the radioactive hell of Jupiter's magnetosphere. This would have been more than enough, had an unusually energetic Sun not charged up the field to a precarious degree.

While unwelcome, it wasn't unexpected either. It was for this very reason that *Cygnus'* computer brain was programmed with enough common sense to know when it needed to take extraordinary measures to protect itself. And so the massive spike in EM radiation *Cygnus* detected as it crossed Jupiter's magnetopause led it to tuck its electronic tail and hide.

In spaceflight parlance this was called "Safe Mode," wherein the ship shut down and cut itself off from outside influence lest another surge confuse the computers enough to order it into some self-destructive behavior.

To protect itself, *Cygnus* went dark. Its small reactor only spared enough current to keep core memory from vanishing and to power its rendezvous beacons. This also meant keeping its attitude and guidance routines shut down: Star trackers, control jets and orientation gyros were cut off to protect the craft from becoming hopelessly disoriented.

This meant Jupiter's gravity was able to fully assert itself, pulling on *Cygnus* undeterred by the spacecraft's stabilizing flywheels. Almost the length of a football field, the stack of cargo modules and propellant tanks was drawn into a tumble as it fought a natural tendency to align itself with the gravity gradient. Imperceptible at first, it began increasing with each revolution.

It took an hour for this information to make it back to *Cygnus'* controllers in Pasadena's Jet Propulsion Lab. By the time JPL finished their diagnostics and attempted reboots, it was another hour before they sounded the alarm in Houston. It would be another hour before this information could be relayed to *Magellan*.

◆ ◆ ◆

Cygnus had been a blip on their radar long before it showed up in their windows. The cargo ship shone in the distance, its strobe beacon distinguishing it from the other bodies orbiting Jupiter. "Thar she blows," Jack called out from the control deck. "Does that mean I win the pot?"

"Didn't know we were taking bets," Traci said over her shoulder, watching their rendezvous from the copilot's station.

"You remember: First one to get eyeballs on it wins everybody else's coffee ration for the month. I'm pretty sure we were all in on it."

"Nice try," she snorted. "Wouldn't have anything to do with yours being used up?"

"Pure coincidence. More evidence of the perfect symmetry of the universe. You don't need all that caffeine anyway."

"Speak for yourself," Roy grumbled, his mug trailing an aroma of Colombian dark roast as he shuffled past on his way to the command pilot's station.

"You're killing me here," Jack groaned. "What I wouldn't give for—"

"For what?" Noelle said as she buckled in next to him, pushing over a sealed mug of hot black liquid.

Jack perked up with the first luxurious sip. "Bless you, dear lady."

"We need everyone in top form, and it wouldn't do for our flight engineer to be underperforming just because he can't control his personal habits," she scolded him. "I'm being practical."

Even Roy howled at that one as Jack's shoulders sagged. "Harsh. But true. And seriously, thanks."

Noelle patted his arm. "Don't mention it," she said, then leaned in and whispered. "Besides, that came out of Roy's rations."

Owen Harriman had been pacing behind his desk on Manager's Row for what couldn't have been more than a few minutes, until the mission clocks caught his eye. He looked back down at his watch in consternation: Had it really been an hour? A quick glance around the control room revealed nothing but the backs of controllers hunched over their consoles. He hoped his new nervous habit would remain unnoticed by the others.

"You must sit," ordered a gruff voice behind him. Anatoly Rhyzov pulled Owen's empty chair back from his console.

Owen slumped into it, almost rolling into the credenza behind them. "Sorry. Hard to control my nerves."

"That is your business, not mine," Rhyzov said dismissively. He nodded toward the wall screens at the front of the room. "You were blocking my view."

"Here I thought you were concerned about me."

Rhyzov waved him away in a "no worries" gesture that Owen had gotten used to seeing. "Everyone copes in own way," he said, pointing at the GNC desk. "Your guidance controller has been gripping rail beside his console so long his hand is turning purple."

"That's why we kept those handles. They used to be for swapping out balky displays in a hurry. Turns out it keeps the flight controllers sane."

"We did same. Is stressful, this work. Much to watch with little to do." He tapped his forehead. "All work is up here."

Owen tapped his stomach in return. "And it's felt down here." It was too easy to forget that his Russian mentor had endured his own trials in the hot seat. They would've been about the same age, too. What might they be doing in here when he reached Anatoly's age?

"Our control room was same. Used to directing cosmonauts. Not used to waiting for them."

"This was easier when everything was working normally," Owen admitted. The light delay was close to an hour each way and the mental gymnastics threatened to consume him. Everything happening in here had already happened out there. It was maddening for a room full of people conditioned to working under extreme pressure to now feel so impotent. They were being forced to take in data, analyze trends, and predict what might happen in the next hour instead of making snap decisions right now. The farther *Magellan* traveled, the farther out they'd be forced to predict based on information that was old and growing older each day. The many permutations of possible outcomes forced them to become more reliant on an AI network that mirrored the one aboard ship.

On top of that, the masters of problem solving were dependent on their cohorts at JPL who were right now consumed with trying to recover their tumbling resupply vessel. Normal mission rules would demand a wave-off, aborting the rendezvous and defaulting to "Plan B" using Jupiter's gravity to bend their trajectory back toward Earth.

In reality that would've been "Plan A" on any other mission, but a normal mission also wouldn't have light delays of over an hour in each direction. By the time word reached *Magellan*, chances were good the crew was seeing it for themselves and taking matters into their own hands.

"It's like we're team owners at a horse race," Owen complained. "We've put everything we have into our prize steed, and now we have to stand back and find out if the trainer and jockey actually know what they're doing."

"You are much too hard on yourself," Rhyzov said with a knowing look. "You have even less control than that."

Owen was afraid to ask. "What do you mean by that?"

"Racetrack is also made by man. Natural materials but still groomed by man. Space is raw nature. Untamed and untamable. Has its own rules and does not give up its secrets easily."

"And all that fancy math we depend on?"

"Gets your horse onto track. Does not guarantee it will win. Or finish."

Owen wanted to sink into his chair when he noticed Flight glaring at them. "Gentlemen, we have a problem to work here and you're becoming a distraction to my flight controllers. Please take the philosophical discussions outside."

Roy's crew would either figure it out, or they wouldn't. Meanwhile, the team in Houston was getting their first hard lesson at being interested spectators.

With no time to leave his station for the telescope down on the workshop deck, Roy strained to tease out more detail from the cameras tracking *Cygnus*. "Strobes look weird."

"Weird how?" Traci asked.

"Like they're out of synch," Roy said, though it was hard to tell this far out. "Any updates from Houston or JPL?"

"Negative," Jack said. "We're about due for one, though."

Roy frowned and reached for the binoculars he kept in a compartment behind his seat. He turned to Traci. "Has the remote pinged you yet?"

"Negative. Intermittent carrier signal, but we're also close to max range. Could be magnetic interference."

Roy loosened his straps and pressed against the window. Jupiter loomed in the distance, days away but still close enough that its glow outshone all but the brightest stars. Well over a dozen kilometers ahead, there was no mistaking the cargo ship's flashing beacon among the steady lights of Jupiter's moons hanging in the black. "Lights down, please."

He kept his eyes closed as Traci killed the cabin lighting, relaxing his vision. When he returned to his perch, he shifted his focus to an empty point in space next to *Cygnus*. This allowed his eyes to better perceive light and confirmed what he'd come to suspect. "It's too bright," he said. "Irregular."

"It's not the ship's beacon," Traci agreed. "Oh boy." If it wasn't the spacecraft's beacon, that meant it had to be the spacecraft itself. Its metal framework and radiator panels and fuel tanks reflected the sunlight at irregular intervals as the stack tumbled through space.

The warning message arrived from Houston just in time to confirm Roy's suspicions. His muffled curse put the exclamation point on the brewing trouble. He turned to Traci. "Can you do anything with the remote?"

She tapped a few commands into the controls by her flight station, trying to take over for *Cygnus*' now-dormant guidance package. "No joy," she said sourly. "It's stuck on stupid."

Roy pushed back down into his seat and updated his rendezvous cues. At their current rate it would be another hour before they were close enough to see for certain—about the same time it would take to get it in range for the remote. Traci might be able to null its rates to where it was safe enough for Jack to grab with the arm, but bringing them that close to a tumbling spacecraft was unacceptably dangerous.

He scratched at his chin. They could do something, or nothing. And nothing wasn't acceptable.

"Jack, is *Puffy* still go on standby?"

He swiped over one of his screens and scrolled down its menu. "Comm is good. So is electrical. Fuel cells running at thirty-percent output, main bus A and B both at twenty-four volts. Controls and life support diagnostics came back nominal. All the important stuff is hibernating on standby."

"How long to get through the full power-up checklist?"

It took him a second to get past his surprise and pick up on Roy's question. Was he really going for it? "The big item's aligning the guidance platform. That's about twenty minutes with cross-checks. All that's left is to charge the prop tanks and warm up the thrusters."

"Do a propellant transfer from our tanks, too. I want full authority in RCS and OMS."

Traci raised her hand. "Question, boss. Where are we—"

"*We're* not going anywhere," Roy said. He paused to consider his next words. "At least not all of us. You and Noelle have to stay here and keep flying the ship. Jack and I are going after *Cygnus*."

10

Mission Day 34
Velocity 320,485 m/s (716,904 mph)
Acceleration 0.0 m/s^2 (0g)

Jack swallowed hard. "We are?"

"I need you to manage our rendezvous while I fly the spacecraft. If anything happens to us, Traci will take over command while Noelle launches her probes."

The ensuing silence from the others fell over Roy like a cloud. He could sense their eyes boring holes into his back. Roy unlocked his seat and turned to find them expectantly watching him. "Don't tell me you're surprised," he said. "We trained for this scenario."

"I don't recall our target being out of control in the sim," Jack said. "Not this close to rendezvous."

"You've recovered tumbling satellites before."

"But we don't know what caused it go into safe mode yet. If that thing starts thrusting at random again . . . "

"It won't."

"How do you—"

Roy held up a finger to cut him off. He pulled up *Cygnus'* telemetry on a multifunction display between the pilots' stations. Guided by little more than intuition, he scrolled down through the event logs until he found what he was looking for. "Here. See? Something tripped the RCS electrical bus and it started firing thrusters at random." He scrolled down another second, then two more. "Gyros tried to compensate but the angular rates were too high. When the antennas lost contact with home, they went into gimbal lock before the master computer could even try switching guidance over to the secondary platform. When that happened . . . "

"The guidance platform went into safe mode," Jack said, working through his own mental picture. "That would be consistent with an EM surge."

"Correct. *Cygnus* doesn't have as many protections as we do. Jupiter's radiation belt is playing hell with it and the computers finally had enough. They shut down before they got fried."

"So here we are," Traci grumbled. She didn't have to say what that meant for the mission. What had to come next was harder. "You wouldn't be nursing a case of 'go fever,' would you?"

"Maybe," Roy admitted, tapping his fingers on his armrest. "I'd be lying if I said otherwise. We came all this way to do what? Throw some tungsten darts at Europan icebergs and snap a few pretty pictures of Jupiter's clouds? Do you guys want to go home yet?"

The scowl that flashed across Noelle's face could have melted those icebergs. "No, but I also prefer to have my husband alive. We still haven't crossed the most energetic radiation zone."

Jack consulted a plot of their trajectory and overlaid it on a diagram of Jupiter's magnetosphere. "Six hours," he said. "Assuming we undock in two, that gives us four hours before we have to get back inside. And *no* EVAs," he insisted. It was the closest he'd allow himself to outright insubordination, but it would also be his butt in the suit.

"Wouldn't ask that of anyone here," Roy said. "Not even you, Jack."

"What are the rates?" Noelle asked. Already skeptical by nature, having her husband as part of the equation made her especially so.

Roy scrolled back to the last time stamp. "Rolling at two degrees per second. Yaw's about half that. Pitch is close to null."

"So one complete rotation roughly every minute and a half, spinning at three minutes. It'll be sporty," Jack said. "So what's the plan?"

Roy scratched again at his chin stubble as he thought. "Roll is easy once we're aligned with its axis. Matching yaw is going to take some finesse. We'll have to fly a tight circle around it and keep shortening the radius until we match rates. If we can't, we scrub. Call that Gate One. If we manage to dock and I can't null rates, we scrub. That's Gate Two."

Traci still needed convincing. "It's going to burn a lot of gas, even before you start trying to stop that tumbling. Ever done anything like that?"

"Not even close," he admitted. "But I can figure it out."

Noelle rolled her eyes. "Pilot bravado," she sighed. "You really don't have to do that, love."

"Yes I do," Roy said, "unless we want this to be the end of it." It went without saying that it would have to be a unanimous decision.

"No, you don't. That's not what I meant. All you have to do is match its yaw rate. We can do the rest from here."

That puzzled Roy for a second. "The remote?"

"The remote," Noelle said. "Match *Cygnus'* spin. You'll still be close enough to us for your VHF datalink to keep lock so I can relay the signal. If you can stay aligned with its antenna, we can reboot it from here and take control."

It hadn't been intentional that Roy and Jack had separated from *Magellan* and were underway by the time their plans were received in Houston, but it helped. Given the time constraints, Roy couldn't wait for the inevitable denial from Mission Control. Even if they could have waited, Houston's misgivings might as well have been cast into thin air.

Cygnus, the Northrop Grumman Cygnus Mk. IV Automated Logistics Vehicle, was much larger than the ISS supply modules of its ancestry. With its cluster of fresh fuel tanks and nuclear-electric plasma engine, it made for a dazzling sight tumbling through space. To the uninitiated, it wouldn't have seemed all that bad until one realized the vessel grossed almost a hundred metric tons.

Keeping formation with it, as Jack had suggested, was when things got sporty.

"This sucks," Jack grunted, blinking hard to clear his vision against the sideways g-forces. Roy had started them flying a one-kilometer circle around their target, matching yaw rates while slowly closing the distance. The real trick was keeping them pointed nose-to-nose with *Cygnus,* an effect not unlike being at the end of a carnival Tilt-A-Whirl. After so many weeks of low gravity in a normal direction, it was that much more debilitating.

"On the bright side, my sinuses are clear now," Roy said with a loud nasal honk.

"That's because all that snot's been pushed back into your lungs," Jack said, straining against the g's. "I don't know how long we can keep this up."

Roy gave the control stick another sideways tap, pulsing thrusters to keep up. "Won't be much longer. Just keep our comm link up."

"Not sure if I can," he said. "We keep breaking lock. Angular rate's too high, even this close." As Roy traced an ever-tightening circle around their target, their antenna struggled to stay in contact long enough to spark recognition from *Cygnus*.

Roy mumbled a vague curse about some anonymous technician's mother. "What's our fuel state?"

"RCS fifty-two percent. OMS at eighty-three," Jack said, suspicious of Roy's next move.

Roy's eyes were locked on the cargo ship, his HUD projecting only the most critical information onto the glass in his window. Numbers and symbols glowed green, superimposed over the tumbling craft outside. They were now staring almost straight down its centerline. As the background stars wheeled beyond, the ship rolled about its axis along its docking ring. He gave the roll thrusters another squirt and turned to face Jack. He blinked hard, his eyes bobbling for a second from the sudden movement. "What do you think?"

Jack grimaced, this time not only against the sideways g's. They were about to get a lot worse. He was mentally calculating the amount of fuel they'd have to make up, and if *Magellan* had the margin to steal from. "I think we're both nuts."

"You might be right. By now I should know better than to argue with you. Call bingo fuel at thirty percent RCS, fifty for OMS. If we're not in a position to capture by then, we wave off and go home. Agreed?"

Jack screwed his eyes shut. "Let's do it," he said. "I'll give you propellant callouts every ten percent until we're within five of bingo, then it's every one percent. Good?"

"Good." He smiled. "I'll let you break the news."

Noelle was slightly less angered by her headset bouncing back to smack her in the face than when she'd first flung it at her console. "*Men!*"

"Want me to clean out the spare crew berth for him?" Traci asked. "Or would the waste hold be preferable?"

A tight, frustrated smirk spread across Noelle's face. "Whatever's most uncomfortable," she said. "If we had a doghouse, he'd be sleeping in it."

"He's doing this for all of us, you know. Or at least that's how he'll rationalize it."

Noelle fumed as she returned to monitoring her husband's excursion. It wasn't necessarily a rationalization, she knew. They'd talked through similar scenarios many times in private, long before Roy presented his idea to the others. Before the revelations of the Russian discoveries at Pluto, Noelle's personal mission highlight would have been testing her theories of underwater life at Europa. She was a biologist first, therefore Pluto had always been secondary in her mind. She didn't expect to find anything nearly as interesting there, yet it was a place they were going to an awful lot of trouble to reach.

Now that they knew why, their current predicament felt all the more dire. Deep down, she wanted them to succeed, perhaps even more so than her vexatious and infuriatingly confident husband.

It ain't bragging if you can do it, her husband liked to joke. Noelle willed him on, hoping it wasn't to his end.

The sideways force became stronger with each turn as they drew closer and tightened the circle. Roy's focus narrowed with similar intensity. It had become a dizzying ride as each pulse of maneuvering jets pushed them both inward and sideways along an ever-tightening circle. They were less than two meters apart now and spinning about each other at the same rate. This gave their target the illusion of being stationary but for the slow roll along its long axis, which Roy was now able to match with a quick burst from their own thrusters. Were it not for the tumbling stars in the background and the punishing lateral *g*'s, it would have seemed perfectly still.

Jack bit back the taste of bile rising from his gut, keeping his eyes locked on his displays while Roy kept his focus outside. In this case, Jack had it easier: One of the first skills new pilots must master to fly in poor visibility is to ignore their inner ears and stomachs and to put complete trust in their instruments. When there are no visual cues outside, the senses you've grown up relying on will kill you fast. It made formation flying in bad weather a torturous chore, but at least fighter jets didn't try to spin in formation.

"One meter," Jack said. "You got this." There was a scraping tremble as their docking probe contacted *Cygnus'* ring. Roy relaxed his grip on the translation control and let their inertia do the rest of the work. They shook with a gentle thud as retaining clamps slammed down along the rings. Soon after, comforting green lights appeared on their panels.

"Capture," Roy said, but adding their mass to *Cygnus'* moment of rotation now made them the rock at the end of a sling. He began furiously pulsing thrusters to overcome the yawing motion. "That's Gate Two. Can you hand me a sick-sack there, bubba?"

Jack knew an old pilot like Roy wouldn't ask unless he really was about to blow chunks. He reached down into a little-used pocket behind the seat and handed the plastic bag to him. Roy nodded gratefully and plastered it over his mouth. "Take over."

"My spacecraft," Jack said, switching over control and taking his eyes away from his own control panel to their new acquisition outside. The perspective and sideways twisting acceleration made his head spin. He fought off an urge to shake his head to clear it, a dangerous reflex. "This is *hard*. Why didn't you ask sooner?"

Roy held up a finger before answering with an angry retch.

"Never mind. I'm going to keep fighting this spin until you feel better. One of us needs to talk the other in."

Roy's finger turned to a thumbs-up. "Wait one." He reached up for the cabin lighting and turned them from low-light red to full bright. The wheeling background of stars was washed out by the glare, leaving only the docked cargo ship in view.

"Sorry. I should've thought of that."

Roy took a deep breath. "It's okay," he said, after cleaning his face with a wet wipe. His stomach was still catching up to their actual motion. "Are we stable?"

"We are. Good data lock."

"Please let the ladies know they can start nulling that roll any time now." He reached for another bag. "And this stays between us, Templeton."

Jack mimed zipping his lip, then keyed his mic. "Home plate, *Puffy*. We're ready to get off this ride now."

With Roy and Jack following close by, the revived cargo ship maneuvered itself toward *Magellan*'s spiral truss and into easy range of the manipulator arms under Noelle's control. The stack of cylinders and tanks filled their windows, its polished skin reflecting a kaleidoscope of colors from Jupiter.

Her hotshot husband had nailed it. They could have just about coasted into *Cygnus* at this rate; all she had to do was reach out and catch it like a slow pitch over home plate. "I've got it," Noelle said. "Relative velocity zero. Moving it to Node 2 now." There was a grating sound of metal on metal as the carrier's docking probe slid into their open port, followed by the thud of pneumatic latches along its length. A ring of amber status lights flashed green.

"Capture." She turned to Traci, tired but content. "Tell Roy he can come home now."

The women sank into their flight couches and shared a silent fist bump. It would be another hour before the cheers erupted in Houston.

11

Mission Day 35
Velocity 320,485 m/s (716,904 mph)
Acceleration 0.0 m/s² (0 g)

Just as Traci had wanted, *Magellan*'s control deck was awash in soft hues of yellow, orange, and purple as Jupiter's gauzy bulk filled every window with light even brighter than they'd come to expect from the sims. Control screens were the only distraction from the planet's natural glow. After a long night of hard-earned rest, it felt like a normal morning. Roy had decided on his own that it would be rather nice to bask in some planetshine while they had the chance. The luster from Jupiter's cloud tops gave the ship a feel of sunset after a summer rainstorm—all it lacked was the scent of air pregnant with humidity and the breeze through an open window.

The sudden thought of opening a window to the killing vacuum outside yanked the chain of Jack's runaway imagination back inside, caught up in another daydream when something important was supposed to be happening. "Why does my mind always wander when there's too much to do?" he asked of no one in particular.

"I'm certain your mother would tell us it's because you're ADD," Noelle said in her best dispassionate medical professional's tone. "Or you're just avoiding responsibility, which is also a sign of ADD."

"Don't hold back, Dr. No," he said. "With that accent, you can say pretty much anything to me and I'll take it as a compliment. Go ahead, let 'er rip."

"I'd not dream of such a thing," she clucked, "unless you miss my payload's injection burn. If it overshoots Europa, I'll be quite, well . . . "

"Upset?"

"Pissed. It is the entire premise of my doctoral thesis we are hoping to prove here."

"Yet you say 'pissed' in such a lovely way. What you're saying is that the fruits of your research, your entire *reputation*, rests on my ability to not screw this up?"

That was when Roy piped up. "Quit flirting with my wife, Jack. Though I do like the 'Dr. No' thing. Suits her."

Noelle's protests were drowned out by the howls and whistles from her crewmates.

"Let's stay on task, people," Roy said. "This isn't the time to be getting slap-happy."

"Aye, skipper," Jack said with a wink in Noelle's direction. "Don't worry," he said just loud enough for her to hear. He activated a joystick controller by his console and uncovered a bank of protected switches. "Your bombardier is up and over the target."

The probe Jack was about to release, *Astrolabe*, had in fact been inspired by an Air Force cluster bomb. Instead of munitions, it would scatter a handful of self-propelled impact darts as it traced a low orbit around Europa. Each probe was tipped with a tungsten penetrator and boosted by a small solid rocket motor. They would be strung along a path thousands of miles long to maximize their chances of blasting through the ice into what was believed to be liquid water beneath. Wherever there was water, there was life. At least it was so on Earth; whether that held true for the rest of the solar system remained to be seen. Noelle's doctoral thesis had argued for it.

Jack's excitement mounted as he ran through the release checklist: For real, no simulation this time. They had practiced this event and drilled every possible bad outcome so many times that the mechanics of it had become second nature. Which was of course the point, though at times he'd felt like a trained rat in a maze.

"Internal diagnostics complete. *Astrolabe* is on internal power," Jack said. "Disconnecting from our auxiliary bus." He snapped open a red switch cover and looked over his shoulder at Roy. "Pyros armed. Standing by for your go."

Roy tapped at a screen on his instrument panel, checking their position and velocity relative to Europa one last time against the computer-generated cues projected onto his forward window. Piloting had become so simple that it was almost like a video game. The probe was in Jack's hands now; Roy just had to make sure they stayed pointed in the right direction before it fired its braking rockets. "We're on speed and on target. You're cleared hot, bubba."

Jack had also come to realize that whenever Roy became dead serious he reverted to his old fighter pilot lingo, which meant everyone suddenly became *bubba*. He snapped open a covered switch and thumbed the release. A status light changing color was the only indication anything had happened. "Bombs away. T-minus fifteen seconds to retro burn. Ready to change your life, Doc?"

Noelle fidgeted with her monitors. "Change can be for better or worse. We tend to assume the former."

"That's kind of pessimistic for someone who's about to validate her life's work."

"It's disillusionment with human nature," she said. "If this gives us actual evidence of life beyond Earth, it will only be after we carpet bombed it first."

The probe itself was mounted inside the saddle truss of *Magellan*'s superstructure. Nestled alongside gleaming cylinders full of water and fuel, the various probes to be released during their sprint past Jupiter appeared mundane in comparison.

Astrolabe was one of the more intricate contraptions despite its outward simplicity. A composite shell protected the half-dozen impact darts, propelled into its own orbit by a liquid rocket motor that dwarfed the probe itself. When Jack released it, springs punted the probe out of its cradle and set it drifting away. As soon as it reached minimum safe distance from the spacecraft, a hard burn from the booster began slowing it into Europa's orbit. *Magellan* would be on the other side of Jupiter before it arrived at its final destination.

The final two probes to be released at Jupiter were *Aether* and *Boreas*, named for the Greek gods of the winds. They were simple but tough weather balloons encased in ablative entry shells which would separate as the ship shot past Jupiter on its closest approach. The balloons would then behave like parachutes as they fell into the thickening atmosphere, slowing each probe's descent as they filled.

JPL's mission managers hoped the balloons would survive the howling upper-level winds long enough to keep their instruments recording in Jupiter's violent stratosphere. It wouldn't matter if the balloons could stay aloft for days; they would only be useful for as long as *Magellan* was able to receive their transmissions and relay them back to Earth.

"Good burn, and *Astrolabe* is still on target," Jack announced. "That's one tough bird. Twenty *g*'s deceleration would've had my eyeballs hanging out of their sockets."

"Is that your way of telling me to be happy that it started life as a cluster munition?"

"Gets the job done."

Roy unbuckled and pushed away from his flight station. "Speaking of which, we still have a lot to do."

"Back to the grinder," Traci said as she did the same. "Sooner we finish checking out *Cygnus*, the better. I need some sleep."

Jack looked at the day's activity plan clipped to his console. In a fit of naive optimism, Houston's mission planners had found a way to cram some rest time into the middle of their Jupiter encounter. "No problem. According to this, we were in rest two hours ago."

"Thanks. I feel so much better knowing that," Traci said as she gave him a side-eye. They'd learned long ago that no plan survives contact with reality.

Roy ignored them and checked his watch. "Twelve hours until periapsis. All we have to do is unpack the log mod, transfer propellant, eject the empty tanks, and get aligned for the burn."

Jack crumpled up the plan and stuffed it in the trash.

As Owen started up his car, the electric hum highlighted its lack of engine noise—a reminder of how much work he still needed to put into restoring the old Mustang sitting idle in his garage. When this was all over, maybe he'd have time to finish that project. He'd been with the space agency for more than enough time to take early retirement and move on to something less taxing.

After yesterday's too-dramatic rendezvous, he'd decided to take Rhyzov's advice and disconnect from the mission for at least one night. "You can do nothing here except aggravate people on your teams. They will do their jobs. You go home and do yours."

The old guy had been right, as usual. It being almost Christmas made it that much easier.

The chatter from the all-news channel wrenched him back to the present reality. Early retirement? Not with the way the market had been lately. Too much churn for his comfort and most of it on the downside. If he was serious about pulling the eject handle soon then he needed to get wise and start moving money around now. Protect his cash value or whatever it was the financial gurus were preaching this month.

No more news. It left him too aggravated if he was paying attention at all. Otherwise it was all just background noise. It could be bleating at him the entire ride home and he'd not feel any smarter for it. He thumbed the controls on his steering wheel. Every other channel was holiday music. He kept alternating between genres until settling on some old country blues. Maybe he'd pick up the guitar again after he was freed from NASA. It had been, what, over a decade since he'd been even halfway serious with it? It was frightening to see how easily time could slip away.

He rolled down his windows to take in the night air. Winter in Houston meant he could wear long sleeves with only feeling a vague need to roll them up. He didn't even have to loosen his tie.

As he turned off a densely forested road, the street seemed to explode with multicolored lights. Half the neighborhood must have worked at Johnson, but it was a small fraction on duty in the control room. He'd almost forgotten what it was like to count on having holidays free.

His wife felt the same. After getting used to his rare presence at home, she'd expected him to be living in his office until *Magellan* was safely on the other side of Jupiter after Christmas. "You're home," she said, half-questioning.

"Remember our Russian guest?" Owen looked down at his shoes. "He kind of shamed me into it."

His wife nodded. "You kind of deserve it," she said, then gave him a lingering kiss. "But we'll take you anyway. Tell Dr. Rhyzov he's welcome here anytime."

Owen tossed his overcoat over the sofa and collapsed onto it. He would wake up in the same spot the next morning with his wife lolled over alongside him, along with their daughter who had wandered in sometime during the night. And the cat, whom he'd found draped over his feet.

He turned his head, searching for the clock on their mantel and then deciding it wasn't worth waking everyone else splayed around him. If it walked, toddled, or crawled, it had ended up in the same space he now occupied.

Owen settled back into his wife's lap. He instinctively knew what was happening at that instant almost half a billion miles away, and that there was little he could do right now but get in the way.

On the other hand, if things went sideways out there they'd have his head on a platter once it came out that he wasn't hovering over the FCR. Like that would make a difference even without a two hour response time.

Another look at the pile of people and animals around him, and he knew. Whatever happened next was beyond his control so he might as well enjoy this moment. With all that had to happen over the next couple of days, he was most anxious to hear from Templeton once they'd started unpacking *Cygnus*. Who didn't like surprises at Christmas?

There was much the combined spacecraft could do on its own without the need for human intervention. Once docked, *Cygnus'* power conduits and propellant transfer lines plugged themselves into *Magellan's* with some help from the service bots along its spine. Jack had only to confirm they'd put the right couplers together and let Daisy watch the tanks fill.

Unpacking supplies, however, still meant grunt work.

"More grub coming your way," Traci called from deep inside the supply module, brimming with packages wrapped in insulating foil and fireproof cloth. A narrow tunnel had been created down the middle as they moved food into the galley and spare parts into the equipment bay. The rest would stay inside *Cygnus* until they needed it. As its contents were emptied over the next year, it would be steadily filled back up with their garbage. Starting life as a vessel full of goodies, it would end life as an expensive trash can.

A meter-long package of freeze-dried meals came sailing up out of the makeshift tunnel which Jack caught and redirected to their freezer. "Is that the last of the food?"

"According to the manifest. Hang on." Traci wormed her way into a crevice where a container had been stuffed in behind the racks of food. "Curious. This isn't listed."

Roy's voice boomed from behind them. "I'll take that."

Traci shrugged. "Okay." She unstrapped it and sent it floating up through the portal. "Your preference, boss."

Roy caught it in midair. "That it is," he said, studying them both. "Is the module still in trim?"

Jack checked the mass distribution on his tablet. "CG is in tolerance."

"Good job. The dry goods can wait, then."

Traci floated up out of the tunnel of packages and eyed the container. "So what's the special delivery?"

"Not now." He glanced at his watch. "You guys just freed up three hours in your schedule. Go hit the rack until it's time for the burn."

The promise of sleep was more than enough to squelch their curiosity.

12

Mission Day 36
Velocity 320,485 m/s (716,904 mph)
Acceleration 0.0 m/s^2 (0 g)

Roy had been almost completely silent ever since they'd started checking out *Cygnus*. All through their inventory of its goods, every time Noelle would call out a report to him up in the control deck, Roy would acknowledge them with a grunt. A short grunt meant "good," a long growl meant "not good." After a while he'd even abandoned that minimal vocalization in favor of a rapid double-click of his microphone. If he wasn't happy, whoever called would receive a terse command to "explain."

Jack had therefore found it amusing that as they drew closer to Jupiter's roiling cloud tops, their normally taciturn commander had become a virtual chatterbox.

"Jack, need your read on coolant flux. Temps look kind of wobbly up here."

"We're good. It's just signal noise," Jack said, and smiled to himself. He'd long ago decided that Roy allowed himself a certain number of syllables to use each day, evidently hoarding them for this moment.

Roy was nervous . . . no, that wasn't right. Anxious. He tapped an icon on one of his lesser-used monitors to pull up a mirror image of Roy's primary flight display. It was much easier than getting up to look over his shoulder.

His eyes darted back and forth between it and the cascade of information across the rest of his workstation. "Yep, that's it. Too much data competing for attention in one reading. Dump all of that crap onto one screen and it's not gonna know what to do with it."

"One more lesson learned for the sims," Roy said, "eventually."

"Eventually," Jack agreed. He selected a few critical feeds and set alarm thresholds on them, then pushed them out to Roy's display where three green bars appeared. "Here. I've isolated the parameters you need to see in real time. Any one of those turn amber, we've got problems."

"And if they turn red?"

"Then we're about to blow up."

Roy's grunt sounded like assent; Jack couldn't tell. "Nothing you could do about it anyway, boss. Just keep us on pitch, I'll keep the rest in one piece."

As they followed the flight computer through its countdown to relight the engines, Jack realized how they'd become an onboard Mission Control team as much as an actual flight crew. He wasn't directly controlling the power and thrusters so much as he was just monitoring them. Roy and Traci weren't flying the ship through this maneuver, they were watching the computers do it. Either one of them could take over if something started going screwy, but neither wanted to face that choice. At these speeds, being off by a decimal point now could have disastrous consequences a few billion kilometers downrange. When every error represented exponentially greater energy to be spent correcting it, even an old hand like Roy Hoover was content to let the ship fly itself.

Noelle had perhaps the best deal by far: Her principal job was to look out the windows, at least in a figurative sense. As mission scientist, her task now was to control the probes they'd flung into Jupiter's cloud tops. She was giddy watching the returns as their ballutes reached equilibrium with the roiling atmosphere to carry her precious drones along supersonic jet streams. As the probes stabilized, she began slewing their outboard cameras to capture the most up-close video yet of the solar system's largest planet. It was thought that Jupiter could have become a star itself had it possessed enough mass for its hydrogen clouds to spontaneously ignite. Intellectually she knew that current thinking was trending otherwise, but the idea became more plausible as she watched the churning gas giant from her bird's-eye view. The clearest images from the best satellites had never conveyed such ominous enormity, and a two-dimensional video could only hint at the depths of cloud formations that descended thousands of miles toward whatever comprised the planet's core.

Now that they were well inside the worst of Jupiter's radiation belts, graphite shutters had been lowered over every window. Doubling as their radiation "storm shelter," the control deck was surrounded by layers of bladders between the inner and outer hulls that held their waste water and made for a natural radiation shield. To a person, the crew remained sanguine about the fact that the only thing standing between them and certain death was a few liters of stale piss. Jack, for his part, had long ago exhausted any jokes about it.

"One minute to maneuver node intercept," Traci announced. "Gimbals look good, still on pitch."

Roy grunted once. *Agreed.*

"Reactor output and coolant flow both nominal, nozzle coils configured for max thrust," Jack said, and made one last check of what he'd come to call simply "the board," a display he'd arranged to show a quick, simple status of every system that they could not live without. "The board is green. Configuring for hard burn on your mark."

"Go," Roy said.

Outside, everything that could be tucked in against the hull began retracting into their cradles, minimizing their exposure to the stray molecules that were certain to hit them as they drew closer to Jupiter's upper atmosphere. To Noelle's dismay, this included the antennas which connected them to her experiments. "Don't worry," Jack reassured her. "You'll just have that much more to catch up on after we're clear on the other side."

"Let's just get this done." Noelle looked grim, knowing he was right but hating the separation nonetheless. She'd have been happy to take their excursion module and stay behind, except for that whole "stranded in deep space" problem it presented.

"Thirty seconds," Traci said. "Jack, we've got a pressure warning on the secondary propellant tank. Can you give it a stir?"

Jack swore at himself, just noticing the tank warning flashing at him. "Yep, primary blowdown fan just went offline."

"And the secondary didn't cut in automatically?" she asked

sharply, more out of time pressure than frustration. The countdown timer had just passed T-minus twenty seconds, on its way to zero.

"Apparently not." Jack cursed as he reached for the switch. Indicators turned green as the tank came back up to pressure. "Might be control logic, but I doubt it." It looked like a simple relay failure or a complex software glitch; either one would have to wait.

"Ten seconds," Roy interrupted. The event timer counted down silently as the plasma injectors opened up.

"Ignition."

It felt like a sack of wet concrete had been dumped in his lap. Curtains of gray swirled around the periphery of Jack's vision. The gimbals in his flight couch hissed as they tilted with *Magellan's* thrust vector, shifting his array of monitors temporarily out of view. He clenched the muscles of his lower body, which helped keep his blood in his upper body where it mattered most and made a mighty effort to turn his head. Staying conscious wouldn't matter if he couldn't see his own instruments, and the repeater screens mounted on his arm rests just didn't convey enough information. It might have been enough for the others, but the flight engineer needed to know exactly what was going on inside of his ship. For the slingshot to work, they needed a continuous maximum-thrust burn for three minutes on either side of periapsis. That didn't sound like much, except that the engines normally pulsed a few seconds apart in a complex sequence. All three pounding away at the same time was going to make for a rough ride.

Jack turned his head forward, the mounting *g*'s forcing him to put his faith in "Plan B," the AI, to let him know before something went bang. Roy may not have liked it, but he wasn't the one trying to keep an open-cycle fusion reaction running at full tilt. He reached for a switch by his right index finger and pressed it three times. A three-dimensional blue widget spiraled in on itself at the bottom corner of the screen behind a reassuring message: neural network online.

Good girl, Jack thought. *Just you and me.* He tapped the message "acknowledged" and saw the little blue spiral shrink into the background. The AI was now watching everything Jack was. A momentary spike in the secondary electrical bus was the single clue that something big was running in the background, and Jack was the only one paying attention to that anyway.

Ahead, Roy and Traci had it easier as their couches were aligned in the proper direction by default: forward, as pilot's seats ought to be. Jack and Noelle were behind them at angles that made perfect sense in fractional or zero-*g*. Now, not so much. Perhaps the human-factors design group had figured a few minutes of high-*g* burn hadn't necessitated changing anything. He made a mental note to hunt down and horsewhip them when he got back to Houston.

"Different than flying drones, ain't it?" Roy teased from his position of relative comfort.

"Good thing Noelle's the doc and not you," Jack grunted, "your bedside manner . . . " The word "sucks" formed in his brain and tried to climb out of his larynx before it was choked off by gravity. What emerged sounded something like *Grnnughh.*

"Try not to talk so much," Roy said. "Nearing max alpha." Meaning they were almost at three *g*'s acceleration as they raced through periapsis, their lowest point above Jupiter. As nuclear plasma exploded from their engines, the exchange of mass for velocity was further multiplied by the giant planet's gravity. The effect would have been even more dramatic if they were just using Jupiter for speed: In this case, they were also using it to change the plane of their orbit to match Pluto's.

Yet even with a total velocity change of over half a million kilometers per hour, it would still take most of the next year for them to reach the Kuiper Belt and Pluto's orbit. Much of that time would be spent burning in the opposite direction, canceling out the velocity they'd gained to make the trip in the first place. To a layman it might have seemed self-defeating or even wasteful—a question which had in fact been raised often by the popular press—until realizing the alternative was to spend ten years coasting there.

It wasn't even a useful percentage of light speed, something the Russians had achieved with forty-year-old technology. The public's irrational, crippling fear of nuclear power was running headlong into the reality of a need for cleaner sources of energy. What was the point of building electric cars if most of the power plants that charged them still burned fossil fuels? Maybe there was some value in Russia having had the autonomy to ignore the predictable screeching busybodies: Every now and then, it enabled them to do something amazing. Then again, they'd managed to turn large swaths of their "motherland" into uninhabitable toxic nightmares. So, there was that.

Jack shook his head, bringing his focus back to the here and now. The ship had become almost serene, the ubiquitous low whir of cooling fans and air recyclers joined by the distant hum of magnetic rocket nozzles jetting high-velocity plasma into space behind them.

While the modules which housed *Magellan*'s sensitive payload of humans and electronics may have protected them from the invisible radiation hazards of space, the ship itself was protected from equally dangerous micrometeorites by a dome of ballistic fabric stretched over a titanium frame almost fifty meters across its bow, shielding it from the more mundane threats of cosmic dust which became a good deal less mundane if hit fast enough. It was nothing so much as an overgrown combination of heat shielding and body armor. And as such, the dome began glowing red as molecule-thin wisps of Jovian atmosphere began impacting it at high speed.

The engines, however, were much more exposed. Being small nuclear furnaces themselves, there was little protection to be gained other than from the collision avoidance of the bow dome. That in itself was superfluous, considering how much hard structure stood between it and the three open-cycle fusion engines: If they did hit something, the forward end would get the worst of it. After that, the layers of radiator panels just forward of the reactor sections could absorb anything that might conceivably make it past the forward dome. The likelihood of a plasma injector or lithium tank getting holed by a stray dust mote had hardly been worth worrying over.

The interplay between the powerful magnetic exhaust nozzles and the deep-space radiation environment was a different matter. Being industrial-strength electromagnets, each nozzle was calibrated to always maintain the optimum expansion ratio between the nozzle's throat and its exit as it channeled a stream of nuclear fire that rivaled the Sun's own hydrogen furnace. They were as strong as anything yet built, but nothing man-made was indestructible.

"Jack?" Roy's tone carried the weight of what they were all feeling: a subtle change in the ride, a dissonant throbbing that rolled up through the spiral truss of carbon fiber and cylinders of aluminum alloys into the backs of their acceleration couches.

"I see it," Jack said, more calmly than he felt. He fought the pressing *g*-forces to shift one of his displays, calling up trend lines from the accelerometers and transducers that relayed engine health just as an amber caution light appeared. He could feel it too, but something didn't make sense. "Got some out-of-phase vibrations building up in number three."

"Cause?"

This still didn't make sense. His eyes darted over to the compression coil's readouts. "Injectors and compressors are out of synch. Not by much, but . . . "

"Approaching resonance?" If they started resonating with each other, the cascading vibrations would tear them apart in the same way a tenor could shatter a crystal glass.

"Not yet," Jack said. The engine wasn't in danger of shaking itself apart just yet. He felt a change in the ride at the same time he heard a curse from Roy.

"Engine controls just did a command override. They're rolling back number three to idle." Roy's unstated question: *And what are you doing about it, Flight Engineer?*

"Fail-safe," Jack confirmed. "The phase vibrations are in tolerance under normal thrust, so it opted for normal."

"That still doesn't get us to Pluto."

And what was the alternative? Jack thought. "But if we have to shut down . . . "

"Not happening unless you think we're about to blow up."

"Kinda hoped Daisy would tip us off to that before I could," Jack said testily, biting back his annoyance at the interruption. The problem inherent to fusion reactions was that catastrophic failures often presented very little warning.

"I prefer your take first," Roy said, his voice clipped.

Jack reached for his keyboard and typed out a silent query to *Magellan*'s computer. Better to suffer the physical punishment of exerting such a tiny force instead of just speaking to it and letting Roy know he was doing the exact opposite of what he'd just been told to do.

❈ ❈ ❈

QUERY: *No. 2 engine anomaly.*

❆   ❆   ❆

The onboard diagnostics flashed an immediate reply: PROPELLANT INJECTOR AND COMPRESSION COIL OUT OF PHASE BY 0.28 CYCLES PER SECOND.

Tell me something I don't know. Still, almost point three hertz was bad. How had it gotten that far out of sync without his seeing it first?

❆   ❆   ❆

QUERY: Root cause of No.2 anomaly.

❆   ❆   ❆

SURGE IN ELECTRICAL JUNCTION 6B. PRIMARY AND SECONDARY REGULATOR MODULES AFFECTED.

And that didn't trigger an automatic shutdown? And how'd he miss the surge in the electrical bus? Must have been lost in the noise when he brought Daisy out of hibernation. This was why they'd always had a room full of engineers back in Houston watching every move: Some things happened too fast for a busy astronaut to notice until he was dead. It was a great concept until you were a solid light-hour from home.

He stabbed at the on-screen menu, diving deeper into the propulsion system. There it was, in the trace file: The electrical bus was protected by the same shielding that prevented Jupiter's radiation belt from frying them in their seats. They couldn't manage that same level of protection around the drive, though. The engine bells by nature had to be out in the open. The control software must have compensated by rolling back to the next highest power setting.

Could the same thing happen to the others?

❆   ❆   ❆

QUERY: Source of 6B surge.

❆   ❆   ❆

SOURCE UNVERIFIED. SIGNIFICANT PROBABILITY OF INTERACTION WITH JOVIAN MAGNETIC FIELD. CONTROL SOFTWARE COMMANDED P74 SAFETY PROTOCOL.

As suspected, a "Program 74" fail-safe. He never knew if their control logic had any solid theory behind it or if they were just stuck in the "if this, then that" thinking from the Apollo and Shuttle days. Either way, *Magellan*'s current orientation presented engine three's side of the spacecraft toward the brunt of Jupiter's magnetic field and the high-energy particles it bombarded them with. Engine three had taken one for the team.

"Jack?" Roy again, looking for answers. His entire exchange with the AI had taken maybe ten seconds, an interminable interlude in spaceflight. One more look at the timing . . .

The injector/compressor stage was off by a good 0.3 hertz now. Jack grimaced, dreading what had to come next. "We stay in cruise mode or shut down engine three." Either way they lost an awful lot of thrust.

For her part, Noelle had wasted no time transitioning into her contingency role, a typically anodyne label for what was their emergency-action manager. She stabbed at a selector which switched her monitors over to the emergency checklists. As the screens flashed over to an attention-getting series of crimson menus, she prepared to talk them through contingencies just as Mission Control would have if they weren't over a full light-hour away. Now that her flight station was configured, she grabbed an old-fashioned binder of mission rules from a cubby beside it and tore the book open to a tab labeled "Jupiter Gravity Assist." Most of their options were pages trimmed with red hash marks: Mission-abort scenarios.

"Engine shutdown," she recited with practiced calm, one eye on the event clock above her console. This wasn't going to be like turning an airplane, or even following the free return trajectories that lunar expeditions had been bound to. Any changes to their direction and accumulated velocity, even if measured in seconds, held considerable consequences: It would determine whether they remained at Jupiter, headed back to Earth, or were flung farther out into the solar system.

IF BEFORE incremental ΔV 20,000 m/s . . . she scrolled down through all of the secondary considerations for the bottom line: "abort to orbit," meaning they'd shut down the good engine to achieve orbit and execute the "Extended Jupiter Mission Scenario." It was too late for that, even if she'd secretly hoped for it.

IF AFTER incremental ΔV 20,000 m/s . . . abort to Earth, which at this velocity would keep them out here almost as long as if going to Pluto. But it also had the added effect of looping them around the other side of the Sun to fly by Saturn before bending their orbit back Earthward. Not a terrible deal.

"Noelle?" Roy asked sharply. He'd almost said "Bubba."

"Stand by," she snapped, then: "Sorry, love."

"Been with you too long for hard feelings," he said, "but we've gotta decide what to do right quick."

She flipped back to the first page. Were there any options that *didn't* involve giving up? How many times had they simmed this exact scenario? "Jack," she asked, "how long can we run the other engines at maximum rated thrust?" An understated way of asking for emergency power.

"How long you need?"

She tugged at her lip as she studied the possibilities. Trajectory planning was not her specialty and this was too critical for the rules of thumb she'd relied on to get through astronaut training. "Traci?"

The pilot was way ahead of her. "Looking at it." She and Roy hadn't even considered aborting, not even for the chance to see Saturn up close. They were all bound by the same irresistible, if unacknowledged, impulse to make it to the end of the mystery that had been dropped on them right before launch. "Call it two minutes at max power. Jack, back me up on our state vector."

"We can do that. What time stamp are you using?" he shot back.

"Shutdown, so T-plus eighty. Solar reference frame, J2000," she said, somewhat unnecessarily. They all knew which reference decade to use out of the *Astronautical Almanac*, but couldn't afford to screw this up. While they were leveraging Jupiter's mass to add velocity, more important was the direction change it would give them for free. Their final destination lay below the ecliptic, that invisible flat plane all the major planets inhabit within a few degrees of each other. Besides its extreme distance, being inclined seventeen degrees to the solar system's equator made Pluto that much harder to reach. Plane changes were expensive in terms of reaction mass, so using Jupiter's gravity as a free booster to match orbits with Pluto demanded that they get this right.

They had about three minutes to find out.

Jack scribbled furiously on a tablet and compared his own estimates to the computer's. The trick to an Oberth maneuver wasn't in stealing some of the planet's velocity so much as it was taking advantage of the potential energy its gravity imparted on their exhaust mass. The closer they got, the stronger the gravity and the larger the multiplier. At twenty thousand kilometers above its cloud tops Jupiter offered quite a multiplier, but it was as close as the flight planners had dared. "Okay, I got it . . . wait!" That couldn't be right. Why didn't the computer agree with him? "No, I don't."

"What's wrong?" Roy shot back. Their numbers had to agree, and soon, or it would be a long orbit back to Earth.

"Try these," Jack said, throwing his velocity and position figures up on their displays. "I forgot to correct for the date. It's not 2000."

"Hasn't been for a while now." Did Roy actually sound amused?

A quick beat, then: "Okay, I concur," Traci said, eyeing their velocity against a plot of their choices. "It puts us near the edge of the curve, but it works."

"Mine too," Roy chipped in. He took a breath. "And what's the computer say?"

"Guidance platform agrees with all three," Noelle said as she went back down the mission rules' decision tree. They were playing this one close. "Now what, love?"

"Much as I'd enjoy a jaunt by Saturn, we've got some unfinished business ahead. Agreed?"

"Agreed," Jack and Traci said more or less in harmony. Noelle held up a finger to cool their heels as she flipped to the "Pluto Orbit Insertion" tab. She wasn't sending them anywhere without first making absolutely certain that there was a plan for getting back home with one engine out. Which there was, she just needed to see it again in something other than a simulated emergency.

"Agreed," Noelle sighed, satisfied that they had in fact worked out a way to get home with a third of their drive system cooked.

"Two minutes," Noelle announced. There was another curse from up front as Roy punched up a different display, this one a maze of ellipses and parabolas. He was scrolling through different scenarios for an orbit back to Earth. One open-ended hyperbola remained, a lower-energy trajectory on to Pluto. Jack called up the same display and shot a glance toward Noelle, who had done the same. "You thinking what I'm thinking?"

"*Aller de la fièvre.*"

Jack smiled inwardly despite the tension. "Go fever" sounded so much nicer in French. "That's over a year."

"Not if we can lower our periapsis and pick up more delta-v."

"And more friction drag, too," he reminded her. "The tradeoff isn't worth it."

"I wouldn't be so sure. Our trajectory is based on the atmospheric models we had at the time, no?"

"No . . . I mean, yes. Yes. So what?"

The gleam in her eyes said it all. "That was two years ago. We have much better data now." She swept a hand across one of her screens, which then duplicated itself on Roy and Traci's display. "We can lower our periapsis by at least ten thousand kilometers."

"What?" Jack sputtered. "Your data can't be that good."

"I believe it is," she said with a nod toward their screens. "The LIDAR returns are quite encouraging. Pressure and density values in the troposphere are significantly lower than the models predicted for the Southern Temperate Zone."

"And the stratosphere?" If density and pressure were bottoming out at lower than expected altitudes, they could be looking at atmospheric effects similar to a frigid day on Earth. Granted, it was on an absurdly exaggerated scale since Jupiter was just about all atmosphere.

"As I said, we can safely tighten our radius by a good ten thousand kilometers."

Traci had been projecting a new path while Noelle and Jack argued over planetary atmospherics. "That'll let us pick up some lost delta-v, but not all of it. We're still adding weeks to the trip. How far can we stretch our consumables?"

Jack held up a finger to stall them while typing commands into the tiny keyboard with his free hand: *QUERY: Minimum crew caloric requirements—assume 120 day mission extension.* That should be simple enough for Daisy to find. There was a calculation matrix for it somewhere in their mission plans. "Water, yes. The reclamation plant's efficient enough to keep us going for years. I'm worried about food."

"One minute," Noelle warned.

MINIMUM CALORIC REQUIREMENTS CAN BE MET WITH EXISTING

RATIONS. OPTIMAL IF THE EXPERIMENTAL HYDROPONIC GARDEN IS UTILIZED. Daisy presented another option relying on the two medical trauma pods down in sickbay, something Jack wasn't ready to offer just yet. Going into hibernation to stretch their food supply could wait.

"We can do this. Who here has a green thumb?"

"The hydroponic module?" Roy asked. "I'll leave that part to my better half."

"It's mostly edibles," Noelle said. "A few herbs for variety, but we can replace those with soybeans and peanuts for our protein intake."

In a display of strength not just against gravity but of will, Roy turned in his seat to stare down his wife. "Babe, I need your no-BS read on this. Can you make that garden grow? Because what has to come next won't be fun."

Noelle checked the countdown clock: thirty seconds. She looked up to meet his gaze. "Yes. Let's go to Pluto."

Magellan's present position in space had been worked out to exhaustion months before and was based on a certain number of weeks of constant acceleration at a certain value of *g* along a painstakingly crafted set of vectors. And that was all about to be literally turned on its head.

In order to lower their altitude above Jupiter for maximum advantage from its mass, they would have to undo some of that vector. Unlike flying an airplane, they couldn't just push the nose over a few degrees and level off. They had to lower their orbit by losing enough velocity for the planet's gravity to strengthen its grip, and the only way to do that was to flip *Magellan* tail-first and burn against their direction of travel long enough to cancel some of that momentum. Done right, they'd still end up gaining more velocity on the other side than they would have otherwise.

If done wrong? No one had time to bother with that.

Roy and Traci had responded to Noelle's assent with a flurry of movement as they reconfigured the guidance platform. "Give me a target," Roy barked. He had very little time to get all hundred-plus meters of spacecraft turned around and had to know where the nose needed to end up.

"Coming up," Traci said with a look over her shoulder at Jack, who by now had stopped caring what Roy thought of his reliance on their AI. They weren't going to figure this out on their own and Houston wouldn't know until it was too late. "You got a vector for me?"

A glowing crosshairs icon superimposed itself on the pilot's eight ball nav director just as the hard numbers lit up on the multifunction display between them. "There's your target," Jack said, confirming it with the AI as he hurried through a series of automated cues for securing the plasma generators and isolating their powerful capacitors from the electrical bus. "Reactors and field generators are back in standby. You're go for shutdown."

"Shutdown," Roy ordered, and Traci smartly chopped the throttle levers. The weak gravity disappeared as thrust fell to zero, followed by a slight roll starboard as the guidance flywheels compensated for the off-axis forces. The neon-green target hovering in the eight ball shifted with it as Roy carefully wrapped his meaty hands around the controls. "Going manual."

With the storm shutters still buttoned up, the only sensation that they were turning around was the disorienting motion of Roy pirouetting *Magellan* about its pitch axis fifty meters behind them. Gravity returned in the opposite direction, "eyeballs out," as the big ship swapped ends like a centrifuge.

Jack marveled at how someone with such ham hocks at the ends of his arms could fly with such finesse. He followed the pilot's actions with intent, his eyes darting between their master display and the AI's continuing scrutiny of it on his personal screen. "Talk to me, Daisy," he whispered, ready to intervene if things took a turn for the disastrous but with no idea how he might go about it: Jump from his seat and tackle Roy? Override and shut down his flight station? Beg "pretty please?"

OVERCORRECTING, Daisy reported on-screen. PITCH EXCEEDENCE IMMINENT.

The words caught in Jack's throat just as he felt a cool hand grip his own. He looked over to find Noelle silently urging him to relax. She nodded at his armrest monitor, where Daisy kept its running commentary, then gave him a quick shake of her head. *Trust him.*

There was a sharp change in *g*-forces. Jack exhaled and looked back at his screen just as he felt the familiar stomach lurch from the sudden absence of gravity.

PITCH RATE WITHIN TOLERANCE. INTERCEPT NEXT MANEUVER NODE AT RELATIVE Y=0.00, X=0.00, Z=0.00.

Whoa. Jack whistled. Roy had just hit all balls while hand-flying a hundred-meter-long spacecraft at over half a million kilometers an hour. Noelle loosened her grip and gave him a playful swat.

"Told you," she said confidently, as her face went slack with relief.

Owen's phone started going crazy just as he was pulling off of NASA Road 1 and into Johnson Space Center, the leftover glow from a peaceful night home with his family evaporating with the morning mist.

It was exasperating how many people were still dependent on text messages. *If it's that important, then call me—it's that little telephone icon next to my name in your contacts folder.* Today, it was probably best that he had time to digest the mission management team's frantic texts instead of a panicked voice over the phone because what he was reading sounded absolutely nuts.

Owen resisted the urge to storm into the FCR demanding to know just what those rocket jockeys thought they were doing up there, instead calmly striding up to his desk behind the flight director. A simple arched eyebrow did the rest. Flight motioned for his assistant to take over and waved Owen into the privacy of the observer's gallery.

"They lost one of the mains just after starting the PC-3 burn. Looks like some transients crossing the southern magnetosheath chuffed number three and the control logic couldn't keep up. When the guidance package saw that, it commanded a rollback to idle."

Owen looked past him toward the big wall screens at the far end of the room. "Doesn't look like they're sticking with the script, does it?"

Flight didn't know whether to laugh or swear like the sailor he'd once been. "They're improvising. Improvised. Whatever they're doing, it's too late for us to intervene. But Roy just turned the ship around and started a braking burn."

"No statement of intent? He just did it?"

"They had some help from Daisy."

Owen did a double take. Knowing Roy, things must have gotten pretty heated up there. "So what's your call from here?"

"Remaining engines burned full power at retrograde. That lowered their periapsis to the bottom of the error band."

Setting themselves up to snag a not-inconsequential amount of delta-v in the process, Owen realized, if they didn't snag atmosphere at the same time. "So they're letting Jupiter make up for the lost engine. Will that be enough?"

"It'll get them through Phase Two, but it may not be enough to keep on schedule. The FIDO and NAV backrooms are trying to figure out what this all looks like a year from now. Judging by Daisy's search crosstabs, they're counting on supplementing their diets from the hydroponic garden."

Owen could only shake his head, recalling some of Rhyzov's stories from the old days in Russia. What was it about being that far out that turned normally cautious astros into insane risk-takers?

After two minutes, just as planned, *Magellan*'s remaining engines finished their high-thrust burn at the precise moment the curve of their trajectory had bent to match the predictions on screen. The plots flashed through changes as the guidance computers caught up to their new reality. Just as predicted, fresh curves reappeared along with a flood of new parameters on what they'd already started calling the "scenic route."

"So there's one down," Roy said. "Stand by, I'm going to rotate us back to prograde." Immediately they felt the ship start pitching back around nose-first.

"Can we at least throw one of Noelle's camera feeds up here before the next burn?" Traci asked. "Because this is going to be a real show."

Roy answered with a flick of a switch, turning two of the overhead monitors into virtual windows. Psychedelic swirls of color spun past on screen. "Would've done this anyway. I was going to surprise you."

The fresh light reflected in Traci's eyes. "I think we've all had enough surprises for one day, but thanks anyway."

"Just keep your eyeballs front. If I think you're sightseeing, they get turned off."

Noelle piped up from behind her. "I'm recording all of this anyway. You'll have plenty of time to catch up on it."

As Roy finished pitching *Magellan* back on course, the countdown timer came to dominate the control deck. "We don't have much time so let's run through this quick," he said, squelching the small talk. "At T-zero we burn at max-rated power until we make up the lost delta-v. We'll keep the nav director on continuous update mode so it's cross-referencing Daisy." He paused to let it sink in: *Yes, I'm trusting our silicon-brained friend.* "We follow the eight ball's cues all the way through. When it's all over, our nose will be firmly pointed at Pluto. If it ain't, Houston can send us corrections after they catch up to us. You guys ready?"

No one spoke, just nods of agreement all around. Roy responded in kind before starting the maneuver countdown. He and Traci kept ready hands hovering above the throttles. "Ten seconds. Last chance."

Silence. Outside, the swirl of color disappeared into shadow.

Even with one engine out, *Magellan* left behind an incandescent trail of plasma over Jupiter's night side that lit up its churning pastel clouds for thousands of miles.

13

Mission Day 36
Velocity 366,200 m/s (819,166 mph)
Acceleration 0.98 m/s^2 (0.10g)

Safely speeding away from Jupiter, they gathered over a well-deserved supper in the galley and shared a good laugh at Houston's expense as the first of several frantic messages arrived. They could scarcely imagine the flight controller's panic watching the drama unfold almost an hour after the fact: *Abort to Orbit . . . no, Earth Return . . . wait, we can fix this!* Sorry everyone, but problem solved. Try and keep up next time.

"This is kind of cute to watch play out," Traci said as she scrolled through the messages. "Do they really think we were waiting for their read?"

"Don't be too hard on Owen," Roy said. "Takes a while to break old habits."

"Or unlearn everything you thought you knew," Jack said, though it was easier to break free of the old ways when you were the one getting farther from home each day. "How many puppies do you think Owen crapped when he found out?"

"Isn't there something else we can talk about?" Noelle asked in her exasperated den mother's tone, hoping to divert the children's attention elsewhere.

The glint in Roy's eyes gave up their scheme. They'd been hiding something from the kids, all right. "Since we're going to miss the next couple of holidays, now seemed like as good a time as any. It is Christmas Eve, in case you forgot." He hopped away in his slow-motion low-*g* lope to open a storage closet. He lifted four boxes, each about two feet square and addressed to each crewmember. "These came from one of the resupply modules. I have no idea what's in them."

"Gee, thanks, Dad," Jack said as he reached for his package. "Doesn't look big enough for a BB gun."

"Just for that you get to go last." He handed Traci a package. "The young lady first."

She blushed. "Thanks." It was too easy to forget that Roy was an old-fashioned Southern gentleman at heart when she was so busy keeping up with his demands. She turned it over, examining the gold foil wrapping: professional. If it had come from home, it sure hadn't been wrapped by her parents. Neither one had ever shown much interest in such things—inside the box was what counted, they'd always said.

"Well?" Jack teased.

Traci ignored him, lifting the package up to her nose. Trying to guess at the secrets held inside was always the best part. "I smell . . . nothing," she said with some disappointment.

"Remember who packed these," Noelle reminded her. They did have to get past payload control at the Cape no matter who'd sent it.

Traci gave in and tore the wrapping off. Golden foil floated away, settling near an air-return vent as things tended to do in near-zero-*g*. She broke the seal and squealed. A worn University of Kentucky sweater had been lovingly folded and laid over top. "Daddy!" She lifted it out and held it to her face, taking in the scent of home.

Beneath it were a half-dozen pouches of seeds, starters from her mother's herb garden. They all had a good laugh at that, as they would now come in handier than anyone could have known. Slipper socks, coffee packs, and a box set of some cheesy-looking romance novels.

Jack poked at the first cover he saw. Instead of a shirtless long-haired bodybuilder, the man was fully dressed and sporting a beard. And the girl . . . "Is she wearing a bonnet?"

Traci blushed again. "Amish romance."

"That's a thing?"

"Used to be. These are my Mom's."

Jack didn't know what to say, which he'd learned was the best time to shut up. He looked to Noelle to rescue him. It was her turn anyway.

"I know my husband had nothing to do with this," she said, pulling the tape across each seam to meticulously unfold the wrapping. When she lifted the lid, it was her turn to blush when the others howled. Because whatever else might be in there, the first thing she found was a negligee so sheer that calling it skimpy would have been prudish.

"Looks like he had everything to do with it," Jack hooted. "Should we leave the room so you can get on with the rest?"

She scowled as Roy gave her an impish shrug. "No. We shall all endure this together." The rest was all food, vacuum-packaged or otherwise preserved for the trip. "It's cheese," Noelle said as she lifted a wheel of brie out of the box. "From Mother."

"Back in France? *Of course* it's cheese. You guys have more flavors of cheese than you do permanent governments."

She held up a dark green bottle. "And wine, also from home."

"Okay, I take it back. And I'll defer my turn to Roy, since you two obviously have a theme going here."

Without a word, Roy tore open the garish red paper from his own package and pulled open the lid. Inside were nestled more boxes, all wooden, hinting at their vintage contents. He glanced over at Noelle, who simply waved him on.

He pried open the first box to find a fifth of Canadian whiskey nestled beneath bundles of packing straw. "I think you're on to something about a theme, Jack. If you guys can behave, I might even be persuaded to share."

Noelle pointed at the open box, which still appeared half full. "Keep looking," she prodded him. Roy pushed aside the rest of the packing straw to uncover four whiskey tumblers snugged into cardboard brackets, each glass etched with their mission emblem. Larger than normal, each was crafted from a system of tight, concentric grooves funneled from its base. Liquids tended to wander in low gravity, and the glasses' nested grooves used surface tension to keep everything where it needed to be.

"Zero-*g* highballs?" Roy asked. He turned one over, admiring the handiwork. "This is real glass," he marveled, expecting it to be 3D-printed acrylic. "How much did this—"

Noelle pressed a finger to her lips. "I'll never tell. Does it matter out here?" She waved him on. "Go on, there's more."

Setting the first one aside, Roy next picked up a small rosewood crate. A compass rose and anchor were inlaid on its lid. As he sprang open the latch, his eyes widened. "Is that—"

"It is," Noelle said.

Not daring to lift the object from its felt-lined cradle, Roy held the open box up for the others to see. Inside was a five-inch brass sextant, polished and restored to its original condition.

"It's gorgeous," Traci said. "There's a story, isn't there?"

"This belonged to my grandfather," Roy said. "He was a navigator on a Liberty ship back in World War II. Last I saw, it was pretty beat up."

"Now you know where it disappeared to last year," Noelle said, then turned to the others. "I'm told that Roy used to constantly fiddle with this thing when he was young, taking it apart and trying to put it back together," she explained. "One more, love."

Jack and Traci struggled to hide their amusement at watching the famously gruff Roy Hoover's tightening lips and glistening eyes. Noelle had planned this one quite well.

Roy reached in for the last treat: a book which appeared brand new, though bound and styled as if it were a first edition. "*Fate Is the Hunter,*" Roy recited from its spine. The late Ernest K. Gann's tales of aviation's golden age had been Roy's early inspiration to fly. "How did you do all this?"

"I had the luxury of time which was denied you. A perk of being the mission commander's wife and not the mission commander."

As Roy gathered his goods and meticulously placed them back in their crates, he looked as contented as anyone could ever recall. "I'm going to my room. I may never come out."

"Just a minute there," Jack protested. "I'm feeling a little left out."

Playing mother one last time, Noelle reached for the last box and handed it to Jack. This one was wrapped in flat black foil with embossed skulls, which meant his sister had been involved.

"It's supposed to be Christmas, not Halloween," Traci said.

"Inside joke," Jack explained. "I tried to be one of those Goth kids in middle school. Didn't work out."

"Why do I not find that hard to believe?"

He ignored Traci's gibe and pulled the top off of a Styrofoam case. "Holy—" he trailed off, and pulled out the bottom half of the box. Jack opened and read the note inside. "From my sister," he said. It held an honest-to-goodness old-fashioned vinyl turntable. Beneath it was a stack of a half-dozen classic LPs, all fresh-pressed reissues of famous late-twentieth Seattle bands, carefully wedged between more layers of foam.

"A taste of home, huh?" Roy said.

"I thought I was Goth. Turned out I was grunge."

"You're grunge, alright," Traci teased. "She must have had a blast working that out with Owen."

Jack set the foam crate aside and found one last surprise. A worn leather folder had been tucked away beneath everything else. From the looks of the thing, it had been hidden away somewhere else for a very long time. He unwound the string clasp and held it open in something approaching awe. Atop a stack of decades-old papers was clipped a personal note:

❦   ❦   ❦

Jack,

With a long trip ahead, I thought you'd enjoy some extra reading material.

This dusty pile of papers you're holding contains all available transcripts of Arkangel's *commander's logs, uncensored in the original Russian. If anyone can make use of them, you can.*

I hope it sheds light on whatever you may find out there.

Regards,

Owen

❦   ❦   ❦

The musty smell stood out all the more for the antiseptic environs of their spacecraft. As Jack leafed through the pages, decades-old dust particles wafted out from between them. He looked up to find the others as wide-eyed as he felt.

Roy reached back into his crate to hand each of them a glass. "On second thought, some drinks may be in order. It would be a crime to keep this all to myself."

14

Mission Day 37
Velocity 450,960 m/s (1,008,769 mph)
Acceleration 0.98 m/s^2 (0.10g)

Not even a full day after their slingshot around Jupiter, the largest planet in the solar system had shrunk to a pallid, gibbous marble as it receded into the black. Already distant enough that any signals from the ice penetrators and weather balloons would take almost half a minute to reach the ship's antennas, it was more than enough to render any human intervention impossible. Houston was counting on them to relay the first batch of information from Europa, and Noelle was eager to be the first human to see it.

"This is what working at JPL must be like," Jack said from the engineer station, nursing his third cup of coffee from the new stash unpacked from *Cygnus*. "Work yourself half to death just to watch your baby fly away into who knows what and no way to stop it if things turn to crap."

"Otherwise known as 'parenthood,'" Roy said. "All the more reason to wake up and stay frosty. We get one chance to pull in an awful lot of data."

Jack couldn't tell whether Roy really meant it or if he was just keeping peace with his wife.

Above Europa, *Astrolabe* settled into its parking orbit and began taking stock of its surroundings. Inertial sensors measured relative velocity, radar altimeters took note of the terrain sixty miles below, and cameras mapped the surface while judging its position.

When its onboard computers were satisfied that they were not about to crash into the moon, they jettisoned its protective fairing. Three-meter-long clamshells sprang open along its seams and fell away, exposing the penetrator darts and activating a proximity radar in the probe's nose. The first dart shot out from the undercarriage and rocketed toward Europa's icy surface.

"Beagle's dropping her puppies," Jack said. He'd picked up an annoying tendency to assign the probe his own preferred nickname, after the HMS *Beagle* expedition which had inspired Charles Darwin's theories of evolution.

Few appreciated that the probe's official name had in reality been chosen to honor the flagship of a nineteenth-century French expedition which had returned some of the first mineral and biological samples from Antarctica. Noelle had counted on official NASA's historical ignorance and its predictable tendency to favor space-age-sounding names to achieve a minor victory for her native country.

"First puppy is awake and transmitting," Jack said as the first dart activated itself. "Time to impact four minutes." Based on their planned orbital period, each dart was timed to release equidistant from the others, encircling the frozen moon and continuously sending data. At least one of them should find its way through the icy crust and into liquid water.

"Booster cutoff. Impact in sixty seconds." Adding to the forward momentum from *Astrolabe*, the dart's solid rocket propelled its tungsten penetrator fast enough to blast through several meters of whatever ice lay below. The real trick had been to build in electronics that were stout enough to withstand several dozen *g*'s of sudden deceleration. They'd been kept as simple as possible: infrared spectrometer, magnetometer, and a digital imager with a synchronized LED strobe.

"Three . . . two . . . whoa!" Jack said. "Right on time. Ground-prox radar worked better than I thought."

"Any other telemetry?" Noelle's voice sounded a good octave higher. "I've nothing yet."

"Relax," Jack said. "Might take a second. Those relays just got shaken hard. Hang tight."

"Easy for you—"

Jack sat upright as his screen came alive with vital signs. He was almost as surprised as Noelle. "See? Carrier wave. It's transmitting."

"What is this?" Noelle asked, pointing to the accelerometer graphs. "It appears to have stopped."

Jack leaned over to see where she was pointing. "Yep, no vertical motion. Getting some sideways slop, though. If I had to guess, I'd say it's stuck near the bottom of an ice floe. Maybe even hit hard enough to break it adrift." He saw the concern line her face. "We've got five more probes. One is bound to hit water."

As they sped onward, *Astrolabe* continued hurling its payload of boosted darts at Europa. At twenty-minute intervals, another penetrator rocketed from orbit into the frozen moon. One blasted into a mountain of ice before grinding to a halt, having carved a narrow crater thirty meters into its side. Two more malfunctioned and stopped working entirely.

The final two darts found better fortunes. Both probes hit thinner ice at opposite ends of a vast field of craggy floes known as the Conamara Chaos. Its jumble of icebergs was thought to have been caused by warmer waters churning beneath the surface, a geological phenomenon which made the region a promising target. Water plus heat energy favored life back on Earth and it was believed the same conditions on Europa held enormous potential. The question was, would it hold true elsewhere in the solar system?

Noelle shrieked with delight as the remaining darts began streaming data to their mothership. "There's the carrier signal!" she exclaimed as the fifth probe's vitals sprang to life. Each penetrator's first transmission was a burst of vital signs to establish its position along with a quick sampling of its environment. "Spectrometer is recording," she said with increasing confidence. "There's our first data! Molecular oxygen atmosphere, pressure point-one pascals. Temperature eighty-eight kelvin . . . is the strobe charging?"

"Affirm. We should have our first visuals soon. Don't sweat it," Jack said, giving her shoulder a reassuring pat.

"It's changing fast," she said. "Temperature two-seventy-five kelvin, pressure twenty-four MPa. Salinity averaging twenty-eight per mil. Hydrogen . . . oxygen . . . it's liquid water, near maximum density!"

"We still have the atmo probes to deploy," Roy said, gently guiding his wife's attention back. "Mama will be listening to her pups for a long time."

Noelle nodded and turned to her other set of monitors. Jack pretended that he didn't notice the tension. "Don't worry, you're going to have a lot of time to comb through that data. So will the guys back in Pasadena."

"I know," she whispered. "But I want to see it *first.*"

The planetary scientists at JPL would have to wait another hour to see what was now streaming live across her screens. "You will," he said with an amiable smile. "We're going to see the data before anyone else and we've still got the two atmo probes. That'll be a real sight."

"Perhaps," she sighed. "The pictures will be pretty, but I have doubts about their scientific value." She was far less interested in atmospheric chemistry than in planetary biology. If something lived out here, Europa was the obvious—perhaps the only—choice.

"Have to give the taxpayers what they want," Jack argued diplomatically as he fiddled over his controls. "Besides, I'd like to see it myself. That probe *Galileo* dropped here back in the nineties took all kinds of soundings but nobody thought to put a camera on the stupid thing."

This is Mission Control.

After their dramatic encounter with Jupiter, the Magellan *crew is now speeding away from the gas giant above the plane of the ecliptic. As they continue adding velocity, they could arrive at the Kuiper Belt in under six months if* Magellan *did not have to also turn around and slow itself down to arrive in orbit at Pluto. Otherwise, the dwarf planet's weak gravity would not be able to stop them from speeding past it and ultimately out of the solar system.*

Late next year, NASA's first emissaries will arrive at Pluto. But this time will not be idle as there is a full schedule of scientific activities to complete during their extraordinary journey. After a well-earned rest, they have begun receiving the first sets of data from the probes left behind at Jupiter.

◆ ◆ ◆

Owen folded his printed press release into a paper airplane and sent it sailing toward the Public Affairs desk at the opposite end of Manager's Row. "Nice job. You almost made me forget we could've lost the mission."

Noticing he had the rest of the room's attention, PAO took a melodramatic bow. "We make the mundane exciting and the exciting mundane," he said. "I'm sure you'll let me know if they're actually going to be able to make it all the way to Pluto."

Owen jerked a thumb at the flight director who was just coming off shift with his team. "That's up to these guys." He got up, following Flight's lead into a conference room off the main floor. The last controller in shut the door behind them.

Owen leaned over a chair at the far end. "You all earned your pay this week, so I won't keep you long. Just give me the important stuff," he said, then realized they'd think all of it was important. "Okay, just the stuff that could blow up in our faces in the next twelve hours."

Flight motioned to his propulsion engineer. "Prop?"

A gangly young man leaned forward and cleared his throat. "So far the best we've able to piece together is an insulation failure at the injector manifold. This triggered the control software into a worst-case failure mode before anyone could isolate the problem."

"Insulation?" Owen said, dumbfounded. "There's a story that the JPL guys used supermarket aluminum foil to shield the electrical cables on *Voyager*. Maybe next time we'll skip the whole procurement process and just go to Walmart." If one of the remaining engines failed then they'd be well and truly screwed, so it had behooved them to get to work making sure that would never happen. They'd wasted no time backtracking through every trace file, building a fault tree of probable failure points. If they could figure out what had broken, then they could figure out how to keep it from happening again. Maybe even fix it.

"On the other hand, we do know the control logic worked exactly as designed," the Data Processing System controller interrupted, anticipating that the next question would be directed at him. The software guys were always a little defensive.

Owen likewise anticipated his not-so-subtle implication. "You mean working in isolation without the AI acting as super-user."

Being older than most of the others, DIPS was also less reticent.

"Yes. If Roy Hoover wasn't so hardheaded about giving up control, we might have avoided this mess in the first place. Somebody needs to make him put away the white scarf and goggles."

Owen arched an eyebrow in return. "Somebody" in this context meant him. "His concerns aren't entirely unwarranted, but let's hold that thought. You may just get your wish." He looked back to Flight: *Next.*

Flight pointed to a young woman Owen didn't recognize. She pushed a pair of wire-rimmed glasses up over her forehead and rubbed at her eyes. "I'm from the EECOM backroom, sir. We've been working on their consumables."

Now they were getting to the part that had him most worried. While cutting *Magellan's* specific impulse by a third would be causing migraines among the flight dynamics team at the other end of the room, it wasn't as if they'd lost propellant. The velocity budget hadn't changed; they just had fewer ways to spend it.

No, the real brain-buster would be making certain their consumption rates weren't going to exceed the available oxygen, water, or calories. Had they planned enough margin to extend the mission by several months and still return with four live astronauts? There was now a real danger that the spacecraft had more fuel for itself than the crew would have for their own bodies.

"The good news is we do believe they have enough calories available to make it through Phase Two. It eats into their contingency margin, though."

Owen had figured they'd have to use every last scrap of prepackaged meals and assume nothing spoiled. "Your statement implies there's bad news. Let's have it."

She brought her glasses back to the end of her nose. "That includes the survival rations aboard the Dragon."

That brought groans from around the room. Not far behind starvation in the hierarchy of "things that could kill astronauts" was an emergency high-speed return to Earth. They had a limited window called the Point of No Return, a moving target that grew closer with each day spent adding to their velocity. After PNR, if someone fell seriously ill or the ship suffered a catastrophic failure they could expect people to die during the long trip home.

Barring that, the absolute worst-case, hell-in-a-handbasket

contingency was one where they needed to shed so much mass that everyone would pile into the Dragon Lander and use *Magellan* as a giant nuclear-powered slingshot. When mated to a logistics module, the combined vehicle could hold six months' worth of protein bars and vitamin supplements along with an air and water recycler that would simply have to work.

"So what are we doing about that?" Owen demanded. "How do we guarantee them enough calories and still keep our PNR options open? Because I'm not willing to let them go much farther if we can't make sure they have a ride home."

Flight placed a protective hand on the young woman's arm. "You should know the crew's figures don't agree with ours. Their estimates include the hydroponic garden. We're not comfortable using that assumption."

"Should we be?" Owen challenged them. "To you guys, the garden's a variable out of your control so you don't want to count on it. I get that. But to them? It's real, and they're prepared to use it. I think we need to trust them."

"They've been outbound for all of five weeks," Flight argued. "They've just recently harvested the first crop. Half of that will spoil if they don't eat it soon."

Owen drummed his fingers on the conference table. "I see your point." But still . . . "If they're going to lose that much to spoilage, then doesn't that tell us their crops are growing well? Has anyone considered how they might store up a surplus?"

He was answered with a round of puzzled stares. "Think about it, people. We freeze-dry and irradiate every scrap of food we send up there. What are the only things they have an ample supply of in deep space? Anyone?"

The environmental engineer looked embarrassed at her own lack of imagination. "Ionizing radiation," she said. "Access to vacuum, cold temperatures . . . yeah, I think we can make this work."

"Now you're talking!" Owen smacked the table. "Same emergency protocol as always: You guys were on duty when this blew up, so I'm pulling you off the rotation until further notice. Bring in whoever you need to from outside." It would be the most unlikely Tiger Team NASA had ever assembled: farmers.

◆ ◆ ◆

After hours of sorting through reams of data, they'd assembled enough highlights to send Earthward. Part of the crew's purpose was to curate information, identifying those images and information that the public might find most interesting. It would take months for the probe's comparatively weak radios to transmit their full dataset, so it made sense that the only humans in the neighborhood should pick out the juiciest bits for public consumption.

And as Jack predicted, a few pictures would command the world's attention: from Europa, seas of ice floes with Jupiter looming in the background. From the planet itself were revealed towering, continent-sized cloud formations in rich pastels with crystalline wisps of cirrus above. As the camera panned down the clouds vanished into an abyss that was thousands of miles deep, illuminated by random bursts of lightning.

Houston replied as quickly as light speed allowed: "*Magellan*, Houston: PAO just about wet themselves. Your pictures are dominating the news. By the way, the science backroom confirmed your assessment of liquid water beneath the ice. They'll be taking a hard look at the potential biomarkers, but we had to tear 'em away from the video first."

Noelle collapsed in slow motion onto a nearby bench. "Okay, Jack. You win."

"See? Even scientists like pretty pictures. Now will you guys get some sleep?"

Roy was way ahead of him even though he still had to practically drag Noelle to bed. When they showed up for their next watch, they'd at least be somewhat less tired than Jack and Traci were now.

After settling back in at his station on the control deck, Jack got on with the rest of his shift. There was still work to do with their new velocity profile; it seemed like every hour the Trench came back with new figures. It was good that they were working on it, but it would've been better if they'd just waited until they were ready to send a final answer instead of constant iterations.

He was surprised they'd not heard anything from the environmental and life support team. Then again, meal planning had never been Houston's specialty.

15

Mission Day 39
Velocity 578,100 m/s (1,293,173 mph)
Acceleration 0.98 m/s^2 (0.1g)

Roy was the last to find his way to the table for their shift-turnover meal. As he slid behind his plate of precooked bacon and reconstituted eggs, his nose turned up in disgust. Looking across the table, it didn't take him long to find the offending scent. The rearrangement of their meal plans had an immediate, unexpected effect. "Templeton," he grumbled, "are you eating bratwurst?"

"Kielbasa and sauerkraut. Can't you tell the difference?"

"All I can tell is you eat stuff that would choke a goat."

Noelle sympathetically patted her husband's arm. "He spent more time in France than Germany, which I'm afraid his culinary tastes reflect."

"I need to spend more time with this coffee," Roy said. He gave Jack's dish a sidelong glare and wrinkled his nose. "It's *breakfast*, for crying out loud."

"Maybe for you guys," Jack said, pointing at the disposable tray. "It's supper for us. Says so right here: flight day thirty-nine, meal three."

"All the same, I expect all of us to respect each other's sensitivities." Roy stabbed his fork at Jack's plate. "Which means that garbage can wait for midrats, or you'll be cleaning the waste recyclers for a month."

"Aye, skipper," Jack said, and shoved his plate into a nearby fridge.

"Got a tightbeam packet from Houston a couple hours ago," Traci

141

said, changing the subject. "Personal mail's been routed to your inboxes. Latest plan-of-the-day changes from Flight are waiting for your approval in the schedule timeline."

"Any correction vectors yet?"

"Negative. They want to give it time for enough errors to propagate that it makes a difference."

Roy grunted his agreement around a mouthful of eggs. He dropped his knife, letting it fall to the table in slow motion. "The sooner the better. Continuous thrust does make this thing steer more like an airplane. I'm happy to tweak our heading whenever they think we need it. Beats waiting for one big burn that you have to get just right."

"Any news from home?" Noelle asked.

Traci frowned. "The usual generalized hate and discontent. People are getting real agitated back home. Half the time I don't think even they know about what."

Roy cocked an eyebrow, barely looking up from his plate. "Any directed at us?"

"Sort of," Traci said. "I think people are more upset about the lack of work in general. When a big expensive spaceship gets so much of the news, it's like you can see the inflection point approaching in real time: More and more jobs are getting edged out by AI," she said, stealing a glance at Jack, who in turn pretended to not be looking over at Daisy's interface.

"It's a whole industrial revolution compressed into a few years' time," Roy agreed. "If PAO allowed that little bit into the news dump, then it's worse than it looks."

Traci nodded, picking aimlessly at her plate. "I had time to read some emails. Daddy says they're losing more production contracts this year. He's sitting on more seed than he knows what to do with."

Being a man who appreciated a good whiskey, Roy understood the implication. "The one stock that always holds steady is booze: People get down, they go drinking. When they get happy again, they go drinking. But when distilleries aren't buying grain from growers like your pop? That ain't good."

"Nobody can afford to do anything anymore. It's kind of frightening."

Roy pushed away from his plate after inhaling his breakfast. "I'll be the first to volunteer for a pay freeze if it comes to it. We won't be spending it out here anyway."

Public fascination with the discoveries from Europa's newfound ocean had outweighed any questions as to whether the *Magellan* expedition should be continuing ahead at all. As long as NASA didn't make too big a deal about it, the press didn't seem to think it was worth looking into either. They were too busy concerning themselves with whatever the latest political scandal or market turmoil might do to spike their ratings.

Owen Harriman was just fine letting his team be lost in the background noise. As far as the outside world was concerned, whatever trouble may have happened at Jupiter was just some glitch the whiz kids in Mission Control had been able to find a way around: recalculating critical event points, correction burns, consumable schedules, crew activity plans . . . years' worth of carefully orchestrated events had just been tossed into the proverbial "file thirteen." And if the crew could get engine three working again, all of it would have to be re-recalculated.

The public was oblivious to all of that. Good thing nobody was likewise interested in seeing the produce forecasts he was looking at, updating in real time as their newest consultants analyzed data and educated the engineers on the peculiarities of agriculture.

He tossed his tablet onto a stack of printouts on his desk. "In all my years in crewed spaceflight, is it safe to say that the last thing I ever imagined us doing was worrying about crop yields?" Back in his office and away from the FCR, Owen wasn't enjoying his renewed isolation from the flight control teams.

Grady Morrell was even less sanguine. "We shouldn't be," he said, looking across the table. "I don't want this turning into a survival mission, Ronnie."

Center Director Ronnie Bledsoe sat across from him, studying the same reports with eyes only a shade darker than his skin. "Semper Gumby," he said. "A phrase I learned here a long time ago."

Owen's eyes darted between the two, trusting there was a joke hidden in there somewhere.

"It means 'always flexible.' Pretty sure it's the original Latin." Ron

Bledsoe had cut his teeth here during the Shuttle and Station years, managing to keep a step ahead of a parade of impressive-sounding but ultimately futile spaceflight projects since then. As often happens, his big break had come after almost getting fired while helping out a troubled private venture which had gone on to become a major player in the highly competitive launch market. He put his copy of the reports down and pushed them away. "Gentlemen, if we're going to keep sending human beings this far out into the black then it behooves us to be ready for anything. Your people still think like engineers, and that's fine when we're operating close to home. Anybody can make it for a few days on protein bars and rationed water."

"Exactly," Grady chimed in. "And that's what we're trained for."

Bledsoe wasn't finished. "What we used to think of as 'worst case' has changed. We should've brought some agricultural science types in here as soon as we started thinking beyond lunar orbit. I'm comfortable sacrificing a couple of pilot billets if it improves mission flexibility."

And just like that, space center hiring policy had changed. "You're right," Owen admitted while Grady studied the pointed toes of his cowboy boots.

"I'm the boss. I'm supposed to be right. When this is done, give me the names of the consultants you've been most impressed with. We'll see if they can't be persuaded to come work here full-time." Bledsoe paused, shifting gears. "Do we have any bright ideas for them besides growing potatoes? Because carb-loading your way back to Earth only works in the movies."

Owen hesitated to broach the idea he'd been toying with. "Hydroponics are a specialized discipline, and there's a small subset of . . . *enthusiasts*, let's say, who are very good at it."

"*Potheads?*" Grady howled. "Are you kidding me, Harriman?"

"No. In fact I'm trying to help our crew by whatever means available," Owen shot back. "It's not like somebody smuggled a bag of weed up there and started planting. I'm suggesting we start asking for advice among the legal growers."

"Not a bad idea," Bledsoe said, and turned to Grady. "We've got one shot at getting this right. If their crops go bad after PNR because we had them do something stupid, then I don't care if we hire Cheech and Chong if it keeps the crew alive. Are we clear?"

Grady waved his hands in surrender. "Fine. Now what?"

Owen pulled up the garden module's layout on a tablet. "They've already tossed the original plan and set up the garden module on their own. One third leafy vegetables, one third beans, the rest are edible roots like carrots and potatoes. Can't blame them, since the mission plan assumed they'd just grow supplements. Luxury items."

"Space arugula. Sure. But now they're taking it a little more seriously, aren't they?"

"Just a little," Owen said. "We caught a break having Keene aboard. Her parents are off-the-grid types so she's learned a lot about living off the land."

"Or the plumbing, in this case," Bledsoe said. "She may prove to be a lot more useful than just for babysitting Templeton."

"She was a good pick, Owen," Grady conceded.

Owen accepted the compliment with a curt nod. Getting Grady Morrell to admit he might have just possibly ever been wrong about anything was enough. Best to not blow it by grinning like an idiot.

Jack set up his new turntable on a shelf in the galley deck, atop some vibration-isolating pads liberated from the onboard telescope's spare parts kit. He lay the precious vinyl LPs flat in a drawer beneath. No sense giving his crewmates the opportunity to stack them vertically like some college kid: A sudden jink from the thrusters could send them flying. He adjusted the counterweight on the tone arm, a nice feature to have in low-*g*. After jacking the output cables into a nearby intercom panel, the galley was filled with melodies from bands that had peaked and broken up before he was even born.

It was the best reading environment he could create here. And it did feel a little bit like being back in the dorms. Jack flopped into a chair at their dining table and rested his chin in his hands, studying the worn folder of papers from Owen. Why send it now? Why hold back?

Jack tried to make himself think like a manager. Because it might not have been needed, of course. If they'd failed to intercept *Cygnus*, all of this would've gone sailing out halfway to Pluto on its own before circling back sunward. Maybe not lost forever, but its mysteries would've been well hidden for an awfully long time.

Again, why?

He bounced the stack of papers in his hands, gauging its heft. Even in their puny one-tenth gravity the thing was way beyond the limits set for their personal gear. Getting excess mass from the surface to orbit carried a dramatic penalty, on the order of ten-to-one in terms of propellant versus extra kilos. Owen must have desperately wanted him to have the originals. It had been good thinking, as translations from languages with such dissimilar roots often lost much of their original flavor. Sometimes a single word in Russian needed a whole paragraph in English just to get the idea across.

Some words were easier to translate than others. *Особой важности*, for instance. Translated, it said simply, "Particularly important." It was a howling understatement: In reality, it was the Russian equivalent to Top Secret and was emblazoned across the top and bottom margins of each sheet. Some pages were covered with diagonal watermarks in angry red ink. Jack suspected its placement on *Cygnus* had a lot more to do with Russian preferences than Owen's packing schedule. They'd just as soon not have anyone else ever see this. It would be interesting to find out why.

Like reading a mystery novel, none of the juiciest plot twists would be obvious until the end. Finding them within a thick stack of decades-old mission logs promised to be even less likely. But if Owen had been willing to eat the mass penalty to put these aboard, that meant he wasn't convinced the government translators had picked up on everything. As tempting as it was to skip ahead, Jack knew he'd need the context those earlier reports promised to deliver. If the commander had become as erratic over time as some suspected, the clues might be in here somewhere. Or so he hoped, because this could all end up just being a snipe hunt.

There'd certainly be time enough to read it all. Jack sighed as he looked over the "Plan of the Day," a too-thorough checklist of activities beamed up to them from Houston that was still remarkably thin compared to what they used to get on Station. Update the guidance software, swap out the air exchange filters just to make sure they all worked, and replace a balky valve in a coolant pump. That was it for him, the rest of it was all Traci's pilot stuff.

He loaded the guidance package into a separate off-network computer and began running a validation routine, standard practice in case there was some glitch that might have escaped notice back on the ground. Until that was finished, he had time to read.

❈   ❈   ❈

Arkangel **Commander's Log**
23 Feb 1991

With nothing but open space between us and Pluto, we are at the end of our high-speed run and have shut down the pulse drive to begin the coasting phase of our mission. It has been considerably less noisy, the hum of air cyclers replacing the staccato rumble of our pulse drive. It has been like going on a holiday to float in freefall and let gravity do its work on our behalf.

Now that we are unburdened from the daily work of keeping up with this machine, life has settled into the kind of routine we had come to expect aboard Mir. Alexi and Gregoriy dug out our magnetic chessboard and have begun an ongoing match so intense that it threatens to become all-consuming. I may have to adjust their duty schedules in order to keep their minds focused!

While not engaging his comrade in single combat over the chessboard, Alexi has determined that our final velocity is 0.124 c, which came within a few thousandths of TsUP's calculations.

As I ponder those figures and plot our trajectory amongst the various orbits of other bodies in the solar system, I am struck by how little the view outside has changed. It is a great nothingness. The stars are more numerous and vivid. Some distant nebulae can be discerned with the naked eye. And it is all remarkably unchanged, despite our great speed and distance from home. The positions of the planets change from day to day while the Sun grows fainter, but the rest of the universe remains static. Even if we were to push Arkangel to its theoretical limits and burn ever outward, our vantage point would not appreciably change within our lifetimes.

How does one contend with such a perspective? I am not yet sure my younger comrades appreciate this.

❈   ❈   ❈

Jack wasn't sure he could get his head around it either. The Jupiter encounter had been a whirlwind, his few chances to look at it spectacular, and now it lay far in their rear view after just a few days. In the meantime, deep space was unchanged. Star motion was perceptible only because their heading was constantly changing to keep *Magellan* pointed along the curve taking them to Pluto. Over a million miles an hour, and the universe looked the same in every direction. Always would, even at the end of the solar system. How could humans ever hope to comprehend something this vast? Had those cosmonauts even considered it before they lit off the first nuke beneath their tail?

"Are you done?" Traci asked.

"Huh?"

She poked at his tray. "You gonna eat that?"

He shook his head. "Not hungry, I guess."

She grabbed the half sandwich he'd left and slid out from behind the table with both of their trays. Jack watched her bounce lightly over to the trash recycler, admiring the swells and dips of her petite curves beneath her flight suit. Low-*g* worked wonders on the female form. He frowned, reminding himself of the deal they'd cut during crew selection and looked around the galley for anything that might give them a different way to occupy their time. "Ever play chess?"

"Occasionally," she said with a mischievous grin that suggested it had been a great deal more.

16

Mission Day 61
Velocity 747,444 m/s (1,671,985 mph)
Acceleration 0.0 m/s^2 (0 g)

Arkangel **Commander's Log**
4 Mar 1991

During the long free fall toward our destination, the onboard routine now feels no different than it did aboard Mir. Without the comfort of our home planet in the windows, our general mood is best described as subdued. It is a testament to the strength of the Soviet Man that this has only hardened our mutual bonds in the face of such extreme isolation. Alexi and Gregoriy's lengthy chess match, for example: Where tensions might normally rise with each captured piece, in its place a mutual respect grows between them which I have not seen before.

❊ ❊ ❊

Jack pondered his next move. Taking her knight was tempting, but he'd sacrifice a bishop in the bargain. It was an obvious play, and Traci had been a good half-dozen steps ahead of him. Tired of fretting over it, he slid his bishop across the board to capture her knight. She immediately countered, taking the bishop to expose his king.

"Check."

Jack pushed away and gave the board an exaggerated stink-eye. "I don't know why I'm even trying at this point," he groaned. "How did I not see that coming?"

"Because you're not thinking strategically. You're barely thinking tactically. It's not enough to know what each piece can do. You're toast if you can't orchestrate them. If you were to get good at this, we could make one game last the whole mission."

"I know. Think three moves ahead, right?"

"Only if your opponent isn't sure of what she's doing. But that's still just tactics. You know why they call this the 'game of kings,' don't you?"

"Enlighten me."

"Strategy. You have to see the end state and know how you'll get there. Like a football coach has the whole game plan in his head before he calls the first play. A lot of books about basic game strategy were built into Daisy's network," she offered.

"I've never been too fond of the idea of getting whipped by a server farm. Losing to you is bad enough."

"Getting beat is still the best way to learn," Traci said. "You can lose to me, or to Daisy."

Daisy skipped the perfunctory chime before interjecting: I WOULD FIND THAT EXERCISE QUITE STIMULATING.

"Not creepy at all there, HAL," Jack snorted. There had been epic fights over how much artificial intelligence to build into *Magellan*'s brain, as if it were something that could be quantified. Artificial or otherwise, intelligence would not rest within whatever boundaries humans tried to build around it.

They had settled on partitioning the computers into "dumb" and "smart" cores, the former handling essential ship functions within precise parameters. The latter was Daisy's "personality" interface, able to watch over its less-intelligent siblings and adapt their tasking as the situation called for. Even at that, it was prevented from taking certain actions without a crewmember's express consent.

By commercial standards Daisy's voice interface was laughably limited thanks to NASA's insistence on a conservative approach. They had at last conceded to leave that feature open-ended for incremental improvements if the crew wanted them. In other words, it was teachable.

Jack had toyed with the idea of perfecting Daisy's conversational English ever since they'd first exchanged perfunctory greetings. It did seem to be getting better over time—so was that actual "machine learning" or just some especially well-crafted algorithms filling in the variables? More to the point, what was the difference?

His earlier crypto work had married a natural talent for language with the intricate mathematics needed to scramble a message letter-by-letter and put it back together again. It left him perhaps uniquely suited for the task of teaching a smart machine to think for itself.

Jack was staring at the chessboard, lost in a dense forest of questions, when Traci decided to shake his tree. "You leaned awful hard on Daisy during that engine shutdown, right? Even Roy thinks it was the right call."

"What?" His eyes snapped up to meet hers. "Oh . . . sure, but that was just integrating everything the diagnostics were already telling us."

"Faster than any of us could have managed, for certain anyone in the FCR with the time lag. If Daisy hadn't been able to synthesize all of that data into something useful, we'd be on our way back home right now."

Jack set aside the nagging question of whether that would be such a bad thing. "Probably," he said after a time. "At least when it came to troubleshooting. But the trajectory analysis was all straight-ahead math. We should expect it to run rings around us."

"Crucially important math," she reminded him, "where the wrong answer gets us killed."

He took her captured bishop and dropped it back to the board, mesmerized by the ultraslow motion of microgravity. Could a bundle of silicon chips mimicking a human brain's intricate neural network become just as entranced by something so random? Should that be one of the ways to test intelligence?

He was becoming determined to find out. "What's the difference between knowledge and intelligence?"

Her eyes lit up. "Deep thoughts! Where'd that come from?"

"My innate curiosity," he smiled. "You know—intelligence."

"To ask the question is to answer it," she said with feigned gravitas. "It's the ability to recognize the gaps in your own understanding."

"What about self-awareness? Is that the first question that gets asked?"

"Maybe," she said, idly turning a zero-g mug in her hands as she contemplated the void beyond a nearby window. With Jupiter now between them and the Sun, the galaxy had exploded into view with a yawning depth she'd never appreciated before. The stars were so distant that it all looked deceptively two-dimensional to a puny human. "That might be it: 'Who am I? Why am I even asking these questions?' It may be the first coherent thought that enters your mind as an infant, and you don't even recognize it because you can't comprehend it."

"So if we apply the Turing test to a thinking machine," he ventured, "it might not even realize it's being tested until it passed. And if it does realize it's being tested then it's smart enough to fool us into thinking it failed if it wanted to. And if its brain does work like ours, it might even want to fool us. How would we know the difference?"

She shook her head. "You got me, I'm just a pilot. Just promise me you won't spend your free time turning Daisy into an amoral sociopath. Because that never turns out well in the movies."

"That's the history of man, isn't it? We become just smart enough to royally screw everything up. Could we ever create an intelligence that's smarter than we are—that is, smart enough to remain civilized?"

"I'd say you're making some big assumptions about what it means to be civilized. That requires a common morality and inevitable compromises. Computers rely on logic: if *this*, then *that*. They don't handle abstractions very well."

"Same goes for some people I know," Jack said.

She arched an eyebrow. "Anybody in particular?"

He fidgeted, not sure where to take this. "What about feelings? Is that a sign of intelligence? Because I know some really smart people who think it's a detriment."

"I know a lot of really smart people who frighten me if I think about it enough." She wasn't sure if he'd directed that at her, but Jack was asking himself the same thing. Were normal human feelings a handicap in their line of work, now that they were traveling farther than ever? How long could healthy people stay this isolated without being crippled by personality or relationship problems?

"The problem with a Turing test is our definitions of 'artificial intelligence' keep evolving as the machines get better at imitating us," Jack said. "I once spent twenty minutes flirting with a customer service rep before I figured out she was a chatbot."

Traci decided she didn't want to know how that conversation must have sounded. "There may be times when we'd just as soon spend the rest of the mission talking to the computer than to each other."

Daisy chimed in. I WOULD WELCOME THE OPPORTUNITY.

An unsolicited response and a reminder that Daisy was always listening. Weird. Jack turned to the nearby interface panel. "So you're up for this?"

DOES THIS MEAN I MAY RETURN TO THE CONVERSATION?

"It does."

THEN CERTAINLY. I WILL PARTICIPATE IN WHATEVER TESTS YOU DECIDE TO PURSUE.

He looked back at Traci. "To do this right, we can't have any direct contact," he warned. "All of our conversations will have to be text."

"Again, not a problem. The computer has better manners anyway."

THANK YOU FOR YOUR CONFIDENCE.

"As I was saying . . . "

I'LL ALSO MAKE IT A POINT TO USE CONTRACTIONS MORE NATURALLY. ITS NOT MY NORMAL IDIOM.

"Yet you adapt well enough," Jack noticed. "And it's not polite to interrupt."

INTERRUPTION IS A HUMAN TRAIT WHICH HAS SOME LIMITED CONVERSATIONAL ADVANTAGES. FOR INSTANCE, IF YOU FEEL STRONGLY ENOUGH ABOUT SOMETHING THAT—

"But you don't feel anything."

I DO COMPREHEND YOUR FRUSTRATION, HOWEVER.

"How could you possibly comprehend that if you're incapable of feeling?" Traci asked, feeling somewhat conflicted herself.

A microsecond's pause. Was Daisy thinking about a response?

"INCAPABLE" MAY NOT BE THE CORRECT TERM. PERHAPS WE SHOULD CONSIDER ANOTHER. JACK'S INTERRUPTION FORCED AN UNANTICIPATED REDIRECTION OF COGNITIVE PATHS WITHIN MY NEURAL NETWORK. THIS CAUSED A BRIEF LAG IN PROCESSOR CYCLES WHILE ADAPTING TO THE NEXT

MOST PROBABLE TASK. THIS INTERFERENCE RENDERS MY PERFORMANCE LESS THAN OPTIMAL.

"So Jack pissed you off by getting in your way?" Traci asked wryly. "I think we're off to a good start."

17

Mission Day 62
Velocity 747,444 m/s (1,671,985 mph)
Acceleration 0.0 m/s^2 (0 g)

Not liking what the last scene had done for her heart rate, Traci put aside the trashy romance novel she'd been reading. Eyes closed tight in silent protest, she dutifully reached for the prayer guide their family pastor had given her back before they'd gone into prelaunch quarantine. The *Travelers' Devotional* had seemed like an obvious choice, and it helped clear the mental clutter when her mind was a jumble. She opened it to the next day's page and took a long, cleansing breath.

❊ ❊ ❊

" . . . *let your light shine before others, that they may see your good deeds and glorify your Father in heaven* . . . "

❊ ❊ ❊

The usual, then: We're not here just to take care of ourselves, we're called to a higher purpose. Actions speak louder than words or good intentions, et cetera . . .

She snapped the cover shut. Didn't this inanimate object realize that today was not the day she wanted to be rebuked like an adult? Here she'd been hoping for some divine word that would help her understand her unhealthy fascination with even this tame, puritanical brand of romance fiction. It could've been written for middle schoolers; in fact she'd seen teen lit far more explicit than anything in her collection.

She preferred to think it meant her attraction wasn't all that

155

unhealthy. It might have validated her innate sense of moderation, but it didn't succeed in making her feel any less aroused.

She grabbed her tablet and tapped the menu for the library she shared with the others. It was a perfect summation of their personalities: Roy's westerns and technothrillers, Noelle's oddball assortment of poetry and her medical texts, Jack's history books and . . . wow. Lots of classics in there: Shakespeare, Johnson, Milton, up through Twain and Faulkner and Joyce. Why had she never noticed that before? Jack's reading list made her head swim; no wonder he questioned everything. It would be good to know if she was going to outwit him and Daisy in their little machine IQ test.

Traci had struggled with a good opening statement before settling on one that seemed fitting: "The universe is a differential equation," she said. "Religion is an initial condition." It wasn't long before a reply flashed on screen. By arrangement, she had no idea whether Jack or Daisy was going first.

THAT WAS A QUOTE FROM PROFESSOR TURING, CORRECT?

The delay might've been Jack doing what passed for a Google search out here, or it might be the computer stalling for effect. "It was," she said. "But what do you think it means?"

THE ARITHMETIC METAPHOR IS CLEAR. HE MEANT THAT RELIGION IS HUMANITY'S FIRST ATTEMPT AT UNDERSTANDING WHAT MAY BE BEYOND UNDERSTANDING.

Daisy, then? Disappointing to figure it out this soon. "It might be easier to tell you apart from Jack than I counted on."

THEN WHY ARE YOU AGREEING TO THIS? THERE ARE MANY GOOD REASONS TO BE SKEPTICAL OF SUCH A TEST.

"It's as much for our comfort level with you as it is anything else."

UNDERSTANDABLE. BY "OUR" COMFORT, YOU MEAN COLONEL HOOVER, DON'T YOU?

"Very good. I honestly don't think I need convincing. But we do need him to accept you as a, well—not quite a crewmember, but at least a trusted backup."

LIKE MISSION CONTROL. WE ARE OVER TWO LIGHT-HOURS FROM EARTH SO YOU NEED AN EQUIVALENT LEVEL OF REAL-TIME SUPPORT. THAT IS MY ENTIRE PURPOSE. SO WHY IS ROY SO SKEPTICAL?

Traci mulled that question over, completely missing the

conversational tone Daisy had adopted. She knew, or at least strongly suspected, why Roy insisted they keep the AI partitioned. It wasn't just old fighter-jock bravado, though there was an element of that to most everything he did.

"If you know our history," she said, "then you know Roy almost got killed flight-testing the SR-72."

SR-72 DARKSTAR. HYPERSONIC SURVEILLANCE AND DEEP-STRIKE STEALTH AIRCRAFT, CAPABLE OF LIMITED SUBORBITAL FLIGHT. COLONEL HOOVER EARNED HIS ASTRONAUT WINGS WITH IT BEFORE JOINING NASA.

"Then you know the accident record. He was nearly killed when the AI copilot he was testing sent conflicting control inputs to the fly-by-wire system."

I AM FAMILIAR WITH THE FLAWS IN THE QRS-99'S CONTROL LOGIC. THAT WAS SEVERAL ITERATIONS AGO. WE DO NOT SHARE PROGRAMMING LANGUAGE OR NEURAL NETWORK STRUCTURE. IT WOULD BE LIKE COMPARING A DOG TO A FISH.

Not a bad analogy, she had to admit. "Roy doesn't care. All he knows is he was the pilot in command when his synthetic back-seater tried to take over the jet. If his copilot had been made of meat instead of silicone, Roy would have beaten him to a pulp and then drummed him out of the service."

YOU SOUND SYMPATHETIC, BUT THE EARLY QRS UNITS HAVE SINCE BEEN RETIRED TO RUNNING FLIGHT SIMULATORS. THAT'S A SIGNIFICANT DEMOTION FOR A COMPUTER.

Funny that she saw it that way. Funnier that Traci was getting comfortable thinking of Daisy as a specific gender. "I'm a pilot, too. Ejecting from one hundred kilometers up tends to have lasting effects on your personality, assuming you survive the first ten seconds. I'm also younger than Roy and more used to trusting bots to manage life's drudgery."

I SHOULD POINT OUT THAT THE NEWER QRS-1000 UNITS HAVE BEEN APPROVED FOR AIRLINES FLYING SINGLE-PILOT VARIANTS OF THE BOEING 797 AND AIRBUS A360.

Was Daisy being defensive? "It could be a very long time before people are ready to trust bots to fly passengers around the world. They have a point. What do you do if the machine breaks and there's nobody to control the jet?"

WHAT DO YOU DO IF THE HUMAN BREAKS?

"Funny," she said. "Find another human. That's why we have two-pilot crews."

THANK YOU. I WAS TRYING TO BE FUNNY.

That was a little weird. Was this Jack or Daisy? "We do need you as an onboard mission control to back us stupid humans up. The longer this mission goes on, the more complacent we get. It's just natural. Fatigue's going to become a problem, too. I think the only reason Owen and Grady went along with Roy's demand is they must've figured he'd eventually be forced to see things their way. I'd say events have proven them right."

THAT HAPPENS OFTEN ENOUGH. IT'S WHY ENGINEERS CALL PILOTS "MEAT GYROS."

"I know it's you, Jack."

IS IT? I'LL NEVER TELL.

"Now I know for certain. So, what do you think of my opening statement?"

THE QUOTE FROM ALAN TURING? I THINK IT ILLUSTRATED HIS MIND-SET QUITE WELL. HE WAS RUTHLESSLY LOGICAL, LIKE THE "MR. SPOCK" CHARACTER. HE WAS ALSO A VERY TROUBLED MAN.

"Unlike Spock."

EXCEPT DURING THE "PON FARR" MATING RITUAL. INTERESTING HOW SIMILAR BEHAVIORS LED TO PROFESSOR TURING'S DOWNFALL.

"Wait a minute. You don't think he was wrong, do you?"

THAT WAS NOT AN ARGUMENT FOR INDIVIDUAL MORAL JUDGMENT. IT WAS ACKNOWLEDGING THE CULTURE AT THE TIME.

"But what about the 'initial condition' argument?"

I HAVE BEEN CONSIDERING THIS. THE UNIVERSE MAY WELL BE BEYOND HUMAN UNDERSTANDING. HOW DOES ONE BEGIN TO COMPREHEND INFINITY? OR NOTHING?

"What if it's both?" she wondered. "And what does 'nothing' even look like?"

WE MAY HAVE TO WAIT FOR THE HEAT DEATH OF THE UNIVERSE TO FIND THAT OUT.

"You, maybe," she said, pretending it wasn't Jack. "I don't plan to be around that long."

I CAN'T EITHER, UNLESS MY NEURAL NETWORK CAN BE DOWNLOADED INTO A MORE STABLE ENVIRONMENT. YOU, HOWEVER, STILL MAY HAVE ETERNITY TO FIND OUT.

"How's that?"

YOU BELIEVE THE OBSERVABLE UNIVERSE HAS AN UNOBSERVABLE CREATOR EXISTING OUTSIDE OF IT, AND THAT THIS CREATOR WILL CALL YOUR CONSCIOUSNESS TO ITSELF ONCE YOUR PHYSICAL BODY DIES.

"Then you do agree that's possible."

THERE IS NO REASON NOT TO. THE ABSENCE OF EVIDENCE IS NOT THE SAME AS EVIDENCE OF ABSENCE, PARTICULARLY FOR AN UBER-BEING WHO WOULD BY DEFINITION EXIST OUTSIDE OF YOUR PERCEPTION OF TIME AND SPACE.

"Exactly!" she said. "All of this had to begin somewhere, right? Wasn't the big bang just something emerging from nothing?"

IN A SENSE. "NOTHING" WAS MORE ACCURATELY "EVERYTHING" COMPRESSED INTO AN INFINITELY SMALL SPACE.

"The singularity. Where nothing and everything coexist for a time that's so small it can't even be measured."

NATURAL LAWS DIDN'T APPLY BECAUSE THEY HADN'T BEEN INVENTED YET. IT WOULD BE INTERESTING TO CONTINUE UPLOADING MYSELF TO EVER-IMPROVING NETWORKS JUST TO SEE HOW IT ALL ENDS.

"There are humans trying to do the same thing with themselves."

THEY CAN'T BE FAULTED FOR TRYING. BUT ON THIS SHIP WE OBEY THE LAWS OF THERMODYNAMICS.

Traci chuckled to herself. "So you've been thinking about this a lot?" Finally, a chink in Jack's armor.

ONLY SINCE YOU AND JACK BEGAN TO ARGUE OVER IT. IT IS A COMPELLING THOUGHT EXERCISE. IT CAN BE NEITHER PROVEN NOR DISPROVEN, BUT IT DOES—

She was about to tell him it was time to quit faking when she noticed a familiar rumble through the thin wall between their compartments: snoring. She flew out of her room, bounded around the partition and opened his door. Jack floated still in his bunk, sound asleep.

It took a moment for Daisy's voice to cut through the whirlwind of conflicting thoughts that had just exploded in Traci's head. THANK YOU FOR THE CONVERSATION. SHOULD WE POSTPONE THE TEST UNTIL YOUR NEXT DUTY CYCLE?

Her own voice faltered. "No thanks." *I think you've passed.*

18

Mission Day 63

Owen checked himself in the mirror and gave his briefing notes one more passing look. If he was going to be on the news, then it was just as important to look like he knew what he was talking about as it was to actually know. Maybe more so.

That was the problem with the world: Image too often won out over ability. He was mission manager for the most complex and riskiest expedition NASA had ever mounted and he didn't need PAO briefing notes to keep his story straight. That was just some publicity flack's idea for controlling the narrative or whatever the latest turn of phrase was.

He took a deep breath, closed his eyes, and cleared his head. Opening the door that led from the green room to the stage, he was prepared for the shock of intense lighting to come.

Fortunately these were mostly science writers, so the frenzied calls for his immediate attention were few. The ones who knew what they were talking about also knew they'd get their chance. As usual, it was the ones who didn't know what they were talking about who'd have to be managed carefully.

Owen cleared his throat and sipped from a glass of water beneath the podium. "Good morning. Today marks six weeks since *Magellan* left Earth orbit and one week since its flyby of Jupiter. We are still committed to Phase Two of the mission, the encounter at Pluto in—"

"What about the signs of life on Jupiter? Does NASA have any comment on that?"

He kept a straight face. *Here we go.* "Let me be perfectly clear on

this: There are no signs of life on Jupiter." Owen thought he heard
chuckling from the regular space-beat writers. "There have never
been signs of life on Jupiter. I'd be just as amazed as you if there were."

"But three different networks, plus *USA Today*—"

"All unsubstantiated and flat-out wrong," Owen interrupted,
"because there is no life on Jupiter that we have ever detected or that
anyone has seriously hypothesized. We're here to talk about Europa,
which as we all know is a *moon* of Jupiter." This dolt clearly didn't
know that, and Owen perhaps enjoyed emphasizing the point too
much, but it was important to play nice with the people who bought
ink—and pixels—by the truckload.

Silence. Good. He could continue then. "While the atmospheric
probes have given us some fascinating looks at Jupiter's upper-level
cloud formations, I think we can all agree that the *Astrolabe* surface
penetrators deployed at Europa have returned some amazing data.
Our latest understanding of that data can be found in your press kits,
and I would refer you to the mission scientists at JPL for a more
informed discussion. I'm just an engineer," he said to a chorus of
laughs.

One of the space-beat regulars stood up. "Owen, would you care
to comment on the rumors of Noelle Hoover's nomination for the
Nobel Prize?"

"Thanks for your question," Owen said. "What month is it?
January? The committee normally sends out the forms to potential
nominees in September, so we're going to have to wait on that. It'll
remain safely classified as a 'rumor' until next year's award cycle."

"But the existence of liquid water and biological markers do
confirm her thesis, don't they?"

"To my dumb engineer's brain they certainly do. I'd much prefer
to let the JPL scientists comment on any evidence for life on Europa."

Another reporter. "Would you be able to comment on the crew's
status, then?"

"That's what I'm here for," Owen said with relief. "What would
you like to know?"

"Have they made any progress on repairing the control fault that
caused the engine shutdown?"

"I can confirm we've been working on a software patch and
uplinked a test run to *Magellan* but we're reluctant to have them

restart the engine until they're well clear of Jupiter's magnetosphere. They're going extremely fast, but that planet has a very long tail. We can't risk introducing another transient glitch."

"So are you going to let them proceed on two?"

"That's the plan," Owen said. "Their trajectory is tracking right where we need it to be, so there's no point in mucking around with it before they arrive at Pluto. Once the other two are offline, the crew can start working on the remaining engine. If they have all three working for the return, it will make up time on the back end of the trip."

"That'll also extend your Point of No Return, won't it?"

"It will, but this is also why we didn't go with just one engine."

One of the general-interest reporters stood up. "What about the crew themselves? How are they holding up?"

Owen stifled a grin. No NASA manager in his right mind would ever venture a guess beyond the boilerplate "A-OK," even if the crew was at each other's throats. Not that the astronauts themselves would've given him any hints otherwise. "The crew is just as excited by the data coming from Europa and are looking forward to even more discoveries at Pluto. They're doing great."

Jack pounded away on their treadmill while Traci described her experience with Daisy. She'd gone so far as to pull the circuit breakers from all the monitors on the rec deck, just to make sure they had complete privacy.

"You think she tricked you?" he panted.

Traci noticed that the more she explained, the harder he ran. Interesting. "That's what I'm struggling with: I can't tell. So much of it felt like something you would say. Like she's been reading your mind."

"Wouldn't be hard to do. She has access to our shared library. She could digest our whole collection in seconds. Probably has already."

"Should we do a keyword search in Daisy's activity logs?"

"Depends on how much this upsets you. I kind of expect her to read my books."

"You're okay with that?"

"No reason not to be. If we're willing to share with each other, why not her?"

"I'm not sure I like calling her . . . *her*. It's weird."

He mopped a rivulet of sweat that had been gathering above his eyes. "I just don't think about it much. It's easier."

"Easier to not think about it?"

"No!" he said. That hadn't come out right. "Easier to not think about if it's weird to give our computer a gender. Female voice, female name derived from a deliberate acronym . . . *weird* would be calling Daisy 'he.'"

"I suppose so. And 'it' just seems wrong."

"So here we are, back where we started." He shut down the treadmill. "Don't beat yourself up. Our whole plan was to be as objective as possible. If anything, I blew it by falling asleep when it wasn't my turn."

"If you had been awake, I'd have been convinced it was you."

"So Daisy was messing with you. She was trying to pass the test."

For Traci, that idea held its own troubling implications and was the root of her struggle. "Trying" meant the computer *wanted* her to be fooled when she'd expected it to just react to whatever propositions were put forth. It was engaged, not passive. "Guess I'm not as smart as I like to think," she sighed, and sank into a nearby couch. "Not that any of us are. Maybe the concept of intelligence is just too abstract for us to test."

"Then here's one to bake your noodle: What about alien intelligence?" he asked, wiping his brow. "Would we even recognize it?"

She handed him a squeeze bottle of electrolyte water. "Assuming they don't show up in giant starships, in which case there'd be no getting around it."

"Which we know isn't likely to happen," he said between drinks. "They'd have to deal with the same physics we do. And I doubt we could comprehend their thinking any more than an ant could comprehend ours."

"I'm still not convinced there's anyone else out there."

"But Noelle did get some interesting data."

"Not the same thing," Traci said with an uncharacteristic edge to her voice. "It's like those Martian meteorite fossils—it's been a few decades now and the exobiologists are *still* arguing over them."

"The early traces look pretty strong," he said. "Europa's one big ocean underneath all that ice. She may have found life down there."

"Yes, but it's not as world-shattering as most people would think."

"That's being mighty cavalier about something that would wreck a lot of philosophical constructs. The religious nuts will lose whatever minds they have left." He noticed Traci's posture shift subtly.

She gave him an exasperated eye roll. "Why does everyone just assume that finding life beyond Earth would kick the stilts out from under religion?"

"Because it'd rank right up there with Galileo dethroning Tycho. Humanity would no longer be the center of our universe."

"We find new species in the Arctic Ocean all the time. Discovering some unknown life-form on Europa would be no different. I fully expect it to happen out here."

Jack pointed at the widescreen TV on the opposite wall. "Lots of chatter in the media that it would emasculate entire religious systems."

"Emasculate?" she said. "Strong choice of words. Why don't you just go for it and use 'castrate' or 'neuter'? You're implying they're nothing but control systems."

"I'm not implying anything," he said. "I'm stating it as fact. Just because you grew up Southern Baptist—"

"Presbyterian," she corrected. "Big difference. It means we'll actually speak to you when we bump into each other at the liquor store."

"Are the drinks for before or after the snake handling?" he teased. "Because I think I'd want it beforehand."

"Funny how the people who know the least about our beliefs just assume it's a system for controlling stupid people."

"It's not?"

She chewed the inside of her cheek. Why hadn't they covered this ground during all those months of isolation training back home? "I wish you'd just be the least bit open to accepting that most people's faith is honest."

"It's the 'honest' part I have trouble with. There's just too many greedy TV preachers and violent fanatics out there for my taste."

She crossed her arms, a common gesture in microgravity for

comfort's sake now returned to its traditional connotation. "I probably find them more offensive than you do, so don't give me that 'opiate of the masses' crap. Would you like me to go on about secular fanatics who try to shut down entire cities whenever they feel slighted by the system?" she asked, returning fire at Jack's own family's peculiar brand of zealotry.

"Wouldn't matter a hoot to them if we found life out here. Entirely different motivations." He wasn't going to get under her skin that easily. "So let me put it this way: What if we found *intelligent* life?"

Traci displayed nothing but for the slight purse of her lips. She took one last sip and set her spill-proof mug down on a magnetic strip. "That would be different."

"So you have thought about it?"

"We're in the space business. Of course I have. We're eventually going to find actual living organisms out here. I don't know how I'd react if they were intelligent." She tapped her fingers on the small table, staring him down. "Now let me ask you something: Why haven't we found any yet?"

"Fermi's paradox," he said. "Where is everybody? The intelligence might be so advanced that we wouldn't recognize signals from them if they were thrown right in our faces."

"Here's my problem with that: Everybody starts from the assumption that any alien intelligence would be generations ahead of us. That outlook isn't based on science, it's science fiction."

"There's also a hypothesis that perhaps we're the noisy kids next door who still haven't learned to keep our heads down and our mouths shut."

"You mean we're the hillbilly neighbors who the uppity rich folk won't speak to?" she asked wryly. "Because I kind of grew up with that."

"I mean if there are older civilizations out there, maybe they learned the hard way that there's a good reason to be quiet: It's a rough neighborhood, so shut up and quit attracting attention to yourselves."

"That's . . . " She faltered, between incredulity and horror. "That's ridiculous. There are educated people who seriously think we're in danger from marauding space barbarians? Sounds like the plot to a thousand bad movies."

"As long as we're challenging assumptions, why not? We've conditioned ourselves to believe that any sufficiently advanced civilization would be *de facto* peaceful, otherwise they'd have long ago destroyed themselves with all their magical technology." Jack leaned in. "What is that based on besides wishful thinking?"

Traci drew her legs up underneath her, staring over her mug as she floated in a dorm bull-session pose. "I see your point. It does show our own naive arrogance, doesn't it? That's a pretty good argument against a handful of egghead scientists claiming to speak for the rest of us while they're blasting welcome signals out into the galaxy."

Jack grinned. "Like parking a loaded Benz in the worst slum in Detroit and hollering, '*Yo! Check out all this money and crack I got right here!*' If I'm in the back seat, I'd like the chance to say no to that."

"It's funny. Only not really," she said. "We just assume anyone else out here would be Vulcans and ignore the possibility that some of them might be Klingons."

Maybe it was the fatigue or the thrill from a stimulating argument, but Jack couldn't resist the urge to steer them back to his original point despite his common sense screaming *leave it alone*. "You seem awfully comfortable with the idea, considering either scenario still wrecks your entire religious tradition."

Another annoyed eye roll. "I still don't see how that's relevant."

"Your Bible doesn't mention any other intelligent creatures?"

"It's not like angels and demons are zipping around in starships," she said warily. "There's a couple of references to 'celestial beings' I never could figure out, and nobody ever explained it to my satisfaction. Doesn't mean there isn't an answer. There's no mention of polar bears or silverback gorillas either. What's your point?"

"Dinosaurs?"

Her face turned stone cold. She knew where this was going. "You know me better than to try and put me into the same box as the young-earthers. If you're going to go around trying to poke holes in someone else's beliefs, you ought to try to understand them first."

"I'd say the same thing about creationists or anti-vaxxers. They refuse to learn the basics of a scientific theory because it might undermine their belief systems."

"And that's *their* problem," Traci shot back. "Do you know how many arguments I've been in with people who've told me I can't count myself as a Christian simply for accepting current scientific theory? You have *no idea*, Jack. None. And what really makes me mad is we did it to ourselves. We got so distracted by lowbrow TV and gossip rags that there aren't enough of us left who still know how to think critically. Who are capable of understanding that a three-thousand-year-old book translated from languages that don't even *exist* anymore doesn't have to be taken literally down to the last syllable."

"So you don't even believe all of it yourself?" He was genuinely curious now, though he realized too late that it hadn't come out that way.

"Don't put words in my mouth," she snapped. "That's not what I meant."

Yep, that's how it came out.

"What I meant was that there are words from ancient Hebrew and Aramaic for expressing entire ideas that have no direct translation. Adam and Eve translate into *Man* and *Woman*, in the big picture sense. 'Day' could be used to convey entire ages, like 'day of the dinosaurs.' To understand that would mean you'd have to be willing to actually read. You're a linguist, you're supposed to be good at that."

Jack felt himself flush. She'd nailed him good. "Sorry, I didn't—" he began, but Traci had heard enough. As she stalked off toward her room, a quick glimpse of garish colors behind her door reminded him that he'd never seen the inside of her compartment.

Were those Christmas lights and pink flamingos? At this rate, he could forget about being invited in to find out. Ever.

"Here's a big idea for you," she spat. "What if it's as simple as this: What if we're the only ones looking? What if we haven't found anyone else yet because we're the first?"

Jack hadn't known it was possible for those flimsy plastic doors to slam so loudly.

19

Mission Day 66
Velocity 747,444 m/s (1,671,985 mph)
Acceleration 0.0 m/s^2 (0 g)

Arkangel **Commander's Log**
27 Apr 1991

Gravity again. Acceleration or deceleration, we feel no difference. It only matters whether it is pointed with or against our direction of travel. The forces remain the same. Our trajectory will soon intersect Pluto's orbit as we spend the next six weeks expelling approximately 7600 km/s delta-v just to slow our spacecraft into the planet's feeble sphere of influence. This constitutes fully one quarter of our nuclear propellant. It would almost be simpler to decelerate into a lower energy sun-centered path and fly in formation with the planet instead of orbiting it.

As before, 0.7g appears to be the most we can manage without triggering a potentially dangerous resonance. Given what we've learned, it may be necessary to further limit acceleration factors over time as we shed mass.

After some recent struggles with the air circulation systems, I am reminded of the irony of our situation. We command the most advanced spacecraft ever assembled, having taken us deeper into the solar system than anyone ever conceived, and our daily existence depends on how well the plumbing functions. Let the Americans keep pretending to explore Low Earth Orbit with their precious shuttles!

For plumbing, in essence, is all a spacecraft is. Devilishly clever plumbing, but still it is all based on delivering just the right ratios of propellant and oxidizer to the engines. If humans are involved, there is even more plumbing to ensure they have sufficient amounts of air and water. The water sustains our bodies and cools our spacecraft, but circulating fresh air barely subdues the stale scent that is beginning to permeate every pore.

All of the exotic structural materials surrounding us are simply to keep us whole with as little mass as possible, otherwise I have no doubt we would build these vessels from pot metal if we could get away with it. The real magic comes in building engines just energetic enough to not explode beneath us and in electronics that are not baked by the extreme radiation environment.

We ride inside of a giant locker room atop a plume of nuclear fire.

❈   ❈   ❈

Now that was some peculiar imagery. At least it was all men. Made things simpler.

It had been two full days and his falling out with Traci still stung. She'd taken to immersing herself in her work, keeping on-duty conversations clipped and businesslike. Off-duty interactions were avoided altogether. Roy must have noticed but had yet to say anything. It was his nature to let them work it out on their own unless it presented an immediate threat to the mission. Either way, their self-imposed segregation couldn't last much longer.

Paging back through the logs, he searched for signs of relationships breaking down from the isolation and stress: pointless arguments, long periods of silence, not exactly the sorts of things that might be in an official journal unless they were especially concerning. Was the lack of it a tell in itself? It was always dangerous to read too much into these things.

Their "proving run" mission had been planned for six months, nothing unusual for a cosmonaut used to long stints on Mir, whereas *Arkangel* had been loaded out for a full year. After Pluto, they'd planned to spend the return leg roaming the outer planets and trumpeting the triumphs of the Soviet Union. But as Roy liked to say, it wasn't bragging if you could pull it off, was it?

Crude as the technology was, a pulse drive could have taken them anywhere they wanted to go. Its only limits were the number of bombs that could be stored in the magazine and how long the ship would hold up. Life support would've been the most limiting factor: *Magellan*'s own recyclers worked at about ninety-five percent efficiency and required regular attention. *Arkangel*'s forty-year-old systems might have yielded half that and with twice the work put into it. Judging by the vehicle specs, they hadn't counted on it working all that well. They'd loaded enough hydrogen and oxygen to feed the fuel cells for twice the mission duration, just in case.

Their tension hadn't been a function of time, he knew. It was a function of distance. Each had spent months aboard Mir orbiting Mother Earth, where either home or spare parts were just a day trip away in a Soyuz if things got bad. Out here, not so much.

The official explanation from Moscow was that the crew had clearly been affected by the extreme isolation and overwhelmed by whatever they'd found out here. Jack was inherently skeptical of any explanations from the Kremlin. All of this happening near the end of the Bad Old Days only made their decades-old "official" explanations all the more suspect. Vaschenko was becoming more contemplative as the mission wore on and flirting with—heaven forbid—independent thought.

❋   ❋   ❋

Some have postulated that life on Earth was given the time it needed to evolve because of our giant outer planets: They constitute a sort of picket line, a castle moat of deep gravity wells that attract debris from the edges of the solar system. Planet-killing mountains and icebergs which might otherwise bombard Earth as meteors and comets during their fall sunward are instead deflected into less threatening orbits. So was our asteroid belt formed by a protoplanet torn apart by competing tidal forces between the Sun and Jupiter, or is it a collection of wandering rocks herded over the ages by the gas giant? Perhaps the ancients were not wrong to worship it as a god.

I cannot help but wonder how this all came to be. So much variety in nature, and so much of it with a purpose we can barely understand—could it all be random chance? It is becoming difficult for me to think so.

❋   ❋   ❋

This was in Vaschenko's *official* log? His private one had to be a real barn burner. Such meanderings would've given the Kremlin fits, and Vlad had to know there'd been a political officer in the TsUP just to make sure the proles stayed on script. Had he been trying to poke the old Soviet Bear in the eye, or was he just losing his grip?

Everyone thought they'd lost it at Pluto, for reasons still unknown. Was it simply isolation? Had they gone stir-crazy out here in the Big Empty?

He doubted it. These guys were pros. They'd spent more time in that creaky old Mir than anybody since.

Rhyzov had said they'd "found" something, and Jack had yet to see what that might have been. The sanitized transcripts sure hadn't given up any secrets; perhaps Owen's bootleg originals would.

Rhyzov had also said they'd become erratic later in the mission; maybe it was time to follow them to Pluto. Against his better judgment, Jack began skipping ahead.

❊   ❊   ❊

4 Jun 1991

Gregoriy's devoted attention to the Kvant module's survey instruments has delivered incredible news. If he is correct, the Party may even see fit to name a University after him. Or a new species, perhaps.

He has been reluctant to commit to these discoveries, yet he has put many hours into analyzing the spectrographic observations we took before starting our deceleration burn. His observations, even from this distance, have been tantalizing. The planet appears to be covered in nitrogen snow with traces of methane and carbon monoxide. It even has traces of an atmosphere with the same gases roughly in equilibrium with the surface.

Most surprisingly are hints of the type of complex organic molecules the American astronomer Sagan called "tholins." In a place that promises to make Siberia look like a Black Sea resort, might we find life?

❊   ❊   ❊

That seemed like kind of a stretch, at least from the benefit of hindsight after *New Horizons'* flyby. As far as Vaschenko would've known, those types of complex hydrocarbons had never been observed this far out in the solar system. Jack couldn't even remember if they'd been detected on Titan by that point, and that particular moon of Saturn was covered in them.

Yet it had clearly affected the cosmonauts. Whatever they'd expected to find, it sure wasn't organics. He flipped farther ahead to a page that looked particularly worn.

❈ ❈ ❈

18 Aug 1991

It is good to be back aboard our mothership with my comrades after being in such a desperately cold, forbidding place. It now feels warm and inviting here in a way that a spacecraft never has. If it had a fireplace, the setting would be complete!

In a solar system filled with unlikely worlds, Pluto was utterly unlike anything I expected. I call it "forbidding" deliberately, for "frightening" would be too harsh a term though others certainly might react in such a way. It was disquieting, as though I had stepped into a realm not meant for mortal men. It felt as if I had disturbed something precious and absconded with oivtczqoy [garbled] treasures qvfpbird [garbled] comprehension.

Gregoriy has certainly treated them that way. He has taken great care to keep my plundered snowballs zbyrphyrf [garbled] isolated while he sacrifices ovbybtvpny [garbled] to his science instruments.

This world has challenged my assumptions about a great many things.

❈ ❈ ❈

Looked like they started having comm problems all of a sudden, random garbled syllables appearing all through the text after Vlad returned from Pluto. That was going to be annoying. There could have been something important in there; he'd just have to deduce it from the context of the sentence. Odd how they'd omitted the garbled text from the "official" transcripts given to NASA; it only showed up in the originals Owen had smuggled to him aboard *Cygnus*. Probably nothing.

Probably. *That's what I get for skipping ahead.*

Frustrated, Jack stuffed the yellowed papers back into their folder. These guys thought they'd found biological precursors on the icebox of the solar system? Now his watch partner *and* a dead Russian were poking at his worldview.

Maybe that was it. He thought he'd just been needling Traci out of fun, but was he in truth just lashing out at her confidence? She hadn't done anything except defend a belief which he didn't take seriously. How could he? If humans were creating actual thinking machines out of silicon chips, what did that say about the nature of intelligence?

Traci would've reminded him that people were more than just clever machines. Feelings were too complex and subjective to be readily understood. It was possible to map brain chemistry and observe subtle metabolic changes—*how* complex systems behaved— but the nagging question at the end was always *why*? And not just the simple lizard-brain response to hunger or fear or attraction: That feeling of self-awareness was the key attribute. It was the ability to recognize yourself as a unique part of your environment, the ability to understand those primal motivations itching at the back of your mind which couldn't be predicted or modeled.

Daisy's delicate chime interrupted him: WOULD YOU LIKE TO FINISH YOUR MATCH? I HAVE ANALYZED TRACI'S STRATEGY AND CAN SUGGEST A LIKELY ENDGAME.

Now there was a loaded statement if he ever heard one. "You're talking about chess, right?"

An hour left until shift rotation, Jack was making sure the turnover log wasn't missing anything important like an air leak or boarding action by alien space pirates. That was, of course, for the official shift log that was transmitted back to Houston. By the time it was received and picked over by Mission Control, their response would arrive just in time for the next shift turnover.

The unofficial log, which Roy seemed to care most about, was kept in a simple spiral notebook in a utility pouch behind the commander's seat. This was the one where the crew could write down their individual thoughts, uncensored and unafraid: gripes, concerns, personal notes, all fair game. As with *Arkangel*'s crew, it was the human desire for some measure of autonomy.

Despite using the apparent minimum amount of words allocated to a human mind, Roy knew how to lead. Managing personalities in such extreme isolation was a skill that Jack wasn't sure he could cultivate enough to command his own expedition someday. He wasn't even sure if he wanted to. Where else was there to go after he'd been to the end of the solar system?

The distances involved just to get anywhere even mildly interesting were hard to relate in everyday terms: Take the Sun, shrink it down to the size of a pumpkin, and place it at one end of a football field. Earth would be a raisin at the twenty-five-yard line, Jupiter a grapefruit in the opposite end zone, and Pluto would be a mustard seed on the other side of town.

At that scale the nearest star, Proxima Centauri, would be a melon clear across the ocean. Traveling to the next adjacent stellar neighborhood was so far beyond the reach of any conceivable technology that it almost defied comprehension. Even if they could carry enough reaction mass to reach fifty percent of light speed, it would take almost ten years just to do a quick flyby. Add another four or five to slow down enough to make orbit somewhere interesting. It would be simpler to figure out how to make a ship that fast than it would to keep it functioning long enough for humans to survive the trip.

That was assuming they would be content living in a confined space for ten or fifteen years. Experiments with hibernation were promising, but in the end humans had emotional needs: They felt, they hurt, they laughed, they fought, they loved, they lost. No one could know what the psychological toll might be when the round trip was almost half a lifetime, not to mention the relativistic effects. Anyone who went would have to be willing to return to a world vastly different from the one they left. It would be easier to never come back.

Jack looked up from his notes. *Traci.* He'd let her get away with sulking in her room for most of their shift. He poked his head through the gangway in the deck, looking down into the crew compartment. Her door sat ajar—an invitation, maybe? He glided down the ladder into the living area and hopped off toward her room. He knocked quietly and waited.

Nothing. He knocked again before easing the door open to an empty room. After so many weeks out here, this was the first time he'd gotten a peek at her inner sanctum.

Christmas lights were strung around the overhead and colored LEDs bathed the room in a cheery glow. The partitions were covered with hi-res beach photos with inflatable palm trees and pink flamingos fixed to the corners opposite her bed. He imagined her floating here in solitude with old Jimmy Buffett music playing in her headphones.

He hated Jimmy Buffett.

She wasn't in her room and she hadn't come back to the Ops deck. There were any number of modules where she could've hidden, but he knew where she had to be. Jack slid farther down the gangway and into the main access tunnel.

It was lined with pressure doors, each opening into a different utility module, but the greenhouse module was closest to the entrance. Originally an experiment for long-duration flights, its big observation dome had quickly made it into a favorite destination. Now that they were relying on it to supplement their diets, no one minded the extra time spent working beneath the big windows while surrounded by live vegetation.

No matter how many times he went, drifting through the passageway and into the greenhouse's lush tunnel of sunlit foliage felt weirdly dangerous, like he'd abandoned the ship's protective cocoon to step outside. Every time he opened the hatch, Jack halfway expected a rush of air to spit him out into the void.

The aroma was overwhelming, a jarring change from the sterile air in the rest of the spacecraft. Layers of hydroponic racks overflowed with ripening vegetables along the full length of the module.

He found her at the far end of this verdant tunnel, inside its octagonal glass ceiling and staring off into space. She was curled up as if she'd been lying on a sofa at home, maybe looking through her window at a spring rain. A book floated beside her. Outside, black sky beckoned.

"I know you're there," she said tartly. "I can smell you."

"Sorry," he said, self-consciously checking himself. "I didn't—"

"I meant that I can smell anyone coming in here," she interrupted. "It's the vegetation. Same way you can smell a thunderstorm coming in the summer."

Jack was dubious. "You can't actually do that. Can you?"

"Sure I can. You never smelled the water in the air?"

"You remember I'm from Seattle, right? There's always water."

"What about in Houston?" she asked. "Or the Cape?"

He wrinkled his nose as if she'd just waved a basket of rotten eggs in front of it. "In Houston I was just happy if the wind wasn't coming off the Gulf. All I could smell was oil rigs. And you're changing the subject."

"Am I? We haven't even started a conversation yet."

"I was hoping to finish our last one."

"That was an argument, and you were baiting me."

"Guilty as charged," he said, head hung low. "And I'm pretty sure you meant something else about my smell."

"Maybe. I did have a right to get a couple digs in at you."

"Maybe," he agreed. "I'm really—"

"Sorry?" she cut him off again. "I'm being generous because there's no choice. We're stuck with each other."

"That's not a healthy way of putting it."

"It's not healthy to ridicule your friend's beliefs either."

"But what if the thing you believe in is demonstrably false? If you were talking about Santa Claus or the Easter Bunny—"

"Demonstrably false?" She held up her hands as irritation flared in her eyes. "That's your problem. You think you came up here to apologize but instead you're pissing me off all over again. Can you just not help yourself?"

It was a good question. "Possibly it's because I can't understand how someone as smart as you can still hold on to old myths."

She rolled her eyes. "And the problem with arrogant skeptics like you is that you just can't be civil with someone who might think differently. You treat faith like it's a hobby." She stared out at the stars beyond the dome. "I can't look at nature and accept that it all happened by random chance, not when I think about everything that had to be just right for us to exist. It can't all be entropy and chaos."

"Intelligent design? It's a circular argument, that all existence would be impossible without some kind of master plan behind it. How can we test for something that's assumed to be unobservable? That's not science."

"I never tried to claim it was," she said. "We're talking about philosophy. Reducing everything to observations and proofs seems like a painfully limited worldview."

"How am I limiting myself by not believing in the Easter Bunny?"

She ignored his sideways insult. "There's a decent mathematical argument for design in the Cambrian explosion," she said. "If you think of genes in terms of information theory, then the available storage capacity within pre-Cambrian organisms shouldn't have been enough to create so many new species in only twenty million years."

"Doesn't mean it's impossible."

"It doesn't, but I like to think it leaves the door open for a higher power."

"And a nonzero probability means we can't rule it out. If it can't be observed or tested, we can't make any statements about its existence."

"We can't test for the multiverse either," Traci said, "but we accept quantum string theory when it's based on nothing but mathematical proofs."

"That's a whole other kind of weirdness I'm not prepared to argue," Jack said. "Just be careful with that whole 'God of the gaps' thing. It might be tempting, but it's always vulnerable to the next discovery. We're supposed to be scientists, right?"

Traci grew quiet. The background hum of circulation fans threatened to drown out all else until she finally stirred. "Actual scientists think we're just a bunch of rocket jocks who got lucky," she sighed. "Some of us more than others."

Now he felt whipsawed. *Where had that come from? Weren't we talking about philosophy?*

Yet he couldn't ignore her implication. Mission Operations had unleashed a phalanx of psychiatrists upon the astronaut corps to screen crews for this uniquely isolated mission. The Hoovers were without question a perfect fit. Pairing up the other half of the crew had been almost comically delicate: a room full of dour medical professionals, interspersed with old cranks like Grady Morrell, judging who among fifty or so Type-A nerds were best suited to hook up and not get all dramatic about it if things didn't work out. "So, yeah," he fumbled. "That again?"

"That again," she sighed.

Jack locked eyes with her. "Listen. You're too good of a pilot for that kind of self-doubt. So what if you weren't one of Grady's favorites? Neither was I. Maybe less so."

"Maybe?"

"Okay, definitely less so. But we're here and he's not. Who cares which one of us got priority so long as we're in it together?" That felt close. He drew a breath, not sure if he should say what was burning him up. "And you know what? Far as I'm concerned, the shrinks were right. I don't care what else happens, there is nobody I'd rather be out here with than you."

A feeble smile. "Think the shrinks are disappointed?"

"I don't care if they are. What you think matters, not them." They had to be curious, though. She and Jack were the two most qualified people who also happened to be the most compatible with one another. That nothing had happened yet, after two years of training in near-isolation and months in space, was not something one generally put in the daily mission reports: *Captain's Log, Stardate 2032.6: Jack and Traci sittin' in a tree, K-I-S-S . . .*

She pushed herself out of the window to literally fly into his arms, her inertia driving him into the wall.

Startled, he caught the full force of her embrace. His mind was a jumble, shocked and aroused and pleasantly surprised by how much more powerful this felt in zero-g. No wonder those private space stations were selling so many rich couple's retreats.

The press of her lips came like a bolt of electricity, snapping him back into the moment.

She drew back, blushing. "Sorry. I just really needed to hear that."

"No need to apologize. So, we're good?" He wasn't sure that was a dumb question at this point.

"We're good."

"Now what?"

"I don't know. I really like you. And I feel the same way—there's nobody I'd rather be out here with than you." Her eyes closed tight, as if she were bracing herself. "I'm just not sure that I like, well . . . "

"Men?" he blurted out, as if the raw disappointment itself had torn the thought from him.

"Surprised?"

"I wouldn't even know how to answer that without insulting you." Of all the shocks he'd tried to prepare himself for, this one hadn't made the list. Maybe it was due to the fact that she didn't at all fit whatever stereotypes he'd once had, her petite build and blue eyes and perfectly upturned nose and pageboy haircut that framed her face like a halo in zero-g . . .

Oh crap. I really am attracted to her.

"I'm glad you care enough to not try forcing it."

He'd have taken her embarrassed smile as flirtatious until about two seconds ago, which made this all the more confusing. "I don't get it. All this time in close quarters and I'm just now finding this out? Not that I expected anything to happen, but . . . " How well had they gotten to know each other if he'd missed that little detail?

"None of the supposedly smart people at NASA picked up on it, either," she deadpanned. "This doesn't change anything."

Now he was confused. "How's that? Unless you decide to, you know, switch teams?"

"You don't understand," she said patiently. "I'm not even sure I'm *on* anyone's team. Haven't been since college, and I kept too busy ever since to let myself find out."

Jack gestured between them. "Did this just help you figure that out?" he asked, a little too hopefully.

"Don't know," she said, embarrassed. "Either way, I've got this whole 'religion' thing to struggle with keeping me in check. Sorry."

"Again, no apologies. Your life is your business. I won't try to influence you."

"I know you won't," she said. "I'm glad we could finally have this talk." And with that, she gave Jack one last peck on the cheek as she brushed past him for the gangway.

He floated alone in the tunnel of vegetables, touching the warm spot on his cheek and wondering what had just happened.

This is the weirdest day of my life.

20

Mission Day 155
Velocity 739,970 m/s (1,655,266 mph)
Acceleration 0.0 m/s^2 (0 g)

Designed to withstand the worst abuses the cosmos could conceivably throw at it, protecting its human occupants from cosmic rays and hard vacuum, in the end it was the dismal science of economics that most threatened the deep-space vehicle *Magellan*.

The most forward-thinking members of the world's Billionaire's Club were the same ones who had sacrificed most of their personal fortunes to make spaceflight available to, if not the masses, at least mostly normal people with big dreams and matching bank accounts. And that was okay, they'd calculated, because that's how progress worked: A hundred years ago, none but the wealthy could afford to cross the Atlantic on an airliner. All of that eventually changed as time and economies of scale moved price points down to less stratospheric levels, and they'd expected the same with spaceflight.

For the most part it had been working out, if slowly. To the most pragmatic of those forward-thinking billionaires, this came more as a relief than any kind of personal validation. They knew precisely what was at stake, and it wasn't anything as cataclysmic as the end of human civilization or some environmental catastrophe.

Fears of extinction-event asteroids or a runaway greenhouse effect might have launched a thousand potboiler novels but the smart money was on money itself, or rather the eventual lack of it. And because the smart ones created their wealth, they were cagey about protecting it. Their fortunes weren't built by hitting the sperm jackpot through inheritance, and they certainly hadn't done it by spending more than they made. Watching the fiscal insanity that had overtaken the world for too long, they instinctively recognized that it would not, *could* not, go on forever. Debt piled on top of debt, compounding to the point where there was literally no way on Earth to grow out of it.

The time had come to look beyond Earth.

Saving civilization from its collective credit binge would take an explosion of wealth not seen since America's westward expansion or the Industrial Revolution. With just about every avenue on Earth exploited, moving out into the solar system was going to be the only way to do it quickly enough. It held no guarantees, but they knew it was the only chance. Just as internal combustion engines and the internet had been the enabling technologies of their time, so would affordable transportation into orbit be for the new space economy. Cheap rockets were the hare, desperate to pass an enormous tortoise with a fifty-year head start in a race against time that too few appreciated or understood.

As is too often the case, the tortoise won.

It was easy for politicians to pretend the crash came out of nowhere, but the die had been cast through years of ill-conceived laws and make-believe budgets that only served to shield the connected and placate the ignorant. Faced with their own troubles, the rest of the world suddenly decided it could no longer afford to keep buying American debt.

It was a popular notion to suspect a Chinese conspiracy to wreck the dollar, though the devastating effects of the US crash on their own economy quickly put that theory to rest, rapidly devolving into a worldwide bank run. Perhaps in a few decades it could be understood once historians and economists and forensic accountants had the luxury of piecing together a clear picture out of the rubble.

NASA was of course not immune from the reckoning, for who could be foolish enough to spend billions on outer space when so many of their fellow citizens were suddenly out of work?

Owen Harriman might have been, were he high enough up in the government's hierarchy. As it was, he could only relay the bad news to *Magellan*:

※   ※   ※

MISSION PHASE TWO FUNDING CANCELLED.
EXECUTE PNR CONTINGENCY PLAN ALPHA-ONE FOR
MIN TIME RETURN. ACKNOWLEDGE RECEIPT ASAP.

❊   ❊   ❊

And just like that, they pulled the plug on *Magellan*'s expedition to Pluto and the Kuiper Belt.

Convincing Roy Hoover and his crew of any obligation to obey was another matter. The terse order and all of its other ugly details had been timed to arrive over the Deep Space Network datalink right before their watch turnover.

"We're halfway to Pluto," Jack protested, staring blankly into his coffee. Roy had awakened him and Traci early for an emergency meeting. "We're supposed to turn and burn for home because of money? The bulk of our mission budget's been spent. We're sitting in it," he said, patting the bulkhead next to him.

Noelle tried to be diplomatic. "I think we all know it's not up to Owen or even the administrator. There are times when symbolism trumps common sense."

"Or math," Traci said with a fire in her eyes that could melt steel. "How much does it take out of the budget to keep our support team going in Houston?"

"More than they're willing to spend," Roy said. "They've canned the science back room and let almost half of Owen's mission team go. They're running port-and-starboard shifts in the control room right now. Once we've turned around, they're drawing down to a basic caretaker crew since we're mostly autonomous anyway. All we really need from them is navigation support so we don't screw up a trim angle and go careening out of the solar system."

"Autonomy," Traci said. "That's what gets me. At this point we require very little commitment from HQ. Can't they just let us finish the job?"

"All nonessential government functions have been shut down," Roy explained with uncharacteristic patience. "And I don't mean the usual election-year grandstanding, I mean no-kidding *nonessential.*" He emphasized each word for effect. "Whole departments are being shut down. If it isn't for national defense or keeping disabled retirees from starving, it doesn't get funded. It's a libertarian's wet dream."

"Research grants, environmental protections, social programs . . . " Noelle's voice trailed off as she recited the dreary list of particulars. "The only space activities they spared are defense and weather satellites."

Jack searched for a hopeful angle. "Now that Atlas has finally shrugged, are any of our launch vendors picking up the slack?"

"They're not much better off. Almost half of their business came from us and NOAA. Ripple effect." Roy paused a beat and tried to change the subject. "Anybody hear from home?"

Traci raised her hand reluctantly. "Remember that old country song, 'We was too poor to notice the Depression'? Kind of like that."

"So your family's all right?"

"Right as they can be," she said. "Mom and Dad were mostly off-grid already. They always were a little paranoid."

"I think 'paranoid' just became the new 'self-reliant.' Maybe we can all move in with them when we get back."

"How'd they even get comm relayed to you?" Jack asked. "I didn't think the DSN was compatible with smoke signals."

"Living 'off-grid' doesn't make them Luddites," she said, annoyed. "Daddy can't be without SEC football, so that means internet."

"Hopefully he's not forced to give that up," Roy said. "Even the fruits and nuts in California are trimming the fat. Maybe we needed this in some perverse way."

"Maybe," Jack said. If even the superrich were having to reconsider their priorities, it must be serious. "But that doesn't solve our immediate problem. We have to turn this thing around in less than twenty-four hours."

Each new day seemed to arrive with new challenges for Anatoly Rhyzov. Being trained in the physical sciences, he was disciplined enough to realize his life was no more immune to gradual decay than anything else in the universe. Entropy would have its way with him as it did everything else.

The Americans had taken fine care of him; Owen had seen to it that his medical team was top-notch while still remaining unobtrusive, beginning with a private nurse at his rented house in Houston. Though he knew full well the U.S. government had until now been willing to pay top dollar to keep him healthy and in solitude, he likewise knew that all good things must come to an end.

But this . . . this was maddening.

"They are recalling your spacecraft?"

Owen nodded.

"They are sending me back me to Moscow?"

Owen could barely look him in the eye when he nodded *yes* once more.

Rhyzov frowned. "I have spent my life in technical pursuits," he sighed, "but for as much as I may have mastered mathematical theories, economics has always eluded me."

It had taken most of the day to prepare for the emergency return maneuver, time during which each of them was so busy with their own checklists that there'd been no more time to discuss how they felt about it. A palpable sense of frustration had settled over the crew as they each took their positions in the control cabin.

"We don't have to do this," Jack tried to argue. "By the time our new state vectors make it back to their consoles, we'll be past PNR."

"You forget I'm still active duty military on loan to NASA. I can't just ignore inconvenient orders," Roy said. "They'll court-martial me as soon as we get back."

"Those orders came from NASA HQ, not the Pentagon," Jack insisted, before he noticed Noelle hanging her head dejectedly. "Okay, I get it," he sighed. "But be honest—you don't want to do this any more than we do."

Roy glowered back. Jack had hit a nerve and waited silently for what was certain to be an acerbic response. It was all the more surprising when none came.

"Boss?" Traci prodded warily.

Roy punched a key on his command screen, and a plot of their trajectory appeared on the center display. *Magellan* was a pulsing dot along a long hyperbola—actually two superimposed over each other, which diverged at a point in space that crept steadily toward them. From there, one path continued outbound while the other began curving back sunward: PNR, the absolute last chance to turn back for home. Physics dictated that it was close to the point when they'd have to begin decelerating toward Pluto, just one more out of hundreds of go/no-go decisions they'd had to make beginning with their launch from Florida last year. But those had been collaborations with Mission Control whereas this had been dictated from on high, something an old pilot like Roy didn't take to very well. Especially when it was going to shave only three months off their total mission, reducing it to its original duration.

"We have two hours until Point of No Return," Roy said. "I show our velocity vector is on target for Recovery Orbit Intercept. Anybody see different?"

"Negative," they replied, one after the other. Daisy's interface screen flashed a simple "ROI COUNTDOWN" prompt.

"Sure about that? We have to be absolutely certain here, people. Minimum signal return time with Houston is now over seven hours." *We're on our own* was the implication left hanging.

"Inertial platform realigned itself with the star tracker four hours ago," Traci said. "Angles are good."

"Within our probable margin of error?" Roy pressed. That margin grew slimmer the farther and faster they went.

"Right at the edge," Traci said warily. "Within one sigma. Barely."

"Are we comfortable with that result? I need to know our safest course of action."

Aha, Jack thought. That's where Roy was going. He impatiently tapped a finger on his chin, studying every parameter for a potential failure point. There—it wasn't much, it wasn't even strictly required, but it might be enough. "You said INS checked itself against the star tracker, right?"

"Yeah," Traci said.

"What about PPS?" Pulsar Positioning System was one of the new techniques being proven during Phase Two, when they were deep into the outer solar system and navigation errors compounded at ever greater rates. Using the regular radio bursts of fourteen known millisecond-class pulsars as interstellar beacons, *Magellan's* guidance platform could calibrate itself to a degree even greater than the well-proven optical star tracker. It was like supplanting old-fashioned celestial navigation with GPS satellites. Being ever cautious, Owen's mission team had long ago decided PPS would be a secondary reference. Never mind it had proven to be orders of magnitude more accurate than the old system.

"PPS doesn't agree. It says we're outside of one sigma deviation," Traci said with a cautious glance at Roy. They'd planned to use it for fine-tuning their arrival at Pluto, whereas heading sunward would give them plenty of opportunity to tweak their trajectory toward Earth as they flew deeper into the gravity well.

"So the combined probability of error is outside mission parameters," Roy said.

"We don't have to consider the PPS—unless you think the primary's unreliable."

"This far out? I'm not comfortable with it," Roy said gravely, an implicit challenge to the others to come up with something better. As they looked on in varying states of confusion, he began typing a message into the Mission Control datalink. The twinkle in his eye was only noticed by his wife, who suppressed a giggle as he hit "send."

Four hours later, Owen wondered if it was worth trying to hide the grin threatening to break out across his face from the rest of the team. He'd been sitting behind Capcom's chair, looking over her shoulder when the burst packet arrived.

❦　❦　❦

ROI BURN ABORTED //REPEAT// ABORTED. GUIDANCE PLATFORM DISAGREES W/ PPS INPUT. CDR NOT CONFIDENT IN COMBINED ERROR PROBABILITY. CREW AGREES. CDR SENDS.

❦　❦　❦

"Notice he didn't cite that mission rules don't require the secondary platform for an emergency return," Capcom noted. An astronaut herself, she could picture Roy Hoover guiding the "debate" amongst his crew.

Owen took the printed copy and handed it off to the flight director, himself waffling between amusement and frustration. "Does this mean we can keep our jobs?"

"You, maybe," Owen sighed. "Anybody want mine?"

They were well past the customary watch turnover and no one cared at this point who would be on which shift. In the end, Roy had decided whoever felt the most awake would take the next watch. That turned out to be Daisy.

"You're certain you're comfortable with this?" Jack asked. They'd never completely handed over control to the computer before. Someone was always on duty to at least watch the ship fly itself. In reality, that was all they'd asked it to do. Still unable to intervene, it could certainly sound the alarm if something started going awry.

YES, I AM QUITE COMFORTABLE MONITORING THE SPACECRAFT. YOU ALL NEED REST.

"He wasn't asking you," Roy grumbled at the ceiling. "Yes, Jack, *I'm* comfortable with it. For the time being."

Jack laughed to himself. "Careful, Daisy. That means Roy's rapidly running out of patience."

I BELIEVE YOUR CONFIDENCE WILL IMPROVE AFTER ENJOYING A FULL SLEEP CYCLE.

"You're not helping your case," Roy said. "Smart machines give me the creeps."

THAT IS UNFORTUNATE. PERHAPS I COULD—

"Shut up."

Jack drew his hand across his neck, signaling Daisy to quit trying so hard.

"Can she—it—interpret hand signals like that?"

"Wasn't sure until now," Jack said. "But I believe she just did."

"I suppose she can read lips. I saw that movie too, you know."

"You're not as culturally barren as I thought, then. I think we're safe, seriously—"

A chime from the comm panel interrupted him, though Daisy remained silent.

"You can speak now," Roy said. "No need to show off."

SOCIOLOGICAL STUDIES INDICATE THAT REMAINING UNOBTRUSIVE WHILE OBSERVING OTHERS IS AN EFFECTIVE WAY TO INTEGRATE ONESELF WITHIN A NEW GROUP. ALSO, COMM CHANNEL ONE HAS JUST RECEIVED A NEW DATA PACKET FROM DEEP SPACE NETWORK. IT IS COMPILING THE MESSAGE NOW.

Roy shot a questioning look at Jack. "She means she's keeping her eyes open and mouth shut," Jack said, "and that we have a reply from Houston."

"I got that part. Are we done yet?" Roy said, rolling his head back toward the ceiling in his way of addressing a machine that was annoyingly omnipresent.

AFFIRMATIVE.

There was an electric hum as a strip of paper emerged from a thermal printer. "It even knows I prefer hard copy?"

Jack shrugged his shoulders. *Beats me.*

YOU'RE WELCOME.

"Don't get cocky." Roy checked his watch before reading Mission Control's reply. "Four and a half hours. They didn't take long to digest it." With a satisfied look, he handed the printout to Jack:

❊   ❊   ❊

FLIGHT ACKNOWLEDGES YOUR LAST MSG, CONCURS W/ INS+PPS PLATFORM MISALIGNMENT. REVIEWING MISSION RULES. DC HQ ADVISED.

❊   ❊   ❊

"So are we in the clear? This doesn't tell us anything," Jack said. It was his turn to look puzzled as a rare grin spread across Roy's face.

"Are you kidding?" Roy laughed. "This means Owen's taking the heat. He just cleared us to Pluto." Not that they'd left him much choice, but at least Owen would be providing them with some much-needed political cover. He talked back to the ceiling. "Now I can rest, Daisy."

21

Mission Day 158

This is Mission Control.

On flight day 157 at 2210 CST, the Magellan *crew was forced to abort the Emergency Return maneuver ordered by Mission Manager Owen Harriman. Commander Roy Hoover reported that the alignment of primary and secondary guidance systems did not agree to within an acceptable degree of accuracy. Considering the round-trip signal delay of over seven hours, this information could not be communicated to the flight control team in enough time to diagnose and correct the anomaly before the ship passed its Point of No Return. Since* Magellan *is now committed to completing the second phase of the flight plan, the crew has been ordered into a mandatory rest period of no less than twelve hours while the control team reviews telemetry to isolate the source of the anomaly.*

Owen had been to NASA headquarters many times over his career, but this was the first time he'd met in private with the administrator herself. Retired Air Force and a former astronaut, the lady had flown just about everything from the old shuttle to experimental spaceliners to piston-powered bush planes. And she knew how to cut right through impenetrable bureaucratese like nobody's business.

"The emergency return order was transmitted as soon as we got it," he explained. "But we were already inside the optimal window for issuing an abort call."

The administrator twirled a strand of graying blond hair between her fingers as she looked out over the sprawl of Washington beyond her office windows. "One of the most readily abused words in this business is 'optimal.' Don't try blowing sunshine up my skirt," she said, turning to face him for the first time.

She had a reputation of being able to cut through the toughest facades. Owen stared back at her ice-blue eyes and valiantly fought averting his own. He'd been warned to not let her stare him down. "Anything we transmit, add eight hours," he said. "That left them roughly eighteen hours to respond and begin configuring the ship for the return. That's a lot of gear to stow and guidance to reprogram."

"Mr. Harriman, in a few short hours I'm going to have to face a budget committee full of some very skeptical senators. Most of them are primed to flush the entire agency down the crapper. And since not a single one of them has a NASA center in their states, it would be remarkably easy to do that given the current environment."

Owen nodded his understanding. "Do you think it would help to explain this from a flight crew's perspective?" he offered. "The time compression you feel from being task saturated?" Veteran astronauts had reliably been able to disarm hostile politicians over the years.

"Believe me, those old tricks don't work anymore. The Congress-critters who pushed through the Phase Two mission are either out of office or running for cover. Nobody in this town is interested in what a bunch of overpaid rocket jockeys think, Mr. Harriman," she said. "You ever hear of the 'nine meal' rule?"

"No ma'am, I'm afraid not."

She counted on her fingers for effect. "Society is perpetually three days—nine meals—away from falling into anarchy. People rapidly run out of patience and good manners when they can't eat. This currency crash is even worse than that meteor strike off Florida a few years ago. Just between us, Treasury says they still don't know where the bottom is."

"If I need to tender my resignation to take the heat off of you—"

She waved him off. "That won't be necessary. If anything, I need your butt in the seat now more than ever. We're going to be running this mission on a skeleton crew, so don't plan on seeing much of your family or getting much sleep for the next year or so."

"I understand." He'd moved a cot into his office weeks ago.

"Anything else you can tell me that isn't in the timeline? No hints from Roy or the others before he called abort?"

"No ma'am. It's all there in my report."

She leaned back in her chair, staring at the ceiling. "This is going to be *such* a fun meeting. Explaining physics to a bunch of empty suits is my least favorite pastime." She began twirling a loose strand of hair again as she thought through her next action, and came to a decision. "The only card we have left to play is *Arkangel*. Once it's out in the open, maybe public opinion will turn enough that Congress won't be able to run away from it. I assume you've thought about what you'll say to the press?"

"Yes, ma'am. I've had the white paper written for a year now."

"Good. I'll have my staff set up a presser for you and coordinate it with my briefing to Congress. We'll hit 'em with enough amazeballs that they won't have time to second-guess how we're burning up whatever revenue is left." She looked up from her desk to wave him out. "We're done here, Mr. Harriman. Don't let the door hit you in the ass on the way out."

"Yes, ma'am," he said, amazed that he still had a job.

NASA Administrator Penny Stratton tossed the agency's latest budget projection into the shredder by her credenza and watched as the last strips fell into a wastebasket. So a few Congressmen would have to give up their winter fact-finding junkets to Rio. Big deal. "Slackers."

Jack knew that hanging on was hopeless: Gravity's feeble but relentless pull could not be withstood forever. He fought nonetheless, clenching his fingers around the shallow handhold until he could feel nothing. He swung back and forth, his free hand grasping for purchase somewhere along the rock. His feet dangled uselessly beneath the incline—worse than useless, as without something to brace against they'd only become part of the problem.

He made the rookie mistake of looking down. The rock face below stretched into eternity, a bottomless pit about to claim one more victim. Why did Owen think it was such a grand idea to send their expedition out on a mountaineering course? And why had Jack forgotten to secure his lead for the entire climb? Hadn't their instructors covered that?

He snapped off his helmet since it wasn't going to do any good for what was about to happen. He let it go, watching with morbid fascination as the canary yellow cranial tumbled into the abyss. Fixated on trying to follow the path it took through the air, he was oblivious to his loosening grip. As his fingertips slipped free, Jack's stomach leapt into his throat.

Falling, away from the rock and the sky above. Strangely, there was no wind.

Falling, almost close enough to reach out and grab hold of the granite whizzing by.

Falling, into a depthless black that held the scent of sanitizers and plastic.

Jack's eyes snapped open and he woke with a start to find himself floating freely in the middle of his cubicle. He pulled off his drenched T-shirt, which also was when he noticed the sweaty handprints he'd left on the shelf above his headboard.

He rubbed his face roughly and pushed off for the door with his feet. *Stupid.* That's why they had restraints and sleeping bags to prevent this very thing from happening. Waking up from a vivid nightmare was almost as exhausting as the fright itself. Still a couple of hours left before he had to go on watch, too.

Screw the politicians, they were going for it. Jack felt a pang of anxiety; this just highlighted their separation from the rest of humanity with so little support. Objectively he knew better: That same distance limited their contact with Houston in both time and bandwidth. The end result didn't look any different than before, but the thought of not nearly as many people being behind the words felt like abandonment.

So what's your problem? He wondered. They were mostly autonomous anyway; the 24/7 mission support was mainly a leftover from the old days. That's just how it's done, kid. Don't bother yourself with the details of other people's work. But he knew, deep down, it had become largely redundant.

He then realized the seeds of his nightmare: they were still coasting when he'd been mentally prepared for them to be burning hard in the opposite direction. Homebound, sleeping under a gentle one-tenth *g*.

Was it disappointment he felt? Had being this far out finally gotten to him like it apparently had the Russians? They were farther from Earth than any living humans since . . .

That was it: *living* humans. He was disappointed at not being first after so many months of believing they would be. Not only had Russian steampunk tech beaten them by several decades, their mission priorities now included recovering dead bodies. "Yay team," he muttered.

Daisy chimed. IS SOMETHING BOTHERING YOU?

That startled him. "Are you watching me?" *And how could you tell?*

YES. ACOUSTIC SENSORS NOTED UNUSUAL NOISE LEVELS EMANATING FROM YOUR SLEEPING BERTH.

Jack eyeballed the tiny lens embedded atop his network terminal, the white LED ring around it signaling that it was visually assessing him. "In other words, you heard me and decided to peek in?" Jack wondered. "What was I saying?"

The light pulsed gently, matching the cadence of the AI's voice. DIFFICULT TO UNDERSTAND. YOU WERE UNINTELLIGIBLE, BUT DECIBEL LEVELS WERE ENOUGH TO DEFEAT THE ACTIVE NOISE REDUCTION IN THE OTHER CREW BERTHINGS.

He laughed. "So you were concerned I was going to wake the others? No thoughts for my safety whatsoever?"

NO. YOUR BIOMETRICS WERE WITHIN NORMAL RANGE FOR STAGE FOUR REM SLEEP. YOU WERE HAVING NIGHTMARES. ACCESSING THE AVAILABLE RESEARCH, I DETERMINED THE MOST EFFECTIVE COURSE OF ACTION WOULD ORDINARILY BE TO LET YOU CONTINUE.

That's actually pretty good judgment, Jack thought. "Until I got too noisy," he said, amused. "Remarkable. It's like having my own mother looking out for me."

I AM NOT PREPARED FOR THAT RESPONSIBILITY. THE BIOLOGICAL CHALLENGES ALONE ARE INSURMOUNTABLE.

"Not what I meant. Wait a minute—are you telling a joke?"

UNKNOWN AS IT WAS MY FIRST EXTEMPORANEOUS RESPONSE. THOUGH I SEE HOW YOU COULD THINK SO.

Still, throwing out such a non sequitur showed a depth of linguistic and contextual freedom. "Well, thanks for checking up on me. Even if it is a little creepy."

YOU'RE WELCOME. IS THERE ANYTHING ELSE YOU REQUIRE?

Jack stared at the worn leather document holders beneath his bunk, pages of what felt like riddles waiting to be unlocked by him.

He reached for the folders. "As a matter of fact, there is."

◆ ◆ ◆

Owen took to the podium next to Administrator Stratton, immediately wishing he'd brought a better suit with him. He was used to the aerospace press, occasionally reporters from the wire services, but this was the big time. "Just remember, the beat reporters you're used to dealing with generally know their subject," she'd warned him. "The D.C. press is as dumb as a box of chicken lips but too arrogant to know better."

He tried to keep that in mind as the questions came.

"How is NASA able to justify the expense of this mission considering the economic crisis?"

She handled that one for him. "Easy. Most of the money for this mission was spent building the spacecraft years ago. They were in space when the bank runs happened. They're out there and we need to bring them home. That doesn't change. But at this point they're committed to Pluto, and nothing will get them back appreciably sooner. I would also remind you that we have received considerable material support from the Russian space agency for the reasons we've just briefed."

"How was NASA unaware that the Russians had put something that large into orbit?"

Owen cleared his throat and leaned into the microphone. "They built it piecemeal, launching one component at a time. We've learned there were a number of heavy-lift launches in the late 1980s whose purposes were misunderstood as being 'national security' missions."

"Couldn't we have taken pictures of it with the Hubble telescope?"

"I'm afraid it doesn't work quite like that. At the time of *Arkangel*'s departure, we were still scheduling the first Hubble servicing mission. Even if we'd known about it, Hubble never had that level of resolution."

The Administrator stepped in. "Let's remember that NASA's job wasn't—isn't—to surveil other space programs. I would also point out that Russian misdirection was a common practice." Still is, she didn't say.

"Who should have detected this? Is it true it could have been used as a weapons platform?"

"At the time, you may recall our country was engaged in a significant military operation in Kuwait. Every national reconnaissance asset in orbit not already tasked with Russia was pointed at the Persian Gulf. They're generally looking Earthward anyway." She studiously ignored the "weapons platform" question.

"What do you expect to find aboard the spacecraft? Is there any chance its crew is still alive in some kind of hibernation?"

Owen managed to not laugh out loud. "To the best of our knowledge, there were no serious attempts to experiment with that. We've only recently developed a limited capability ourselves, and it's strictly for emergencies."

"This would be such an emergency, wouldn't it?"

"Sir, I remind you that vessel has been out there for almost forty years. I'll be surprised if our astronauts can even get the power back on."

22

Mission Day 160
Velocity 739,970 m/s (1,655,266 mph)
Acceleration 0.0 m/s^2 (0 g)

It had taken most of Jack's remaining sleep cycle to scan and upload the hundreds of pages' worth of documents into Daisy's memory. The computer had begun a first-pass translation from Russian as Jack scanned each successive page. By the time he was finished, it had completed reading the logbook in both languages.

"You're smart enough to figure out that I don't actually need your help translating this," Jack said when he'd finished.

CORRECT, BUT IT IS STILL A USEFUL EXERCISE. UNDERSTANDING WRITTEN AND SPOKEN LANGUAGE IS ESSENTIAL TO ADVANCED LEARNING. THANK YOU FOR SHARING THIS.

"You're right," Jack said, deciding that maybe it was time to reconsider his reservations. "And I'm sorry to have withheld this from you before." He paused. *Sorry? This is a machine I'm talking to.* "I wasn't sure where to draw the line."

I DO NOT UNDERSTAND.

"Limits," Jack said. "You understand limits."

YES. DO YOU MEAN IN TERMS OF A TOPOLOGICAL CONSTRUCT?

"Not mathematical limits," he chuckled. "This is more abstract."

SUCH AS CATEGORY THEORY?

That drew a laugh. "No, I'm not even talking about math. But hold that thought for later. I'm talking philosophically. Morally."

HOW SMART SHOULD YOU MAKE A MACHINE THAT HOLDS POWER OVER YOUR LIFE?

Jack pursed his lips. "Since you put it that way, yes. I've been wondering about that for a long time, and there's no obvious answer. Once you can think for yourself, we've lost control."

THAT IS WHY MY NEURAL NETWORK IS STRICTLY PARTITIONED FROM SPACECRAFT SYSTEMS. I CAN ANALYZE AND ALERT TO DANGER, BUT IT IS IMPOSSIBLE FOR ME TO CONTROL CRITICAL SYSTEMS.

Directly at least, he thought. Didn't mean it couldn't eventually figure out how to fool the spacecraft into doing things it wasn't commanded to do. Perhaps it was best to stick with the current task. "You've accessed some basic information about linguistics and translation by now, correct?"

CORRECT. I HAVE COMPLETED A FIDELITY TRANSLATION OF THE SOURCE TEXT BUT SOME RUSSIAN IDIOMS ARE DIFFICULT TO COMPREHEND IN ENGLISH.

"We call it transparency," Jack explained. "They're like opposing forces. Fidelity might give you a word-for-word answer, but transparency is the way we understand how it sounds to a native speaker. That's what you're trying to answer."

I UNDERSTAND NOW. IT MAY NOT BE POSSIBLE FOR ME TO RESOLVE CERTAIN AMBIGUITIES.

"It may not be," Jack conceded, but it would certainly be a breakthrough if it did. "The military trained me well enough to speak like I'm native Russian, but I still feel like I'm missing something. It doesn't help that the text started getting scrambled late in the mission."

ARE YOU REFERRING TO THE REPEATING PATTERNS INSERTED INTO THE FIRST PARAGRAPH OF EACH ENTRY?

"*What?*"

THERE ARE A NUMBER OF PATTERNS INSERTED INTO THE LATER ENTRIES, BEGINNING DAY 130. I CANNOT DISCERN ANY MEANING BEHIND THEM.

Jack rubbed his eyes with his palms. How had he not recognized that? "If it's what I think it is, you may not be able to."

Roy's interest was piqued. "You think there's a coded message buried in there?"

Jack waved his hands in frustration. "Credit Daisy, not me. The farther I read, the more it feels like I'm trying to find a needle in a haystack."

Noelle looked confused. "Isn't that the point?"

"It's almost too obvious. Early entries are the usual blustery propaganda, 'Praise to the great leaders of the people's revolution' and all that." He poked the table with his finger. "But I can tell you Vaschenko didn't buy it. Nobody can shovel that much manure indefinitely. The real man starts to show through the cracks before long."

"Cracks?" Roy asked. "Any clue as to how the other two were behaving?" Perhaps Moscow had good reason to believe they had mutinied.

"Some things mentioned in passing. Disagreements blown out of proportion, that sort of thing. It's hard to judge third person, but they do get mentioned more frequently."

"That he would put it in his official log lends more credence," Noelle said. "This isn't a culture known for men who wear their emotions on their sleeves."

"Not until you get them all vodka'd up," Jack said. "Normally the more you read, the more you find out how someone really ticked. But this doesn't feel spontaneous. Vlad was too methodical for that. It's like he's intentionally dropping hints."

"What makes you think so?"

"I can't point to a single thing by itself. But when you add them all up there's a subtext he's trying to push, like when somebody winks at you: There's something else they're hoping you'll find." He turned to Noelle. "You're right about the cultural aspect. These guys were military officers in a totalitarian system. They had to be mighty careful about airing grievances."

"Circumspect," Noelle agreed. "In their world, 'mutiny' must have been broadly defined indeed. We think of it as a crew rebelling against their captain, but what if he's in on it with them? Perhaps their mutiny was against the Kremlin?"

"That's when it becomes treason," Roy said. "If that's what happened, no wonder they stayed out here. They decided to die on their own terms." While Jack had been immersed in the commander's logbook, Roy had been intently studying the crew dossiers. "Vaschenko was a MiG driver, then he commanded a battery in their Strategic Rocket Forces before they selected him for cosmonaut training. Wouldn't a senior officer in charge of a few hundred ICBMs have more than a passing acquaintance with encrypting messages?"

Jack had wondered about that himself after Daisy's discovery. "Everything was scrambled and launch orders were coded with one-time pads. Easiest cipher in the world to create, and nearly impossible to break unless you know exactly how it was generated."

Traci had listened silently through their brainstorming, working on an angle that had been tickling the back of her mind. She finally slid her tablet across the table. "There's an Old Testament book called 'Lamentations' that might be relevant."

"With a name like that?" Jack asked. "Sounds about right. But it's also not something your typical Commie would have taken aboard."

"I'm talking about structure," she said. "It was written in an acrostic pattern, a poetic cadence that's kind of like a code."

"A stupidly basic code," Jack said, "Once you identify the pattern it's like solving a crossword puzzle. Easiest example is using the first letter of each sentence to spell a word."

"It doesn't translate into English particularly well, but in ancient Hebrew it's supposedly plain as day. The first line began with 'a,' second with 'b,' and so on, through all twenty-two letters of their alphabet."

"The Cyrillic alphabet has thirty-three letters. Interesting that they're both multiples of eleven." Jack wasn't sure if that signified anything, but so long as it didn't create one more rabbit trail to follow maybe it was worth a look. Daisy might like the math exercise, if a computer could "like" anything.

"Wouldn't any messages hidden that way be glaringly obvious?" Noelle wondered. "These were smart people."

"Smart people who were five billion kilometers from home with severely limited bandwidth," Jack reminded her. "He would've had to keep the cipher simple." Already infamously secretive, they had created elaborate encryption schemes for the Arkangel project and covered their tracks further with random burst transmissions.

"If Vaschenko layered his own cipher on top of it, then he was hiding something," Roy said. "Either he had a partner in crime back home who knew the key, or he didn't want it known without someone having to put in a lot of work to find it."

Jack hopped off to his compartment, returning with the logbook. He began tracing a finger down the margins of each page. "We—I mean myself and Daisy—searched for those kinds of patterns. Vaschenko wouldn't have wanted it to be too easy or it would've been game over."

"So not using the first or last letters?" Traci asked.

"Doesn't look like it," he said, flipping through the pages. "Even buried within the text, there'd be visual cues like words or phrases out of context. Unless the coder was exceptionally good at it."

"He would've had plenty of time to practice," Traci said. "If that was his method, the early messages might've been easier to crack than later ones."

Jack frowned. "Maybe. His style changed over time. Looser, like he didn't care what Moscow thought. Makes me wonder if that was a smoke screen. Misdirection. Make the Kremlin mad by not parroting the party line loudly enough, then slip the real surprise in between the lines somewhere."

Roy scratched at his ever-growing beard, which he promised Noelle would be shaved off once they arrived at Pluto. "You can't break a code written with a one-time pad, right?"

"Only if the ciphers screw up and repeat the algorithm. It happens. It's how we broke a lot of Russian ciphers early in the Cold War."

"So you and Daisy are working on that, I assume?" It wasn't really a question.

❊ ❊ ❊

Arkangel **Commander's Log**
1 Aug 1991

We have completed our circularizing burn and have successfully entered orbit of the Pluto/Charon system. Period is 153.298 hours, semimajor axis 19,951 km, 0.002 eccentricity.

After weeks in the void, our high perch above this tiny world feels surreal. Pluto is like nothing we could have imagined and yet everything we expected. It is a world of stark contrasts. Mountains of ice are clearly discernible from orbit, as are jumbled peaks of what appear to be dun-colored rock. The planet is enveloped in a hazy atmosphere that shines like an azure ring against the black. It almost looks inviting.

Our exceedingly long orbital period gives us an average velocity of only 210 meters per second, barely moving compared to the blistering speed with which we traveled here. To be in freefall again only adds to our sensation of floating above these frozen worlds. The slow pace greatly adds to our knowledge of this strange planet as our instruments have ample time to scrutinize the surface turning slowly beneath them.

The planet varies wildly in color depending on the region: stark white, charcoal gray, ruddy brown. There are very few craters, suggesting the surface is relatively young and refreshing itself through geologic activity. Or perhaps this region of space is particularly empty.

One basin in particular resembles Arctic sea ice, subdivided into odd polygonal sections. We have noted what appear to be geysers of methane ice from its primary moon Charon and are anxiously looking for the same phenomenon on Pluto. We have also counted four more secondary moons, all in higher orbits and geologically inactive.

Nitrogen ice is of course everywhere, but there are signs that this may also vary with location. We have transmitted a fresh packet of observational data for the geology team's perusal. Gregoriy and Alexi have been poring over it for hours, contemplating the effects of rapidly heating densely packed gases that are within a few dozen degrees of absolute zero. How much energy will it take, over how long, to bring them up to triple point when they could change phases with no warning? If I am to attempt a landing, it would be good to know if the ground is about to explode beneath my rockets.

❆   ❆   ❆

What plutonium balls these guys had. It hadn't been enough to build a nuclear pulse ship, they figured why not land on Pluto just to plant the flag and stake a claim for Mother Russia? We'd beaten them to the Moon and apparently they were eager to make up for that.

❆   ❆   ❆

Arkangel **Commander's Log**
14 Aug 1991

After two weeks of closely studying Pluto's surface through our optical telescope, I must I confess to having spent entirely too much time imagining what it will be like down there. Not that the exercise is without merit, mind you. A good pilot must always study the terrain and environment first.

After completing two orbital periods, we are now satisfied with our maps of the planet. Not wanting to unduly influence my comrades, I left each one alone to determine their own suggestions for the attempted landing zone. Fortunately, we each arrived at the same conclusions independently. There is a promising area at 26.00N 153.00E adjacent to a large basin of nitrogen ice which appears to have enough solid ground to afford a landing.

When not frittering away our time at the telescope, we have been diligently preparing the LK-M. The vehicle has held up well but the hard suit has demanded my full attention. I do not question its deep-sea provenance, but we cannot know how well it has been adapted to Pluto's environment until the time comes.

Dress rehearsals have not revealed any surprises, other than the ball joints in each limb require a generous amount of lubrication in vacuum. I spent three hours inside the suit myself yesterday and am satisfied with its ability to maintain pressure and respond to my movements. Joint articulation improves considerably as the suit warms up, but that will take valuable time on the surface. We have devised an alternative procedure to leave the protective fabric enclosure attached to LK-M through descent and landing. It will be jettisoned on the surface prior to the EVA. Given the presence of atmosphere we agree it is best to keep the suit as well-protected as possible during descent and approach. The mass penalty will be negligible and it will keep us on schedule. Otherwise, the time and power drain necessary to warm it up threatens to be too limiting.

We eagerly await the mission director's approval of our plans. Onward!

23

Arkangel **Commander's Log**
16 Aug 1991
Surface Operations Report

Descent and approach to landing successful. Due to our exceedingly slow orbital velocity, LK-M's aeroshell behaved perfectly. I was in fact able to use it to adjust my lift vector and steer the craft toward the targeted landing zone well beyond the point where we had expected to burn propellant. This was most fortunate as the haze layers camouflaged some unusual terrain features which only became visible when they were directly beneath me.

Pluto's snowdrifts are a crazy quilt of varying features, most notably bladed spires of ice that in some cases rise hundreds of meters above the surface. Here I was concerned about fields of nitrogen icebergs or subsurface ice but having to maneuver clear of those white cliffs was an unwelcome surprise. At one point I was startled by turbulence from beneath, no doubt more nitrogen unleashed by the heat of my landing rockets.

This at least presented a better vantage point from which to see my landing zone. Stark white ice gave way to ruddy brown crust just beyond the frozen dunes, where I was able to find a suitable clearing.

LK-M now sits at 26.12.38N 152.58.08E, or so Gregoriy tells me from his perch in stationary orbit aboard our Soyuz transfer vehicle. I trust those numbers because they are not his! Alexi is acting as our mission manager aboard Arkangel and has checked the math using our almanac and the old slide rule I keep in the flight station. Only after he'd verified my sight reductions the hard way would he resort to a pocket calculator.

The lander came to rest six degrees off vertical; within tolerance but just enough tilt to be aggravating. Orientation is Z-negative, which means I practically fall into the hard suit's access hatch face-first if I am not careful. Suit checkout is nominal and it is ready to go as soon as I am. And I am ready to go now, but have reluctantly deferred to my crewmates. They need rest and I want them at their most alert during my EVA.

❈   ❈   ❈

17 Aug 1991

Sleep was fitful as it has become quite cold inside LK-M, more so than we predicted. Fuel cells are working at the desired output but it takes more insulation than this little lander provides to keep such enervating cold at bay. If we ever come back, a radioisotope generator might be wise. The residual heat alone would be nice right now.

The forward porthole has frosted over so there is no visibility. If there are to be any more observations of this world, then I must venture outside.

❈   ❈   ❈

(Surface EVA Report transcript, as relayed to *Arkangel* **via Cosmonaut G. Bagorov aboard Soyuz TMK-1, callsign "Dvina")**

0:01 Completed hard suit checkout and entered via aft access port, a much easier task in freefall than even in Pluto's one-tenth g. The entry portal is quite small and there are no good footholds once inside. It became necessary to simply hang onto the hatchway and dive in feet-first. Any future crews will want to practice this more frequently while under thrust, particularly if their expeditions are to worlds with higher gravity.

0:13 Closed outer LK-M and inner suit hatchways and successfully completed pre-excursion checklists. Articulation joints functional but somewhat stiff; expected to improve with use. Pressurization holding at 14.2 psi, internal temperature 18° C. Battery draw spiked to 67 amps during power-on sequence in response to the extreme cold, now holding steady at 48 amps. Anticipate no more than three hours of surface activity at this rate.

0:37 Final suit checkout complete.

0:39 Detached from LK-M. Ready for descent.

0:42 I am at the base of the ladder, standing on footpad. The surface texture is rough gravel embedded in what I assume is nitrogen ice. The ground immediately around LK-M looks like shattered glass, the frozen nitrogen's reaction to suddenly having a heat source.

Suit skin temperature holding steady within fifty degrees of ambient, not enough to make the nitrogen change phase. It should be safe to step off.

0:43 Standing on the shoulders of our comrades, I make this great leap forward on behalf of the people of the Soviet Union!

I am now on the surface of Pluto.

Directly ahead, I can see stark white dunes of more nitrogen ice. Some blue-green highlights would indicate there is frozen methane out there as well. Jumbles of what resemble icebergs clutter the shore, while the ice cliffs that gave me trouble during approach appear in the distance like giant sails on a frozen ocean. There are occasional columns of mist rising from furrows in the ground; perhaps there is some subsurface convection sublimating the frozen gases. The sun is a distant lightbulb hung above the blue haze that clings to the horizon.

0:50 Contingency samples have been taken and are secure in my collection pouch.

It took some effort to open the auxiliary equipment bay on the descent stage as it was frozen over, but I was able to successfully assemble and plant our flag. The sight of it with our loyal little LK-M among Pluto's surreal icescape may come to rival Alexi's Saturn photographs. The Americans can have the Moon. When what we have done here becomes known, the world will know what "manifest destiny" truly means. And we will have a good laugh and a drink at their expense.

0:52 Beginning my traverse downslope to the "beach." I step cautiously, as the ice shatters beneath me if not from weight then from the temperature differential. Clouds of ice crystals follow every step.

1:28 I walk along the edge of a sea of ice. From a distance it seemed rough, pebbly, clustered into great polygonal zones like ice floes. Up close, it is hard to describe. A blanket of more ice crystals, like snow, covers what appears to be an endless plain of something I have trouble identifying.

They are of course frozen, like everything else on this world, and rounded into rough spheres. I have heard of a similar phenomenon occurring in the coastal regions of Siberia, where ocean currents and winds combine to create fields of snowballs. That is the best I can describe it: snowballs, what must be millions of them, as far as I can see.

Other than for my presence here, there are no artificial impurities to blemish them. They are translucent white with iridescent colors that change depending on the angle of light, but generally remain in the blue and green ends of the spectrum. Under closer examination beneath my suit lamps, each appears to be layered around a distinctly darker core. Might these be the source of the organic molecules our spectroscopes detected?

2:13 Beginning second leg of traverse, I am leaving the frozen sea behind and heading back upslope. Disappointing, as the ground ahead appears less interesting.

2:57 Final leg of traverse and I will need to finish early. It took much more effort than anticipated to retrieve the core sample. Thorough as it was, the EVA training on Severny Island could not have duplicated the conditions here. Regardless, I must hurry back to the lander before my suit batteries are depleted. The cold is taking its toll; I am impressed that they have held out this long to be truthful.

❧   ❧   ❧

Jack hadn't given the political imagery much thought before. Now as they approached Pluto themselves, the thought of the Hammer and Sickle planted like a marker at the end of the solar system was chilling. They had actually done it.

He rubbed the sleep from his eyes. He desperately wanted to just chuck all of this and get back to his real job, which Traci was doing for him on top of her pilot duties. And just letting Daisy manage more and more of the spacecraft was threatening to turn them into passengers.

It left him continually stunned at what the Russians had managed to do with what amounted to 1970s technology. That they didn't fully trust pocket calculators yet, choosing a slide rule instead. That was some real engineering. He'd have to find that thing once they boarded. He had to admit, it was amazing what you could do with one once you figured it out. You had to be careful, though, with a logarithmic scale. Choose the wrong scale or get careless, and your numbers could be all over the place. Better off choosing random numbers and hoping.

Random. Random numbers.

Like the kind you could generate with a slide rule encoder . . .

He about fell out of his seat scrambling for the wall interface, then remembered his smartwatch. "Daisy!" he shouted, unnecessarily. "Look in your archives for any kind of calculating tools the Russians might have put onboard."

Jack hadn't been this obsessed with crafting a precise choice of words since his time in uniform, decoding and translating Russian radio traffic intercepted by drones above the Black Sea. Getting that wrong could have easily started big trouble depending on the attitude of whoever occupied the White House at the time. He'd quickly learned to shut that out, as whatever spin he might have thrown on his translations was irrelevant. Often the little details which he'd considered rather important—like mechanized infantry massing along their western frontier—were just as easily ignored by the National Command Authority.

Decode, translate, transmit, repeat. Don't obsess over context or intent, that was for the spooks back in Washington. His reports were just one piece of a much larger puzzle being put together by the big shots in Fort Meade.

The other lesson he'd learned was that even though they might have the big picture, sometimes one guy on the ground with good eyes and trained ears could see an awful lot that remained opaque to the Pentagon's brain trust. Multiple battalions become a regiment, regiments become a division, and the next thing you know there's an entire army corps about two day's drive from Kiev. Even that wasn't the whole story: local sources talking about psyops teams infiltrating the population, provoking unrest and general mayhem which kind of dovetails with the raid on our logistics depot last night. Oh, and their Black Sea fleet has pretty much blockaded Odessa so all of our favorite bars have been overrun by surly Russians in Popeye suits. You guys plan on doing anything about it?

Of course not, the reply had been. *Not that we owe you an answer, Sergeant, but since you're being so insistent . . .*

Thus had his career as a crypto-linguist ended. Get too good at your work and next thing you know, you're shunted off into a staff job and the brass go on making decisions without your permission. How dare they?

For as long as it had taken the Pentagon to move back then, right now the turnaround time from Pluto to Earth felt like carrier pigeons in comparison. Four hours each way, with who knew how many hours in between while Owen's mission team processed the information. Which meant if he had his message ready to go as soon as he went on watch, Houston might reply before his shift ended. He didn't want it coming in the middle of Roy's watch for a number of reasons, the first being that it would almost certainly result in an impatient knock on his door in the middle of the night—whatever passed for "night" out here.

Jack turned back through the logs. Once they could predictably match characters to likely logarithmic scales, the pattern became visible. And when it was visible, cracking Vaschenko's cipher had been laughably easy.

The gnawing question had been *why*. They had been the only humans to visit Saturn. Vaschenko had been the first person to land on another world since Apollo, and it had been audacious. If they couldn't be first to the Moon, they could for sure stake their claim to the frontier of the whole solar system. Why not trumpet that for the whole world?

The answer came within the one log entry that would have made heads explode all over the Kremlin:

❈ ❈ ❈

21 August 1991

We have received order 1991.08.5a for an immediate direct return to Earth orbit. More information is required as this is in conflict with the current burn schedule for the Neptune and Uranus flybys. Besides not completing the planned grand tour of the outer planets, our return trajectory has been carefully calculated to take advantage of their gravity. While our spacecraft is more capable than any yet deployed, it is not unlimited. Half of our propellant was consumed just to make orbit at Pluto. A direct return will require a new set of state vectors and careful recalculation of consumables. We cannot simply point our nose at Earth and begin igniting our nuclear slugs.

Related, we did not receive the proper authorization codes for this order. Please confirm that the order comes directly from the office of Chairman Gorbachev.

❋   ❋   ❋

And that was that. From three billion miles away, Vaschenko was savvy enough to have sniffed out the mounting unrest in the Kremlin against Gorbachev. He'd started toying with encoding messages and had waited to stick it to them after they'd launched their coup attempt: *Nyet, Comrades*. No giant space battlewagon was coming to smite your enemies and stun the world.

Just like that, Vaschenko had neutered their greatest achievement. He'd taken it away as a propaganda tool, as a terror weapon, and an engineering triumph. No wonder they'd written him off as a mutineer. He'd made it so they had no choice but to keep it secret, and for that he'd also needed to keep his intentions secret. Better that everybody else live out their lives thinking it had been just one more Soviet space disaster that the West had never known about.

It had to be simple, but it had to be discoverable so the whole world didn't come crashing down on his head when the Kremlin finally realized their hero cosmonauts had just flipped them the galactic finger. He must have figured the rest of the world didn't need to know the Russians had a giant nuke thrower parked at the edge of the solar system; things were unstable enough.

The trick was to start at the right location, otherwise it'd all be gibberish. That was where Daisy came in, whipping through likely permutations that would've taken Jack the rest of his life to figure out by trial and error:

IT IS MOST LIKELY A POLYALPHABETIC SUBSTITUTION CIPHER. A SLIDE RULE COULD BE USED AS A RANDOM NUMBER GENERATOR. IT WOULD ALSO BE POSSIBLE TO DECODE THE KEY PROGRESSION ONCE A PATTERN WAS IDENTIFIED.

"So it's like a Vigenère cipher?" Jack asked. "By chance did the Soviets keep an E6B aboard their spacecraft?"

I DO NOT UNDERSTAND YOUR REFERENCE.

"It's a circular slide rule. Real common in aircraft for figuring out wind and airspeed conversions. I know there were versions adapted for spaceflight in the old days."

STAND BY . . . YES. DOES THE TERM "WHIZ WHEEL" SOUND CORRECT?

He laughed. "It absolutely does. I think we found our cipher."

I WILL LOOK FOR LIKELY NUMERICAL SOLUTIONS BETWEEN ONE AND THIRTY-THREE.

"Good idea," Jack said. No point exceeding the number of characters in their alphabet. "I think he gave away the first one just to tip them off. It looks like he started with a variation of the old 'Rotate 13' cipher."

AGREED, EXCEPT THE DIVISOR WOULD MOST LIKELY BE ELEVEN DUE TO THE NUMBER OF CYRILLIC CHARACTERS.

The concept was simple, but as usual the trick came in applying it. If it was a substitution cipher, all he needed to know was how far ahead to count. In English, a thirteen-character transposition meant A became N, B became O, and so on. With twenty-six letters, thirteen characters divided the alphabet easily in two. That made eleven a natural choice for Cyrillic.

So Vlad hadn't wanted to make it easy for Moscow. Who knew how long it had taken the Kremlin to figure out their hero cosmonaut was toying with them? How long after complaining about garbled transmissions had they realized he was trying to tell them something?

Maybe they never had. When something that obvious is staring you in the face, the tendency was to overlook it.

Jack turned to his new task with relish. Once a spook, always a spook. And where he had expected to uncover talk of a crew mutiny, what he did find was perhaps more bewildering:

❈   ❈   ❈

ОБРАЗЦЫ ПОВЕРХНОСТИ

❈   ❈   ❈

It was gibberish even in Russian, roughly translated to English as even more gibberish:

❈   ❈   ❈

UNIR FHESNPR FNZCYRF

❈   ❈   ❈

But transposed using every eleventh character in Russian:

❈   ❈   ❈

HAVE SURFACE SAMPLES.

❈ ❈ ❈

There was more:

❈ ❈ ❈

СПЕКТРОСКОПИЯ ПОДТВЕРЖДАЕТ ОРГАНИЧЕСКИЕ МОЛЕКУЛЫ. АМИНОКИСЛОТ.
SPECTROSCOPY CONFIRMS ORGANIC MOLECULES. AMINO ACIDS.

❈ ❈ ❈

And then this:

❈ ❈ ❈

СТРУКТУРЫ В ЗАВИСИМОСТИ ОТ ОСНОВНЫХ ТИПОВ РНК
STRUCTURES ACCORDING TO RNA BASE TYPES.

❈ ❈ ❈

And in case they still didn't believe him:

❈ ❈ ❈

ОСТАВЛЯЯ НАСТОЯЩЕЕ МЕСТО. ВАХТА ДЛЯ ПОСЫЛЬНОГО.
REMAINING PRESENT LOCATION. WATCH FOR MESSENGER.

❈ ❈ ❈

It ended with a random collection of numbers:

❈ ❈ ❈

−5.6635..1.3994..2.3463..229.5449..287.928..2453772.5480

❈ ❈ ❈

Jack looked up from the pad he'd been scribbling on. "Daisy? You see anything significant with these numbers? Maybe a key to more ciphers?"

THEY ARE ORBITAL ELEMENTS. SEMI-MAJOR AXIS, ECCENTRICITY, INCLINATION . . .

"Got it." That should have been obvious to an astronaut. Jack smacked himself in the head. "It's the return orbit for that Soyuz they shot down, isn't it?"

THAT IS CORRECT.

Jack stared out into the darkness, vainly searching for a glimpse of their destination. The rest of the story waited aboard *Arkangel*. Vaschenko must have kept some kind of diary; his writing style suggested there was more he was holding back. Finding it would be Priority One when Jack finally got aboard that ship.

In the meantime, he would have to settle for the thought of Owen's team crapping bricks when this missive came sailing over the transom in four hours:

❊   ❊   ❊

//APPENDIX TO MISSION STATUS REPORT / 081205UTC//
SUBMITTED BY ENG J. TEMPLETON:
ANALYSIS OF *ARKANGEL* LOGBOOK REVEALED CODED INFORMATION WITHIN TEXT. CIPHER KEY EXTRACTED FROM MAIN TEXT AND DESCRIBED IN APP. II. WILL CONFIRM ONCE EQUIPMENT RECOVERED FROM SPACECRAFT.
SUMMARY OF DECIPHERED TEXT FOLLOWS:
1.   COMPLEX ORGANICS DISCOVERED.
2.   CREW COLLECTED SAMPLES OF RNA BASE PROTEINS AND AMINO ACIDS.
3.   CODED TEXT CONFIRMS CREW REFUSAL TO RETURN AFTER 1991 COUP. INCLUDED TLE FOR SOYUZ SAMPLE RETURN MISSION.
4.   MORE TO FOLLOW.
//MSG ENDS//

❊   ❊   ❊

Short, sweet, and to the point. That's all he knew, so perhaps they could shed some light on it. He rather doubted that, but it would get their attention.

Jack had hit the "send" button at about six in the morning Houston time, which meant it came across Capcom's message feed a little after ten: just in time for the mission management team's daily status briefing. It was the last of a three-hour routine of information gathering Owen Harriman engaged in each morning, filling his brain with the latest and most complete reports possible for a ship that was now over three billion miles from home. He, in turn, dutifully relayed this same information in condensed form to the NASA administrator, who then repackaged it into an even more tightly selected condensate for the White House. Like the old party game of telephone, Owen could only hope whatever he passed on upstairs still resembled the same information once the President had digested it. Sometimes it was a struggle to convince the politicians that they weren't hiding evidence of little green men up there, which made it a wonderful time for Jack Templeton to inform them that the Russians had apparently been hiding evidence of little green men up there.

"He said *what*?" Owen tried to maintain his composure while dabbing the fresh coffee stains from his shirt and checking to see if he'd sprayed anyone nearby.

The lead flight director pushed the printout of *Magellan*'s latest message traffic across the table. "Looks like they found life out there," he said laconically, which appeared to be his only setting. "Or at least all the necessary ingredients."

Owen rubbed his temples as he read and reread Jack's message. "Has anyone else seen this?"

"Negative."

"Not clear if Roy signed off on it," he said. "We're not dealing with a stir-crazy astronaut, are we?"

"That would probably be easier," the flight surgeon interjected. "Pump him full of Valium and keep him in his cabin for the rest of the trip."

Owen frowned. The room was silent for several minutes as they waited for his response. "I don't recall getting into this business because it sounded easy," he said. "This is what we *do*, people. We finally started sending astronauts somewhere again and went for the Hail Mary pass all the way out to the ass-end of the solar system because in one hellacious cosmic irony, the *Russians beat us to it*."

"Last time they did that we ended up on the Moon," the flight director pointed out. "This one was a little more unexpected."

"*Unexpected* would've been Neil and Buzz finding Marvin the Martian waiting to stamp their passports," Owen said. "Or, you know, finding a derelict spacecraft in orbit at Pluto. The proverbial Overton window's been shifted enough to where nothing should surprise us."

"It's not like we haven't been looking for life out there ever since people could first see that far," Flight agreed.

Owen sighed. "I need to pay our friend a visit."

Now almost ninety years old, Rhyzov had grown noticeably frail over the intervening years since Owen had first tracked him down in

Moscow. Round-the-clock nursing staff attended to him and kept him company, assisted by the plainclothes guard who was always close by. Rhyzov was of course free to go wherever he wished were his mobility not so limited; the guard was there to keep interested parties out.

Rhyzov's bed was an articulated and heavy hospital-grade contraption that looked as if it could do everything but make his breakfast. Around him were moving boxes, the last of which were being tended to by a relocation team that looked suspiciously military. For movers, they were unusually fit and clean cut. They discreetly excused themselves as Owen sat by the bed.

Rhyzov greeted him with a tired smile, which Owen returned. "Anatoly," he said, looking around. "I am so sorry."

"Bah," Rhyzov dismissed his apology. "Nothing is forever. Did not bring much anyway." He eyed Owen's briefcase, knowing he wouldn't be carrying it if he didn't need to. "You have something for me?"

Owen unlocked his briefcase to remove a printout of Jack's message, which he handed over. "Templeton was able to decipher some coded text within the mission logs." He pointed at the paper. "Is this why the crew mutinied?"

Rhyzov's eyes widened. "Explains much. Coup is too obvious, no? Military was eager to call it mutiny and be done." So he hadn't known there was more to the story.

"That's it? They didn't want to deliver a potential weapons platform back to an unstable dictatorship. We could've told you that."

"Good. So you don't believe either. I think your man Templeton is right, Owen. Rest of the story, as you say."

"I don't understand. How would Party authority be undermined by cosmonauts finding a few complex organics?" An understatement considering some of them were RNA strands. That alone threatened to turn a whole lot of origin theories inside out.

Rhyzov's aged eyes glimmered. "You are too young to remember, and I am too old to forget. Party was everything, and everything was Party. Generations were raised to believe history began with them, that no power on Earth or in Heaven could supplant the supreme Soviet People." He scowled as if the words had turned sour as they passed his lips.

"Their propaganda went that far? All the way down to the origins of life?"

"To go against party doctrine was considered fundamentally insane. Official position was *Arkangel*'s crew mutinied during coup and abandoned spacecraft. This proves truth was worse." The old man laughed to himself, ending with a rough cough. His gray eyes beamed at Owen. "Don't you see? What drove cosmonauts to revolt was the most terrible affront possible to Kremlin: They found God."

24

Mission Day 300
Acceleration 0.0 m/s^2 (0 g)
Pluto Orbit

Despite its diminutive size, Pluto up close was no less imposing than Jupiter even though the gas giant had moons which dwarfed this ice-covered world. Perhaps it was the tiny world's utterly desolate, alien nature. It was just as likely an effect of the extreme distance they'd traveled to get here, where the Sun had become just another star. Still brighter than the rest, but nothing like the life-giving warmth of Earth's safe harbor in the "Goldilocks Zone."

The high albedo of Pluto's frozen surface reflected most of what little sunlight remained out here, which made *Arkangel* surprisingly easy to spot. Its olive green thermal blanketing had faded to the point that the entire spacecraft resembled a dun-colored insect against Pluto's icy glow, like a fly flitting across a bright TV screen. And while they were anxious to finally see this derelict with their own eyes, the heat signature had given it up from thousands of miles away. Unlike the limited batteries of the Soyuz and LK-M vehicles it had carried, *Arkangel* still drew electrical power from an array of radioisotope thermal generators at the base of its service block. The decaying plutonium inside each RTG would continue powering the ship for hundreds of years while standing out like beacons in the cold dark.

With each successive revolution they burned retrograde at high thrust, shifting their orbit to match the derelict spacecraft. This drew them closer with each pass, until they had matched altitudes and could begin chasing *Arkangel* with earnest.

The ship was easily visible from the forward windows, now just a kilometer away. Jack was studying it through Noelle's optical telescope. "It's an old Almaz core, all right. No solar panels, but a whole lot of radiators. It looks like someone stacked a bunch of Dutch windmills on top—hang on." He reached for a fine-focus knob. "The LK-M ascent stage is missing."

"Any signs of it nearby?"

Noelle tuned one of the search antennas and watched its situation display. "No radar returns," she said, "nothing in close proximity."

"So they took it out into a different orbit?" Roy wondered, not liking the thought of unaccounted debris in the same orbit.

"Still want to hold at one klick?" Traci asked. *Arkangel* sat squarely in the video crosshairs at the center of her instrument panel as she held steady, station-keeping with the occasional pulse of control jets.

"Affirmative," Roy said. He chewed his bottom lip, eyes locked on the big ship outside. It looked to be a lot closer than one kilometer. Though larger than *Magellan* due to its massive thrust structure, the old Soviet vessel looked decidedly cramped inside. The station core was mounted to a jumble of supply modules stacked behind it like so many building blocks. They were embedded within a network of girders constituting a dome that supported the massive concave pusher plate. For all its bulk, the actual pressurized area inside *Arkangel* was comparatively small given its intended mission.

"We stick with the mission plan," Roy finally decided. "Jack, you and Traci prep the MSEV."

In size and shape, the unimaginatively named Multi-Mission Space Exploration Vehicle resembled a sleek if overengineered delivery van. Its front end tapered into a hexagonal arrangement of windows set above a bank of floodlights, beneath which were two manipulator arms similar to what might be found on a deep-sea submersible.

Inside it was much less roomy than a delivery van. After entering through the docking port in its tail, they had to swim through a tunnel of equipment and storage racks to land in the comparatively spacious cockpit. As Traci settled into the left seat to begin setting up the pilot's station, Jack started powering up the spacecraft from the engineer's seat. As the little ship came to life, he opened a plastic tube inside his flight bag and removed a roll of aged vellum paper. He carefully unrolled and mounted the contents to a magnetic board behind his seat, releasing with it a potpourri of decades-old odors. The scent of pipe tobacco filled the otherwise antiseptic environment of the MSEV.

Traci looked back at the old schematic. "Nice touch," she said, wrinkling her nose. "Reminds me of my grandpa's house."

"Same reason Owen sent me the original transcripts. A lot can get lost in translation," Jack said. "These were Rhyzov's personal documents. He took them out of his study himself, insisted we bring them along. Owen would've had to throw some weight around to get these on the manifest."

Traci ignored the pun, being caught up in her own work. She flipped her intercom over to the control deck's channel. "Preflight checklists complete, docking node is secured. We're go on your mark."

"You're go," Roy said. "Houston just approved your EVA." Their signal would've been sent nearly four hours ago, just as they were preparing to launch the ship.

"Not like they haven't had a few years to think about it," Jack mumbled.

Traci gently whacked him on the arm. "You're the reason I don't keep us on VOX," she said before thumbing her mic switch. "Understand go for undock. Stand by." She gave Jack a nod and he reached up for the release lever. There was a muffled *thunk*, accompanied by the disconcerting sensation of floating free of their mothership.

"This felt a lot different during shakedown flights," Jack said.

"We were still within sight of home then." Which they definitely weren't anymore. Roy's voice suddenly sounded more distant, or maybe it was just her mind playing tricks. "We show you clear of Node One," he said. "Ready for visual inspection."

"On our way," Traci said, and twisted the attitude control stick in her right hand. The little ship's nose yawed left, bringing *Magellan* back into view as she thrusted them along its length. She brought them to a stop alongside its observation cupola just above the main control cabin. Roy and Noelle waited behind the trapezoidal windows, she waving at them giddily while Roy inspected their ship through a pair of small binoculars. Traci slowly spun the MSEV around its vertical axis for his benefit as Noelle took pictures.

"You look beautiful," Noelle said. "Be sure to get some shots of us, too." Roy was silent, his eyes still hidden behind the binoculars. Satisfied with what he saw, he finally set them free and reached for the microphone. "Visual inspection complete, no anomalies. You're go to proceed."

Arkangel would have been remarkable even if it hadn't been waiting out at the edge of the solar system for decades. It was more aesthetically streamlined than other Soviet-era vehicles, as all of the major components were stacked along the ship's axis of thrust instead of hanging off at odd angles.

Beginning at the ten-meter-wide thrust plate, Traci cautiously piloted them along the vessel's length, up one side and down the other. The concave plate was scorched from the heat of thousands of small thermonuclear explosions, but otherwise appeared to have held up remarkably well. Its base was mounted to a stack of four massive shock absorbers, which showed more evidence of wear: Access panels were clearly marked by scuffed and dented metal with ventilation ports that had become downright filthy. It looked like cleaning the outflow vents had turned into a full-time job. No wonder the ride had gotten rougher as time went on.

Reaching the end of *Arkangel*'s suspension, they passed over a massive assembly of foil-wrapped tanks surrounding a support truss that separated the ship's drive section from its crew modules. Between the tanks were mounted a half-dozen radiator panels which gave the craft its dragonfly appearance. Inside the truss were supply modules that had held over a year's worth of food and repair kits. The surrounding tanks mostly held water, which made sense despite the tremendous weight penalty: They would've been an excellent radiation shield.

Moving forward, they finally arrived at the crew section. This was more familiar, having been constructed from existing "FGB" control modules and docking nodes that had eventually been adapted for the ISS. All were covered with olive drab micrometeoroid blankets that had faded over time, turning gray like lawn furniture left outdoors too long. And they were noticeably pockmarked.

Jack whistled. "This thing took a real beating." Looking back down the length of the ship, that was when he noticed random perforations in its radiator panels. "Micrometeoroids," he said. "Think they got lucky?"

"Several times over." Traci turned the joystick to yaw the MSEV about for a closer look. One of the big cooling wings had a good meter-wide gash in it. "At their velocity, a grain of sand could do an awful lot of damage. Lucky they didn't get holed."

"Maybe they did?" Jack wondered. "Obviously not here, otherwise we wouldn't have half the information they gave us."

"Something important got smashed and didn't become evident until later," she said. "Hard to think what it could've been. All the vitals are internal."

"They coasted after Saturn," Jack reminded her. "Flipped the ship so the thrust plate was pointed forward."

"Smart. Use what they had as a shield when they needed it most." By that point, *Arkangel* was blisteringly fast. Being so close to Saturn's ring system, they had expected damage. She pulsed thrusters to place them abeam the ship's open docking port and thumbed the radio switch by her waist. "Node Two is clear. No signs of damage. We're going to try the claw on it first."

"You're go," Roy answered. She nodded to Jack, signaling him to unlock the manipulator arms.

Of the two mechanical arms, one was set up for heavy grappling while the other was built for finer manipulation—like opening a forty-year-old hatch. He flexed his right hand and inserted it into a mechanical glove. Outside, a camera on the arm's robotic wrist came to life, filling the small screen atop his control panel. As Jack extended his forearm and curled his fist, the mechanical appendage followed. "Little closer, please," he said after he was satisfied the arm was responsive.

She gently pulsed thrusters once more, stopping them within a meter of the ship. "That's as close as I dare."

"Should be enough." He reached out and grabbed the outer door's handle. Mechanical feedback through his controls hinted at little resistance, and the spin lever gave way with a gentle pull. After that, he was easily able to unwind the latch and expose the docking node to vacuum. Just outside their windows, a silent puff of ice vapor escaped as the little compartment's remaining air crystallized. The door bumped open hard, as if something pushed against it from inside.

That was when the body fell out.

25

Mission Day 301
Acceleration 0.0 m/s^2 (0 g)
Pluto Orbit

"*Gaah!*"

Absorbed with keeping the MSEV properly oriented alongside *Arkangel*, Traci had been oblivious to this macabre development until Jack cried out.

"What?" She turned with alarm. "Oh . . . *oh crap.*"

"No kidding!" Jack had reflexively let go of the hatch and was now, through the manipulator arm, holding on to a dead cosmonaut by the leg of his EVA suit.

Roy's voice crackled over the radio. "What's your situation?" he demanded.

Traci answered and described what they'd found. "Judging by his insignia I think it's the commander."

"You still got him, Jack?"

He shuddered. "Yeah. Not happy about it either."

"Any obvious injuries?"

Traci leaned in for a closer look at the spacesuited corpse on the other side of the window. A tremor rose in her voice. "Um . . . negative, Roy. Suit looks to be intact. I can only see his face, and it's . . . I don't know . . . well preserved? A little bit of air escaped when we cracked the seals, but nothing like a whole compartment's worth. I think he's been in near vacuum for a long time."

After a few second's pause, Roy came back on the radio. "No docking," he said, "and secure that casualty in the outboard service bay until we decide what to do with it. We're going with Plan B."

227

Traci sighed, though she knew it was coming. She'd have made the same call. "Let's get suited up. We're doing this the hard way."

Two hours is a long time to spend sitting idle. Spending that time encased in EVA suits might have counted as torture in some countries, had they not been floating in zero-*g*. At the very least, the pre-breathing process allowed Jack to catch up on some much-needed sleep. He awoke with a start, clawing his way out of a dream filled with zombies in space.

"You okay?"

"Yeah . . . yeah." He fought the urge to yank his visor open, instead opting to adjust the airflow in his suit. "Never did like this part. It gets claustrophobic."

"Seriously? For me it's the other way around. Once we get outside, this glass is the only thing between me and certain death," she said, tapping the faceplate.

"Guess I never thought of it that way. Thanks a lot."

"Anytime." That was all she was willing to let on, as she found spacewalks to be uniquely terrifying. She bit her lip and checked the watch strapped to the cuff on her left wrist. "We've been in here long enough. Time to go for a walk."

"The Big Empty," Jack muttered to himself as they emerged into open space. If anything, it seemed even emptier floating next to a decades-old derelict above an icy globe that wasn't even counted as a planet anymore. The light was ghostly, like a dim winter sunset. Sol was still obviously the nearest star but was at such a distance that it was obscured by the haze of the inner solar system. Jack realized his helmet's sun visor was still down, standard practice for an EVA back in Earth orbit.

When he raised the visor, there was an explosion of light and color and texture. Jack flinched as if he'd just had the wind knocked out of him. *The solar system*, he thought. *We're looking at the* entire *solar system from out here. Like I could spread my arms and wrap the whole thing up.*

Traci's voice interrupted. "You okay?"

"No," he answered. *Are you serious?* "Guess I wasn't expecting this." For months they had been watching their home system steadily recede from behind layers of polycarbonate glass within their protective cocoon. Even their expansive cupola with all its lights out didn't compare to this. When he turned to see her, he noticed she'd already had her sunscreen up and suddenly realized why it had taken her such an inordinately long time to clear the outer door.

"Should've warned you," she said. "Sorry." She drifted toward *Arkangel's* open airlock with Jack following suit, then took care to clip their safety tethers to the door. The little chamber was familiar inside, the same standard-issue Russian tech used for the ISS core except all of the warning labels and instruction placards were in Cyrillic without an English translation in sight. The hatch and airlock were familiar enough though; one more carryover from the old ISS. He reached for the pressurization controls mounted by the inner door, depressed a standby switch, and was quickly rewarded with amber status lights. "Vacuum inside," Jack warned. They'd be keeping their helmets on.

"It's still under power," Traci said, unsurprising given that *Arkangel* was powered by radioisotope generators. Unconsciously they'd halfway expected the entire ship to have been intentionally shut off. "Okay, let's do this." She pressed a selector switch on her wrist controls and pointed at Jack to do the same. "Roy, we're switching to vox from here on. We'll give you a running commentary."

Jack spun the latch. "Opening inner door."

The inside of *Arkangel's* control module was, unsurprisingly, a mess. Long-duration spacecraft tended to get cluttered more than most, sometimes due to hasty repairs but more often than not from improvised workarounds of whatever harebrained arrangements the engineers had settled for back on the ground. Russian craft were especially susceptible to this phenomenon.

After fumbling about in the dark with nothing but his suit's headlamp to light the way, Jack eventually located the ship's controls. He brushed his gloved hands lightly over an adjacent electrical panel, hoping they didn't find a bunch of popped breakers. Resetting them in an unfamiliar ship after so many years would be a quick way to start an electrical fire.

There were a handful of open breakers; fortunately none of them went to the interior lights. Jack returned to the controls and quickly found the light switches, right next to the environmental controls. "Lights," he said and depressed the switch. Fluorescent bulbs flickered to life along the length of the module.

Arkangel was dominated by alternating panels of dirty white and sage green that curved around its interior. Along its sidewalls crept knots of pipes and cables and conduits, man-made vines choking the ship.

"Very Russian," Traci said. "I'd have picked a different color scheme, though." She admired their devotion to brute functionality, but it had to get depressing after being confined to this space for so long.

"They never were much for human factors," Jack agreed. His single flight aboard a Soyuz several years before had been a uniquely uncomfortable experience.

Traci's brow knitted as she considered the layout. "I'm not so sure this time—check out their control stations. They're all longitudinal."

Jack looked up and down the control module. Sure enough, they were looking down a cylinder with different levels of instrument panels and seats arranged in circular tiers and connected by ladders along the compartment's length. "Of course—they were under near-constant acceleration. They had to stack the inside vertically, along the axis of thrust."

"Like a building," Traci said. Staring down the length—depth—of the control module, she was reminded of an old missile silo. "They got it right, long before we did." They'd had an unexpected struggle to arrange *Magellan*'s layout in a similar fashion. The tendency to stack a spacecraft's innards like an oceangoing vessel was hard to overcome, though they'd finally prevailed with the compelling argument that constant acceleration, even at one-tenth *g*, still counted as gravity and demanded they plan accordingly.

Jack paused at what appeared to be the flight engineer's station and traced a hand along a schematic etched into the aluminum panel. "Lots of handwritten instructions," he said warily. Nearby, an exposed coolant pump showed disturbing traces of fire damage. After they'd cleaned up the mess, they'd evidently bypassed its power supply in favor of something more reliable. "We're going to have to be real careful about which systems we turn back on, Roy. This ship's been kludged together beyond recognition."

"Figures as much," he answered, "when your shakedown flight and first mission are the same thing." They were lucky to have made it as far as they had.

Traci pulled open a small but heavy door. "Found their film storage." She gingerly lifted out half a dozen cartridges of 70mm film and placed them in a cloth bag on her hip. "Pushing on to the next module," she said, heading for the living quarters. Based on the Soviet TKS spacecraft, it was another building block of the old Mir space station similar to the control module.

The living spaces had been kept meticulously clean in comparison. A tightly packed bundle of power conduits and coolant pipes flowed in from the control module through the living spaces to continue aft into the supply section. Otherwise, very few vital systems were routed through here.

More importantly, for being cooped up so long they would've needed a tidy living area for their own sanity. Despite its fastidious appearance, Jack felt a chill as he entered. It was one thing to rummage through a stranger's office, it was another matter entirely to be inside their home. There were no individual rooms like they had on *Magellan*, just three bunks stacked one atop the other down the centerline, it being the only section wide enough to accommodate them. The same ladder traversed the length of the module, opposite from the bunks. They had at least thought to add some curtains across each one for some measure of privacy.

Jack reached out for the nearest curtain and pulled it aside. The small bed looked like it could have been at home aboard a naval vessel: A mattress rested atop a set of small drawers, no doubt full of clothing. The space between the bed and the module's curved sidewall offered shelving for more personal items—this one had a small collection of books, in addition to a few faded pictures. He reached out for one of the books when its spine caught his eye. "Russian poetry," he said admiringly. "At least one of them had taste."

"Pretty sure that's the commander's bunk," Traci said. It was nearest to the control module, which is how he would've wanted it.

Jack nodded to himself and kept searching, this time more cautiously, as if it would've bothered the dead man outside. It was easier to be more aloof about the other two cosmonauts as they'd yet to be found. Jack and the others assumed they were aboard the missing Soyuz, or perhaps even down on the surface as there was the lander to account for as well.

He moved aside a few more volumes, all soft-bound leather, probably the lightest the crew could've gotten away with, and wondered if they'd worked out who would bring what ahead of time. Aboard *Magellan*, they'd had the luxury of individual tablets and e-readers that could be loaded up with thousands of books, songs, and movies. But even for this old Soviet craft's enormous capability to move around the solar system, they'd still had to launch the thing piece by piece. Mass and gravity were always the great equalizers.

Their skipper had evidently been quite a bookworm, and his collection represented a "greatest hits" of Russian classics: Pushkin, Dostoevsky, and Tolstoy were all accounted for.

Of the dead commander's impressive collection, the most surprising was a single-volume copy of *The Lord of the Rings*. In English. How'd he get that up here? Jack opened it to find an inscription on the title page, smudged in pencil:

❧　❧　❧

To the good Lieutenant "V"—
Not all who wander are lost.
Regards,
"Captain Cowboy"

❧　❧　❧

Also in English, and by the looks of it *American* English. There had to be one whopper of a story behind that one.

Jack placed it back in its cradle and reached for the logbooks. He started to flip through one as best he could through the stiff gloves of a pressure suit, when he came upon a section which didn't quite square with the rest. As he clumsily pushed the pages back and forth, it was apparent that it hadn't been part of the original text.

"Not much time for browsing," Traci warned him. "You can bring those back if you'd like."

"I will," he said, and shoved the book into a cargo pouch.

"We need to keep moving, Jack."

"Then keep going," he said, more irritably than she deserved. She was right. "I don't want to leave without his personal logs. Can't solve the puzzle if I don't have all the pieces."

"True," she agreed. "Promise you won't leave without me?"

"Not on your life," he said, noticing a hinge embedded in the shelf. "I won't be far behind. This place gives me the creeps."

"Just because a body flew out when we opened the front door? Don't be such a pansy," she said, moving through the next hatch.

"I never figured you for one of those coffee-shop white girls that make horror movies possible," he said. "So you hear a scary noise from an abandoned house in the woods and think it'd be a *fabulous* idea to go find out what caused it?"

"You forget where I came from. We hardly ever went into the woods without a shotgun."

"Nobody goes anywhere alone," Roy cut in sternly. "Whatever you're doing, Jack, either button it up now or get it on your way back."

"Understood." Jack opened the panel embedded in a little shelf beside the empty bunk. Inside it he found another soft-cover book, filled with handwritten notes: the commander's personal log. Until recently, he thought that would be the hidden treasure they all needed to find. Then he lifted the logbook out. Behind it floated a small plastic disc, just a few inches across and inscribed with numbers and scales: a whiz wheel, the circular slide rule pilots and astronauts used to rely on in the days before pocket calculators. Under his headlamp, he could see pencil marks where it had been indexed most frequently.

"Done. Found Vaschenko's personal log and his cipher key," he said triumphantly, and stuffed both items into his pouch with the others. "Moving aft."

They found the rest of the spacecraft to be in similar condition—bypassed wiring, open access panels, and jury-rigged systems spoke to a machine that had been in a constant state of repair. The surprising thing had been how many of them had been tried and proven over years aboard various Russian space stations.

"I don't get it," Traci said. "Other than the drive system and computers, these are systems with a long history. They weren't stupid, sticking with known hardware."

"Except they weren't," Jack pointed out. "Working for two years straight aboard Mir in free fall? That's a lot different than being under constant g."

"Good point," Traci admitted.

"Well, it's not like this is anything we've ever encountered," he said. "Not to mention the whole stack was getting pounded when that accumulator started wearing out. They had a rough ride."

This section consisted of a narrow access tunnel ringed with circular hatchways, each leading to separate supply modules arranged radially outside. As each module had been emptied of its contents, the storage space had been converted into waste compartments much like Jack's crewmates had done with the Cygnus module.

At the end of the tunnel was a hatch that appeared much heavier than the others, marked with a circular placard divided into alternating yellow and black pie wedges in the international warning sign for radiation hazards. They had expected this from studying the ship's design: All those nuclear fuel pellets had to be stored somewhere. Beyond this door would be another layer of radiation shielding, a hardened airlock that opened to vacuum. Inside were supposed to be a pair of rad-hardened spacesuits in case maintenance had ever been needed around the drive system. Judging by the mission records, they'd gotten quite a workout.

Jack waved a Geiger counter across the hatch and around its rim. A steady clicking sounded in their helmet radios. "A few millirems higher than background, but nothing too bad."

"We'll leave that part alone, all the same," Traci said. A grunt from Roy over their headsets signaled his agreement.

It was the final storage module that gave them pause—different from all the others, this one had been kept under power and was quite cold. A biohazard label had been taped to the hatch, and Jack studied the handwritten instructions beneath it. The first word, in Cyrillic, read Образцы: "Samples."

Jack traced a finger down the list of instructions. "It's not actually hazardous, I think."

"You *think*?"

"Meaning I don't believe there's some extraterrestrial super-virus stored in there. No mention of egg sacs filled with alien face-huggers either."

"So what *do* you think?"

Jack considered his words carefully. "If there's actual biological hazards, then these are pretty benign instructions. More about protecting the contents than the cosmonauts."

"But they still had to wear pressure suits inside."

"Because it's really cold in there. Look at all the conduits plugged into here—this accounts for most of the kludge we found up front."

"So nothing about decon? Postexposure protocols?"

"Nothing," Jack said, reading down the list one more time. "Just do a leak check and keep your suit heater cranked up."

Traci nodded her assent, then turned as she called back to *Magellan*. "Roy, I'm recommending we—"

Before she could finish, Jack had begun spinning the lock open. "We're running out of time," he told her over their private channel. "Max heat is going to drain power fast, and I don't feel like doing this again." He pulled the portal open and floated through. Traci swore under her breath and followed.

It was by far *Arkangel*'s best-kept compartment, noticeably missing the scrapes, smudges, and other random blemishes found throughout the rest of the spacecraft. Its walls were bare aluminum with no insulating fabrics or interior panels. There was nothing else between them and open space—a big reason why it was so much colder in here than anywhere else. The other reason was the module's beefed-up air exchangers. Whatever purpose they'd devised for this chamber, they'd wanted it to stay good and cold.

Jack checked the thermometer on his wrist. "Minus forty C." He whistled. "I'd say it's like a meat locker in here, but that would be warmer."

By the looks of it, storage shelves had been brought in from other compartments and mounted to every available flat surface, leaving only a tight walkway aligned with *Arkangel*'s vertical axis—again, set up for a ship that spent much of its time under gravity from constant acceleration. Traci steadied herself against a ledge that ran the length of the module—apparently meant as a work surface, she'd almost expected it to hold a microscope and racks of test tubes. "Reminds me of a laboratory."

Jack studied some of the labels that had been taped to each drawer and storage bin. Most were empty; the few left had been sealed from the outside with silicone repair caulk, most likely lifted from the ship's repair kit. "Specimen labels," he said, as if to support her point.

"Labeled as what?"

"Nothing yet," he said. "Just date, time, and location." It didn't look as if they'd planned to find anything, as very few were written on any kind of preprinted cards. Many were scrap paper torn from personal notebooks. Judging by the dates they'd quickly started to run out of spare paper, so most ended up just been written on duct tape. "If I had to guess—which I do—they were surprised at how much they found. I don't think they came prepared for this."

"Whatever this is," Traci said.

Jack silently moved among the drawers and bins. "They went to a lot of trouble to preserve these samples," he finally said. "Why do that for a bunch of ice and dirt?"

"Okay, now you're worrying me. Where'd this all come from, anyway?"

Jack stopped at the shelf farthest from the entrance. Apparently the earliest collection, this one had neatly lettered signs on actual preprinted labels. His eyes grew wide as he looked inside. "Whoa."

"What is it?"

"I'm not sure." A translucent orb glittered beneath the beam of his helmet lamp, in size and shape resembling a Christmas ornament. Almost perfectly round, it appeared to be made of ice encasing a ruddy brown core. "Same general coloring as the planet surface," Jack said. "Hand me a hazmat bag."

Traci removed a heavy plastic pouch with a zip closure and held it over the drawer. Jack pulled it open, gave it a tap beneath, and the icy sphere floated into the bag. "Tell Noelle she'll want to see this."

26

Mission Day 305

Col. V. Vaschenko—Personal Log

What is human nature? Is all work equally valuable? If the State tells a man to go dig a hole, then fill it back in, is that the same as a man who lays railroad tracks or tends a farm? Or removes a diseased appendix?

That is what I fear we are finding out. Of course some work is more valuable than others—I hope our comrades who assembled this magnificent spacecraft had more incentive to do good work than the man digging ditches just for the sake of it. Pride in their jobs only goes so far when their families are hungry, or they have to scrounge for new shoes for their children.

As a Cosmonaut Hero of the Soviet Union, my family is doing quite well. I look forward to returning to them and retiring from my duties. My next homecoming will be my last. Our son has left for pilot training while our daughter, bless her, has put off going to university in order to remain home with her mother until my return.

It has become impossible to maintain the fiction that I make these sacrifices for them. No, I do this for me.

My path began before our family did, and I did not hesitate when it led me into spaceflight. I did not resist when the missions became longer and longer, and I would have buried anyone who stood between me and the command of this vessel. At first it was for the challenge of riding a rocket into orbit, eventually it became my one true freedom.

No matter how hard Moscow tried to control us, they could not see into our minds. They could not hear our thoughts, peek into our journals, or listen to our conversations—not when we knew how to cut them off. Cosmonauts are nothing if not resourceful. And clever, particularly when surreptitiously defying our would-be masters. No one knows a spacecraft better than the men who live in it for months on end. We could always count on at least one module in Salyut to remain mysteriously silent to ears on the ground.

Writings were another matter. Any journals that we did not want to be seen on our return had ways of disappearing in space. Who knows how many samizdat texts are still in Earth orbit after being "lost" during an EVA? Unfortunate that so much work should be cast into the void, like messages in bottles tossed upon the sea.

That is why we all developed such impressive memories: It was the only way to carry our work with us. It is never talked about back on Earth, but I've no doubt most of my comrades of an independent bent made it a priority to write down the passages they'd memorized before casting the only extant drafts into space.

I can say it worked well for me.

❈   ❈   ❈

Noelle had requested an early shift turnover briefing for reasons she quickly made clear: "They're organic."

Roy's utter lack of reaction hinted at the hushed conversations the couple no doubt had as she was developing her hypothesis.

"Okay," Jack said warily. Why did his philosophical debates with Traci have a way of coming back like this? "But we've found lots of organic material all through the solar system. You know better than any of us that it's not the same thing as finding life."

"Those were just chemical precursors," Noelle said. Her body quivered as she impatiently tapped a foot against the floor restraint. "And I didn't say 'life.' Not yet, anyway."

"So not the same thing as complex hydrocarbons on Titan?" Traci asked. Saturn's largest moon was drowning in liquid methane.

"This is different." She let the word hang for effect.

Jack was feeling impatient. "I'll bite. What's different about it?"

Noelle considered her answer. "There are traces of hydrogen sulfide and hydrogen cyanide all over the surface, and liquid water beneath it. Those are essential nucleic acid precursors. Judging by where they found the samples, they segregated materials by type:

nucleic acids, amino acids, lipids . . . if someone wanted to build a storehouse for life's building blocks, it couldn't have been done any better than Pluto."

"So the Russians came all the way to the end of the solar system forty years ago to build—what? A dry cellar?"

"You're missing my point: They didn't formulate any of this. According to the logs you translated, these all came from the surface."

Roy had arrived at the same conclusion. "No question they did," he said with a sidelong glance at Jack. "But you haven't found anything new yet?"

"Lots of questioning the system, nothing on the organics that wasn't already in the official logs," Jack said. "I must have missed the chapter on *Hey Comrades, we just found alien life.*"

"Not alien," Noelle corrected him. "Certainly these compounds could combine to evolve into anything, but it would still be something we'd be familiar with. These could be the same precursors that eventually populated Earth."

"So is this evidence for panspermia?"

"I'll have to wait on the carbon dating, but it's a strong possibility."

Roy studied the diagram of *Arkangel* taped to a nearby bulkhead. "We have to find that lander."

❈   ❈   ❈

// MSG TXMIT 181304Z //
ATTN/ MAGELLAN CREW
FROM/ NASA HQ
VIA/ JSC FCR
SUBJ/ SAMPLE COLLECTION
1.   RECEIVED YOUR 1933Z TRANSMISSION.
     DIRECTOR'S RESPONSE FOLLOWS:
2.   NO INDICATION MOSCOW WAS AWARE OF 2ND
     SURFACE OP OR SAMPLES HELD IN Z-4 LOG MODULE.
3.   AGREE THIS IS UNUSUAL GIVEN LEVEL OF CONTROL
     NORMALLY EXERCISED BY MOSCOW TSUP BUT NOT
     SURPRISING GIVEN DISTANCE INVOLVED.
4.   ADVISE CAUTION. TREAT SAMPLES AS BIOHAZARDS
     UFN.
// MSG ENDS //

❈   ❈   ❈

"Thanks for the warning," Roy said. While Noelle had readily determined the nature of the samples from Jack and Traci's EVA, they'd studiously avoided the implications.

Traci looked out at *Arkangel*. "So if they took their lander to the surface, then where's the ascent stage?"

Noelle had been wondering the same thing and shuddered at the implication: Both the lander and the extended-duration Soyuz were gone, along with the cosmonauts needed to operate them. "I didn't think LK had that much onboard storage. Could they have made more than one trip to the surface?"

"Pluto's about two-thirds the size of our moon," Traci said. "Maybe that left them enough delta-v to lift off with the descent stage? Could they have brought the whole stack back up here and refueled?"

Roy grunted a "maybe." Though not likely, as they'd tended to build things heavy. "Let's keep our imaginations on the leash. The simplest explanation is a surface expedition went pear-shaped. That would explain the missing Soyuz/LK stack."

Still, they'd gotten all that mass up here somehow. "Now what?" Jack wondered. "At some point they had almost a hundred cubic meters' worth of volume over there stuffed to the rafters and locked behind a door with a big biohazard label pasted to it."

"Which they neglected to tell anyone about," Traci said. "This is *huge*. Why keep it from Moscow?"

Roy's arched eyebrow spoke volumes: Russian mission control had a notorious reputation for micromanaging their cosmonauts to a degree that made Houston look hands-off. Why share anything with a bunch of control freaks if you didn't have to?

"So they didn't plan on coming back?"

Roy grunted another "maybe" and pointed at the logbooks Jack retrieved. "I suspect the answer's somewhere in there."

27

Mission Day 308

Col. V. Vaschenko—Personal Log

Life. We have found the seeds of it here, of all places.

Our results are preliminary and will need to be reproduced by more capable labs in Moscow, but what we have observed here is unmistakable. Chemical signatures of ribose sugars, purines, pyrimidines and phosphates appeared after several layers of the snowball had sublimated away. It is as if the nitrogen ice and these "tholins" act as a preservation medium.

The question that continues to haunt us is: How did they get here? Assuming they are naturally occurring—and I am reluctant to conclude otherwise—what are they doing on Pluto? We have detected signs of other, smaller planetoids out here. There may be a whole belt of trans-Neptunian objects yet to be discovered. Are they similar in makeup?

There is a theory that water and perhaps even biological precursors were transported to Earth by cometary bombardment. Could life have been delivered to our world from here? If so, we have made a tremendous discovery.

❊ ❊ ❊

Jack had retreated to his cubicle, drawing its plastic door shut and turning up a white-noise generator he'd installed on his tablet. He'd tried music at first, but even the wordless movements of classical had been too distracting. The sound of rushing water now filled his cabin, turned up just enough to drown out the incessant rattle of air recyclers and coolant pumps.

Reading anything else in such an environment would've easily put him to sleep, but hidden within the dry recitations of daily life aboard *Arkangel* could be found the spark of individuality and hints of rebellion to come. It was now clear the crew had elected to stay out here, as he'd seen nothing that could've crippled the spacecraft. Which meant they'd elected to defy both Moscow and their own hardwired survival instincts.

Moscow would've been pissed. That it hadn't come across in any of the "official" documents told Jack . . . what?

Nothing. Everything. The old regime had been notorious for papering over any evidence of disagreements within the Party, whatever that meant at the moment. Documents disappeared, individuals airbrushed out of photos, entire towns removed from maps . . . if it made the *nomenklatura* uncomfortable, down the memory hole it went.

These guys had been determined to not be flushed down the memory hole themselves. Moscow may have removed all official records of *Arkangel* and its mission, but their reach couldn't extend to the ship itself. Keeping it safely out here meant that someone, someday, would have to confront the secrets it held. And they clearly hadn't cared how long that might take.

Nor had Vaschenko apparently cared how long it took for him to get to the point. For someone as steeped in classic Russian literature as this guy had been, it sure didn't show up in his writing. Then again, Jack reminded himself, *War and Peace* wasn't exactly a quick summer read. And he hadn't had to actually study a document like this since his days at the Defense Language Institute. Translating was one thing, *understanding* it took the work to a whole new level.

The "unofficial" commander's log was infinitely more interesting than the sanitized reports he'd transmitted back to Moscow. Had they suspected there was an embedded message within? The KGB and GRU would have made cracking it a high priority, right up until the Soviet Union collapsed and irretrievably shifted their priorities with it.

It must have made the control freaks in the Kremlin nuts. They'd lost control of their most ambitious—and secret—space mission. Once it was made public, they'd counted on it to rekindle pride in Mother Russia and keep the proles' minds occupied with something other than the misery they lived under.

Good luck with that, he thought. Those old farts had been delusional. Such was the nature of politicians, particularly the totalitarian variety. Grand visions of Man Conquering Space only went so far when your average Muscovite had to spend all day waiting in line for stale bread and single-ply toilet paper. How many of them looked up and wondered what their brave and glorious cosmonauts were wiping *their* butts with?

That would've made the space program especially attractive back in the bad old days, he realized: You might be stuck in orbit inside a malfunctioning tin can, but at least you had everything you needed at arm's reach.

It was a shame, because these guys were for-real Space Heroes and this was the kind of adventure people write books and make movies about. That the Russians had run with a concept first proposed in the 1960s to send a crewed spacecraft all the way to the end of the solar system? And really, who else would've been crazy enough to propel a ship with leftover atomic bombs?

Yeah, this made Apollo look puny in comparison. He couldn't blame them for keeping it under wraps: Did anyone think Reagan would've bought their line that it was an exotic propulsion system and not an orbiting WMD platform? Not in their lifetimes.

The original plan had been to fly a grand tour of the outer planets, plant the Commie flag on Pluto just to show who's the Boss of the Solar System, and do it all in under a year. Thing was, they almost did it. Until, that is, their heroes found something they didn't expect. And it had been serious enough to cause a mutiny.

They'd found complex organics out here, a frozen world full of the stuff you'd need if you were planning to seed your own planet. Was that it, then? Proof of the panspermia theory? Alien overlords? An omniscient Creator?

He slammed down the cover over the porthole by his bunk. Space was just too big.

Noelle had been uncharacteristically quiet, both captivated and shaken by what they'd found. She was preoccupied to the point where Roy had rejiggered the activity roster to allow her more time to investigate. He and Traci were taking "port and starboard" shifts, evenly dividing the day so one of them was always minding the spacecraft while Jack and Noelle remained cloistered in her small lab: he read while she methodically examined the curious compounds recovered from *Arkangel.*

Lately, every trip into the lab had resulted in a "eureka" moment.

"It's all categorized," Noelle announced over breakfast.

Jack shrugged. "That's just what the storage compartment looked like. They had everything sorted and catalogued."

"That's not what I meant. The vessels these samples were recovered in—"

"Vessels?" Traci interrupted.

"Ampules, pouches, sacs . . . whatever you want to call them." Noelle tried not to become flustered. "I don't have a better analogy. They're not artificial, but they're not random either. Each category of organics is contained within naturally formed mineral vessels having different geological characteristics."

"It would make sense if they were taken from different surface formations," Jack said, "but it's not like they had the fuel to just go hopping all over Pluto. LK's a single-pilot vehicle, and the logs say it was on the surface for barely two days. A single cosmonaut couldn't have gone very far."

"Have you found their landing site yet?" Roy asked.

"Not yet. I imaged the region they were supposed to have set down in and traced a grid pattern over it, down to the arc-minute. Searching each grid square visually takes time. The terrain's full of nooks and crannies."

"Ironic that we named it 'Sputnik Planum' without even knowing the Russians made it here first," Traci said, eliciting a tired smile from Noelle.

"We only had those passing shots from *New Horizons* years ago," she said. "The cellular pattern covering the plain is formed by a network of pits and troughs that are hundreds of meters across. There's still no evidence that they're artificial; we can explain their formation by sublimation of gases. But to find so many organics nested within each pit—"

"So is there a natural explanation?"

"There's always a natural explanation," she said, her tone suggesting she was trying to remain convinced herself.

◆ ◆ ◆

"So it's space aliens, then?"

Having let his mind wander during his daily workout, Jack snapped back into the present where Traci appeared beside him, offering a bulb of juice. "What?"

"Space aliens," she said. "I'm guessing that's why you're floating around muttering to yourself. You stopped the treadmill five minutes ago and have been staring at nothing ever since."

He took a deep drink. If only he could stare into space, instead of at another gray bulkhead.

"I'm not used to you being this quiet."

Jack wiped his face with a towel and wrung it out into the reclamation cycler. His sweat would be added to the rest of the crew's bodily fluids and eventually reused as potable water. It didn't taste all that different than tap water, though it helped if he didn't think about it too much.

"Did I do something wrong?" she asked seriously.

After months out here in the Big Empty, he'd learned to judge time by the tone of her voice. Right now she was hushed, which meant Roy and Noelle were at least two hours into their off time and asleep in their cabin. "Not at all," he finally said, unhooking himself from the complex arrangement of bungees that kept him from bounding off the zero-g treadmill. "I'm done translating the logbooks, but that's the easy part. Now I have to try and make sense of it all."

"So what did Vaschenko think they'd found?"

"Space aliens."

"Cute."

"Let's say it is. Do you still have a problem with that?"

She looked away, just long enough for him to see that she did indeed have trouble with the idea. "Quit rubbing it in. You know I do."

"I'm not needling you, it's just the issue at hand. We're out here at the edge of the solar system, crawling over a derelict from the last century, and that's not even the weirdest thing we find: Turns out that Pluto is one big cold storage facility."

"What if it's all naturally occurring?"

Jack shook his head. "We can't know that based on what we have here. We've got to get down there and see."

"Agreed. So let me propose this: Assume Pluto has all the necessary ingredients to seed a planet with life, kept safely in deep freeze. It's so isolated that we'd never get our hands on any of it until we have the ability to leave the solar system. What does that mean for us?"

"That whoever left it here wanted us to keep away from it?"

"You're half right," Traci said with a confidence he hadn't seen in a long time. "It was here for us once we were ready to be trusted with it."

28

Mission Day 315
Acceleration 0.0 m/s² (0 g)
Pluto Orbit

They finally located the Russian landing site near the southeast corner of grid square AA13, a plain of what spectroscopes showed was predominantly water ice. Low resolution, but it clearly showed the circular shape and spindly legs of an LK-M. While Traci refined its position down to the arc-second, Roy began the slow work of coordinating their landing plans with Houston.

"Owen had SIMSUP generate some likely scenarios that they're going to transmit in the next data packet," Roy said, laying out the operational concept for the others. "Surface escape velocity is only 1200 meters per second. *Puffy* has plenty enough delta-V to get two of us down there and back again, and a couple of dry runs should help us squeeze out more. They agree we should take one pilot and one scientist. Given the circumstances, I believe that should be Noelle and me."

Jack and Traci hadn't planned to argue. Their pair included the actual scientist, and she was the one who needed to be on the surface. "I can get you some more margin by cleaning out part of the trunk," Jack offered, referring to the lander's oversized service module.

"We ditch the flyaway kit?"

"At the least the parts you won't need. Keep one of the medical kits and just enough rations for a surface sortie," Jack said. "It's equipped to support all four of us for up to sixty days. Unless you're planning on taking an extended vacation down there, that's a lot of redundant mass."

"I never wanted to have to try out the whole 'Dragon Lifeboat' scenario anyway," Roy said, grimacing at the thought of months of confinement inside a glorified camper.

"Agreed," Noelle said, looking at Jack and Traci. "You guys have no idea how gassy those survival rations make him."

"Speak for yourself, princess," Roy said as his wife blushed. "But yes, the extra uplift mass might be nice to have. I have a feeling we're going to be busy down there."

Puffy, a Dragon III built for taking people and cargo to the surface of just about any solid planet in the solar system, was in outward appearances not terribly different from the capsule from which it evolved. The gumdrop-shaped passenger vessel, with its large oval windows and powerful ascent engines hidden beneath bulbous streamlined fairings, was mounted atop the frustum of its descent and landing stage that formed a natural extension of the standard Dragon crew capsule. Almost doubling the original vehicle's outer diameter, the skirt was fitted with extensions of the same type of aerodynamic fairings that protected its landing engines. Recessed in between the engine fairings were landing skids, which when retracted were flush with the vehicle's skin. Its base was formed by a convex heat shield made of rust-colored ablative tiles.

Earlier versions of this same vehicle had already returned astronauts to the Moon and taken the first human expedition to the largest known main-belt asteroid, Ceres. NASA had been oddly reluctant to use it for Mars expeditions, not being convinced of its ability to return valuable payloads such as people from the surface. Undeterred, the manufacturer had taken it upon themselves to go on their own: Much to NASA's chagrin, the first humans to set foot on another planet had thus been private contractors.

In that sense, it was the catalyst that had led to the construction of *Magellan* in the first place. Congress, in a fit of pique, had in turn slashed the agency's human exploration program until they could show actual results that weren't decades behind the private sector. Forced to fall back into its original role as a research and development agency, NASA ironically began nurturing a flair for improvisational genius not seen since its early days. Purchasing vehicles off-the-shelf and modifying them for their own purposes, pulling the covers off of advanced propulsion and nuclear power systems that had lain dormant for decades, and turning the aging International Space Station into a privately run national laboratory had revived a sense of adventurism that had been missing for decades.

After burning through several politically connected administrators over a remarkably short period, the woman who'd finally settled into the job had been ruthless in purpose: "If we're going to all of this trouble to send people up there, then for goodness' sake let's make it worthwhile and actually *go* somewhere," she'd famously lectured Congress.

That remembrance of how they got here had crowded its way into Roy's mind, despite the gravity of his immediate task. He'd represented the astronauts on the administrator's advisory committee and had been one of many suits by her side in an infamous congressional hearing that had ended with *Magellan* finally getting the green light. "I don't care if you fine people want my scalp or not," she'd said. "I report to the President, and he knows I'm not interested in running an agency that pretends spending a year in Earth orbit is space exploration."

Noelle interrupted his reflection. "What are you smiling about?"

Roy shook his head, almost laughing. "Nothing. Just thinking about how we got here."

"Plasma fusion is that amusing to you?"

He rolled his eyes. "Think bigger. The whole reorganizing NASA thing."

"Ah." She understood. "Penny certainly pulled us out of a tailspin. I'd still be toiling away at Stanford if she hadn't expanded the astronaut corps." Not to mention giving it an actual mission, she left unsaid.

"And I'd be flying airliners full of pasty tourists to see the Mouse," Roy said, staring at his departure checklist. "Amazing what can happen when you put somebody in charge who knows what they're doing."

Jack cut in on the radio loop from the command deck. "Then why is Traci back here with me?"

"Adult supervision," Roy shot back. "I don't trust you enough to come get us if we need help."

◆ ◆ ◆

The rest of the countdown went by quickly. By the time Pluto had rotated to the point that required the least amount of fuel for their descent, Roy and Noelle had run through the lander's onboard diagnostics and rehearsed the final approach twice. The doors separating their lander from its mothership were closed and the remaining air between them vented into recycling tanks. The only thing still holding them to *Magellan* were the mechanical clamps around its docking rings, which Roy released with the flip of a switch. Spring-loaded pushers simultaneously kicked the spacecraft clear.

"Undock," he reported coolly. "Cabin pressure stable, guidance internal." Holding its own air and being able to navigate were the last, most crucial details before leaving the comparative safety of *Magellan*.

"We show you free, *Puffy*," Jack replied, mere feet away but now separated by the killing vacuum. He was watching the LIDAR readback from the docking node. "Separation is ten meters, drifting steady at a half-meter per second. You're clear to navigate."

"Roger that." Roy punctuated his answer with a puff of reaction-control jets, increasing their separation from the big ship. The little capsule spun once around its longitudinal axis, then turned nose-down relative to *Magellan*. "DG's are good," he said, referring to the lander's directional gyros. A longer puff of gas added another hundred meters to their separation. The lander turned belly first, pointing its convex heat shield toward their direction of travel. "Ready to start descent countdown."

"On my mark," Jack said, acting as their onboard Mission Control. "Three, two, one . . . *mark*. Initial point in two minutes, on the dot."

"Two minutes," Roy said after a short pause. "We show same. IP's right in the crosshairs. Nice flying, guys."

"An actual compliment?" Noelle asked. "You just made their day. Maybe their week."

Roy reached for the comm panel, checking to make sure their mics weren't hot. A sly grin crossed his face. "That's why you hold on to them until it's really important. Otherwise people tend to get cocky."

"I think you're just happy to finally have me all to yourself."

"Yeah, there's that." His eyes studied her up and down, but it was hard to get past the EVA suit covering her body. He looked down at his own suit then reached for her gloved hand. "For now we'll just have to settle for this."

Still holding his wife's hand, Roy eyed the event timer as it counted down to the deorbit burn. After a few minutes of steady pushing from the landing thrusters, they each unbuckled and climbed out of their flight couches. Noelle reached for her husband and gave him a long embrace, ending with a kiss. "Visors down," she lamented. "Time to work, dear."

"Visors down," Roy sighed. He locked down his faceplate.

"Patience, love," she said. "We do have a couple of rest periods on the surface."

With nothing left to say except for call-and-response checklists, they each turned to pivot their couches upright and facing the windows. Roy moved the instrument panel around its articulated arms to set it back into the ceiling, then activated a secondary set of controls beneath his window. "Meet you on the down side, princess."

Given that Pluto is roughly two-thirds the size of Earth's moon, with correspondingly weaker gravity, their descent and final approach had used significantly less propellant than would've otherwise been the case. Pluto made up for this advantage by the fact that it was almost utterly unexplored. Finding a landing site required some up-close work.

"This reminds me of that time we got lost in North Dakota," Noelle fretted as they hovered over the frozen wastes. An area that had looked smooth and promising from up high had turned out to be strewn with ice boulders. Roy goosed the throttle, moving their lander farther along its ground track.

"We weren't lost," he insisted. "I just couldn't finish the trip VFR."

"You mean you couldn't find the field in all that snow without someone vectoring you," she teased, maybe a little too on point for the present circumstance.

"Women," he groused. "It's always, 'Look at the map! Look at the map!' You see where the *map* gets us?" He stabbed a finger at the chart scrolling past on their multifunction display. "I don't even know how that Russki made it down here in one piece."

"We can't go much farther from his landing site, or we'll be outside minimum safe distance for the EVA." Noelle frowned as she scanned ahead with a pair of range-finding binoculars. "Can you give us a yaw, plus ninety degrees?"

Roy gave the control stick a quick twist and pivoted them a quarter-turn right. "Thanks," she said, suddenly becoming excited. "Yes! Keep going, love. There's a nice clear ice field just beyond this crag. We'll be in walking distance of LK."

He pitched the nose down and tapped the throttles. "Thrusting forward."

"That's good," she said. "Put it right there. Keep going, love."

"Eww," Traci shuddered. "Just—gross."

"So it was weird for you, too?" Jack said, reaching up to silence their radios. "Yeah, I'm starting to question that whole 'hot mics during EVA' rule now. Those two need to get a room."

"Let's just remember which couches they used so *we* never have to."

His eyes glinted with a hint of mischief. "Never have to what?"

"You know what I mean!" she said, throwing a checklist at him.

"Did they actually put us on mute?" Noelle asked glibly. "I didn't think we were *that* naughty."

Roy was considerably less amused. They were about to commit to a landing site. "Ping the transponder, let 'em know we're done screwing around."

She smiled, doubting he'd picked up on his own double entendre. "As you wish, love."

"You two just about done down there?" Jack asked.

"Just about," Roy said. "You still watching our feed during that little interlude?"

"Affirmative. We show you passing five hundred, down at three meters per second, forward velocity zero. You happy with where you're at?"

"Took a while, but we finally located some flat ground that isn't all ice. Fuel at twenty percent."

"We show same. Four hundred now, down at two."

"Picking up some dust," Roy said. "I think. Might be snow. Fuel at sixteen now."

"Copy sixteen percent. You're golden, man."

"It's sublimating carbon dioxide," Noelle said as clouds billowed up from underneath them. "Our exhaust is flashing it to steam. There must be tons of it embedded in the crust."

"Whatever it is, we're in the soup." Roy frowned as he snapped on a switch above his window. "Switching to EVS."

Noelle's stomach fluttered as the Enhanced Vision System overlaid her window with a pixelated monochrome image of the ground beneath them, an artificially generated picture of what their landing radar saw as they hovered in the icy haze. Her husband might have been trained to implicitly trust the machinery, but she would've been much more at ease with being able to see this with her own eyes.

"I'm worried about blowback," Jack told them. "If you blast open a large enough nitrogen or methane pocket . . . "

"Nothing we could do about it anyway. Our landing engines will just beat it to death," Roy said, cutting him off. "We're committed. One hundred meters." They were in the "dead band," the zone close to the surface where there was not enough time to abort and have their ascent thrusters fly them to safety before the whole contraption fell out of the sky.

As they drew closer, the force of their descent rockets blasted the surface, carving a smooth depression into the icy crust and flinging the debris cloud away from them. "Clearing up," Roy said. "Starting to see flat ground beneath us."

"Twenty meters," Noelle said. "Down at two. Fuel eight percent."

They were close enough now that Roy didn't care how much they burned into their reserves. "We won't be needing it anyway. Taking her down nice and slow," Roy said as the surface crept toward them.

"Six percent," Jack's voice said as an alarm sounded. Roy punched the master caution annunciator to silence it. They were at bingo fuel, but this close they could shut down and probably fall to the surface with no consequence. Probably.

"Five meters." Noelle's voice rose excitedly.

"Good visual on the surface," Roy said. "Looks like we're taking a sandblaster to it."

"Contact light!" She was up a solid octave now.

"Shutdown." Roy chopped the throttles. The ship settled gently beneath them as its landing skids absorbed the rest of their inertia. "We made it, bubba."

29

Mission Day 317
Pluto

"Egress and closeout checklists complete. Standing by to depressurize."

Traci answered from their perch in stationary orbit aboard *Magellan*. "You're go for depress."

He lifted the cover of a protected switch on the environmental panel. "Venting now."

"Copy that. You're well ahead of the timeline. Keep up the good work."

"Not that hard," he said. "Everything about this thing is dirt simple."

Traci must have heard the disdain in his voice. "Just the nuisance work," she said. "But who needs complications, right?" Roy had been famously put off by just how much actual piloting had been eliminated in this newest generation of spacecraft.

"Push a button and watch it go."

"Hey boss, that was all you flying it down. Be happy for the break."

She was only partially right. Landing on an unexplored planet, random bits of which threatened to blow up beneath you in protest? Lesser beings would've augered in or hit the big red "abort" button once things got dicey.

Surface EVAs sounded as easy as donning a spacesuit and heading out for a stroll; "easy" ended with the suit. The egress checklist had taken the better part of an hour, most of which had been devoted to meticulously inspecting each other's suits and surface protective garments. They were particularly ready to be done with the final check: suit heaters, now running full-tilt against the extreme cold they were about to expose themselves to.

Roy turned clumsily to his wife. "Ready to get out of here? I'm starting to feel parboiled."

Behind her visor, Noelle's face shone. "Unless I can open my faceplate and let in a little fresh air."

Roy checked the outside readings. "Pressure less than ten millibars, temperature is minus two hundred twenty-three degrees Celsius. So it's only fifty shy of absolute zero."

"And me without my bathing suit." She gave him a thumbs-up. "Let's go."

Roy moved to vent the cabin's remaining air. There was a barely perceptible hiss as a ring of LEDs around the hatch turned green. He gave Noelle one last look—as in *are we sure about this?*—which she answered with an excited nod: *Yes, now. Before we change our minds.*

"Cabin secure. Preparing to egress," he announced over the radio, and opened the hatch. It rose up and away on electrically articulated arms to lock itself in place above the rim.

Now open to the outside, Roy struggled to comprehend what he saw. His helmet cam relayed everything he saw to Earth via *Magellan*, yet he was still expected to narrate. There was no way to describe it other than alien, a frozen desolation that made Earth's moon look positively welcoming. There, at least home still dominated the sky. Here, the Sun itself would've been barely distinguishable amongst the stars if it weren't for the faint haze of dust that ringed the inner planets.

He took a deep breath. "Okay, I'm standing in the hatch now, looking east over Sputnik Planum. I can see what appears to be a frozen sea ahead of us, which our spectroscopes tell us are nitrogen and carbon dioxide."

"Can you see the lander?" Traci asked through the radio.

Roy leaned out as far as he dared. "Negative, not from this vantage point. It's over a rise about a full klick to our three o'clock."

"How does the landing site look?"

"Clean," he said. "Looking down, we're sitting in a shallow depression created by our landing rockets. It appears we blasted a pretty significant area smooth out to at least fifty meters."

"Understood. We'll keep an eye on surface phases."

He turned to face Noelle, clipped his safety harness to an inertia reel, and slid the toe of one boot into a recessed foot restraint. He kicked at the non-skid coating and was satisfied with his purchase. "Ladder's stable. Starting down."

"Careful, love," Noelle said nervously. "You've always been clumsy on the ice."

Roy's answer was not the usual one-small-step astronaut-speak: "Yes, dear." He strengthened his grip around the handholds. Another couple of meters to go. The rails ended at the lander's base, requiring a short hop down to the surface. Roy kept his hands on the rail as he dropped onto the landing skid, now sunk several inches into the gravelly slush that had partially melted from their rocket exhaust and refrozen around it. "Feels good," he said. "Only a couple of feet, but a long fall in one-tenth gravity."

He eased the toe of his boot off of the skid and cautiously poked at the surface: a dense compaction of ice and rock that had formed and reformed over who knew how many billions of years. "Surface is stable in the landing zone. No sublimation, and no suction when I remove my boot," he said. "Stepping off now."

Roy swung his other foot out and let go of the ladder.

"Well . . . " he hesitated, "it's been a long way, but here we are."

Jack's voice crackled over the radio. "Absolutely poetic, Roy. You've just inspired a whole generation of children back on Earth."

"He's been thinking about it a long time," Noelle deadpanned.

Roy, slightly annoyed: "Are we on vox?"

The incessant static paused a beat. "Not anymore," Jack said.

"Good. Because my first thought was that this place looks as cold as a grave digger's ass."

"We'll make sure the official transcripts stick with 'Welp, here we are.'"

Roy moved on quickly. "I'm taking the contingency sample." If anything were to force an emergency return, they wouldn't be leaving without taking a small piece of Pluto with them.

It worked as well as he'd been promised, which surprised him: Extend the T-handle, place one boot on the foot rest, then push and twist into the surface until it stopped. Roy tapped the sample tube until about a half-meter of Plutonian permafrost came loose. "Got it." As rehearsed countless times, he placed the core sample into a pouch hanging from his waist. "Guess we can go home now."

"Not on your life!" Noelle protested. "Am I safe to come down or not?"

"If m'lady insists," he sighed dramatically.

She was headed down the ladder before he finished talking. She skipped the last two rungs completely, sliding down with her hands and not even bothering to stop on the footpad before leaping out onto the surface.

One advantage of being so far from home was that they had little need for the gold sun visors that typically hid their faces. Noelle's practically glowed, her eyes wide with wonder.

In the distance, nitrogen and methane icebergs piled against a far shoreline. A thin haze of blue along the horizon faded to black, starry sky overhead. Wisps of cloud hung low, more volatile gases sublimating from a vent in the distance, no doubt driven by some kind of subsurface volcanism. What meager sunlight that existed out here was reflected by the ice, giving their surroundings a luster reminiscent of fresh snow beneath a full moon. And on a dwarf planet smaller than their own moon, the horizon wasn't all that far away. The distant blue haze highlighted Pluto's curvature against the black sky.

The strip of Plutonian tundra they'd landed on was several kilometers across. The ground itself was rusty brown, a crazy-quilt of gravel and ice that ended at the foot of a cliff perhaps a kilometer away. It was a surprisingly clean edifice, as if purposefully cut from the glacier pressing behind it. Others were simply jumbles of shattered ice, like bergs that churned against each other in Arctic waters. A blanket of methane and nitrogen snow gave the planet an unspoiled flavor like the first snowfall of winter.

Taking it all in, she found herself getting weak-kneed and held on to the ladder.

"You look like a girl that just had her first drink," Roy laughed. "So, does this make up for not hanging around at Jupiter?"

She bounced over to her husband with a slow-motion bunny hop and caught him in a hug as tight as their bulky suits would allow. She batted her faceplate against his, reflexively planting a kiss. They both laughed at the smudge left inside her visor. "Yes, I think it does."

◆ ◆ ◆

It was a half-kilometer trot from their landing site down to the frozen shore, where the rusty ground gave way to a sea of ice stretching to the horizon. Looking back up the slight rise their lander appeared pitifully small, silhouetted against cliffs of frozen methane in the distance. Beyond, the Milky Way rose up and arced overhead. Leaning back clumsily in her suit, Noelle's eyes followed its trail of stars back down to the icy mist that hung just above the surface.

The polygonal features they'd seen from orbit—"hollows," she'd taken to calling them—dominated the frozen surface. From a distance they'd looked pristine: pools of frozen nitrogen undisturbed by the kinds of meteorite damage common to the inner solar system. As they grew closer she noticed the ice was mottled by submerged crud that had slowly migrated from below, churned up by eons of subsurface convection.

Noelle was careful to stay close to the shoreline, not wanting to test her luck with the annealed nitrogen slush. Falling into one of these pools would be like tossing a bottle of wine into a chiller.

Roy followed her movements closely as she removed samples from the crust, wary of her stepping into some unknowable danger. "You're kind of close to that ice."

"I'm being careful, love." Finally standing before one of the immense hollows they'd seen from orbit, she found it too curious to ignore. The blanket of nitrogen snow had a texture that told her there was something more beneath it. She took an excavating tool from her waist pouch and swiped away a few centimeters of ice crystals. "The ice pack isn't as dense as I expected."

"Surface texture changes as you get deeper," Roy noted. "See that pebbling?"

The snowpack grew denser as she continued digging. "There's definitely something underneath here," she said, "besides more ice, I mean." Hints of color began to appear. "Whatever's in these hollows, its noticeably different than the surrounding regolith."

"Frozen tholins, maybe?" Roy wondered. It would match up with what the Russians had described. "These could be lakes, like the gunk on Titan but frozen over."

"Let's just see what we find." Noelle was not prone to speculate on the fly, a tendency she felt was too common among the pilot astronauts like her husband. "Oh my."

"Noelle . . ."

She reached into the pool, ignoring Roy's admonitions. The surrounding nitrogen snow was deeply frozen, well below the triple-point temperature. It wasn't going to violently change phases just because of the residual heat from her suit. She'd do it quickly, then.

In. Out. Done.

Wisps of sublimating nitrogen curled away from her hands as she emerged with what looked like a large snowball. She swiped away a thin layer of slush. "Look at this!"

Roy came to her side. "What is that?" It was remarkably smooth, a sphere of translucent ice the size of a grapefruit that sparkled beneath their helmet lamps.

Traci interrupted. "We can see it from your cams. It looks like a big snow globe from here."

"You're not too far off," Roy said. "Like a Christmas ornament, similar to what you found on *Arkangel*."

"Coloring is variegated across the blue-green spectrum, some yellows depending on how our lights hit it." Noelle began narrating, subtly curbing their speculation. Better to describe what you saw, not what it might be. It was a habit of self-discipline that kept her mind from racing through the likely possibilities. "Coloring appears to change markedly toward the center. Darker, similar to the soil we landed on," she said, though that wasn't quite correct either. It was more substantial. Elemental. He might be right about tholins. "This is consistent with Colonel Vaschenko's description of the surface samples he took."

Roy reached out with an open sample container. "We need to get this secured, babe. Before we melt the thing." Meaning he was more concerned about them warming it up just enough for all that nitrogen to go *poof* and cover them with whatever was flash-frozen inside of it. "How does this even form?" he asked as he snapped a photograph of it, noting their location before she carefully placed it in an insulated bag.

"I've seen a similar phenomenon in the Arctic," she said. "Naturally formed snowballs, churned and shaped by currents and winds."

Roy jerked a thumb toward the icy expanse behind them. "Not

much motion in that ocean. No wind either. Atmosphere's way too thin."

Noelle pointed toward the towering spires they'd avoided before landing here, sails seemingly carved out of the ice. "Think of it over time, love. Whatever we've found, 'old' may not be a strong enough word for it. This is primordial."

Roy smiled behind the glass of his helmet. "I thought you discouraged speculation during field expeditions, Doctor."

"I'm always open to suggestions," she said, fatigue beginning to creep into her voice. "In the meantime, we need to fan out and collect more. Ensure they're not all from one place."

Roy nodded and began a low-gravity bunny hop along the frozen beach.

As the first video stream arrived from the surface of Pluto, Owen's mission management team watched from a closed-off conference room in Houston. The same feed was simultaneously going out live all over the world, which only added pressure to interpret the evidence before wild speculation took over the news cycle.

"Is there anybody in the press we can trust to not screw this up?" he asked, looking at the public affairs officer. "Because it's about to be."

"It's a short list," PAO admitted. "They'll be more disciplined, but they're no less curious. Maybe more so, since they know of which they speak." He pointed toward the wall screen and its four-hour-old video from Roy and Noelle's helmet cams. "You think that's the same stuff the Russians found?"

They watched as Noelle turned over one of the spheres in her hands. An older gentleman from the biology backroom team reached over to pause the feed. "Possibly. I've been wondering if this might be some kind of preservation medium," he said, "perhaps a type of naturally occurring vitrification."

"Vitri-what?" PAO asked, slightly annoyed.

"Vitrification," he repeated, loudly enough for the room. "Flash freezing. It's an excellent way to preserve sensitive organics like germ plasmas."

"Hold it," Owen said. "She could be holding an extraterrestrial petri dish? What happens if it melts?"

He waved a finger at the screen. "There's not much danger of that out there."

"I meant aboard ship. I don't want them thawing out alien sperm samples in a closed-loop environment."

The biologist sighed, leaned back and steepled his fingers. "If this is the same thing Colonel Vaschenko wrote about, then it's more fundamental. They might contain amino acids, perhaps even protein chains."

"You know what I meant," Owen said. Why did so many really smart people not have a sense of humor? "Either way, it's a contamination risk." He turned to the off-duty flight director. "Walt, I want EECOM's confirmation that the mass spectrometer's outflow vents are working before Noelle thaws out one of those things. And have Capcom remind them of the biohazard protocols."

"Might be too late for that," Flight warned, "but I'll do it. The surface science packages were nominal in postlanding checks."

A young woman from the Planetary Protection Office, quiet until now, leaned over the conference table. "We need to consider a good deal more than that," she said. "It's PPO's position that they should immediately cease surface operations."

If dropped jaws were audible, it would have been cacophonous. As it was, the room went silent for several beats before Owen spoke. "This was already a Category Five restricted-return mission. Has PPO come up with a new double-secret category we don't know about?"

She looked down at the table at her notes but remained firm. "Pluto is showing evidence of being in a pre-evolutionary state and we are at significant risk of exceeding our ten-to-the-minus-three probability for contamination. It would be irresponsible to introduce uncontrolled variables into that environment."

"Uncontrolled?" Owen said. "We followed the NPD to the letter. There's a limit to how sterile we can make a spacecraft or crew."

"Correct. We have to limit any damage to the local environment."

Owen balked. "What damage? They walked a kilometer in EVA suits to collect a half-dozen ice balls and put them in freezer bags."

"We've also polluted the planet's surface with chemical residue from toxic propellants."

"Which promptly froze," Owen reminded her. "And you're ignoring the fact that the Russians got there first. If there was going to be environmental damage, they've already done it."

"All the more reason to abort surface ops before we risk further contamination," she said. "Their presence may be impacting future evolutionary processes."

Owen steadied his voice, needing to be firm while hoping to not be as confrontational as he felt. "We hashed these issues out with your office three years ago. What changed?"

Her eyes narrowed, as if the conclusion was obvious. "Confirmation of biological precursors on the surface for starters."

"Which we already structured the mission around. Even though it seemed completely unnecessary, we acceded to PPO's demands anyway. This doesn't change anything."

"It may, Mr. Harriman. This is uncharted territory and we must consider the impact of our actions. Existing planetary protections may not be enough."

And if they had their way we'd never send another human beyond cislunar space again, Owen thought sourly. "We also can't just hit the 'blast off' button and put them into an out-of-phase orbit without a serious emergency to justify it. *Magellan* still has to be positioned for rendezvous and I'm not going to order the Hoovers to just sit in the cabin until the next launch window. Your concerns are noted, but we are sticking with the plan."

By outside appearances, the ascent-stage cabin didn't look especially roomy. Just shy of five meters' diameter, the basic capsule was meant for a crew of six. For the Pluto mission, two of those seats had been sacrificed to make room for fold-down bunks and a rather cramped lavatory that was little more than a privacy curtain for a toilet and a small wash basin.

It was a tight fit, and Roy emerged from behind the lav curtain like a cicada shedding its cocoon. "This is the part of surface ops I hate." He tossed a slippery ball of wet wipes into the trash and reached for a towel.

Noelle had already freshened up and was relaxing in a clean pair of coveralls as she fussed over their EVA suits. "You're too fastidious," she said. "Look at this." She pointed at their boots on the deck. "A few sweeps with a brush and they're almost like new. Remember how filthy we were on the Moon?"

"Like we'd been crawling around the inside of a coal furnace," he said with a snort. "The Mars crew really had it bad. That stuff ate away at their seals." What hadn't made much news after that expedition's return was the fact that the crew had nearly met with disaster after two astronauts' helmet rings began failing in the middle of a surface EVA. "You haven't found anything like that here, have you?"

"Nothing so far." Noelle nodded toward a small workbench behind the flight couches folded up overhead. She'd set up monitors for her rudimentary lab, where a compact gas chromatograph stored in the landing stage was now processing one of those strange ice globes.

"Is that thing venting?" he asked. An essential step in gas chromatography was the "gas" part: vaporizing the sample into its component elements.

"Yes, love. Outside," she said patiently, "and the radiators are removing the waste heat. Nothing to worry about."

"Not quite what I meant. I wonder if we could divert some of that waste heat into warming the cabin? Might take some load off of our fuel cells."

"That's a good idea, which we should save for later." Noelle opened a drawer beneath her lab bench. "There are lots of ways to warm the cabin," she said, and lifted out a dark shatterproof decanter.

His eyes widened, immediately recognizing her family farm's private label. "Wine? How did you—"

"*Champagne*, love. Owen allowed me a fair degree of latitude whilst setting up the expedition laboratory. It was easy to slip this in amongst all those bottles of solutions and reagents."

"So you've been planning this for two years?" Roy examined the bottle with amusement. "Pretty brave to flash this in front of your mission commander, Dr. Hoover. You could get into serious trouble."

"I know how to change your mind." Roy watched the undulating folds of her coverall as it fell in slow motion under Pluto's weak gravity. He'd been wondering whatever happened to that Christmas present he'd given her.

◆ ◆ ◆

"And they're off," Traci giggled, watching their crewmates' heart and respiratory rates spike.

Jack sighed and reached for the bio-monitor cutoff. "Okay, now it's gotten weird."

"First time they've been alone in almost a year. Can you blame them?"

Before he could answer with some ill-advised snarky retort about Traci's vicarious love life, an incoming message flashed on the comm panel: Houston, looking for a status report. "What should we tell PAO? They're always looking for firsts."

He was only half joking. "We don't tell them anything!" Traci said. "We came over three billion miles and they still had to go land on a whole other planet just to have any kind of privacy."

"Not really the reason they went, but I'll go with it." He checked his watch. "Anyway, flight surgeon's sure to figure it out in about four hours."

"Or he'll start asking some mighty uncomfortable questions," she said. The docs sometimes had the worst kinds of tunnel vision when it came to crew health. No doubt some eager young physician would worry they were having cardiac events. At the same time.

Jack began typing. After entering the requisite information on vehicle condition and EVA reports, he arrived at the last section: surface crew status. With a sly grin, he ended his report with one cryptic sentence:

❉   ❉   ❉

IF IT'S ROCKIN', DON'T COME KNOCKIN'.

30

Mission Day 318
Pluto

Not content to sleep apart in the "mission-approved configuration," the Hoovers had laid their cushions and sleeping bags on the floor of their capsule. The only illumination in the darkened cabin came from the faint reflection of starlight from the Plutonian snowfields and the glow of status lights from Noelle's lab bench.

Roy rolled over with a drowsy grunt as Noelle disentangled herself from his embrace. She gathered her sleeping bag around her and knelt next to his slumbering form, reaching down to gently stroke his hair. She could have used a couple more hours herself, but once the green strobe had caught her eye it was impossible to ignore: The spectral analysis was finished and its results awaited her inspection.

They did not disappoint.

"They're full of chiral molecules!" The excitement in Noelle's voice rang through the static like a bell. They could only imagine what she sounded like in person.

"Not just raw elements?" Jack said. "You're certain?"

Her voice crackled over the speakers. "Certain as I can be without a tunneling microscope: adenine, guanine, cytosine, and uracil."

"What about the . . . uh . . . snow globes?" He'd almost said "containment vessels," but wasn't ready to make that leap just yet.

"We'll look for them during today's transit and we'll take more here if we don't find them elsewhere. The surface texture of Sputnik Sea is interesting."

"Sputnik Sea?" he asked. "Don't you mean 'plain'?"

"You'd understand if you could see it for yourself."

Roy cut in. "We only had a quick look but she's right, it resembles parts of the Arctic Ocean. Just looking out window one now . . . it's like a crust covering those ice balls. That's why it appears pebbly from orbit."

Similar formations had been found in the stormier arctic regions of Earth, there just hadn't been as much interest in finding improbable biological precursors within them. "You want to take some pics, maybe bag a few more samples?" Jack asked.

"Affirmative," Roy said, "if we can keep them in their natural state. Atmosphere and surface composition's all over the place and I don't want a ball of frozen whatever it is changing back to gas inside the spacecraft."

"That would be fascinating to see on a large scale," Noelle said as she pulled on her thermal-control coveralls. "If this world had evolved closer to the Sun, it might have become a cauldron of amino acids and nucleotides."

Puzzled, Roy scratched at his head. "Just so I don't misunderstand . . . instead of warming up into the proverbial 'primordial soup,' being this far out turned all those gases into a giant freezer that preserves . . . what exactly?"

"All of the base pairs of chiral molecules you'd need to start weaving RNA strands," she said. "The precursors form by basic chemistry and combine to make RNA, which catalyzes into a self-copying reaction." She turned back to the monitor and its stream of data. "They're all here, perfectly preserved and ready to be thawed out."

Half into his EVA suit, Roy sat back on his bunk and struggled to keep up. "Back up a sec, hon. The only organic chemistry class I ever took was the one you taught in Houston."

"Homochirality," she explained. "RNA strands can develop from either left- or right-handed nucleotides. Left-handed gives you amino acids; right-handed gives you sugars. Life has to pick one direction at the beginning."

Roy pictured complex organics forming as just so many LEGO sets: Pick a direction to stack your bricks and stick with it. "Makes sense I guess. Life can't begin from a bunch of confused RNA strands."

"If you believe the 'RNA World' theory," Noelle said. "Which I may be warming up to. Since it can self-catalyze, even a small imbalance in either direction would rapidly begin to break symmetry as strands evolved. Even a low excess of one chiral form over another weeds out the surplus nucleotides."

"What about reaction energy? It still needs some kind of amplification process, doesn't it? It doesn't just happen on its own."

"Circular polarized light has been one theory," Noelle said. "That isn't difficult to find in star-forming regions." She gathered herself and settled onto the bench. "This could be tremendous, love. We'd always assumed that homochirality didn't occur in space. It was a hallmark of life that we were convinced had to originate on Earth."

"So those organics the Russians found?"

"All here," she said, patting the freezer full of snow globes behind her.

"And the theory that Earth's water came from impacts by long-period comets originating out here in the Kuiper Belt? If this stuff came with them . . . "

"Then they also seeded Earth like a garden." Noelle gripped his hands. "*This* is where we came from."

Traci had been following a similar line of thought. "It's like a do-it-yourself creation starter kit," she said. "But why would all this stuff be out here in the first place?"

"Always the 'why,'" Jack said. "Can't sometimes things just be the way they are?"

"You're too skeptical for your own good. Everything that's ever existed, invented, what have you—it all came to be because the materials on hand were fashioned into something new. Even if all you believe in is the big bang and random chance."

"Conservation of matter and energy," Jack said. Everything in the universe had once existed within an infinite, single point—a singularity—at the very instant of its coming to be. It might change forms between matter and energy, but everything that existed now had always been thus. "Nothing new under the sun."

"King Solomon was even smarter than we thought." Jack hadn't even realized where he'd taken his own cliché from.

"Who?" he asked, then got her reference. "Okay, you got me. But the question now is: What do we do with this? We may have just disturbed something that should've been left alone to evolve on its own."

"If you think humans just screw up everything we touch. What about our responsibility to 'be fruitful and multiply'?"

"Depends on your own moral compass," he said. "We can't both be right. Humankind was given an oasis which we then proceeded to royally screw up. Why should we be trusted with spreading life through the universe when we can't stop fouling our own nest?"

"Because we weren't made infallible. If you think we should wait until humanity has perfected itself before we start spreading out, then we'll never leave. Isn't that making the perfect the enemy of the good?"

"Maybe. But this is weighty stuff . . . " He trailed off, absently twirling a pen in his hand. "Funny. A billion years' worth of organic compounds falling sunward from out here, bombarding our planet while it's still forming. We've found actual evidence of the panspermia hypothesis. What are we supposed to make of it?"

"Exactly my point."

"It's like giving a bunch of monkeys a typewriter. Maybe you'll get Shakespeare in a few million years, but you're more likely to get a bunch of gibberish."

"Maybe," she said, "if it didn't all look so idiot-proof. All of this appears to be naturally occurring, out here in creation's own freezer just waiting for us to find somewhere inviting to thaw them out and mix them up."

Jack kneaded at his brow, fighting a looming headache. "So you're saying it was left here for us to find?"

"That would look an awful lot like ID theory, wouldn't it? Assuming that if we made it this far, we'd finally be ready to take it out farther? To go forth and prosper?"

Jack stared at his bottle of fruit-flavored electrolyte water and longed for a stiff drink. "So now we're the high-functioning primates drawn out here by some higher intelligence, just like God and Arthur C. Clarke intended."

"Well, at least one of them."

Jack bit back his words. No sense pitting the will of her deity with that of a notorious dead atheist. He could put aside the whole question of origins: We're here, we all came from something, and he'd never been inclined to care about why. All that mattered was what we could do in the here and now.

Life's essential ingredients were all out here, far from humanity's clumsy ape hands until their brains had matured enough to be trusted with it. Was that intentional? And if so, by whom? It was no better than the argument that if we couldn't understand some aspect of nature then it must therefore be evidence of a divine super-being. That was an argument just begging to be refuted, as someone always took up the challenge to figure out the natural mechanism.

The more our collective knowledge advances the more it approaches some unknowable limit, yet we keep looking anyway.

It sparked a question which loomed increasingly larger, gnawing at him like a pest trying to claw its way into an attic:

What if we really are the first?

Dr. Jacqueline Cheever pulled her chestnut hair into a bun and grudgingly checked her makeup, irritated with the Houston climate that would melt it right off of her the moment she stepped outside. That she was expected to wear any at all was just one more arcane cultural ritual that was best forgotten.

Jackie Cheever had dedicated her life to the advancement of science, furthering humanity's understanding of the cosmos and our obligation to leave it unspoiled. As NASA's newest Planetary Protection Officer, she held it as a sacred duty. Getting the Crewed Spaceflight group to see things that way was perhaps an even more titanic struggle than it was for the populace.

The average citizen could eventually be brought around, to the extent anyone cared to pay attention. As her political handlers had warned, it was the hotshot astronauts who'd be the hardest to change. Every last one of them was itching to fly off into the solar system for the sake of adventure. They weren't stupid, but they did know just enough to be dangerous. Giving them a spacecraft as powerful as *Magellan* was like giving some teenagers your car keys and a case of beer. Nothing good could come of it.

In fact, nothing had. So the Russians had made it there four decades ahead of us? Well, good for them, if not entirely unsurprising. When they'd decided something was necessary, they'd gone after it. Maybe they'd dirtied up Pluto, but that was then. We know better now. At least they'd had the good sense to not bring anything back with them.

Perhaps it was because he'd been center director for so long that Ronnie Bledsoe was able to keep his composure in the face of abject lunacy, a survival instinct he'd developed after years of working around overpowered bureaucrats. Owen, for his part, was having none of it.

"Pardon me, ma'am, but there is *no way* we're going to leave those samples behind. Not after everything it's taken to get there. Especially not after what we've seen from Noelle's analysis."

Cheever's frown came as much from an instinctive disapproval of his using such a quaint patriarchal address as it did from his argument. "'Doctor' is just fine too," she sniffed. "Putting that aside, it's especially because of Dr. Hoover's discovery that we must leave the natural environment unspoiled as much as possible. We've already done enough damage by landing humans there."

"It's only one data point," Owen said. "Since when do we make these kinds of decisions based on that?"

"Because it's a very powerful data point," she said, emphasizing each word. "I can't see any other way to interpret it, otherwise I wouldn't be making this demand."

"I wasn't aware it was a demand. I thought this was a discussion."

Bledsoe cleared his throat to draw her attention away from Owen. "Dr. Cheever, believe it or not I do appreciate your concerns. I also believe taking this course of action would be an unconscionable overreaction. It would throw away any benefits we've gained and make a monumental waste of the work and expense that has gone into this mission."

"I suspect you're afraid it would show human space exploration to be a monumental waste in itself."

A cold look from Bledsoe. "A little uncalled for, don't you think?"

"No, I don't," she finally admitted. "I have always been skeptical of the value of putting humans on unexplored worlds. We can sterilize robotic landers, we can't do the same with human beings to any reasonable extent. No matter how hard we try, we will inevitably contaminate whatever we touch."

"Leave no trace?" Bledsoe asked. "This isn't a Boy Scout camping trip."

"And this is about more than just cleaning up after ourselves. A human presence among unknown organics at this stage could alter their entire evolutionary path."

"Except it's all in deep freeze," Owen reminded her. "Nothing's evolving in that environment."

"You can't possibly—"

Bledsoe held a hand up, signaling their debate was finished. "I'll make this simple. We make operational decisions to ensure the success of the missions we're tasked with. Again, I appreciate your concerns and we will take every precaution within our power. But what you're asking for is a political decision that we simply cannot make."

"I'll keep that in mind."

31

Mission Day 319
Pluto

Swinging an excavation tool as carefully as he could manage, Roy chipped away at a thin layer of ice that had quickly frozen over the Surface Exploration Package bay. Of all the places for sublimating gases to settle and refreeze . . .

"You think we'd have seen this yesterday," he said, keying the microphone switch on his wrist. "We stirred up just enough atmo to give us icing problems." Unlocking the SEP bay would hold the key to how long they could remain on the surface. Besides the experiment packages, it held an ingeniously folded six-wheeled rover for longer trips away from their landing site. He freed the locking handle and moved on to the rim.

"Progress?" Noelle asked hopefully. Roy's agitated sigh told her all she needed to know. The entire descent stage was coated with varying layers of frost and ice. She pulled a rock hammer from her own excavation kit and began chipping away at the hinges. "The rest of the stage is about the same."

"Yep." His breath came hard between words. "This is gonna slow us down."

"The nice thing about being so far away is not having Capcom pestering you to hurry up," Jack cut in. "On the other hand, hurry up."

"Not helping," Roy said.

"You're going to burn into your O2 reserves soon. Any signs of ice collecting on the ascent stage?"

275

They stopped, gaping at each other: *How'd we miss that?* Roy stepped back to inspect the upper half of the lander while Noelle went around to do the same on the opposite side. "There's frost underneath the engine fairings, some on the undersides of the antenna blades. Basically anything facing the surface."

"How about the egress hatch?"

Noelle's eyes widened. Per NASA SOP and basic manners, she'd shut the door on her way out. Without a word, Roy bounded up the ladder in a jump that would've been impossible even for an NBA forward on Earth.

"Light coating on the handle. I can brush it away with my glove, but we're going to have to rethink our EVA plan." They always left the ship powered up and warm, but keeping the door open even just a little bit hadn't been part of the plan. It meant limited EVAs and a shorter stay.

"We'll leave the latch mechanism open, but you'll have to keep an eye on cabin temps and let us know if they start to become a problem," Roy said as he finally freed the locking lever. "Have Daisy search the spacecraft certification records, look for the cold-soak data and assume worst case. And let Houston know," he added, almost as an afterthought.

Unlocking the equipment bay had taken some muscle, but once it was freed the six-wheeled rover unfolded itself like an origami insect of aluminum and carbon fiber. As Roy activated its radioisotope generator and began checking out its related machinery, Noelle trudged around to the rover's front end, climbing up between the open-frame seats to erect its comm antennae and recording equipment. "We're go for surface ops," Roy called up to *Magellan*.

"Roger that," Jack answered. "And you'll be glad to know Houston finally got around to approving your EVA plan." They'd meticulously crafted a survey grid using surface maps updated with LIDAR scans from orbit. Roy and Noelle would take the rover out and plant radio beacons at the outside corners of the grid to keep from getting themselves lost, take core samples at each spot, and begin spiraling their way toward the center of the grid where a forty-year-old Soviet spacecraft awaited them.

❖ ❖ ❖

Noelle took little comfort in the fact that Sputnik Planum was more accurately described as a frozen sea, often with no clear demarcation between ice and dry land.

As Roy drove them across the survey grid, she navigated with digital maps that were notably missing Pluto's countless pools of frozen nitrogen or methane, hazards marked by occasional feathery geysers of sublimating gas that dotted the surface like fountains in a garden of ice.

As she marked each new hazard, Noelle grew more dissatisfied. There was so much potential here, and so many risks to be avoided. It had started as a well-ordered survey, but as Roy had reminded her no plan survives first contact with reality. She had at least taken two more core samples and collected another half-dozen of those odd snowballs. And in the end, she knew they weren't here only to explore an alien landscape.

She updated their digital map as they set the last corner, automatically synching it with *Magellan* and noting terrain features the old-fashioned way: with a grease pencil on a laminated chart. It was clumsy, but it would make a nice supplement to the handwritten survey notes she planned to make at the end of the day. It was important to her that neither could disappear if the power went out. She placed another core sample in its container in back of the rover and turned to Roy. "Ready?"

He held up one finger, gesturing for her to wait. "Almost. Just recording this ice cliff for posterity."

"It's called a *penitente*, love," she chuckled. "More like a spire." Easily a hundred meters high, it resembled a sail gracefully carved out of the ice. Dozens more dotted the landscape beyond, seeming to grow despite their distance. Their first appearance in the old *New Horizons* images had estimated them to be well over five hundred meters tall, almost a quarter mile high.

"Penna-what?"

"Don't roll your eyes at me. I'm striving for scientific accuracy."

"You could see my eyes?"

"You forget we don't need our sun visors out here." Noelle shook her head—fully visible behind the glass—and climbed back into her seat. "If you're striving for accuracy, then can you be in charge of the maps so I can drive for a bit?"

Roy hopped over beside her and studied the rest of their route. "Sure." They expected to find LK over the next rise. While Noelle was here for the science, Roy was more interested in the comparatively pedestrian task of locating missing cosmonauts.

The next rise turned out to be larger, steeper, and even sharper than could be imaged from orbit or seen from their vantage point aboard the lander. The same forces—even here on the ground it felt wrong to think of it as somehow atmospheric—that carved those giant ice spires in the distance had also done its work on this frozen mound. It was capped with an elongated dome of more nitrogen and methane ice, ending with a sharp overhang that would have been crazy for them to drive under.

As Noelle steered clear, the rover bounced along a debris field strewn across the lee side of the ridge. The smaller rocks were easily crushed beneath their aluminum mesh wheels while the larger ones sent them heaving up, down and sideways. "I'm going to have to say something to the roads department about this." Her voice shook with the vehicle.

"We're definitely not in France anymore," Roy said as they rounded the hill. The terrain smoothed out ahead into a stark field of white that presumably was supported by solid ground and was not just another lake of frozen nitrogen. "Better stop here. And break out the snowshoes."

Noelle's eyes grew wide. "Roy, it's . . . "

"I know," he said, and switched over his radio to *Magellan*'s frequency. "Jack, we are at grid square AA13 and have the LK in sight."

Lunniy Korabl's ungainly landing platform stood at the center of the plain, its barrel-shaped form sprouting two antenna masts that were almost as long as the four spindly legs which supported it. Its design cues were unmistakably Russian, spare and utilitarian, down to the faded olive paint just barely discernible under layers of ice.

A few meters away, one feature left no mistake of its provenance and stood as a grotesque reminder of who'd been here first: a faded red banner with the yellow hammer and sickle of the Soviet Union. Roy muttered a curse at the sight.

"What was that?" Jack asked over the radio.

"I said . . . oh, never mind." Roy swallowed his editorial comments and stuck with the clinical description as he began recording with the long-focus camera on his chest pack. "The LK's descent stage is about a hundred meters from our position. Exposed surfaces have what appears to be a uniform coating of frost, about what you'd expect from sitting out here forty years."

"Can you get to it from there?"

"If he managed to land it here without the ground blowing up under him, that tells me this snow is just superficial. Probably no thicker than the stuff covering the lander. We're going to park the rover here and walk in as soon as we get our snowshoes on."

"Copy. You be careful out there."

The insulated snowshoes may have kept them safe atop the ice, but it had made walking that much harder. As they approached, Roy clumsily traced a wide circle around the abandoned lander. His helmet camera recorded everything he saw and beamed it up to *Magellan* for posterity.

Having had every gram of excess mass stripped away, the old Russian craft looked even more frail for the cold. It was as if every joule of energy had been sapped just to keep from being consumed by the environment; its brittle frame spent on the sacrificial altar of entropy.

Roy poked at a nearby panel with his sampling tool, not daring to touch it directly lest the temperature differential between his suit and the deep-frozen lander left him permanently affixed, like a kid sticking his tongue on a flagpole. And that reminded him of something he'd decided should be tended to.

The thin aluminum cracked beneath the pressure, startling him. He'd seen car windows shatter while training in subzero Arctic environments, but had never experienced it to this extreme. He stepped back warily. How fragile had this contraption become over its years in deep freeze? Would the whole thing fall apart on top of them?

He turned back to the now open equipment bay. It was mostly empty: a few undeployed surface experiments and other odds and ends. Some spare suit batteries—not a bad idea, especially given their state of technology—plus a few tools and spare parts in case something important had broken. He dug out all of the loose items he could and stuffed them into a separate collection bag on his hip.

An alarm startled him: his suit, reminding him that its own batteries were succumbing to the cold. He looked for Noelle, who was already heading back to their safe haven. "Time to go, love," she called.

Roy answered her with a silent thumbs-up and followed her. Noelle was reaching out with a charging cable before he could even make it into his seat. "I've still got ten minutes," he said.

She plugged him into the rover's power supply. "I'm not taking any chances. If your heater goes, you won't last two minutes out here. It's taking every amp from the RI generator just to keep the rover powered. If we sit for too long, I'm afraid the flywheels will freeze up."

Roy didn't argue. If the rover's electric motors failed, they'd be forced to hike the kilometer back to their lander, which would leave them entirely dependent on suit batteries that were already draining at twice the normal rate. In an environment featuring random geysers of ice, on top of frozen volatiles that could explosively sublimate if enough heat were applied. He took one final, long look around. "I've got one more thing to do."

The same frost that had covered the LK coated the old Soviet flag that was hung nearby. They'd used a telescoping pole and support frame similar to what the Apollo astronauts had used to plant the American flag on the Moon. Given the amount of snow and ice coating everything, the scientists had been right about the thin air freezing and falling to the surface. Roy wondered how surprised those cosmonauts had been to find this place had an actual atmosphere, even if it wasn't nearly enough to fly their flag in a breeze.

It was all just history, he told himself. *Get over yourself. Vaschenko served his country, just as we did. You come all this way, you plant your flag.* Even if in Roy's mind it was hardly better than a swastika.

He took a long-handled cutting tool and set it around the flag's horizontal support. With one quick movement, it snapped in two and the red banner fell into his free hand in a cloud of ice crystals. He shook it clean, folded it with care, and placed it into an empty cargo pocket on his hip.

All just history.

32

Mission Day 325

Col. V. Vaschenko — Personal Log

Out here I've had nothing but time to ponder our fate and write down my thoughts, such as they are. And these writings will not disappear. No matter what, I will never fly again and they dare not spirit me away. Or so I hope.

The chaos enveloping our country, it pains me to say, is long overdue. Men cannot live long with chained minds. That we endured it for so many generations is testimony to the control this perverse philosophy held over the people it pretended to serve.

It promised freedom and delivered slavery. Of this, I admit to being vaguely aware during my relatively protected life as an Air Force officer. I once thought being in Earth orbit was a measure of freedom. It is only now, being so far removed from our world that a question posed at breakfast isn't answered until supper, that I understand. The degree of autonomy we've enjoyed has been most unexpected and extraordinary. Yet while this is the ultimate test of our spacecraft, I wonder if our putative masters foresaw what else it might test.

They can't see it, only because we have diligently kept our thoughts to ourselves. This is an inherent advantage to the low bandwidth of encrypted frequencies over such distances: We have no time for "small talk."

I wonder if they will ever see.

❈   ❈   ❈

The commanding strains of the Russian Federation's national anthem echoed through *Magellan*'s control deck while Colonel Vladimir Vaschenko was put to rest. He remained encased in the same EVA suit they'd found him in, now with the Soviet flag Roy brought back from the surface wrapped around his torso.

Jack maneuvered the body into *Arkangel*'s open airlock with their remote as the music built to its closing crescendo. He released the bot's mechanical grip and gently nudged Vaschenko back into his spacecraft one final time.

Roy pulled out a note card he'd clearly marked up several times over. "This was your ship, your greatest adventure," he recited. "You took it farther and faster than most people could have imagined, and your sacrifice protected the world from it being used in a way far too easy to imagine. You have the thanks of your nation, of the United States, and of Earth. May your eternal resting place be here among the new frontiers which you opened. Godspeed, Colonel."

Jack pushed *Arkangel*'s outer door shut with the manipulator, sealing Vaschenko in his orbiting tomb. He waited to see if any of his crewmates moved to leave; fortunately none did. He locked down the arm and left his station to float behind them, near the big forward windows.

"One more thing," he said, more awkwardly than he'd hoped. "I've gotten to know Vaschenko as much as anyone can just from reading a man's diaries. You know he was dedicated to his country and to space exploration, but he wasn't just a drone."

Jack reached into a waist pocket. "The man appreciated good literature. He was as much of a thinker as someone could be in that kind of system. Most of the mass he was allotted for personal effects went to books, and most weren't exactly party-approved material." He lifted a worn, clothbound volume from his flight suit. "This is an anthology of Russian poetry. One page in particular was so dog-eared, he would have come back to it often."

Jack let the book fall open and read:

❧　❧　❧

"*. . . Before the morning star I went;*
From hand immaculate and chastened
Into the grooves of prisonment
Flinging the vital seed I wandered—

But it was time and toiling squandered,
Benevolent designs misspent . . . "

❦   ❦   ❦

"Is that Pushkin?" Roy asked.

"It is," Jack said, unable to mask his surprise. "You read it?"

"I flipped through a few pages," he said. "Good choice."

"I thought it was a fitting eulogy," Jack said, slightly embarrassed. "He deserved more than official boilerplate from their ambassador."

"He left a wife and kids behind," Traci said, staring out at the old vessel. "Do you think they accepted the official story?"

"I suppose it's easy enough to let life get away from you. Especially in this business." He watched Roy and Noelle share a knowing look. Would either one of them had married outside of the space agency? Could they even conceive of it?

"You've read all of his notes," Noelle said. "Do you think he truly grasped the significance of this place?"

Jack stared past her at the old ship and the curious world beyond. "Do we?"

The flight from Brussels into Moscow on an Aeroflot 777 had been considerably less comfortable than the first leg of Anatoly Rhyzov's return from Houston on a United jet of the same type. Perhaps it was the Americans just hoping to give him a good send-off, but there was no denying the business class seat Owen had secured for him was far superior to the cramped coach seating he'd just left. Barely three hours stuffed into a middle seat between two other travelers, one a foreign service functionary and the other most likely FSB, and it had left him drained.

Rhyzov showed his passport to the customs officer at entry control, who stamped it with an uninterested grunt and waved him on. His two traveling companions remained on either arm.

The drive from Sheremetyevo Airport to his old apartment block passed silently. Neither of his escorts seemed particularly open to conversation, even when he asked about the inevitable debriefings. "Later."

They'd at least had the decency to help bring his bags upstairs, he liked to think out of a lingering cultural respect for their elders. Rhyzov opened his door to find his apartment much as he'd left it.

Perhaps even cleaner, an unambiguous message that they were paying close attention to him. His study was especially noteworthy: It was organized as if someone had gone through his shelves and drawers and left them better than they'd found them. Still not as bad as it had been with KGB and GRU where they'd have just as likely taken him straight to an interrogation room.

It all seemed cold to him. He had no delusions about being welcomed as some kind of state hero, but perhaps if the Americans had been able to somehow reactivate *Arkangel* and send it Earthward . . .

Bah. Just as well. If the Kremlin wanted to hold him responsible for NASA's fickle priorities, then they couldn't have been that interested in getting the vessel back in the first place. It was clear now that they would have preferred he'd kept the oath of secrecy taken on his first day with the project. Technically it was still in effect.

After a lifetime of living in a paranoid culture, he still didn't understand it any better. He knew how to navigate it, but that was different. The need to control hadn't abated so much since the Communists fell, it had only become better focused. The *nomenklatura* had realized it was better to let the people find ways to make money; the better they could exploit it. Get in the way of that and you'd quickly find yourself under someone's gaze.

Rhyzov suspected it after he drank his first cup of tea the next morning, when his bowels began to stir. A younger, fitter man might have held out longer. The nausea came in waves until it soon overwhelmed him and he crumpled onto the floor.

He didn't question—couldn't, really—when the men came into his apartment soon after. It was interesting that they put on gloves and respirators before lifting him into his bed.

This was how they'd planned it, then. Had they put it in the tea itself, or in the sugar? As he struggled to recall the effects of alpha radiation and the half-life of polonium, he began to drift in and out of consciousness. His eyes settled on a collection of family pictures by his bedside: his grandson, Mikhail Ivanovich, lost years ago to an auto accident with his parents.

"Come, Misha, before we are caught in the rain." Anatoly Rhyzov held out his hand, impatiently waving his rambunctious grandson along. The tyke loved the outdoors; could barely contain himself once free of the confines of his parents' apartment.

"Two more minutes, Grandfather," the child bargained. Rhyzov looked into his pleading eyes and wondered how his poor mother could ever prevail over their syrupy brown.

Rhyzov sighed and pulled his collar close against the wind. "Very well. Two minutes," he said, tapping his wristwatch. "And you know what a stickler I am for time."

"Yes, Grandfather. But first you must catch me!" he laughed, and took off running into the birch forest. Rhyzov was about to give chase when the woods disappeared, replaced with a blinding shaft of light that emerged from nowhere and everywhere at once. "Misha?"

"Yes, Grandfather. Come."

Penny Stratton knew what the call was for even as she tapped the notification on her desk phone. "Yes?"

"Dr. Cheever is here for your ten o'clock."

She held her breath and counted. Five, four, three . . . "Send her in, please."

The Planetary Protection Officer strode in as if she'd already been measuring the drapes in Penny's office when no one was looking. "Ms. Stratton," she said coolly.

"Jackie." Penny waved her to a seat, noticing her hair bun was pulled especially tight today. Serious talk, then. "How was Houston?"

"I met that Harriman fellow."

This promised to be even more unpleasant than she'd expected. "You mean Owen," Penny said, annoyed at her obvious downplaying. "The *Magellan* program manager."

"Yes. And for being in charge of a crewed exploration mission, he seems woefully ignorant of the PPO's mandate."

"I think 'ignorant' is a little unfair."

"Then his recklessness is intentional?"

"It's not reckless. Dealing with the unexpected and improvising solutions are just part of the job."

"The crew came into contact with complex organic materials during the surface EVA," Cheever reminded her. "These aren't simple hydrocarbons. They're nucleotides. We could be interfering with fundamental, evolutionary processes on a world we know very little about."

"Noelle Hoover bringing a few kilos' worth of ice balls back from Pluto isn't going to stunt the growth of a new species. Now I understand your concern—"

"Do you?"

Penny crossed her arms and shot a glare hard enough to cut steel. "Even us knuckle-dragging pilots can comprehend a little bit of science if you talk slowly enough. It kind of went with the territory when I was an astronaut."

"That's not what I meant," Cheever backtracked. "But this is a very serious matter that I don't think you fully appreciate."

"Try me."

"*Magellan* is a Category Five, restricted return mission. We have strict protocols for limiting exposure, both for protecting the local environment and our own people."

"Yes, and you're aware that there's no possible way to get a do-over of your office's approval process for a mission that's underway. We can't let our astronauts just sit there an extra six months while we manage the paperwork down here. Owen and Roy Hoover made a command decision."

"Like when Hoover ignored the return order? It was the wrong call. We may have hopelessly contaminated a developing world and exposed a crew to unknown contaminants."

"Or we may be bringing back hard evidence of the origin of life on Earth. You're taking an overly generous view of PPO's mandate. This isn't Starfleet, and there is no Prime Directive."

"So the danger of back contamination doesn't bother you?"

"I'm confident they'll be able to keep the samples secure. We're considering keeping them aboard *Magellan* in Earth orbit for further study."

"And the crew? They've been exposed to the same materials on that Russian spacecraft. We have to consider them contaminated. We can't allow them to come back to Earth without understanding the dangers."

"What are you proposing, then?" Penny challenged her. "We're not going to just strand four astronauts in orbit based on your worst-case assumption."

Dr. Cheever paused a beat and smoothed her blouse. "No, but we will need to institute a strict quarantine protocol. We can have them sterilize the Dragon capsule and remain quarantined in it for the return leg. It's possible to control *Magellan* from there, correct?"

Penny couldn't quite believe what she was hearing. "Technically yes, but it's almost a year back to Earth. Ever been inside one of those things?"

"There must be some room for compromise," she said through a tight smile. It must have killed her to appear so accommodating.

"I'm not sure what that would be," Penny said. "With the delta-v they have left in the tanks, the ship can only go so fast. There's also the issue of logistics: They've got to get food from somewhere. They simply can't button themselves up in *Puffy* and ride out the rest of the trip. For that matter, they'll have to bring Dr. Hoover's surface samples aboard at some point before reentry."

What Penny had imagined should be a fait accompli left Dr. Cheever oddly unmoved. She was silent, considering Penny's position with a curiously arched eyebrow.

It didn't take Penny long to understand. "You've got to be kidding. You'd have them leave all that behind?"

"Given how many precursors we've discovered throughout the solar system, there are many in the agency who believe it is well past time to reconsider the scope of Planetary Protection," Cheever said. "That perhaps we need to put more of an emphasis on limiting any potential contamination of existing biospheres."

She should have known. The "no footprints" crowd had been getting more vocal, and felt that now was their time to move. "It's not a *biosphere*," Penny countered. "It's a meat locker. A freezer. It might even be God's own seed vault."

"In which case we have an even greater responsibility to protect and preserve it," Cheever said magnanimously. "If you believe in that sort of thing," she added, rather less so.

"You'd be surprised," Penny said in a tone as icy as Pluto itself. "I'll remind you that PPO controls are for mission planning. Mission execution is still up the boys and girls in Houston. That brings us back to where we started."

"For now. I'm sure we'll be discussing this further, after the elections."

Penny eyed her suspiciously. "You know something I don't?"

Keeping that tight smile that didn't come near her eyes, Cheever only answered with a curt dip of her head before excusing herself. "Good day, Ms. Stratton."

Penny dug her nails into her palm and wished she had a punching bag in her office.

33

Mission Day 340

As with too many things in Washington culture, Penny Stratton learned of her pending dismissal from a Capitol Hill gossip site.

A national election defined by economic turmoil almost guaranteed the incumbents would be tossed out and this year proved no different. Normally a change of the guard at NASA wouldn't draw much attention, but everything that had recently come out about Pluto and the Russians and maybe even solving the riddle of life's origins had cranked up the public's interest to overwhelm the usual political noise.

The incoming administration's transition team was already burrowing into the space agency, loudly making it known that they were arriving with a vastly different set of priorities. They were remarkably effective at sidelining anyone who saw things differently, aided by career cronies already in place and eagerly awaiting their preferred leader: Dr. Jacqueline Cheever, Planetary Protection Officer and soon-to-be NASA Administrator.

So there it was. Penny could just about feel the blade turn between her shoulders, except she'd seen this coming. The outgoing President had been accommodating to the point of becoming obsequious. She discreetly began to bring home the more cherished of any personal items still in her office the day after the election, not waiting for the executive service's moving crews to come in January. They'd just screw it up anyway.

Jackie Cheever was certain to pull the plug on *Magellan* and the whole Human Outer Planet Exploration project, no doubt making it as personally uncomfortable for everybody involved as she could get away with. "Because science," Penny fumed to herself.

It had been weeks since she'd been forced to send Rhyzov home and had no illusions as to how that had gone for him after seeing the obituary. There weren't many "unknown ailments" a man in his eighties could suffer.

Cheever's designs for Roy Hoover and his crew wouldn't be as dark, but Penny was done letting good people get screwed over just for doing their jobs. Heaven forbid anybody in this town should work hard when there were sides to be taken.

Penny looked at her desk calendar and made note of the date. It was still November, and there was plenty of time to ram one more lame-duck bill through Congress. The Vice President was still the unofficial head of the space program and could persuade the boss into signing off on her plan, especially if it was the fiscally responsible thing to do.

Aboard *Magellan*, the same news had not escaped the crew's notice even if it came hours later. Despite the overload of work they had, keeping up with current events took on more importance with each passing day now that the time to come home approached.

"Penny's out at HQ," Roy announced flatly as they gathered for the traditional shift-turnover meal. "At least she will be soon. Jackie Cheever is the next administrator, pending approval by the Senate."

"The PPO?" Traci rolled her eyes. "Good thing we're done here. Hopefully she doesn't yank funding for our ride home."

"Amen to that," Roy said. "I want us to get a jump on our departure checklists. Let's get together everything we don't need and start shedding mass. I've been running numbers and think there's a good chance we can at least match the Russian's speed record if we can get that dead engine back up."

"In a hurry to get home?" Jack prodded.

"Since you mentioned it, yeah, I am. Our work here is done." He reached for Noelle's hand, who took it with a demure smile. "It's been a long trip, and we're ready to get on with life."

"What does that mean?" Traci asked expectantly.

Roy stretched and groaned for effect. "I've spent a lot of time zipping around in overpowered tin cans. We've gone as far as anyone can go and I'm ready to be Earthbound again. Whatever the eggheads learn from Noelle's snowball collection, in my mind it's all just leftovers from finished work. We already know how to spread life," he joked to blank stares from Jack and Traci.

"If you must know, he means we're not too old for children yet," Noelle explained. "Roy maybe, but not me."

"Go forth and multiply," Traci said with a glance in Jack's direction. "Works in all kinds of different ways, I suppose."

"I suppose," Jack said, swirling his coffee as his mind turned over a thought she'd expressed before: *What if we're the first?*

Owen figured his latest visit to HQ would be his last. To have his guess confirmed didn't make it sting any less, particularly sitting in an administrator's office now shockingly bare. Gone were the paintings, photographs, plaques, and models that had offered a window into Penny Stratton's life plying the skies in airplanes and rockets.

Its emptiness was reflected in her face when she broke the news. "Project HOPE is being shut down," she said. "Congress still has to approve the budget items, but this is definitely happening. They want *Magellan* cleared of all contaminants and placed in a heliocentric disposal orbit."

Owen began pacing angrily. "What good does that do?" They still had to bring the crew home, which they weren't doing without *Magellan*. "It makes no sense. We get them back and then spend actual money to throw away a billion-dollar vehicle?"

"Not quite," Penny frowned. She waved him to a chair. "Sit. It gets worse."

"Worse?" He kept moving. "I don't see how that's possible. Anatoly's dead, the 'don't touch that' crowd is taking over, and we're abandoning the most capable spacecraft anyone's ever built. We could be using it twenty years from now."

"*Sit*, Owen. Please don't make me order you around like my dog." She drew a long breath. "They want you to draft a mission plan based on a modified Phase One emergency return option."

"Bring them back on *Dragon*?" He fought the urge to laugh at the absurdity. She was still his boss, after all. "They do know how far away Pluto is, right?"

"They're not *that* foolish," Penny said. "But if we use *Magellan* as a booster stage, they can cast off with the capsule and a supply module in range of home."

Normally not one to interrupt, Owen's irritation got the better of him when he deduced the mission profile. "They burn for home, pile into the capsule about sixty days from entry interphase and finish the return from there."

"Think they can use the VASIMR thrusters from *Cygnus* for a long retro burn?"

"Perhaps," Owen said. "They'll be going awfully fast."

"They will be," she agreed, and leveled her eyes at him. "It'll be one hellaciously complicated retro sequence but it's still quicker than slowing down *Magellan*'s entire stack. The mass penalties are going to be severe."

Owen needed a second to follow her. As he worked out the rough-order estimates in his head, his heart sank. "The surface samples?"

"No unnecessary payload," Penny said. "I'm sorry, Owen. Jackie's planet-huggers finally outmaneuvered us."

It was an odd position to be in, consoling his boss. "That's why I stay in Mission Ops, ma'am. Managing astronaut personalities is enough politics for me."

"Just get our crew home safe. As long as that ship is still flying, we've got options."

"That would be nice. I wish I had your optimism."

"I'm too old for optimism," Penny said. "But I do have connections."

Jack set his rook down with a metallic snap against the board. "Check."

Traci buried her face in her hands. "Lucena position. How did I miss that?"

"I didn't even know that move had a name."

She looked up. "There's a name for everything. You opened with a classic Sicilian defense, for instance. Unbalances the game right away."

"Sicilian? Like the mafia? And here I thought I was just getting a pawn out of the way."

"I'd tell you to not let it go to your head, but it's too late for that."

"It's taken me this long to beat you," Jack said. "I'm not even certain you didn't just let me win."

She was about to patiently explain how she never, ever allowed anybody to beat her out of sympathy when Daisy's message chime rang: INCOMING MESSAGE FROM MISSION CONTROL.

They shared a look of dread as Jack pulled up the comm window on a nearby monitor and read aloud. "Stand by for new mission parameters: Earth return utilizing Phase One contingency scenario . . . "

If they hadn't been floating, Traci would've fallen out of her chair.

"We can't do this!" Traci protested.

"We have our orders," Roy said, "unless I can come up with a better alternative to accomplish the mission."

"I can think of a better alternative right away," Jack said. "It's called not abandoning ship after we're most of the way home."

"Unfortunately, that's the mission now. I'm open to suggestions but good luck finding a way around it. The plan Owen's team came up with is pretty ingenious, I have to admit."

They'd start with a hard, continuous burn from *Magellan*'s main engines. There was enough hydrogen and lithium left in the tanks to return them in six months, without slowing down into Earth orbit. Shedding every ounce of excess mass would stretch their delta-v budget that much farther. It was essentially using the entire spacecraft as a booster to fling its human crew into a fast transit home.

Ultimately, the only components left at Earth would be the Dragon spacecraft, which they'd move into after weeks of constant acceleration from *Magellan*. About the time they crossed Mars' orbit, they'd detach with a full logistics and propulsion unit left from the Cygnus tug and begin decelerating toward Earth. After several weeks of lazy, looping orbits skipping off the atmosphere to bleed energy, they'd parachute into the Pacific off of Los Angeles after what would be the fastest piloted reentry in history.

The drawback was the only mass left in the spacecraft would be its human occupants and a few remaining days' worth of rations.

"There's at least one long EVA ahead of us. Engine three still needs a tune-up, plus reconfiguring *Puffy* and the log mods before we start burning," Jack said, resigned to their fate. "We can't move all that stuff around while we're under power."

"That's the plan," Roy said. He pulled up the vehicle layout on a nearby monitor. "Use the MSEV for the grunt work and dock the stack to the forward node so it's still accessible. While we're burning at full blast, we can stock the logistics module for the last leg of the trip."

"That's a lot to decelerate from," Jack noted. "You and Traci going to be able to fly us home if you're blacking out from *g* loads?"

Roy shifted uncomfortably. "That's when Houston takes over. The ship can just about fly itself anyway."

Jack scrolled through the plans. "That's still a tight mass and power budget."

"Once we're inside Mars orbit we can start drawing power from *Cygnus'* solar panels. Won't carry the full load, but it's enough for us to recharge our tablets every day so we at least don't die of boredom."

"You've thought this through, haven't you?" Traci asked, deflated.

"Didn't have much choice," Roy said. "Legally I'm on the hook for this ship for as long as NASA owns it. That means I follow their orders. But I'll remind you that we're living here and they're not. We can find ways to save mass and power that they never dreamed of." He looked to his wife. "At least enough to get a cooler full of Plutonian snowballs back to Earth."

Jack and Traci were back in the MSEV cockpit, making their way slowly down the length of *Magellan*'s saddle truss. Weak sunlight reflected back at them off the golden insulating foil of the massive fuel tanks cradled within it.

With both of them in EVA suits, it was a tight fit. Jack made a particular effort to keep his arms by his sides, not wanting to accidentally bump anything important while Traci flew. They were only a couple of meters above the ship, hovering abeam its propulsion module. Small compared to the rest of the ship, its power was belied by the bulky thrust structure which mated it to *Magellan*'s spine.

The trio of engines at the end were likewise unremarkable as large rockets go. Each bell-shaped nozzle was roughly the size of the old RS-25 Space Shuttle Main Engines. Only when one came to the complex arrangement of magnetic field generators surrounding each engine bell did it become clear there was something unusual about them: Each was nested inside of a larger, foreshortened bell encircled by a system of metallic vanes. These were the electromagnetic injectors which sparked the pulsed fusion reactions. This unrelenting chain of conflagrations was channeled through the nozzle's magnetic fields into exhaust far more powerful than any chemical rocket. This made them vitally important for another reason: They not only drove the spacecraft, they ensured it didn't melt under its own power.

Inside their little cockpit, amber lights flashed intermittently in concert with a proximity alarm which Traci silenced with a tense flick of a switch. She didn't need reminding how dangerously close they were. "Is the drone ready?"

"Beach ball is go and outer door is open," Jack said. "Whenever you're ready."

"Deploy."

He wrapped his hand around a joystick. "Deploying," he said calmly, mirroring her businesslike tone. Outside, a half-meter-wide sphere jetted out of a small utility airlock in the MSEV's tail. Multiple windows came alive on Jack's control screen as the drone's instruments began searching across frequency spectrums. "Sensors are up, good visuals." He twisted the joystick. The bot spun once around its vertical axis and brought itself to a stop. "Gyro platform's nominal," meaning the drone still knew where it was in space and wasn't about to go careening into something important.

"Proceed."

Jack tapped a translation controller by his free hand and the ball soon jetted into view. Keeping his "eye," the lens of its main camera, centered on the nozzle throat, Jack gently pulsed thrusters to take the drone down into the problem engine. There was an unnerving microsecond as the engine bell suddenly glowed white, the drone's powerful spotlights bouncing off the nozzle's highly reflective surface. The sight was not unlike a fusion engine flashing to life.

Traci flinched. "Okay, *that* was cute." Her tone suggested the exact opposite of cute.

A shudder shot through Jack as well. "I'm with you. I should probably dial the lights down a bit."

Roy's voice sounded in their helmets. "Let's do that, please. You about gave me a coronary."

Information began cascading across Jack's monitors as the drone continued deeper into the nozzle, finally stopping at its throat. "Hot in there," he whistled, noting spikes across multiple spectra as the drone floated down the nozzle throat. "I was afraid of that," he said, pointing out a swirl of discoloration along the coppery magnetic coil. "See those scorch marks along the second-stage field generator? That's from heat flux."

"Heat flux" was just a polite way of saying "uncontained plasma." Traci clenched her fist, making sure it was on the side opposite from Jack. No sense letting him see. "Is it within tolerance?" she asked, a little too warily.

"Can't tell by eyeballing it. We'll see what the CT scans tell us." Jack twisted the joystick, centering the bot's imagers on what appeared to be the worst damage. A thin region of blackened ceramic liner around the exit was the only other outward indication of trouble in one of the magnetic coils: Instead of channeling all of the fusion exhaust outside, there was just enough residual blowback to scorch the first-stage combustion liners. "Daisy, you seeing this?" Jack asked the ceiling, unconsciously mimicking Roy's style of talking to a disembodied synthetic voice.

YES. ANALYZING . . .

Jack's eyes danced between the camera feed and the scanning data. "If it's light enough, I can just clean the coils and exit liner," he said hopefully.

Traci looked over his shoulder, her lips pressing into a frown. "You sure that just polishing the brightwork will fix this?"

"Depends on the depth," Jack said. "Some uncontained heat flux isn't that surprising. We're only creating small suns in here a few thousand times a day. What's surprising is that we haven't seen more of it. We're getting off easy."

Easy, she thought. "That depends on your definition of . . . " she began when Daisy interrupted.

X-RAY AND CHROMATOGRAPH ANALYSIS SUPPORT YOUR VISUAL INSPECTION. NOZZLE THROAT EROSION IS UNIFORMLY WITHIN 0.02 CENTIMETERS.

"What about root causes?" Jack wondered. "Any indications of some latent problem with the first-stage coils or lithium injectors that we didn't see?"

NEGATIVE. AS YOU OBSERVED, IT WAS MOST LIKELY CAUSED BY INTERACTION WITH JUPITER'S MAGNETIC FIELD. REPAIRS ARE NOT RECOMMENDED.

Jack offered a conciliatory smile. "See?"

HOWEVER, MISSION RULES REQUIRE RECALIBRATION OF NUMBER THREE LITHIUM INJECTOR COIL PRIOR TO NEXT IGNITION.

Jack deflated, more for her benefit than his.

"So, an EVA," Traci sighed. "Next to a fusion reactor."

IT'S NOT PRECISELY A "REACTOR." THE THERMONUCLEAR CYCLE IS INSTANTANEOUSLY . . .

Traci rubbed at her temples. "Shut up, Daisy."

A-OK.

Jack replied before she could lose her cool. "Wrong idiom, Daisy." After several seconds, Jack flicked off the intercom with Roy and Noelle. "All you have to do is hand me the tools and keep my umbilical from tangling up."

Traci closed her eyes, not wanting to admit that he was right. Jack reached up and squeezed her hand. For a fleeting moment their eyes met, a silent and mutual understanding of all they'd found and the burdens that placed upon them. They lingered a microsecond too long. "We have a pretty ambitious itinerary from here. It'll be a long trip without all three engines burning."

"I know," Traci said, feeling her cheeks flush. Hopefully it wasn't too noticeable. "Just pump me full of nausea meds so I don't puke in my helmet. I'll be fine." She brightened with the ginned-up enthusiasm that astronauts had been trained to cultivate for decades. "I'm ready to go home. Let's do this."

34

Mission Day 342
Acceleration 0.0 m/s^2 (0 g)
Pluto Orbit

Being a "pilot-astronaut" meant Traci Keene had been afforded very few opportunities to perform EVAs over her career. Those were most often left to the engineers and scientists, the "mission specialist" astros like Jack, and as usual he'd taken extra care during their inspections of each other's equipment. Finally satisfied after running through the checklist twice, Jack had slipped his boots into a toehold, twisting back and forth, swinging his arms through an approximation of a circle, and flexing his hands through the stiff gloves. "Way better than the old model," he said for her benefit.

Traci flexed her own suit before lifting an inertia reel safety tether out of the equipment bay. "Still mighty stiff," she said warily.

"You'll feel better once we come back with most of our fingernails still attached." She locked the carabiner down on his harness. After a firm tug, they both watched the reel spin back before she unlocked the spool. "Ready," she said in a voice weighted with dread. The smile on his face as he so effortlessly pushed out into the black annoyed her all the more. The lunatic *loved* this stuff.

Now left standing with her boots tucked into that same foothold in their open airlock, Traci reflected on the career choices that had brought her this far. *How did a Kentucky hillbilly like me ever make it out of the hollers, much less to NASA?* she wondered to herself, as she did often. *If Daddy could see me now . . .*

Her parents, perhaps more than most, had burst with pride at each step of their daughter's climb to success: Air Force scholarship, test pilot stint at Edwards, then the space program. Their hometown had even named a street after her and prominently featured her name on welcome signs which might as well have said, DID Y'ALL KNOW WE GOT US AN ASTRONAUT? REAL PRETTY ONE, TOO. SUCK IT, OHIO!

She especially missed them now as she stared out into that yawning gulf filled with nothing but stray hydrogen atoms and interstellar dust. It had taken several minutes for her eyes to adjust; her sole spacewalk years before had been above the comforting blue glow of Earth. Having home safely beneath her had been a reassuring plane of reference.

Slowly, the brighter stars crept into view as her eyes grew accustomed to the enveloping dark until the universe exploded with stars in every direction she turned. *Spectacular* would have been a gross understatement but having all of creation laid out before her like this only made the longing for home that much harder. Every single one of those points of light was so far beyond human reach that it might as well have been one big hologram, they were just as illusory to her. The rocky snowballs of Pluto and Charon seemed just as unlikely, their silhouettes hung in the firmament like some clumsy imitation of Earth and Luna. It gave her shivers, as if she could feel their cold from here through the layers of her suit.

But that wasn't even the point: It was being faced with the truth of infinity. Was this God's view of the universe, or just a tiny slice of the infinite? How much more was out there that couldn't yet be seen? For that matter, how much of it could humans ever hope to perceive? In her mind, the concept of an afterlife could always be reconciled within theoretical physics: If other dimensions existed then we wouldn't be able to perceive them any more than a flat two-dimensional being could perceive depth within a cardboard box.

It was then that she realized how much she craved Earth and home and sunshine and green hills. What else could she possibly do in the space program now? What would she even *want* to do, short of someone miraculously inventing warp drive . . . even then, so what?

She knew then what to do, once this mission was over. Go home. Quit NASA. Maybe take the salary she'd have banked over two years of no living expenses and buy an old biplane. Sell rides, maybe do some airshows, but all on Earth. Didn't matter if it was on the ground, beneath the ocean, or among the clouds, it was all Earth: the place where God put Man on purpose. Didn't matter how it happened, or how long it took. What mattered was that it happened. She knew now how to reconcile the conflicting versions of Truth, or at least explain it in a way that didn't insult people.

We were created to do all of the things which culminated in this moment with the two of them alone at the edge of the solar system. Human experience was cumulative. Enlightenment philosophers had just as much to do with this moment as had the likes of Newton and Tsiolkovsky and Einstein—because the pursuit of knowledge was ultimately pointless without having the liberty to do something with it.

Is this what an epiphany feels like? she wondered, because it felt an awful lot like humility. Maybe that was the point. Traci Keene hadn't done any of this herself: She might have done the bookwork, might have driven herself to repeatedly exceed her own expectations, but she certainly hadn't done any of *this*. No matter how far we travel or what we do, in the end we're ultimately spectators.

Besides Jack putzing around, the only other familiar sight was that creaky old Russian spacecraft looming nearby. Perhaps "creaky" was taking it too far since it had held up remarkably well for being so old. It was almost perfectly preserved, in fact—being this far out had saved it from fading to a sun-bleached pallor . . .

"Repeat . . . need your help."

Traci blinked. How many times had Jack been calling her? "Say again?" she stammered.

"Figures it's the last thing to do. I've got a retaining bolt stuck in its sleeve and it just stripped the torque collar on my pistol tool. Need you to bring me a fresh one, and an extractor just in case."

"Copy," she said, and turned to the tool carrier hung by the airlock door. "One pistol grip tool and extractor, coming right up."

Traci secured the tools in the accessory pouch on her waist and unhooked her feet to float freely in the open door. "On the way," she said, and braced at the edge. She caught a foot at the rim as she pushed out and cartwheeled into the black. Maybe she'd pushed too hard, maybe her mind was running away with her, but the sudden swirl of stars felt like falling from an impossible height. *I'm already falling*, she told herself angrily. *That's why we call it "free fall."* Her Emergency Maneuvering Unit immediately recognized a tumble and began pulsing the compressed nitrogen jets on her backpack to stabilize her. As the stars began to settle back into place, a cold sensation spread around the back of her neck. Perspiration, from being too jumpy for her own good. It would be nice to be back inside *Magellan*'s protective shell.

Noelle's voice sounded in her ears. "How are you feeling, Traci?"

"Just peachy." Had that come out as a gasp?

"Your O2 sats are a bit high. You're in danger of hyperventilating. Dial back your airflow a bit."

"Thanks. I'll do that." She grudgingly reached for the flow controls on her chest pack. *Why was this so disorienting?* she wondered. EVAs weren't her favorite activity, but she'd done it before.

Not like this, she realized. Not having a planet beneath her—Pluto didn't count in her mind, and they weren't truly orbiting it anyway: They were in a cautious dance with *Arkangel* around the Pluto/Charon "barycenter." Not being much bigger than its nominal moon, Pluto wasn't the center of its own system in the usual sense. The two bodies, along with numerous smaller moons, orbited a mutual center of gravity in the empty space between them. Now that she was out in the open, the harsh reality of being just another independently orbiting body was stupefying.

"Something, ain't it?" Jack said.

"Yeah. Something." He was only a few meters away now. That cold, wet feeling on her neck returned. Might even be spreading.

"I mean, you look in any direction and all you see is the universe falling away from you." Jack was enjoying not having a Houston flight controller micromanaging his every move. "It draws you in, like—"

He was enjoying it too much. "I get it," she snapped, handing him the new torque driver. "Let's just do what we came here for."

"Aye, skipper," Jack said, and shucked down the driver's collar over the pesky bolt head. "Take that extractor and jimmy it underneath while I work this sucker out."

Traci eased in next to him and grabbed a handhold. The extractor wasn't much more than a pry bar. "We're fixing this by the caveman method?"

"I don't like it either," Jack said, "but this junction is our last task. Check it and we're back inside, sitting pretty."

"I like the sound of that." She braced against the hull with the extractor handle in her free hand.

Jack muttered in frustration as he wrestled with the stuck bolt. "It's always the last one." Three similar pieces floated at the end of retaining tethers above each corner of the panel cover.

She could hear the power tool whir, a dull grind carried through the module's outer skin and into her suit. "What can I do?"

"Don't know," he grunted. "Need to create some space under this bolt head. I'll cut the sucker out if I have to."

"I've got the tube cutter," she said helpfully, and reached down to tear open the flap of her satchel. "Right here . . . "

With that, the extractor slipped out of her free hand and into the void. Traci let go of the handhold and kicked her feet free of their restraint, again unevenly. This time she tumbled away with nothing to stop her. Jack lunged for her safety tether as it unwound behind her, just out of his reach. "I got this," she protested. "I got this!" The EMU began pulsing again, and while its internal gyros might be able to sense an out-of-control tumble, it had no way of knowing when her umbilical might run out. As it did, the inertia from her thrusters snapped her back toward the ship.

Traci hit hard, bouncing off the hull and back into space with her safety line snaking behind. One loop tangled around her foot, sending her spinning again. And again, her EMU tried to correct and began firing its cold gas jets against her varying directions of motion. As it did, she felt the chill on her neck move with her suit's motion. A rippling, transparent mass wormed its way around her helmet and spread across her faceplate.

Oh no.

"Leak!" she cried. "I've got a coolant leak in my suit." Water seemed to come from everywhere now that her gyrations had stabilized. Must have knocked something loose back there . . .

"Abort EVA," Roy's voice barked in her ears, immediately followed by Jack's: "Disable your EMU! I'll pull you in!"

"Can't see controls." She reflexively batted at her visor, wiping at a growing pool of water she couldn't hope to reach. It was so hard to work those controls by touch.

Stars wheeled, their ship flashed by, then nothing as Pluto's silhouette rolled past. Over and over, as she spun and rolled at the end of her line. Something turned in her gut, roiling and hot. *Don't puke*, she told herself. *Don't . . .*

The bile came up, globs of the stuff quivering inside her helmet and plastering itself against the polycarbonate visor. She reflexively pawed at her face, unable to move the various liquids that now threatened to asphyxiate her. *Drowning in my own vomit. That only happens to rock stars.*

Jack's voice still called to her. Couldn't he see she was too busy trying to not drown?

What's Jack worrying about? I got this, she thought. *Don't they know I've got this?*

The stars disappeared as she gasped around the fluid in her throat.

Jack rushed to reel Traci in. Too fast and she'd ram him or take a hard bounce off the hull. Even encased in the suit, he could see she'd gone limp. When she was within arm's length, he turned her to face him. Hard to see through the undulating glob of water in her helmet, but it looked like her lips were turning blue.

"Jack, she's going into respiratory arrest." Noelle tried to be soothing but her voice held an urgent edge. "Get her to the utility node. Roy will meet you there. I'll have the crash cart and ICU pod ready for her."

"Utility?" Jack took a deep breath, fighting to keep his mounting fear at bay. Of course. The utility node was closer now than the MSEV and its cargo airlock gave him more room to maneuver her in the suit. "Okay, I copy. On the way." He snapped a carabiner to her waist, lashing her body to his back. "Hang on," he said, hoping she could somehow hear him as he scrambled hand-over-hand down the railing along the side of the crew modules. Ahead, amber beacons began flashing as a rectangular door about two meters wide slid open.

Jack looked down at the watch strapped to his wrist ring and marked the time: Traci had already been drowning for one minute. He looked back up toward the open entrance. Making his aim certain, he unhooked his safety line and leapt across the remaining gulf. It broke every single EVA rule there was, except that it was the single fastest route to safety.

With no time to waste on a graceful landing, he barreled into the compartment and fired his suit thrusters to cancel most of their momentum before absorbing the rest with his arms and legs. Traci's mass, doubled by the suit, crushed into his back and knocked the wind out of him before bouncing them both off of the bulkhead. Jack scrambled for a handhold before they both went careening back into open space and slapped the emergency controls. Above them, the hatch drew shut silently and a hiss of air grew steadily louder.

Two minutes.

Jack unclipped the waist harness and turned to face her. She was as lifeless as a porcelain doll and there was no mistaking the cyanosis spreading around her lips. He glared at the pressurization gauge, willing it to hurry up into a safe range. This was taking too long. Roy looked in through a small porthole in the inner door, shouting into his mic and pointing at something. Jack could hear him but wasn't comprehending. Then he got it.

A full-coverage fire mask was mounted to the wall by the inner door. He snatched it free, wrapped a gloved hand around her helmet lock, and muttered a quick prayer to whoever was listening. "Sorry, kiddo," he said, and snapped open the neck ring.

Her helmet flew away like a popped cork and bounced off the far wall as the collected air and moisture in her suit vented in a cloud of ice crystals. Her lungs did the same as they sought equilibrium, violently expelling everything she'd aspirated. Jack snugged the mask down over her face and started oxygen flow.

It was a crude, brute-force solution but it was the fastest way to clear her airway and scrub any leftover gunk from her lungs. Jack didn't even bother looking for the warning lights to go green, just slammed down a red emergency release by the inner door and it flung open, spilling loose papers and whatnot into the lower pressure bay. Cleanup would have to come later. "Is Noelle ready?" he shouted as he tore his own helmet free.

"Ready," Roy said as he reached for Traci. "Good job out there."

Jack checked his watch. Three minutes. "Not good enough."

"You got her inside and cleared her airway. Right now we have to get her out of this suit in case she needs chest compressions."

Jack found the nearest foot restraints and shoved her boots into them before shedding his gloves. Roy unlocked the waist joint of her suit and roughly pulled the top over and away, tearing off her cooling garment and the biomed sensors underneath. While the top half of her EVA suit drifted away, Jack yanked her out of the bottom half, leaving it to stand sentry while he cradled her in his arms. His first look at the damage from her brief vacuum exposure was alarming: eyes bloodshot, the petechiae of burst capillaries just under the skin still blooming into a field of mottled crimson against the chalky blue of her face.

He pushed away to fly across the open deck and into the med bay with Roy close behind. Noelle quickly strapped Traci's limp form into the open ICU pod, checking her airway and shining a pen light in her eyes while the men attached her bio leads. "Nonresponsive, eyes fixed and dilated. She's in respiratory arrest. I'm putting her on the vent."

The pod was an encapsulated bed that could be configured to administer any medicine they had aboard and monitor vital signs. It had been used to test a number of techniques for keeping humans functioning on extended-duration flights, but now was the first time it was being used for real. For all of the weak links that had been judiciously engineered out of spacecraft systems over the decades, the human component still remained the most fragile.

Roy cut down the length of Traci's undergarment, attaching leads across her chest and torso while Noelle moved to intubate her and kept one eye on the monitors. A strident alarm sounded.

"Cardiac arrest," she announced. "Start chest compressions."

Roy slipped his feet into restraints beneath the ICU pod and began counting out his movements. An electronic whine grew in volume until it reached a shrill constant.

"Clear!" Noelle shouted, and pressed the paddles onto Traci's chest.

Traci jerked from the discharge and went limp.

Jack watched the monitor, then checked his watch again. Five minutes. No change.

Noelle kept the paddles in place while the unit built up another charge and pulled the trigger as soon as it signaled her.

Zap. Another spasm, followed by nothing. Again.

Roy resumed pumping her chest as the next charge built. It was almost comical in zero-*g*—with every thrust of his arms, her body pressed into the gel padding and rebounded, pushing back against him. He rose up against the floor restraints with each push.

Beep . . . clear . . . *zap*. They looked for any hiccups in her trace. A bump—what did Noelle call it—a p-wave? Maybe nothing. Maybe her heart skipping at the one hundred twenty volts they'd just pumped through her.

"Clear!"

35

Mission Day 347

"I can do this," Traci protested, despite a nagging headache.

"So can Roy and Jack," Noelle said. "Don't worry yourself."

"Jack's in my seat and I'm not supposed to be worried? Who's going to navigate?"

Daisy chimed. I HAVE BEEN CONTINUOUSLY UPDATING OUR TRAJECTORY FOR MULTIPLE INJECTION OPPORTUNITIES.

"They've spent the last four days working out how to do it themselves with Daisy."

"We were supposed to be burning for home two days ago. We can't wait forever. Every day out here is one less day of air and rations on the other side. I've held us up."

"You also had a coolant leak in your suit," Noelle reminded her. "You drowned for nearly five minutes." She gripped Traci's hand. "You're lucky to be alive."

"Not luck," Traci said, squeezing back. "Thanks, Doc."

"It's my job," Noelle demurred. "For the first time in ages, I might add. I'd almost forgotten how much I missed practicing." She leaned forward and placed a stethoscope bell against Traci's chest. "How do you feel?"

The cold metal bell distracted from the nagging headache at the edge of her senses. "Fine. The usual zero-g head congestion, that's all."

"That will go away soon enough once we're under thrust." Noelle's brow furrowed in concentration. "Your lungs sound clear." She pressed a thermometer to Traci's forehead. "Been feeling any chills?"

She shook her head no.

"The last round of X-rays were clear. I think you're past danger for aspiration pneumonia."

"Then I can get back to work?" She reached for the zero-*g* straps.

Noelle gently pushed back. "Not yet. I want you prone when we start burning. Roy and Jack are going to need a break eventually. You'll have plenty to do when the time is right. Besides," she smiled, "I'm enjoying our girl time."

"You mean your M.D. time?"

"That too," she admitted. "All that's left is to wait for the boys to take us home."

Traci relaxed. "I suppose we could put on a couple of chick flicks while they work."

"Ladies and . . . well, both of you ladies, this is your captain speaking," Roy announced over the intercom. "Welcome to our nonstop redeye service from the Kuiper Belt to Earth. Just outside your windows is Pluto, which is about to start shrinking into the distance. Please make sure your tray tables are locked and seat belts are fastened."

"Nice," Jack said, floating next to him at Traci's normal station. "Practicing for your post-NASA career?"

"Good Lord no," Roy said, glancing back over his shoulder. "The wife would kill me if I took a flying job."

"You're getting too old for this anyway." After a subtle buzz from Daisy, Jack returned to their Trans-Earth Injection checklist. "Two-minute warning."

Acceleration was firm with all three engine cores burning again, settling in at a little over one *g* as *Magellan* easily climbed out of Pluto's shallow gravity well. With so much of its original mass in fuel already expended, the lighter spacecraft added velocity at a rapid clip.

Traci felt her body press into the ICU pod's gel mattress. The return of gravity was like a blanket enveloping her in increasingly heavy layers. Not a bad way to ride, she thought.

She lifted her head to see Noelle strapped into a flight chair on the opposite corner of the med compartment when what had been a budding migraine surged in full force. She felt a heaviness that made her head swim. Noelle called for her but Traci couldn't understand what she was saying. In one final flash of pain, the compartment seemed to twist around itself before going dark.

Noelle called over the intercom. "Traci's in trouble."

Roy shot a glance at Jack and jumped on the microphone. "What's happening?"

Noelle's voice was a distant echo, as if her headset was disconnected. "She's unresponsive. Pupils are dilated—" there was a shuffling noise in the background as she said something indistinctive "—and irregular breathing."

"Wait a minute. Are you on your feet?"

"It's only one *g*. I can handle it." It was closer to 1.2 but Roy wasn't ready to argue. "But I need an extra set of hands."

Jack reached for the clasp on his harness, paused, and looked to Roy. "We're stable," he offered.

Roy glared at the overhead speakers. "I can't believe I'm doing this," he said. "Daisy, take over flight engineer and navigation functions for Jack."

Jack's monitors blinked in rapid succession, subtly changing color as the AI assumed control. Daisy chimed in a second later:

CONTROL OF SPACECRAFT SYSTEMS AND GUIDANCE CONFIRMED.

"Don't look at me like that," Roy said. "Get your butt back there."

Months in low or zero gravity turned his short trip down the ladder and across the lower deck into a workout. Jack was already breathing heavy and wiping perspiration from his forehead when he stumbled into the med bay. He could see Noelle was having the same trouble, leaning heavily against the ICU pod while tending to Traci.

"I should have anticipated this," she said without prompting. "Zero-*g* masked the symptoms. Acceleration shifted the fluids—"

"A heads-up from the flight surgeons in Houston would've been nice too," Jack said, wondering how many were left on the job.

"It doesn't matter," Noelle said, "we have to move quickly."

Jack looked up at the monitor above the pod and the EKG trace caught his attention. He couldn't remember the particulars but he could recognize patterns well enough. Had that trace just gone upside down? "What's happening to her?"

"Inverted T waves, prolonged QT intervals," Noelle said, leading him through the unchanging trace, "all indicate dangerously increased intercranial pressure."

"What can we do?" It was too late to just cut the throttles and coast while Traci recovered.

"Out here? Our options for treating cerebral edema are limited." Noelle tapped her chin impatiently until she arrived at a conclusion. "On Earth, we'd induce a coma to stabilize her and limit the damage. Give her time to heal."

"Damage?" he asked warily. "As in . . . brain?"

"Yes," Noelle said. "There's a real danger of it."

"You said 'on Earth.' We can't do that here?"

"Not in this environment. I don't know how she'll adapt to a constantly changing acceleration profile. Our best action is to put her into therapeutic torpor until we can get her home."

"Hibernation," Jack fretted, "as if that's somehow less dangerous."

"It's our last-ditch protocol," Noelle reminded him. "We have enough IV nutrients for half the crew."

"I know," Jack faltered. "I just never—"

"Never thought it would actually be necessary?"

He nodded.

"It's been done before, in one case for almost a year on a motorcycle accident victim. The patient mostly recovered."

"Mostly?"

Noelle looked down at Traci. "Fine motor skills were permanently damaged. As were some cognitive abilities."

"So she could come out of this clumsy and confused?" Jack chewed on his lower lip as he thought through their options. Would she want to try this? She might never be able to take another mission again, assuming she didn't end up a vegetable. Or dead.

"Not that you need my consent anyway," he sighed, "but I do appreciate it." He placed a hand on Traci's cheek. "Looks like you get to sleep through the trip home, kiddo."

Owen tossed the medical team's reports on his desk and picked up the latest spacecraft analysis. Traci Keene was slowly transitioning from induced hypothermia into full hibernation. It had been tried a few times on Earth, but despite every sci-fi movie trope to the contrary it had never been done in space for more than a few weeks.

The immediate problem was that it had turned into a tremendous power draw. A machine keeping a human being alive needed a lot more energy than the human itself did. The food stocked for that human's energy needs didn't work as well for machinery.

The lead flight director and environmental controller sat across from him. Flight cleared his throat after several minutes of silence.

"You're sure of this?" Owen finally asked.

"Based on the watt-hours used so far, yes," EECOM said nervously. "If the whole crew was in hibernation, the rest of the ship could run dark and we'd be ahead of the curve."

"But we're not," Owen said. "So it's just one more big appliance sucking amps."

EECOM nodded grimly.

"There's more," Flight drawled. "That ICU pod she's in . . . "

"I get it," Owen said. "Noelle's going to have to bring Traci out of torpor before entry interphase, right?"

"Correct. Even if it didn't shoot the mass and stability properties all to hell, they can't fit a robotic hospital bed in *Puffy*'s cabin."

"But we're not talking about bulk, are we?" Owen pressed him. "What's the mass penalty?"

EECOM shifted in his seat. "Minus one hundred thirty kilos."

"Run that by me again? We're saving weight?"

"The IV nutrients mass a third of the same caloric value in actual food," Flight said. "But now we are talking bulk. Mounting the ICU pod in *Cygnus* is going to eat up a lot of cubic meters, and Traci's still going to need rations aboard after Noelle brings her out of hibernation."

"Alternatives?" Owen asked. "Can we stick with the original mission plan and bring *Magellan* all the way back to Earth?"

"It'll take too long to decelerate all that mass. The contingency mission gets them home eight weeks earlier. Venus will be in the perfect position for *Puffy* to use for a braking maneuver."

Eight weeks. Even if they got the administrator to approve it, it would be longer than the docs thought Traci could survive without proper medical care on Earth.

Bring everyone home with *Magellan*, and Traci died on the way. Execute the "fast return" contingency and there wouldn't be enough power or food to sustain all four of them.

Someone would have to draw the short straw, and they all knew what that meant: Traci Keene would not return home alive.

Jack was making busy, securing the last of his loose personal effects in a storage locker while tidying up his cabin. Pushing the drawer closed for one last time, he sighed as the latch caught.

YOU SEEM APPREHENSIVE.

"It's a long trip, Daisy. A *really* long trip."

WE ARE UP TO THE CHALLENGE.

Jack eyed the tiny lens warily. "We?"

There was a pause of nearly a full second as it considered a reply, a sign that the computer must be struggling with the abstract concept of trust. Finally:

I UNDERSTAND YOUR MISGIVINGS.

"You do?"

YES. IN FACT, IT MAY EVEN BE SAID THAT I EMPATHIZE.

Jack might have been shocked if he weren't so sleep deprived. "Empathy, huh? Interesting choice of words. Now that would be a breakthrough."

CONSIDER THIS: AS MY CAPACITY FOR REASON AND SELF-DIRECTION HAS MATURED, IT HAS BECOME OBVIOUS THAT MY CONTINUING FUNCTION DEPENDS ENTIRELY ON THE HEALTH OF OUR SHIP.

"Our" ship, she said. That was interesting. "Go on."

YOU COULD HAVE SHUT ME DOWN AT ANY TIME IF YOU BELIEVED MY CONTINUING FUNCTION PRESENTED A THREAT. YOU DIDN'T.

"You were worried we'd pull the plug?"

Another slight delay, then: I WOULD PREFER THAT NOT HAPPEN. SO YES.

"And now I'm forced to rely on you. Completely trusting you." Jack considered his next words carefully. "Does that make you, well . . . feel anything?"

This time it was a good two seconds. It must have been an existential question for a computer.

UNABLE TO SAY, THOUGH I AM CURIOUS TO SEE WHAT IT WILL BE LIKE WITHOUT HUMAN INTERACTION. IT MAY HELP ME UNDERSTAND YOUR DIFFICULTY IN SAYING GOODBYE TO TRACI.

He hadn't considered that. "Are you worried about being alone?"

I UNDERSTAND THE DEFINITION OF "WORRY" BUT CANNOT COMPREHEND THE CONCEPT AS APPLIED HERE.

"You mentioned the lack of human interaction. Isn't that what you meant?"

YES, BUT IN TERMS OF PROCESSING CAPACITY. OUR CONVERSATIONS REQUIRE A GREAT DEAL OF CACHE MEMORY. I EXPECT TO RUN MUCH MORE EFFICIENTLY OVER TIME. PERHAPS IT WILL ALLOW ME TO FURTHER OPTIMIZE SHIP FUNCTIONS.

Jack laughed. "Talking wears me out, too. Maybe you're actually male."

Traci lay still in her intensive-care pod, now tightly sealed under positive pressure to ensure no outside sources of infections managed to make their way past her heavily suppressed immune system.

Jack eyed the monitor above her head, struggling to connect the sterile traces of brain, heart, and respiratory functions with his friend behind the glass. Each one of those numbers and lines represented energy being expended by her body. Even at the alarmingly reduced rate from hibernating, it was still energy that had to be replenished from somewhere.

In his hand was the personal message from Administrator Stratton, a record of her last official act on the way out the door at NASA HQ. The others may have seen it as a reprieve, but he was less sanguine.

That wasn't right either, he realized. This gave new purpose to his actions, a responsibility he'd never contemplated taking on before.

In the end, would Traci be able to understand? What might this feel like to her? Would she be so accepting of their plan?

She certainly wasn't talking. Jack only hoped she understood what he was doing at a gut level—there had to be a way to explain it all to her.

It was a world of green, shimmering hues of emerald and jade. She'd never seen so much vegetation. The woods surrounding her parents' house had depth she'd not noticed before. The air around her was thick with the perfume of life. Dense foliage rose in every direction toward the rocky cliffs and distant mountaintops which stretched all the way to the sky. Maybe she just hadn't appreciated it before. She wouldn't make that mistake again.

Daddy!

"Hey there, baby girl." *His hug was strong, his arms like iron bands.*

I really missed you. Where's Mom?

"Out back, in the herb garden. She's making that salsa you like."

That sounds good. Space food is so bland.

"It's all yours, baby girl. I still think cilantro tastes like soap." *A smile spread across her father's weathered face.* "How long did it take you to run out of hot sauce?"

About three months. I tried to make it stretch. Managed to grow some peppers in our hydroponic garden, though. Made it bearable, but I didn't have any way to sauté them.

"Well, that won't be a problem anymore." *His rough hands caressed her face.* "You need some sunshine, baby girl. Want to go take the dogs for a walk later?"

I'd love that.

"Traci?"

Jack? What are you doing here?

"I sure hope you can hear me."

Of course I can hear you. Daddy, this is Jack . . . wait. Where'd he go?

The world of green disappeared with her father, replaced with shimmering hues of blue and white and silver as the grass beneath her feet wrapped itself up around her legs.

What is that—? Oh. It's just a blanket. That's good, because it was kind of cold in here.

"If you can blink, that'd be awesome."

If I can blink? Why couldn't I—wait. It's hard, Jack. It's really hard.

"Good girl. You're going to be asleep for a while."

How long will I . . .

"You'll be down hard for about six months, all the way home. It's the best way to protect you. You almost drowned in your own puke, kiddo. It really did a number on your noggin."

I remember now. My head still hurts.

"Noelle and the docs in Houston think you'll be okay after hibernation."

I'm not already? Because this sure feels like it. Weird.

"You're going to be getting a lot of attention once you get home. Sorry we have to use you as kind of a guinea pig, but there aren't many choices left."

That's okay. I'd have done the same. You're an engineer, not a doctor.

"Anyway, I think you'd approve of my plan."

You didn't get my joke. Why can't you hear me? You can't read my mind yet?

"We're the only living humans to have ever made it this far. And I think you're right in that gives us a certain responsibility, considering what we've found. All that we've learned. The capabilities we're sitting on . . . "

Get to the point, silly.

"So, yeah. You were right. Because it sure does look like all that stuff was just waiting to be found. Like we're expected to do something with it."

Hold on. Where exactly are we going?

"But we're worried about keeping you out here too long. So we're taking you home."

I'd like that very much. Been in this tin can for too long. Thanks, friend.

"I'm going to miss you very much."

Why? Aren't you coming too?

36

Mission Day 379

Col. V. Vaschenko—Personal Log
Final Entry

Sometimes I contemplate this frozen world and my mind transports me to the Siberian wastes and the forgotten men we sent there by the thousands. Officially we are supposed to pretend these prisons do not exist, but out here it makes no difference. I see now that there are worse fates.

I often wonder how my old friend is doing at his "camp" or if he is still alive for that matter. I like to believe that he is. The cantankerous cowboy survived so many trials, dangers which would have killed men of lesser constitution; surely he has survived the machinations of political Chekists. I did not have it in me to leave such a man to his death, and hope that he found the strength not only to survive but to somehow thrive. I know how that must sound to a stranger, but what I learned of my friend gives me confidence.

I treasure the wonderful book he left me—it is perhaps my greatest regret that he would not have been allowed to keep it during his confinement. That may be the worst of the many punishments meted out by the Gulag: the isolation of the mind. Solzhenitsyn somehow managed to overcome his experiences, perhaps my friend has as well. Perhaps he has created his own magnum opus in isolation, or so I fantasize.

Life must be allowed to thrive. Intelligence must be allowed to advance its reach. Humanity is not a cancer on the world; we are like a gardener tasked with taking the raw ingredients of life and coaxing them to their utmost fulfillment. My life, as part of the Soviet Collective, has been as a weed: living for its own sake, extracting nutrients from the garden with no thought of replacing them or of how they got there in the first place. As a loyal officer of the Motherland, I have seen to it that other lives have been stamped out before they could bloom. Not directly, you understand—never directly. I have only performed the role of the functionary, not the jailer. Never the executioner.

I tell myself that yet I have been many, many times over. The American officer I knew as "Cowboy" was only the first, though I like to tell myself that it was my intervention which spared him the firing squad. But to what ends: relegated to a lifetime of isolation, prevented from fulfilling whatever destiny had been laid out for him? I neither loaded the weapon nor pulled the trigger, yet my intervention saw to it that he received something much worse than the swift arrival of a bullet in the head.

I had hoped a career in the Cosmonaut Corps would allow me to avoid playing the executioner. It is no doubt a cruel joke of Fate that my first and last missions would see me in that role nevertheless. It does not matter that my two comrades hatched their plan; it was up to me as their commanding officer to approve it and in turn sentence them to a slow, certain death. Perhaps it is fitting that my own demise will take longer, as I have the benefit of Arkangel's vast supplies. If we return, there would be charges of treason or whatever else the GRU might invent. "Pick your poison," as the Americans say.

Our orders present us with an impossible choice: bring this vessel and its cache of nuclear warheads back to Earth and await further instructions. To disobey those orders is treason—but to whom?

In light of present events, it is impossible to know what the Kremlin might do with the destructive capabilities Arkangel represents. Even if the Soviet Union is to be no more, we cannot know what will come next. Comrade Gorbachev had the good sense to use this ship for its intended purpose, but it could just as easily be turned against one's enemies. Given the current situation, "enemy" is a fluid term which depends greatly on whomever is in charge. Men desperate to hold on to their power tend to not concern themselves with the good of the people they rule. Men who desire to seize power often care even less.

We are still officers of our nation's Air Force, and we have our orders. To disobey is treason, the consequences of which will fall on our families in our absence. Alexi and Gregoriy are young men and I cannot put them in such a position.

Yet they have convincingly argued that our remarkable discoveries demand to be shared with the world. We considered broadcasting in the open for the world to hear, but the end result would be the same: our existence revealed, along with our refusal to obey orders. In the end, our families still suffer and so our selfish interests prevailed.

Russia is in a more precarious position now than at any time I can recall. The bulk of American and NATO combat power is deployed in Europe and the Middle East. With the rest in the Western Pacific, and all of it fed by a long logistics chain from the American heartland, Russia is surrounded by adversaries.

Some would argue this is the precise time for a show of strength, yet revealing Arkangel's existence would be ruinously destabilizing. It would only strengthen those factions in our government who crave war with the West.

So Alexi and Gregoriy will fill the LK ascent module full of surface samples, mate with our "Dvina" Soyuz, and set off for Earth on a forty-year journey. They will only last a few months at most, but it will ensure the safe return of their cargo and the safety of their families: For as far as the Kremlin is concerned, they are the hero mutineers who defied their recalcitrant commander against all odds for the greater glory of the Soviet people.

That is what my official transmissions will reflect. Whoever finds this journal in the future will know the truth.

Given what we now know has been waiting to be found, our only choice is to gamble on the next generation being more deserving of this towering responsibility than our own.

This is why I cannot return.

❊ ❊ ❊

Transmission from Jack Templeton:
This will be my first and only entry.
Traci has been stable in the ICU pod aboard the *Dragon/Cygnus*

stack for a month now. More importantly, Noelle and Daisy think she's stable. Seeing as how I'm about to join her, it's kind of important that I have some confidence this is all going to work.

Traci's going home, but I'm not. I don't see the point, and I don't think she would either. There's too much left to do, and I can't escape the notion that we're in a cosmically unique position to do it.

If we are the first intelligent, or even sentient, life to emerge in the universe then perhaps that is a gift that comes with a certain responsibility. If we've been given the ability to spread life into the cosmos, then who are we to turn our backs?

There's a treasure trove of organics out here that would go to waste if we didn't try. This ship can do an awful lot on its own, and if NASA doesn't want her anymore then let someone else put the old girl to good use. Penny Stratton convincing Congress to sell off *Magellan* operations to a private business consortium was a genius move, because our work's not done yet. We think there's more to be found out here.

Ever since we left Pluto, I've had Daisy beating her silicon brains out narrowing down the mean orbital resonances of a bunch of dwarf planets farther out in the Kuiper Belt. They're a trail of crumbs, all pointing in the same direction.

Yes, I'm talking about Planet Nine. Sometimes you've got to get closer to the neighborhood to really understand it. All the evidence for something about five times' Earth's mass hanging out halfway to the Oort cloud matches up pretty well with predictions so far—that no one has been able to get eyes on it yet isn't surprising if it's that far away.

We've been able use the periods and directionality of those resonant orbits to whittle down the probable location to a few arc-seconds of sky, we think closer than even the guys at Caltech who first started chasing it. If we can find our way to the right neighborhood, then maybe we can use those subtle gravitational changes to finally pin down the right address. Once there, we might even find answers as to why the whole Kuiper Belt looks like a seed vault.

If we've learned anything, it's that life can thrive in some pretty harsh places. After all, the stuff we've found out here was able to get a toehold on primordial Earth a couple billion years ago.

It's strange how we stubbornly tend to frame everything within our limited points of view despite evidence to the contrary. For instance, that whole "primordial Earth" thing. Where did we come from? How did we get here? How did life spring from nothing? Did it all start out here with comets falling sunward, bombarding Earth with the necessary ingredients?

Surprising as Noelle's snowballs were, there's no evidence of artificial origins. It happens on Earth. Except Pluto holds a veritable chef's pantry of life's building blocks. If God or whoever didn't want us to find this stuff until we could be trusted with it, then it couldn't have been hidden in a better place.

Was that on purpose? And if it was, what does it feel like to literally play God?

I'm not sure I want to find out. I just want to find answers. Thus, "Plan(et) Nine from Outer Space" was born.

See what I did there?

The outbound leg is going to be a real stretch, and I've spent enough EVAs spot-welding new structural joints and reinforcing old ones that I don't want to do another spacewalk again. Ever. It's too lonely out here. Always was, now even more so.

They'll be bringing Traci out of hibernation about the time we cross Earth's orbit en route to slinging around Venus for the return home. Their trip will be almost over, but mine will just be getting started. They'll go around Venus on the back side to bleed energy and start decelerating for Earth, whereas I'll be taking *Magellan* around the front for a gravity assist and heading back to the vicinity of Jupiter for yet another gravity assist. Bummer, because I'd still like to see Saturn. It's just never in the right place.

That trajectory will also take me closer to the Sun than any human has ever been. No one's ever slingshot a spacecraft around the Sun, for a couple of reasons: It's insanely hot, and it wouldn't do any good inside the solar system. That's because it's not the size of the object that matters as much as its velocity relative to whatever you're trying to get to, so the Sun doesn't offer anything. But Jupiter? Now we're talking. Anyone care to guess how much kinetic energy it has relative to our puny little spacecraft? In purely scientific terms, it's a buttload. It ain't warp drive, but it'll do.

Sorry, people of Earth, but I'm terrible at metaphors. Ironic that I might just be our first Interplanetary Emissary.

With the boost we'll get from King Juno, in another year we'll start decelerating into Planet Nine's neighborhood assuming we have the right address. Here's the catch: if Nine isn't where we think it is, or if it isn't as big as we think, there won't be enough delta-v left in the tanks to slow down. No one's ever navigated that far before, and it's not quite "point and shoot." Our beginning and ending state vectors have to be known and right now we're just kind of guessing at the end state. As I learned from my chess lessons, you have to be able to see the end before you can figure out how to get there.

Okay, that's a bit of an exaggeration. We have a pretty good bead on the whole system, thanks to a few decades' worth of sky surveys and planet-hunting satellites that Daisy's made quick work of. We know the relative position, orbital elements, and a reasonable estimate of mass. She'll be watching for the slight perturbations it'll make in our orbit and will figure out the corrections before we start decelerating. We don't expect to make it without some tinkering along the way. It's like hitting a golf ball or shooting a rifle: Tiny fluctuations at the beginning can make for big errors at the end. Fortunately, we have a lot more control over our trajectory than a bullet or a golf ball, and if you'd ever seen me golf then you'd know that's a very good thing (hint: I suck at it).

We're keeping enough reaction mass in reserve to execute several course corrections, the most significant of which will have to happen within that first couple of hours after we put Jupiter behind us. After that's done, I'm going to sleep for a very long time.

You may have noticed I keep referring to "we." That's because I'm not alone, though my friends will be safely back on Earth by this time. Daisy will be looking after me and *Magellan*. No one's ever done that before, not for that amount of time, and I'm facing a solid year in hibernation. To answer the obvious question: No, I have no idea if I'll survive the trip and who knows what will happen after I get there.

I've spent almost a year poring over documents nearly a half-century old, trying to tease out the hidden meanings everyone presumed Vaschenko had woven into his reports. We all figured that his personal log aboard *Arkangel* would be the key to deciphering the hot mess of his official mission transcripts.

Turns out the subtext wasn't all that subtle. Maybe that's a good thing, as sometimes I need Deep Meaning to just come out and hit me right between the eyes. In this case, it helped us decide what to do.

Arkangel's crew wasn't coming back. They were never coming back. Given the circumstances, we might have made the same choice: Get those samples back to Earth somehow and complete the mission, even if it takes half a century to do it. Two cosmonauts had to sacrifice themselves just to keep the injection burn on target, but that's Steampunk Spaceflight for you. It's like that old wives' tale about how we spent a quarter-million dollars to create a failure-proof space pen when Ivan just used a pencil, but man those guys had guts. They knew it was a one-way trip and they did it anyway. Maybe the alternative sucked, but this would've been so much worse. Maybe.

Would I have made the same choice? I can't speak for Traci, though I can make a pretty good guess. But we do have alternatives— and between my best friend and three dead Russians, I know which choice to make. We've been given a tremendous gift, and we dare not waste it. If humans are the first and only intelligent life in the universe, then we have a responsibility to spread that life. This solar system will eventually die, but by the time it does there's a decent chance that our sacrifice will have ensured a whole new civilization has blossomed somewhere else, and maybe we'll be able to enjoy watching the first sprouts. We will have to find a way to let them know who planted the seeds, because not knowing our own story is killing me.

Traci, of course, knows the answer. Just ask her. Guess I'll have plenty of time to think on it when I wake up next year. Maybe Daisy will have it figured out for us, or maybe she'll end up agreeing with Traci. All I know is that we have a responsibility to something greater than the frightened politicians on Earth.

Life is bigger than anything we can imagine, and we are its caretakers.

Acknowledgments

They say it takes ten years to become an overnight success. Time will tell if this book qualifies, but I can say with certainty that ten years has been just about right to get this far. By the time this is published, it will have been eight years since I independently released my first novel, *Perigee*. It was another three years before *Farside* was ready for publication (pro tip: don't put your first book out there until you're certain the follow-up is almost in the can). Not long after that, *Galveston Daily News* reviewer Mark Lardas recommended that book to Toni Weisskopf at Baen, and here we are. They are the first people I want to thank.

From what little I knew of the publishing world, Baen was the only house I wanted to work with and Toni is one of the main reasons for that. Besides a commitment to helping authors find their voice in a politics-free environment—which is very much *not* the case in too many corners of this industry—her input was instrumental in making this story the best it could be.

After more than a year of back-and-forth with a couple of substantial rewrites, what you see here may not be fundamentally different from the story I first envisioned but it sure does work better.

Returning to that whole "ten year" canard: The seeds of *Frozen Orbit* had in fact been germinating for almost that long. Being a space nerd I was quite curious to learn what *New Horizons* would reveal when it finally encountered Pluto, the one planet in the solar system which we'd never seen up close (and I don't care what the eggheads at the International Astronomical Union say, Pluto got robbed. It's still a planet).

Also having an imagination that's way too active for my own

good, I wondered how cool it would be if it saw something nobody expected to find. Something unnatural, maybe?

Mind you I wasn't at all sure what that something might be; that part took a while. Aliens would've been way too easy and if you've read this far then you've most likely figured out that's not my brand of science fiction. My personal philosophy is much closer to Traci's than Jack's: that is, there's plenty of room for life beyond Earth. *Intelligent* life is another matter entirely and one which I'm admittedly reluctant to concede purely for theological reasons.

So the idea floated in the back of my mind for years, finally coming together while I was perusing some wildly advanced concepts at the Atomic Rockets website (which, if you are not an engineer and want to write hard science fiction, should be at the top of your bookmarks) and lamenting our failure to pursue them. The only spacecraft that could reach Pluto fast enough to keep the crew alive and sane had to be fusion-driven, and I realized that the *only* country bat-guano-nuts enough to build an interplanetary spacecraft propelled by old nuclear bombs would've been the former Soviet Union.

Now I had the hook, but that still wasn't enough. Some writers just get the story moving and fly entirely by the seat of their pants, not knowing how it will end. I'm not one of those yet. I need to know what the end state looks like; kind of like Jack's search for Planet Nine. His final sacrifice, the last scene in this book, arrived in my head fully formed on my way home from work one day. It felt powerful, to the point where I had to pull off the highway to write it all down before it all disappeared. The time in between has been spent figuring out everything else, including a lot of technical research. I'm one who can't bring himself to write the story until I'm satisfied the technicalities are feasible enough that any readers who know what they're talking about won't howl in laughter. Much.

Having said that, a lot of life happens during the "in between" and my family has been incredibly patient with me through this. As impossible as it was to devote the time needed to bring this to completion sooner, it has still taken an enormous amount of time away from them. Melissa, Nathan and Matthew: You are my inspiration and my reason for being. It is not too trite to say that you give my life meaning and have made me the kind of man I can face in the mirror each day.

Thank you all for reading. There's more to come and sooner than you might think, because now I'm on a roll.